A BOARDWALK STORY

A
BOARDWALK
STORY

A novel by
J. Louis Yampolsky

Plexus Publishing, Inc.
Medford, New Jersey

First printing, 2009

A Boardwalk Story

Copyright © 2009 by J. Louis Yampolsky

Published by:
Plexus Publishing Inc.
143 Old Marlton Pike
Medford, NJ 08055

Cover: Boardwalk illustration copyright © by Paul Lovett

Page 253: Cartoon by David Low, "Rendezvous," originally published in the *Evening Standard*, 20/09/1939. Reprinted with permission by Solo Syndication on behalf of Associated Newspapers Ltd.

This is a work of fiction. Names, characters, places, and incidents either are the product of the author's imagination or are used fictitiously. Any resemblance to actual persons, living or dead, is entirely coincidental.

Library of Congress Cataloging-in-Publication Data

Yampolsky, J. Louis, 1928-
A Boardwalk Story / J. Louis Yampolsky.
    p. cm.
ISBN 978-0-937548-72-1
1. Atlantic City (N.J.)--Fiction. 2. World War, 1939-1945--Fiction. I. Title.
PS3625.A67225B63 2009
813'.6--dc22

                                                                        2009011825

ISBN 978-0-937548-72-1

Printed and bound in the United States of America.

President and CEO: Thomas H. Hogan, Sr.
Editor-in-Chief and Publisher: John B. Bryans
Managing Editor: Amy M. Reeve
VP Graphics and Production: M. Heide Dengler
Book Designer: Kara M. Jalkowski
Cover Designer: Lisa M. Conroy
Copyeditor: Pat Hadley-Miller
Proofreader: Barbara Brynko
Sales Manager: Linda Chamberlain
Marketing Coordinator: Rob Colding

www.plexuspublishing.com

To Betty and Lou

Acknowledgments

DEBT OF gratitude to:

My granddaughter Lauren—our talks about American life before World War II led me to write this book.

My wife Judith—my muse and grammarian.

My dear friend Susan Ditmire, who introduced me to Plexus Publishing, Inc.

The wonderful gang at Plexus—especially John Bryans, Amy Reeve, Heide Dengler, Lisa Conroy, Kara Jalkowski, Rob Colding, and Tom Hogan, Sr.—whose ideas, comments, and tireless efforts improved the story and the book.

Thanks to all of you.

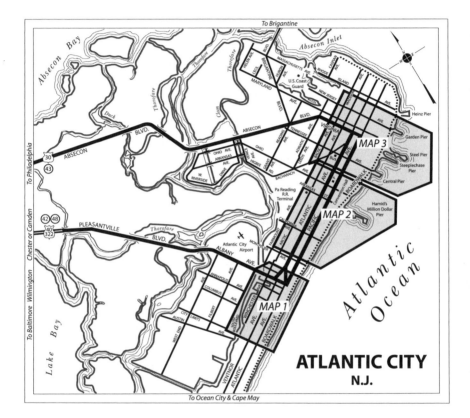

ATLANTIC CITY
N.J.

Map © Rand McNally, R.L.09-S-30

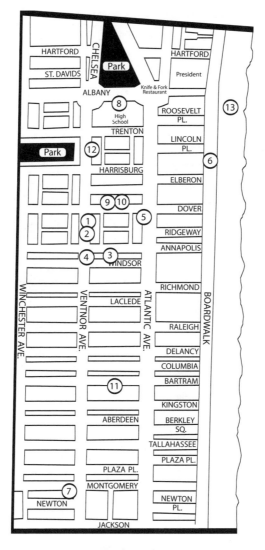

Map 1

1. Michaelson's Bakery
2. Dunauskas's Polish Delicatessen
3. Mackeys' House
4. Mackeys' Corner Hangout
5. May Incident with Mackeys
6. October Incident with Mackeys
7. Goren's Apartment
8. Atlantic City High School
9. Bernie's House
10. Blinky's House
11. Alice's House
12. Frederick's Pharmacy
13. Beach Party

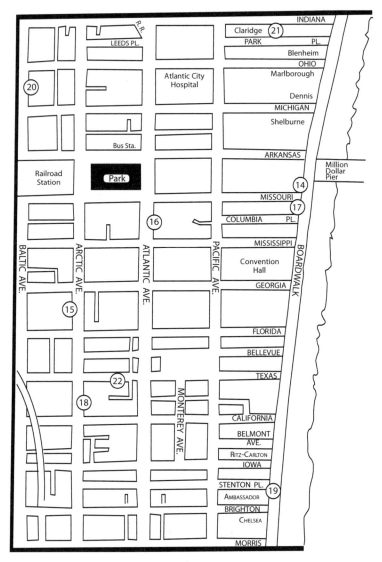

Map 2

14. Waldorf Grille
15. Trucci's
16. Nu-Enamel Paint Store
17. Zena's Parlor
18. First Errand for Bobo

19. Second Errand for Bobo, Ambassador Hotel
20. Abortionist
21. Patti's Apartment, The Claridge
22. Gracie's Apartment

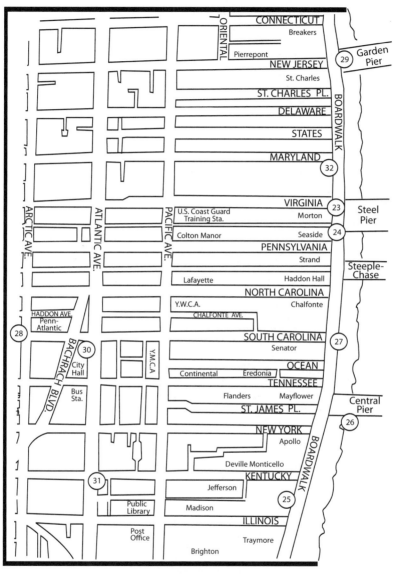

Map 3

23. Krilow's Kitchen Gadgets
24. Vi-de-Ian Studio
25. Royce's Shooting Gallery
26. Krieger and Son
27. South Carolina Avenue Pavilion

28. Mrs. Ormont's Boarding House
29. Garden Pier
30. Courthouse
31. Lawrence Durells, Esquire
32. Rolling Chair Storage Shed

1

An Autumn Sunday

THERE WERE TWO of them. The bigger one leaned against the wall. The other against the light pole on the sidewalk. They studied her through half-closed eyes as she approached. She was young and pretty. She had a bounce in her step.

She saw them. A fleeting apprehension. She should turn back. Too late. The bigger one pushed off from the wall. Two quick steps, cat-like, and he had her from behind, his right arm across her chin, her cry smothered in the crook of a fleshy elbow. A low animal grunt escaped from him as he dragged her backward into the alley.

The other one moved to the entrance of the alley, blocking it from view.

***

I'm ahead of myself. That hadn't happened yet. It was several months away.

My story begins in April 1939. I was fifteen, living in Atlantic City. I'm Jack Laurel. This is my story.

2

History Belongs to Historians

MY IMAGES OF earlier times are gray and indistinct, as though the colors of earlier times were muted and the people knew that their society was primitive compared to what was to come. Not so, of course. Every age thinks it is advanced. We think we are modern. Future generations will think us primitive. It is always the way with history. The times are not understood by the players. Only later is it understood what was happening and why.

Those of us who remember World War II, and the historians who write about it, divide the twentieth century, conveniently, between *before the War* and *after the War*. In 1939, we were living out the final days of a dying era. We didn't know it then, but now we see it clearly, that everything changed in the beginning of September, when the War started with the Nazi invasion of Poland and a new chapter in world history began.

3

April 1939

OUR FAMILY LIVED in a rented two-bedroom apartment in Atlantic City, on the third floor, above Michaelson's Bakery. We were four: Father, Mother, me, and my thirteen-year-old sister, Evie. Times were hard. Until a year earlier, I shared a two-tiered bunk bed in a bedroom with my sister. Mine was the upper. When Dad decided that Evie and I shouldn't sleep in the same room any more, he bought a fold-up cot for me. It stood in our pantry. I wheeled it into the laundry room at night and unfolded it, but my clothes and the rest of my stuff stayed in the bedroom with the bunk bed and Evie.

Dad was the manager of the Nu-Enamel Paint Store, uptown on Atlantic Avenue, near Missouri Avenue. He worked all the hours that the store was open, from 8:30 in the morning until 9:00 at night, Monday through Saturday, and Sunday from 10:00 to 1:00. Sunday afternoon was his time off. That spring his salary was thirty dollars a week. A year earlier, his salary was thirty-five dollars a week, but the district manager cut it as part of a cost-cutting program. Business was bad. It was the tenth year of the Great Depression. The company was losing money. Jobs were scarce. Dad thought himself lucky to have a steady job.

He wore a three-piece suit to work every day, with a white shirt and necktie. He owned two suits: a navy blue and a dark gray. They came from Sears Roebuck. They cost $14.95 each. He owned four white shirts, four neckties, and two pairs of wing-tip shoes, a black pair and a brown pair. Nothing was superfluous in his life.

He was in the American Expeditionary Force during World War I. He served in France in 1918, but he never talked about it. He was a quiet man. I always thought he was retiring and non-confrontational, but there was an incident, three years earlier, that showed him differently.

It happened in mid-summer in 1936. It was a Sunday afternoon. Our family was crossing Ventnor Avenue, on the way to Mom's cousin's house for Sunday dinner. A big stake body truck with a smelly cargo of noisy hogs was stopped at the traffic light. The driver, a husky fellow, maybe twenty-five or so, leaned out of the window of his cab and looked down the front of Mom's dress. She was dressed modestly, as always, but her dress had a scoop neckline, and I suppose the truck driver was able to see a bit of her upper bosom.

He leered at her, "Nice tits, lady."

Dad stopped. He stopped the rest of us with an outstretched right arm, Mom, Evie, and me. Keeping his eyes on the driver, he pushed his outstretched arm to return us to the sidewalk.

He never said a word. With a quick fierceness that I had never seen before, he pulled open the door to the cab, grabbed the truck driver's left foot and dragged him out of the cab. The driver, caught by surprise, tried to stop my dad by holding on to the steering wheel and kicking with his left leg. "Hey, what're you doin'?" He tried to keep from being pulled out of the cab. He was too late. It all happened in a few seconds. Dad yanked at him so fast and so hard that the driver slid out of the cab and bounced down onto the running board. As he started to pull himself up, Dad socked him in the chest, right below his breastbone. The driver fell back against the cab. Dad stood over him and said, quietly, "Watch your tongue." Then he motioned us to follow him. We crossed Ventnor Avenue. I looked back and saw the driver climbing back into his cab, bent over, holding his chest. Dad didn't look back. "Sorry," he said, grimly, not looking at us, looking straight ahead, talking into the air, "he needed a lesson."

That was it. He did the thing so matter-of-factly you might have thought he did it once a day. I was astonished. None of us ever spoke of it to him, or he to us. I talked to Mom about it. She just said, "That's the way he is. He would rather take a beating than endure an insult." Evie, who was only ten at the time, asked me if I would do the same thing for her. I said, "Sure."

Mom stuffed envelopes for a direct marketing company for extra money. Its office was all the way uptown, on Arctic Avenue, almost three miles away. She walked there almost every weekday to deliver her work and pick up a new supply of boxes of envelopes and marketing pieces. Each pick-up was 2,160 envelopes and the same number of flat marketing pieces. She worked at her own pace, but she had to return the pick-up within two days. They paid her sixty cents per load. She was fast. She could fold and stuff at the rate of five seconds each. She could stuff 700 in an hour. Some days she picked up and delivered two full loads. That was $1.20, but most days she could only manage one load, squeezed in among her household chores. Her evenings were usually spent in the kitchen listening to the radio and stuffing envelopes until Dad got home. Supper was always waiting for him. They talked about the day while he ate and she stuffed envelopes.

Dad couldn't afford a car. Most days he walked or rode his bike to and from work, two-and-a-half miles each way. Sometimes in heavy rain he took a jitney; they were limousines outfitted to hold six passengers. They cruised along Pacific and Ventnor avenues, stopping at any corner to pick up a waiting passenger or let one out. Fare was five cents. My father did not take the jitney often. He did not waste nickels.

For my parents, it was a hard life. No frills. But they thought they were doing fine. They managed to make do and stay out of debt, and they even saved money. One day, I saw the Boardwalk National Bank passbook on the kitchen table and looked in it. The balance was $1,720.86. I thought that was a lot of money. And the passbook interest rate was two percent. *Oh boy*, I thought, *that's almost seventy cents a week! For nothing. Just for the money sitting there in the bank. Why didn't the bank charge my dad to hold his money for him?* I imagined a box in the bank, labeled with my father's name, with his $1,720.86 in it. Why would the bank *pay* my father to hold his money? It did not make sense.

America was different then, and I was still a boy.

4

America 1939

IF YOU COULD be transported back to 1939, the first thing you would notice is the way people dressed. Clothing was more formal. Even leisurewear had a degree of formality. Women's wear was not revealing. Dresses and blouses were designed with lots of pleats. The purpose of women's wear was to cover up the figure, not to display it. You would see no women wearing pants. Only a few Hollywood stars wore slacks. It was daring and sexy. Only young starlets could get away with it.

Except for guys with blue-collar jobs and in industrial work, men wore suits and ties everywhere, to work, to the movies, to visit friends, to sporting events, even to a summer outing in the park. All men wore hats or caps. So did boys. Boys wore knickers up to about age fourteen. I was wearing long pants only for the past year.

The big buildings were not as tall. They were brick or stone or concrete block, decorated with columns and capitols, and some with gargoyles. There were no steel and glass skyscrapers.

We thought our cars looked sleek and modern. Not by today's standards. Cars wore dark colors. Most were black. There were some deep maroons, dark forest greens, chocolate browns. A parking lot full of them looked monochromatic, all dark.

Most men smoked. Cigarettes were twelve cents a pack. Men smoked everywhere—on the streets, on the job, in the movie houses, on trolley cars and trains, in restaurants, at home, while visiting in the houses of friends, in church, in hospitals, and in the doctor's office. Any roomful of men was full of cigarette and cigar smoke. Dad smoked. He was not sure if it was harmful, but he knew it certainly wasn't good for you, so he made me promise not to smoke until I was twenty-one. Fewer women smoked than men and those who did were more discreet about it. Women who smoked usually smoked at home, rarely in the workplace. Sometimes women smoked in public places like restaurants or the movies. That was rare. It was vulgar for women to smoke in public. At home, women smoked while breast-feeding, while doing the laundry, while cooking dinner. It was all right for men to smoke anywhere, but the rule for women smoking was to keep it at home.

There was no air conditioning in 1939. In the heat of summer, the only relief was from fans and the coolness of nighttime and early morning. Tourists came to Atlantic City in the summer to cool off and catch the ocean breezes. The Atlantic City Chamber of Commerce advertised: *Atlantic City—Playground of the World, Fifteen Degrees Cooler.* Despite summer heat, the correct dress code for businessmen was hat, suit, and necktie. A few modern movie houses advertised that they were *air-cooled.* The cooling was done by running a waterfall down the face of a metal grill in front of a fan. The fan pushed a column of air through the waterfall, cooling the air as it was pushed into ductwork, which carried and distributed it. It was not very effective, but it helped a little.

Things cost a lot less in 1939. A new Packard sedan, one of the most expensive and luxurious cars, cost $900. The 1939 Buick Eight cost $860. The Studebaker top-of-the-line car cost $800. It was called the Studebaker Dictator. In mid-year, in view of the unpopularity of dictators, such as Hitler, Franco, Stalin, and Mussolini, Studebaker changed the name to the Studebaker

President. Studebaker also introduced a new lively, smaller car, aimed at younger buyers. It was called the Champion. It cost $660. A new Plymouth cost $640. The Dow-Jones Industrial Average stood at 92. The stock market had never recovered from the 1929 crash and the Depression that followed.

There was a different sense of what was OK and what wasn't. There was more respect for government and the law. Sexual displays were taboo. There were no sexually provocative magazines or books. The movies had a strict morals code, supervised by a congressionally appointed committee, the Hays Office. In the movies, the bad guys always lost, and sex didn't happen, and married folks slept in twin beds. Premarital sex was rare and shameful. No one ever heard of joints and fixes.

Rogers Peet Men's Stores advertised their Palm Beach men's suit for $12.50, slacks for $5.95, Jantzen bathing trunks for $1.49, Arrow dress shirts for $2.95, Nunn Bush shoes, 100 percent leather wingtips in black, brown, or brown and white, for $8.95.

Women's fashion dresses went for as little as $4.95. A full-course dinner on Saturday evening or Sunday, in a moderately priced family restaurant, was $1.30 to $1.75.

The New York World's Fair opened in April of that year. Admission was 75 cents for adults, 25 cents for children. The price of a pound of cocoa beans on the New York Board of Trade was four cents—more about that later.

5

The Playground of the World

ATLANTIC CITY OCCUPIES the northern five miles of Absecon Island, a ten-mile-long barrier island, one of the ten barrier islands along the southern New Jersey coast, separated from the mainland by shallow bays and marshes. Three other cities occupy the lower half of Absecon Island. They are Ventnor City, Margate City, and Longport City, bedroom communities for Atlantic City. The island's industry, business, and hotels are concentrated in Atlantic City. A sandy beach lines the ocean side of the island. Atlantic City's main attraction is its boardwalk, built along the western edge of the beach. In 1939, the boardwalk ran from the northern tip of the island, all the way south, through Atlantic City, Ventnor, and Margate. Longport never had a boardwalk.

The Atlantic City boardwalk was, and still is, the heart and life force of Atlantic City. In most places, it is fifty feet wide; in some places, sixty feet. In Ventnor, it narrows to eighteen feet. In 1939, there was a ten-foot-wide boardwalk in Margate. In the mid-forties, Hurricane Hazel swept away most of Ventnor's boardwalk and all of Margate's, and one of Atlantic City's favorite piers, Heinz Pier, where they gave away free samples of some of Heinz's 57 varieties. The hurricane also damaged Atlantic City's boardwalk, but it was repaired. Ventnor's boardwalk was completely rebuilt, thirty feet farther from the ocean than the old one. Margate's was torn down completely and never rebuilt.

Hotels, stores, restaurants, and amusement arcades lined Atlantic City's boardwalk. The hotels were splendid. The shops were of all kinds, from typical tourist shops and hot dog and ice-cream stands to the most elegant and pricey high-style clothing, jewelry, and antique shops. In 1939, despite the Depression, Atlantic City still drew the big crowds. The city came alive in June, full of visitors, crowded shops, and hotels. Like a perennial flower that opens in the spring, Atlantic City displays its glory for thirteen weeks, then loses its bloom and goes to sleep until next year.

Atlantic City's permanent population was less than thirty thousand. The summertime head count swelled to several hundred thousand. The permanent residents felt a sense of camaraderie. We were the permanent cadre. We manned the post and struggled with winter's cold and hard times. We longed for the arrival of tourists and summer. We needed the tourists. We lived on the thirteen-week burst of activity they brought. Like the locals in every other resort town, our need and appreciation for tourists was mixed with contradictory feelings of servitude and superiority.

My family lived in a three-story brick building, one of a row of similar buildings, on the 3900 block of Ventnor Avenue, between Dover Avenue to the north and Annapolis Avenue to the south. Each building had a basement, a ground floor store, and two apartments above. Our apartment was on the third floor. The Michaelson family owned the building as well as the bakery on the first floor. They lived in the second-floor apartment. Their basement was furnished and laid out like an apartment. In the summer, the Michaelsons rented out their second-floor apartment and moved into the basement. The second-floor apartment brought in a summer rental of some three hundred dollars, more than enough to compensate for the annoyance and discomfort of spending the summer in the basement.

It was a strange custom, the Michaelsons moving out of a comfortable apartment, turning it over to strangers for two or three months. Strangers slept in your sheets, cooked in your kitchen, ate with your dinnerware, relaxed on your sofa, listened to your radio, carried your beach chairs to the beach. Money was the reason. In 1939, money, or not having any, was the central issue in the lives of most families. A supplement of a few hundred dollars was important. Lots of Atlantic City families did what the Michaelsons did.

The Michaelsons had a daughter, Rhoda. She was a beauty. I thought her the prettiest girl in my school. She was my age and in most of my classes at school. She was a cheerleader, an all-American girl. She was popular with the boys. She had a smile and a cheery greeting for all the boys, but she only socialized with boys who were several years older. I adored her. To Rhoda, I was just the kid who lived upstairs, sort of a non-person.

Once the previous December, I asked her to go to the movies with me. "Rhoda," I stammered, "I'm going to the Warner on Saturday. There's a real good movie, *Lost Horizon*, wanna go? I mean, can I take you? Will you go with me? I'll buy the tickets."

She touched her hand to my arm and smiled. "Jack, that is so nice of you to ask me. But, you'll have to excuse me. I'm going to a frat dance on Saturday. But tell you what; stop in to the bakery Saturday afternoon. I'll pack a couple of cinnamon buns for you." I think I was glad she turned me down. I wouldn't have known how to behave if she accepted.

Rhoda was embarrassed every summer when the Michaelsons moved into the basement. The basement apartment had only two small windows, high up on the front wall because most of the front wall was below the level of the pavement. The sun's rays had trouble finding their way into the narrow windows. Only a pale indirect light made its way into the dark apartment.

"I like the basement," Rhoda lied to me once, flushing as she mouthed the official Michaelson family lie. "It's cool. We don't cover the cement floor because it keeps the apartment so nice and cool."

"Sure," I thought. "Nice and cool. Damp and dark, you mean. What a bummer!"

I thought the Michaelsons were prosperous. They owned the building. I admired and envied their bakery. It was so clean. And it smelled so wonderful, and Mr. and Mrs. Michaelson were so pink and cherubic in their white aprons and white paper caps. Rhoda worked in the bakery. She was a wholesome beauty, all in white, except for her rosy cheeks and red lips and dark eyes and flowing black hair. I ached for her. Whenever I had reason to visit the bakery, Mr. or Mrs. Michaelson or Rhoda gave me a muffin or a square of cinnamon bun, or whatever else I might select. Such casual generosity. "They must be well-off," I thought. Once, I asked my father if the Michaelsons were rich. He didn't know. "I think they make a living," he said, "how much, I can't guess. They seem to be doing pretty good."

I tried to figure out clues. I weighed the visible facts.

Rich facts for the Michaelsons:
They own the building.
They collect rent from us.
They collect rent from their apartment in the summer.
They own a business.
They dress nice.

Rhoda has nice clothes and at least five pairs of shoes. I have one pair of shoes and one pair of sneakers. My sister's clothes look drab. Evie has one pair of beat-up saddles and a scuffy pair of loafers.

Their apartment looks nice. Their furniture looks good. Their rugs look new.

They have a private telephone line. Our telephone is a party line (two households sharing one line and one phone number).

Our apartment could use a painting, and our furniture looks dreary.

We have yellowing window shades that are getting stiff and cracking; the Michaelsons have bright, new-looking drapes, lined with white lace.

Mr. Michaelson has a nice bike. Rhoda's bike is new. My father's bike is about ten years old. He bought mine for two dollars at a yard sale.

Poor facts:

They do not have a car. Neither do we.

They never go out for a meal in a restaurant. Neither do we.

They never take a vacation. Neither do we.

Rhoda works in the bakery every day after school and all day Saturday except for cheerleading. In the summer, Rhoda works full time every day except Sunday.

They move into the basement every summer. They must need the money.

After considering all the facts, I couldn't reach a conclusion. Dad's summing-up was, "I guess they are doing OK, but I wouldn't want to be in business with things the way they are. A good steady job is better. Like mine. My pay envelope is there every week. If Michaelson has a bad week, he must have trouble paying his bills. He has to pay suppliers, and gas and electric, and repair his oven, and I think he has a mortgage on the building. He has to pay for insurance and real estate taxes. And fix the roof when it leaks and heat the building in the winter and shovel off the sidewalk when it snows. I think *we* are doing OK, without all those problems. We don't owe anybody any money, and we have some savings, and we are going to send you to college. You are going to have a better job than me. Maybe you will be a doctor or an engineer. I'm doing pretty good for a man with only a high school education. You will do better than me."

I wanted a dog. Dad said we can't afford to waste money on a dog. The Michaelsons had a cat. His name was Mendelsohn. He was not a pet. Mendelsohn worked for his living. He spent his nights in the basement. He was a skilled mouser, a valuable employee. A bakery invites mice and other creatures. But there was never a mouse or any other undesirable creature in Mr. Michaelson's building. Mendelsohn saw to it. Once, when my father asked me to take the rent money downstairs, I saw Rhoda reclining on the sofa with Mendelsohn curled behind her knees. Mendelsohn had a good life.

***

My best friend was Eddie Dunauskas. His parents came to America in 1910, from Lithuania. His family owned the building next door, which, like the Michaelsons's building, had a basement, a store, and two apartments. Mr. Dunauskas's store was a Polish delicatessen. The Dunauskas family, like the Michaelsons, rented out the third-floor apartment and lived in the second-floor apartment, and like the Michaelsons and so many others, they rented out their own apartment for the summer and moved into the basement.

Eddie was a month older than me and two inches shorter. I was skinny; Eddie was broad and muscular. Eddie was dark and good-looking. I was non-descript. My hair was light brown, straight, and unruly. I had a fair complexion with a hint of freckles across the top of my cheeks and nose. Except for the two inches I had on Eddie, he was superior in every way. He was smart and strong. He had a serious manner. He spoke slowly, deliberately. He was curious about everything. He had to know how things worked. He was a tinkerer. He could fix just about anything: bikes, lamps, radios, even cars. He worked in a gas station. He told me he would have worked for nothing, just to watch the mechanic and learn about cars. He said he would buy a wreck and fix it next March when he turned sixteen. I had no doubt that Eddie could do it.

At age fifteen, neither Eddie nor I had much time for girls, except that I had a crush on Rhoda. It was a good thing that Eddie had no interest in her. I think she would have made an exception for Eddie in her boys-over-seventeen dating rules. So I had the Rhoda field to myself, except that Rhoda did not have the slightest interest in me.

Eddie and I had two other good friends; one was Bernard Resnos, who lived around the corner on Dover Avenue. Bernie's father was from Greece. He worked in the kitchen of the Olympus Diner on Albany Avenue. The other was Harvey Geek. What a name. Harvey was little, a wiry little kid. We were all about the same age, but Harvey looked two years younger. We couldn't call him "Harvey" or "Geek," so we called him "Blinky" because of the way he squinted so hard when he was trying to concentrate. He lived next door to Bernie. His father was a debit man for Metropolitan Life Insurance Company. He sold small life insurance policies door-to-door and collected the premiums weekly. The policies were typically $1,000 ten-year term policies. The insurance people called it industrial insurance. The premiums averaged 25 cents a week.

Eddie and Bernie and Blinky and I were always together. We took the same classes, played ball together, and ogled the girls together. We played Pinochle every Thursday night in Blinky's house. Blinky's father taught him the game and Blinky taught us. Blinky's father and his father's three friends played every Tuesday night. They played four-handed Auction Pinochle. We were allowed to watch their game whenever we wanted to. They were skilled players. We learned and improved our own game by sitting behind them and absorbing their play. Blinky, who was the most outspoken, often questioned his father after a hand about the way his father played the hand. The rest of us were embarrassed to be so impertinent. We merely sat and watched, quietly. That was the rule, you can watch the game, but only in silence. No kibitzing.

Blinky was easily the best player of the four of us. We all knew the rules and the basic strategy of the game. But Blinky was different. He had a special talent. Eddie, Bernie, and I could develop a sketchy idea of what each player had, from the way the bidding went, and from each player's meld, and the cards that fell on the first couple of tricks. Blinky, however, after the first two tricks, seemed to know just about every card remaining in each player's hand. I tried mightily to do what he did, but I never mastered it.

He would say something like this to me (I was his partner): "I knew Bernie didn't have the King of Spades because he melded a Pinochle (a Jack of Diamonds and a Queen of Spades), without a marriage (without the King of Spades). When it got down to the last two tricks, there were only two Spades left, the Nine and the King. I had the Nine. I knew Bernie didn't have the King. How about Eddie? Eddie played the other Queen on the first round of Spades. So Eddie didn't have the King or he would have melded the marriage. So the King had to be in your hand. That's why I pulled the last trump with my Ace and came back to you with the Nine of Spades. If I saved the Ace of Trump so we'd get last, and played the Nine of Spades, Eddie would have trumped it. Eddie still had the Trump Queen (of Hearts)."

It was as if Blinky could see each player's cards. A lesser player would not have known that Eddie had the Trump Queen and a small Club and no Diamonds and no Spades, and that Bernie still held the Jack of Diamonds and a King of Clubs. So for Blinky, the last Trump lead was not guesswork. For the rest of us, by that stage of the game, it would have been largely guesswork. But Blinky knew. Blinky's team usually won, regardless of who was his partner. Sometimes Blinky's father even let Blinky take a few hands in the grown-ups game, he was that good.

My father didn't play Pinochle. He didn't play at anything. His life was work. Of all our fathers, I suspect that mine must have had the lowest income.

***

Then there were the Mackey brothers.

They lived on Annapolis Avenue around the corner from me, between Ventnor Avenue and Atlantic Avenue. They were eighteen- and twenty-year-old school dropouts. They were big and mean. Their father was a giant of a man. He was an over-the-road truck driver. He drove a big rig for a long-distance freight hauler. Sometimes Mr. Mackey was away for two or three weeks, driving thousands of miles. When he was home, he spent his days on the front porch, drinking beer and playing the radio too loud. Mrs. Mackey was almost as big as Mr. Mackey. She had huge flabby arms and hands like fat, fleshy hams. The sons, Tom and John, were proof of genetic theory. They were big, sullen, sort of flabby, but powerful. They worked for the same freight company, as warehousemen. They were inseparable. They liked to hang out on the corner of Ventnor and Annapolis, smoking and drinking beer. We saw them almost every day. It was not a good idea to talk to them. There was always the tension that one of them would say something insulting or mean, and we would have to bear an insult without responding. We couldn't be near them for more than a few minutes before the insult came. The best thing to do was to avoid them, or to keep any encounter brief, limited to a hello. A prolonged encounter was bound to lead to an insult. Best not to let that happen, as we were not about to respond in kind or challenge them. How many times had Tom, the older Mackey brother, called to Eddie, "Hey, Dun-owski, I hear you're not even a Polack. What the fuck are you? A Jew? A Russky?" Tom thought that was so funny. He would slap his younger brother, John, on the belly with the back of his right hand, and laugh, a low, harsh, ugly laugh, more like a sneer. John always joined in, like it was the funniest thing. John's laugh was a snicker, somehow uglier than Tom's.

Tom's favorite line for Bernie was, "Hey, Resnos, I hear your father and mother are getting married next month," followed by hilarity.

Or to Blinky, "Hey, Geek, is your pecker a little fella like you?"

To me, a favorite taunt was, "Jackie-boy, I hear you sleep with your sister. Is she any good?" Another favorite name for me was "Jack-ass." What could we do? Our response was feeble. Something like, "Hah, hah, very funny." That one was safe. Anything sharper was liable to bring on dangerous consequences. Usually we didn't respond at all, just kept on walking, in silence, feeling demeaned and embarrassed. I hated them, and I hated my weakness and disgrace.

One day, Tom hurled this one at me in a reference to my mother's envelope-stuffing: "Hey Jack-ass, your mom must give great tongue with all that lickin' practice." I felt the heat rise, and I lost control. I shot back, "Your mom's a fat pig, and you suck hind tit!" Tom was stunned. He actually took a step backward as if I slapped him. His eyebrows raised in surprise. Before his surprise could turn to rage, I turned and walked away. I felt his eyes burning into my back. I knew I was going to pay a price for my outburst. With difficulty, I forced myself to walk, not run.

6

Showdown

EDDIE WAS WITH me. He witnessed the incident. When I turned to walk away, Eddie ran two or three strides to catch up. Neither of us spoke. Tom recovered from the shock of my insult. "Hey, come back here," he hollered. "You little bastard, I'm gonna beat the shit out of you." We kept on walking, ignoring Tom's shout. To reach Eddie's house was only some thirty steps. It seemed like a mile. One more bellow from behind, "Get back here, you little prick." But neither Tom nor brother John moved toward us. At last, the safety of Dunauskas's Market. We scooted inside, through the store, up the back stairway to the Dunauskas's second-floor apartment. "I thought he was going to kill me," I said, still trembling. "Why didn't he?"

"We'll know tomorrow," Eddie said. "Maybe he was too surprised to do anything. He ain't smart, you know. We'll see what happens tomorrow. But don't go near him by yourself. Wait 'til I'm around, or Bernie or Blinky. And if he comes at you, run. He'll never catch you, that fat piece of shit."

I managed to stay away from the corner where the Mackeys hung out. The fear of the next encounter was with me all the time, draining the pleasure out of everything I did. I wanted the showdown to happen, so I could get past it, but I dreaded it. I rehearsed my steps. I would walk by as if nothing happened. I would count on my reflexes to bolt at the first move toward me. I knew I could outrun them. They were slow-moving, mountains of knotted muscle. I imagined Tom coming at me. In my imagination, he was lumbering toward me, like an elephant, slow, huge. I practiced in my mind how I would run a dozen steps, then turn to face him. I imagined him standing still, frustrated by my quickness. I imagined him breathing heavily, glowering at me. What would I do then? I might just turn and walk away, nonchalantly, but turning my head just enough so I could see him out of the corner of my eye, ready to run again.

I imagined another scenario, in which after I turned to face him, I extended my right hand in a peace offering. I practiced the words, "OK, Tom, let's call it even." But I knew it would not work. Was I forever to remain in fear of Tom Mackey?

The corner where the Mackey brothers hung out was where Annapolis Avenue crosses Ventnor Avenue. Ventnor Avenue is the long north–south street that runs parallel to the beach, two streets inland. Michaelson's Bakery was on Ventnor Avenue between Dover Avenue to the north and Annapolis Avenue to the south. Just about everywhere I went was up-island or north of where I lived. I could avoid the Mackey's hangout corner, even though it was only a half-block away, because it was down-island. School, center city, hotels, the Nu-Enamel paint store where my father worked, the marketing company where my mother picked up and delivered her mailing pieces, all were up-island. There was hardly a reason to come out of our apartment and turn left, or south. If I had to head south, I could bypass the dangerous corner by walking around the block in the other direction, by heading north instead of south, then east to Atlantic Avenue, which is the first street that parallels the beach. Ventnor Avenue is the second. Once on Atlantic Avenue, I could head south, and cross Annapolis Avenue where it intersects Atlantic Avenue instead of where it intersects Ventnor Avenue. For me to go to those lengths to avoid the corner of Ventnor and Annapolis avenues was proof of my fear. I fooled my inner voice by giving myself no reason to head down-island.

Eddie and I talked about my problem. Bernie and Blinky, too. Bernie didn't share my optimism that I could quickstep away from Tom Mackey.

"He is quicker than he looks," was Bernie's opinion. "John will hold you, and Tom will beat you," Bernie said, dolefully, shaking his head from side to side to emphasize the negative outlook for what was bound to come.

Blinky had a different view. He squeezed his eyelids closed as he offered his opinion. "Jack, you should apologize to Tom. Holler, *Tom, I want to apologize.* Say it before you get close enough for him to grab you. Let him know you are going to apologize. Then say you are sorry. You did not mean to insult him or his mom. Then say, *Are you going to accept my apology?* See what happens." Blinky's idea was to buy peace at the price of self-respect.

Eddie spoke for me. "No good, Blinky. Jack ain't gonna back down. Tom is the prick. Jack ain't gonna apologize. He didn't do nothin' wrong."

"Yeah," I muttered. "Apology is out." Much as I feared a beating, I knew I could not bear the humiliation of such a craven solution. Eddie and I agreed that one beating was a better deal than carrying around the shame of begging forgiveness from that son-ofabitch bully. Tom Mackey ought to be apologizing to me. The problems were these: how bad a beating would I suffer, and would there be more than one.

***

May came, a season of promise for Atlantic City folks. The bleakness of winter was over. Days were getting longer. The promise of summer was in the air. The visitors would soon be here. Fresh money was coming. There was a sense of congratulation among the residents, having made it through another winter, about to reap the largesse of summer. The sun was climbing higher every day. Sitting on a boardwalk bench, you could trace the path that the sun would follow that day. High, reaching higher, a great arc. A great ball of fire rising out of the ocean, shrinking in size as it climbed into the sky. Why does the sun get smaller as it climbs higher? Sailing high in the midday sky, the sun is less than half its size at sunrise. And it gets bigger again as it sinks into the Western sky, behind the distant line of trees on the mainland. Why? Thirty years later, a physicist gave me the answer to that one, quite by accident.

One sunny Sunday afternoon in early May, the four of us got together for a two-hand touch football game on the beach, me and Eddie and Bernie and Blinky. We walked up, north, to Dover Avenue, then east, across Atlantic Avenue, and on up toward the boardwalk. At the foot of the ramp up to the boardwalk, I hollered, "Last one on the beach is a rusty mule," and the four of us sprinted up the ramp onto the boardwalk, and like a team of acrobats, we flipped the rail, in unison, our four sets of legs flying over our heads into the air, in unison.

Here is how you flip the rail: The railing is made of stainless steel pipe, about two-and-a-half inches in diameter. There is an upper, a middle, and a lower rail, supported by stanchions made of the same stainless steel pipe. The upper rail is forty-two inches high. The middle rail is twenty-eight inches high. The lower rail is fourteen inches high.

To flip the rail all in one smooth motion, you run toward the railing, your left hand grabs the top rail, palm out, fingers down. As you are grabbing the top rail, you hoist yourself so that your stomach is lying on the rail, as a pivot. At the same time, you throw your legs high in the air, over your head. Your weight comes off your stomach as your body turns upside-down, vertical, on the outside of the railing. You grab the outside of the lower rail with your right hand, fingers down. For a moment, you are held vertically upside-down by your left hand on the top railing and your right hand on the lower railing.

As your body completes the big circle and as your legs head downward, you push off with your right hand, twisting your body at the same time so you face the ocean, rather than the boardwalk, and to make sure you clear the edges of the boards, which protrude about eight inches beyond the stanchions. You complete the somersault in the air; the circle completed, you land on your feet on the beach. In some places, the beach is only four or five feet lower than the boardwalk. In other places, it is as much as ten or twelve feet lower. Flipping the rail is the fastest way down. The entire maneuver takes only two or three seconds. You could climb over the rail and position yourself on the outside edge of the boardwalk and then jump down to the beach, but that is the long way. And besides, flipping the rail is sort of an acrobatic feat—graceful, makes you feel a little like Douglas Fairbanks. All of my friends were accomplished rail-flippers. It also works on fences and brick walls, if they are not too high.

It was a warm day. We took off our sneakers and T-shirts. We wore only our all-purpose short pants. They were our everyday shorts. They doubled as swim trunks. They were made of heavy canvas-like cotton. After coming out of the ocean, they stayed wet for the rest of the day, their heavy cold wetness clinging to our legs all afternoon. They must have been very uncomfortable, but fifteen-year-olds don't feel any discomfort. If the day was hot enough and the sun strong enough, the pants might dry out by dinnertime.

The touch football teams that day were me and Blinky versus Eddie and Bernie. The team with Blinky always lost.

We played for an hour, then we raced into the ocean and showed how tough we were by diving into the first breaking wave. It was too cold, but the sun was bright and the air was warm. A lot of splashing and shouting helps to make the cold water tolerable. Then we ran out of the surf and threw ourselves prone on our backs, spread-eagled on the warm sand.

"Hey, guys," Blinky asked, "what's the plans for the summer?"

Eddie announced that he was going to spend the summer on his uncle's farm in Ohio, near a town called Coshocton. It was news to me.

"When are you going?" I asked.

"Right after school's over."

"When did this happen?" I asked.

"My father told me this morning."

"Will you come home on weekends?"

"No, the farm works seven days a week, and the bus takes a whole day to get there. I won't be back until Labor Day."

Boy, that was heavy news. I couldn't imagine summer without Eddie.

"What about you, Jack?" Eddie asked.

"My father got me a job at Krilow's Gift Shop on the boardwalk. Fifteen cents an hour. I'll be working in the kitchen gadget booth on the boardwalk in the front of the gift shop."

"Hey, that's good money," Bernie said.

"What about you guys?" I asked Bernie and Blinky. Bernie's aunt and uncle had a diner in Asbury Park. They had no children. Bernie was going to live with them for the summer and start learning the diner business.

"How 'bout you, Blinky?"

"Michaelson is giving me a job in the bakery. Ten cents an hour."

Really, I thought. *Why didn't I think to ask Michaelson? That sounded better than Krilow's. And Blinky would be working alongside Rhoda. What a deal!*

"Well, Blinky," I said, "it looks like it's gonna be just you and me this summer."

We lay on the sand, looking up at the sky. A few cottony clouds drifted by, slowly changing shape. Sea gulls circled above, their cries a musical background to our thoughts. *Cah, cah, cah.* We spoke to the sky.

"Guys," I said, "I have to tell you something. I have the *hots* for Rhoda Michaelson."

"She's pretty enough," said Bernie.

"It's not just that," I said, "she is ... just ... terrific. And what a figure!"

"She looks like the other cheerleaders."

"No, no," I disagreed. "Rhoda is different. She's like silk. I love to watch her."

"Why don't you take her out?"

"I tried. No deal. She goes out with guys seventeen, eighteen, even with some college guys. To her, I am a boy. Anyhow, I wouldn't know what to do."

"What's to know?" Blinky asked. "You grope her and kiss her and feel her up. When she gets hot, you go for her panties."

"Sure, Blinky, voice of experience. Did you ever kiss a girl?"

"No, but I know what to do when I get the chance."

"How 'bout you, Eddie? Did you ever kiss a girl?"

"Sort of," Eddie answered. "When we went to my uncle's farm last Christmas, the daughter of one of the farmhands took me in the barn and let me feel her up. Then she wanted me to kiss her."

I was aghast. "You never told me, Eddie."

"Nah, I promised her I wouldn't tell anybody."

"What was it like? Was she pretty?"

"She was old, maybe twenty-five. She was big and she smelled bad. She was full of pimples."

"Did it turn you on?"

"Naw, I wanted to get away from her. Then she grabbed my cock. It got hard and big. I don't know why. She sure wasn't pretty or anything."

"What happened?"

"I came in her hands. Boy, did I feel shitty. I wiped myself off with my shirt. I couldn't wait to get away from her. Then she grabbed my head and tried to kiss me. I wanted to pull away. She stuck her tongue into my mouth. Ugh. It was terrible. Then she made me promise not to tell anybody. She said her old man would beat the shit out of her. And me, bein' the boss's nephew and all. She said she would let me do some real good stuff to her if I wanted. But I just wanted t'get away from her. She wanted to know didn't I like what we did. I said *yeah, it was great.* She said *come on back here and we'll do some more.* I said *no, I gotta go.* I couldn't wait t'get away from her.

"Is that what it's like?" Bernie wondered.

"The way the big guys talk about it, it sounds better than that."

"She was too old," I observed, "and the pimples—ugh."

"Yeah," agreed Eddie, "I thought about doing that with somebody young, and pretty, like Rhoda, maybe. The idea makes me feel squirmy, like I could come just from thinking about it."

"Hey, lay off Rhoda," I almost snarled.

"Hey, take it easy, Jack. I don't mean Rhoda. I mean somebody like Rhoda. Don't get excited. I'm not going to move in on your girl."

"My girl. What a joke. Like Gene Tierney or Hedy Lamarr is my girl. To Rhoda, I am the little boy upstairs."

"Well, anyway, Jack," Eddie said, "you don't have to worry about me. If I wanna do any of that, I'll do it on the farm. I'll be goin' there soon. Those farm girls do all kinds of stuff. They know what to do. From watchin' the animals, I guess."

"How 'bout you, Bernie?"

Bernie confessed that he tried to kiss Alice Keever at the school Christmas party, but she turned her head away.

Blinky said he thinks about it all the time. He said he found a picture in a Western Stories comic book of a beautiful cowgirl tied up to a post with her hands behind her and her skirt above her knees. He said he gets turned on every time he looks at her. He keeps the picture folded into a textbook. He said he studies the picture every night. The rest of us were too kind to ask Blinky what else he did besides studying the picture.

"By the way, Jack," Blinky said, "your sister, Evie, is getting to be a looker. You ought to keep an eye on her."

"You stay away from her, Blinky," I warned. "She is just a kid."

I changed the subject. "My father says there will be a war before this year is over."

"Who cares," said Bernie. "It will be the Germans and the English and French. It ain't gonna involve us."

"My father says we'll get pulled in." I told them that he was in the World War. He says it will be just like that again. All four of us could be in the Army in a couple of years.

Bernie had an idea. "If there's a war, let's us all join up together."

"If there's a war, I'm gonna be a pilot," Blinky announced. "They like short guys 'cause there's not enough room in the planes, especially in a fighter plane."

"Sorry, Blinky, I can't picture you flyin' a fighter plane," Eddie responded. "Those guys are the best. They're strong and tough and smart."

"They are just guys," answered Blinky, "like us, only a few years older. What do you think—they are supermen? No, just guys like us."

"Me for the Navy," I declared. "My father told me the Army is the worst. He lived in mud and trenches the whole time. The Navy is clean."

"Yeah," agreed Bernie, "but when your ship goes down, everybody goes down with it."

And so it went, on a bright blue spring day, at age fifteen, still boys, full of the bloom of vigorous health and energy and the suppleness of youth. Adulthood and careers and responsibilities were still something in the distance, nothing to be concerned about, not yet.

Time to head home. We raced into the surf and dove into the first wave. We dropped our trunks halfway to let the ocean wash out the sand. We emerged clean, shining, smooth. On with the sneakers; T-shirts rolled tight and worn like neck bands.

"Race ya to Atlantic Avenue!"

It was a dead heat. The four of us pulled up at the same moment. Uh oh, across the street were the Mackey brothers. There were two other guys with them. I didn't know them, but I recognized them as sometime companions of the Mackeys. What were they doing on the corner of Atlantic and Dover? It was not their hangout corner.

The Mackeys spotted us, across Atlantic Avenue. They stopped their conversation and stood still, watching us, expressionless and silent, lions waiting for the gazelles to approach. The time had come. Confrontation time.

7

The Fight

ICOULDN'T TURN away. It would be a disgrace. Blinky tugged at my arm.

"Jack, tell him you're sorry." He blinked, furiously. I pulled away from Blinky and his appeasement sentiment. I heard Bernie whisper, "Jack, don't cross the street. Let's head up to Elberon" (the next street in the up-island direction).

Eddie spoke up, "C'mon, Jack, let's cross over and get it over with."

Eddie and I started across the street. Bernie and Blinky followed, a few paces behind. I tried to recall my imagined rehearsals, how I would quickstep out of his reach. I couldn't remember anything. My legs felt weak.

I reached the corner. My idea was to say *hi, guys* and walk right by. I was ready to bound away at the first sign of attack.

When I was within ten feet of the Mackeys, I started to say it. *Hi* was as far as I got. Tom Mackey sprang at me like a cat. His left hand shot out and grabbed my upper right arm. He struck me on the left side of my head with his right fist, a sledgehammer. I would have fallen from the blow, but he held me up with his left hand, like a vise grip, and he beat me again on the left side of my head. I felt myself losing consciousness. Before he could beat me yet a third time, Eddie jumped at him and began to pummel him in the face with a torrent of punches. Tom let go of me to deal with Eddie. I fell to the pavement. Eddie's arms and fists were a whirlwind, beating at Tom's chest, shoulders, and head. With a grunt, Tom drew his left arm across his chest and with a great sweeping backstroke, he knocked Eddie to the ground with the back of his hand. I got to my feet and rushed at Tom. I butted him in the stomach with my head and tried to get my arms around him. He was like a mountain. He slapped down at me with his huge ham of a right hand and knocked me down again. Bernie and Blinky backed away. They stood motionless at a safe distance.

Eddie and I got up and charged Tom again, together. We almost knocked him down. He staggered back a couple of steps, then he punched me to the ground again with his right fist and at the same time, he slapped Eddie to the ground again with the back of his left hand.

I started to get up again. Tom kicked me in my ribs. I felt a rib crack. A wave of stabbing pain. He lifted his leg to kick me again. Eddie grabbed his foot and with a mighty twist, he brought Tom down. Before Tom could push himself up, Eddie and I were on him, pounding and pounding. We were going to beat him up! I was in a blind rage. Tom tried to brush us off, but he couldn't get leverage. He was flat on his back, using his arms to fend off our blows.

Two great hands grabbed at the backs of Eddie's neck and mine. It was Tom's brother John. Another vise grip. It felt like he could lift me in the air by the back of my neck. He pulled us off of Tom, and with a big push he shoved us away, more like he threw us away.

"Get goin', kids," he said, threateningly. "I don't wanna hurt you. Stay away from us. Next time, you won't get off so easy." Tom was up on one knee. He snarled, "I'll kill you, you little pricks." John repeated, "Get goin', if you know what's good for you."

My head was bursting with pain. My left side had a sharp stabbing pain. I could barely stand. The pain in my ribs kept me bent over. I limped away, full of pain and humiliation and rage. Eddie threw his right arm around me to help me along. Bernie and Blinky joined us, their heads hung down in shame. "I'm sorry, Jack," Bernie apologized. "I should have jumped in."

"Yeah, me, too," Blinky pleaded. "I'm sorry, Jack."

I didn't answer them. I didn't go home. I went with Eddie to his house. He only had some bruises. The left side of my head was on fire with heat and pain. Eddie wrapped ice in his T-shirt and held it to my head. He probed the left side of my head with his fingers, trying to feel if my cheekbone was broken. It hurt something fierce.

"I don't think anything is broken here, Jack," he said, "but you're gonna swell up like a balloon. How does your side feel?"

"It hurts bad, Eddie, and when I inhale, it's murder."

"I ought to get you to the hospital." Eddie was worried.

"No. I don't want my folks to know about this. How 'bout you, Eddie? Did you get hurt?"

"I skinned my knee and my left arm when I hit the pavement. But, Jack, you gotta get some help, if you got broken ribs. I read that a broken rib could puncture your lung. And that would be ballgame."

I answered in a whisper. It hurt to talk. "I read that the only thing to do for broken ribs is to tape yourself up. If my lung was punctured, I would know it by now. You can't let my father know about this. He will try to fight Mr. Mackey. He won't let anybody get away with an insult. Mr. Mackey is a goddamn mountain. He'll kill my father. I'm telling my folks that I got beaned on the side of my head with a baseball. That has to be our story."

So Eddie took a dollar from his secret money box under his bed and ran to the pharmacy and bought some two-inch tape. He taped me up, real tight. It eased the pain, but I had to take shallow breaths. We talked about the debacle and how to restore our self-respect, but we couldn't find an answer.

"I was real disappointed in Bernie and Blinky," I told Eddie. "They should have helped, or at least tried."

Eddie was more philosophical. "You can't blame them, Jack. It's just as good that it wasn't a real fight. We all coulda got hurt real bad. You and me got off lucky. Those Mackeys are like supermen. They must weigh 250. And did you see how quick Tom was? Like a cat. He grabbed you so fast. I never thought he could move like that."

"I never saw it coming," I winced as I spoke. "I thought I could dodge him and dance around or I never would have come so close. He was like lightning. And his hand was like a damn vise. It felt like he could break my arm just by squeezing."

"So what do we do?" Eddie asked.

"Steer clear of them," was my answer, "but sooner or later, we gotta even the score."

"Yeah," Eddie repeated. "Sooner or later, we gotta even the score."

"Yeah, but how?"

Eddie and I swore Bernie and Blinky to secrecy. Bad enough we had to live with our humiliation. No need to broadcast it.

My father never heard about my beating. Neither did Mr. Dunauskas. Not then, anyway.

***

Eddie and I became closer friends than ever. We shared the shame and frustration. Bernie and Blinky apologized for their behavior. Eddie and I accepted their apology, but our closeness with Bernie and Blinky was damaged. We hung out together like before, except something was different. We were all ashamed; Eddie and I for the beatings, Bernie and Blinky for holding back. We never spoke about it. The easy laughs became rare. We went through the motions of being carefree fifteen-year-olds. It didn't work. Eddie and I knew that a showdown finale had to come. We were scared of it. The longer the delay, the more ominous the dreadful anticipation.

By Memorial Day, I was all healed in the ribs and cheek. I was looking forward to summer vacation and starting my summer job at Krilow's. I was going to avoid the Mackeys and not think about them all summer. I wanted to put off the showdown until the fall.

8

Memorial Day

MEMORIAL DAY! BRIGHT and sunny, with a light spring breeze. The ocean sparkled like a million diamonds. Memorial Day was my favorite day. It was a day of promise—the promise of summer, end of school, return of the tourists, and good times. Atlantic City celebrated Memorial Day with a wonderful parade on the boardwalk. High schools from a dozen nearby towns brought their bands and drum and bugle corps. The Army, Navy, and Marines sent small contingents to the parade. Local businesses joined in the parade. So did some national companies like Coca-Cola, Lucky Strike, Wrigley's Spearmint chewing gum, Colgate (the smile of beauty) and Sal Hepatica (the smile of health), Hershey's Chocolates, Texaco, Philco, and others.

I was going to the parade with Eddie, Bernie, and Blinky. Evie planned to go to the parade with three of her girlfriends. Mom insisted that I take Evie and her friends with us. Mom didn't want the girls to be alone in the big crowds.

"Aw, Mom …," I protested.

"Sorry, Jack, if it will be an annoyance for you and your friends. I won't let Evie and her friends go by themselves. They're children, Jack. They can't be by themselves in the middle of those crowds. You have to take care of your sister and her friends."

Dad's store was closed for the holiday. He was going to march in the parade with some of the World War veterans. Mom decided to stay home. She said it was a good opportunity to do some spring-cleaning and finish stuffing two loads of circulars.

So the eight of us started out early to beat the crowds. We walked on the boardwalk, uptown to the Dennis Hotel, which was about halfway along the line of the march. Eddie and I stood on the top of the boardwalk railing, on opposite sides of a light pole. I balanced on the rail and supported myself from falling off by wrapping my left arm around the light pole. Eddie, on the other side of the light pole, did the same thing, supporting himself by wrapping his right arm around the light pole, right beneath my left arm. Bernie and Blinky did the same thing twenty feet away, at the next light pole. The girls sat on the railing, between the two light poles. They balanced themselves by locking the right foot behind the middle rail and resting the left foot on the lower rail.

By the time the parade started, crowds were thick on both sides of the boardwalk, three and four deep. Lots of folks carried and waved American flags. It was all very colorful and cheerful. Bunting and banners were strung up along the entire line of the march. Every hotel wore the colors on this day.

A blast of bugles! Here comes the parade! First came the Atlantic City High School Drum and Bugle Corps. The snare drums rattled their message, *rat-a-tat, rat-a-tat.* The bugles spat out their tattoo from the opening bars of a Glenn Miller march, *daaadadadadadadah*! The bass drum thumped. *Boom! Boom! Boom!* Then came the flag bearers, followed by the Atlantic City High School Marching Band led by twelve baton-twirling majorettes. I loved the way the majorettes looked in their white patent-leather boots and prim blue-and-white military jackets, peaked officer's caps with red, white, and blue cockades, and their short pleated skirts, white with blue pleats peeking through.

The armed forces were represented by a Navy band, a platoon of soldiers with their own drum and bugle corps and color guard, and a platoon of Marines. Slow-moving open convertible cars were scattered throughout the parade, some carrying dignitaries, some carrying advertising banners of the participating national companies, others carrying the banners of popular hotels, restaurants, stores, and so forth. Every car had a pretty girl seated on top of the rear seat, smiling and waving to the crowd on either side of the boardwalk. Every car flew two American flags upright on their front fenders. The high school marching bands and drum and bugle corps were spread throughout the parade. Their music filled the air, from the band just passed and the band that was passing to the band that hadn't yet reached us; all of it mixed together and blanketed the crowds with spirited sound.

Representatives of the wars were formed into marching platoons, each platoon carrying an American flag of its time and a number of regimental flags. The World War was represented by three platoons of forty men each, marching in good order. They wore their World War doughboy uniforms for the most part, with a sprinkling of sailors in Navy blues. The World War was only twenty-one years past. The veterans were men in their forties. Most were getting too big for their old uniforms. I spotted my father in the front platoon. I waved wildly and shouted. He noticed me, gave me a salute and a smile as he marched by. In the middle platoon, I noticed a man who looked out of place. He was wearing a gray suit and hat, with a white shirt and a gray necktie. He looked as though he should be sitting behind a desk in an office, not marching in a platoon of soldiers. He wore a military ribbon on his lapel. I couldn't know then that he was the cocoa man and would become an important part of my life.

There was only one platoon of Spanish-American War Veterans, about thirty men, in their late fifties and sixties. They looked pretty fit for the most part, but their marching was ragged. Only a few were in uniform. Most wore suits. Only their American Legion caps and campaign ribbons hinted at their past military service.

A line of six green Army jeeps were in the parade, each one towing a field artillery piece. A flight of four Kittyhawk fighter planes buzzed the parade. They were painted with shark teeth on their fuselages, like the Flying Tigers, who flew the same planes for the Chinese against the Japanese. The Japanese invasion of China was in its seventh year, the long-playing overture to World War II.

The sentimental favorite of the spectators was the Civil War platoon, a handful of frail men, in their nineties, struggling to keep up. A number of them walked with canes and several were accompanied by young men on whose arms the aged veterans leaned heavily. A few rode in open cars. All of the Civil War veterans were in uniform, faded blue coats and blue trousers and old blue forage caps. The Civil War veterans received the biggest cheers and applause as they passed. One of them stumbled and fell. He was not embarrassed. He smiled to the spectators as three of his comrades lifted him to his feet. He resumed his march to a great burst of cheers from the spectators. Eddie and I shouted, "Hoorah! Hoorah!" and whistled our loudest.

Across the boardwalk, I saw a well-dressed black couple walking up the ramp to the boardwalk. The man carried a little girl on his shoulders. The woman held his arm. I could see over the crowd because I was standing on the rail. A policeman appeared. He barred their way by holding out his billy club, horizontally, with both hands, arms stretched forward. I couldn't hear what he said, but the message was clear. No blacks allowed on the boardwalk. They turned and walked away. The incident went unnoticed. The crowd was facing the boardwalk, craning to see the parade, many on their toes, a few standing on boxes that they brought to the parade. The incident took less than a minute. The general revelry was not disturbed.

As the open cars went by, Eddie and I rated the girls in them. Some were great looking. They must have been models, hired for the occasion, or else the best-looking girl working for that particular sponsor's Atlantic City office.

"Hey, look at Miss Haddon Hall," Blinky hollered over, as a pretty girl went by wearing shorts and a halter. "Look at those legs. Oh, boy!" I agreed.

Near the end of the parade, two boys, who looked to be about seventeen, pushed to the railing where Evie and her friends were sitting. The boys looked drunk. They were carrying beer bottles, which they raised to their lips frequently. They were sweaty and unkempt. One of them put his hand on the railing, next to Evie, and leaned toward her. With a drunken grin, he leered at her and slurred his words, "Hello, Baby, how ya doin'?" He leaned closer. The other boy placed his hand on the railing on Evie's opposite side, so that Evie was between the two boys.

"Hey, you two," I called down, "get away from that girl!"

The boys looked up at me. One of them flicked his fingers under his chin at me in an expression of contempt. I jumped down from the railing. Eddie jumped down a moment before me. Without a word, Eddie moved to the boy who made the gesture and drove his right fist into the boy's face. The boy fell to the boardwalk. Meanwhile, the other boy backed away. I lifted the downed boy and said *get lost*! But instead of moving off like his pal did, he charged at Eddie. Eddie knocked him down again. The crowd closed in on us. A man who witnessed the incident spoke softly to the boy on the ground. "You'd best to be gone, son." The man helped me lift the boy to his feet, and repeated his advice, "Best to be gone, son." The boy wiped his face with his arm and joined his friend. They walked off into the crowd.

"Thanks, Mister," I said.

"Nothing, son," the man said. "I saw the way your friend hit that boy. I did that boy a favor by getting him to leave."

Evie was on the verge of tears. "Thank you, Eddie," she wiped her eyes and smiled.

"Yeah, Eddie," I said, "Thanks. I was gonna talk to him. Your way was better."

We climbed back on the railing to watch the rest of the parade.

A platoon of Atlantic City police marched by, led by a baton-twirling majorette, borrowed from Atlantic City High School. They marched poorly. They sort of strolled along, sort of in formation, nothing crisp or military-looking about them.

"Look at AC's finest," I called to Eddie. "What a sad-looking bunch. Hey, wait a second!"

Behind the police platoon came a white convertible with a uniformed man and a beautiful girl sitting atop the rear seat. The man was a stocky fellow in full, heavily braided police uniform. He sported a thick, black mustache, and he was smoking a cigar. When he waved to the crowds, he waved with the cigar between his fingers. A few waves, then a chew on the cigar as he leaned back and aimed the smoke into the sky. The girl was maybe the prettiest in the parade. She looked to be a late teenager or maybe twenty or so.

"Hey, Eddie, who's that?"

Eddie shrugged. He didn't know.

A nearby spectator turned to say, "That's Police Chief Leonard and his daughter. She is probably going to be Miss New Jersey this year. She's won every beauty contest she has been in so far. If she doesn't make it as Miss New Jersey, the Mayor wants to enter her as Miss Atlantic City. Pretty girl, isn't she?"

Pretty, I thought. *Gorgeous is more like it.* I wished for the next four or five years to pass quickly. I wanted to be nineteen or twenty and dating girls like the Chief's daughter or Rhoda. I thought Rhoda was as pretty as the Chief's daughter, but not as grown up, not as *full*. Rhoda still had some teenage puppy cuteness. The Chief's daughter was all woman.

Memorial Day! I loved it.

On the way home, I told Eddie that I never stopped thinking about the Mackeys. I said something happened every day to make me remember that I had unfinished business with them—or maybe they had unfinished business with me.

"With *us*," Eddie corrected me. "Don't worry, we'll figure out a plan."

"I tell you what, though, Eddie, I learned something today when you beat up that kid. Start swingin'. Walk right up and start swingin'. I didn't know what I was gonna do. Maybe tell the kid to get lost. I didn't figure it was goin' to be a fist fight."

Eddie stopped and faced me. "Listen, Jack," he said. "There's a time for talkin' and a time for punchin'. I didn't wanna get into a pissin' contest with that punk. I wanted to get him the fuck out of Evie's face."

"Your way is the right way," I said, thinking about the Mackeys.

That evening, at dinner, Evie told my mom and dad how Eddie protected her.

"See, Jack," said Mom. "I knew the girls should not go alone."

"I guess you were right, Mom," I said. "Hey, Dad, you looked swell in your old uniform."

"I hope you will never have to wear one," was his reply.

***

School ended in mid-June. Hooray for summer! I was looking forward to it. I had a new job. I knew I was going to miss Eddie, but I was glad to get separated from Bernie and Blinky. I needed time away from them. I never stopped seeing them standing by, fifteen feet away, while Tom Mackey gave me that beating.

Eddie took off for his uncle's farm in Ohio. I went with Mr. Dunauskas to see him off at the bus terminal. When he got ready to board, I stuck out my hand to shake hands good-bye. He ignored my outstretched arm. He embraced me instead and said, "Have a good summer, Jack." Then he whispered in my ear, "Don't worry about the Mackeys. Stay away from them. We'll fix their asses in the fall."

With that, he swung onto the bus, and gave me a wave and a grin.

Bernie went to Asbury Park to learn the diner business. I saw little of Blinky, even though he was working right under my feet, at Michaelson's Bakery.

My summer job was at Krilow's Kitchen Gadgets. That's where I met the great Benny James.

9

Krilow's

KRILOW'S KITCHEN GADGETS was in a booth that opened onto the boardwalk at Virginia Avenue, directly across from the entrance to Steel Pier. Steel Pier was the very heart of Atlantic City. It was more than an amusement pier. It was a wonder. For the thirty-five-cent price of admission, you could spend the entire day there. There were three movie houses. There was live entertainment, the biggest names in show business: Eddie Cantor, Jack Benny, Tommy Dorsey, Frank Sinatra, all the singers, all the comics, all the big bands. There were bandstands and ballrooms and amusement rides. There was a diving bell with glass sides that held six people at a time and took you down to the ocean bottom. Down there, through the glass sides, in a pale green world, you could see fish drifting by, eyeing the diving bell curiously, and sometimes a shark. There were circus acts, a roller coaster, diving horses, wild animals, everything you can imagine, all included for the price of admission.

The boardwalk was not the same as today. There were no casinos. The hotels were grand masterpieces of ornate architecture. There were upscale stores, fine jewelry shops, designer women's stores, expensive antique shops, menswear in the English manner of expensive tweeds and buttery flannels, a few hot dog stands, some frozen custard counters, delicious chocolate and fudge shops, salt-water taffy shops, dozens of restaurants, and dozens of coffee shops; even Mr. Peanut walked the boardwalk, wearing a six-foot-high plaster-of-Paris head in the shape of a peanut with a broad-painted smile, as he hawked his peanuts and peanut brittle. Nothing tawdry. Nothing cheap. The boardwalk was a place of elegance, elegant hotels and elegant stores. And the visitors, they, too, were elegant.

Strolling the boardwalk was a favorite pastime. People dressed fashionably. Men wore hats and suits and ties, or fashionable blazers and ascots and English tweed caps and creamy slacks. The women on their arms wore well-chosen dresses and high-heeled shoes, and stylish hats and long ivory-colored satin gloves above the elbow, and, on cool evenings, fur wraps or fur coats. The boardwalk was always crowded. Except for when it rained, it was always jammed with strollers, all day and well into the night.

A trademark feature of the boardwalk was the wicker rolling chairs. They were open chairs on three wheels: two rear wheels and a single wheel in front. The front of the chair was a curved basketwork panel that gave the rider a feeling of being in a carriage, rather than just sitting in a chair on wheels. Some of the chairs had roofs; others were open. A man pushed the chair for twenty cents an hour. Two could sit comfortably, maybe three, if they were slim or if one was a child. Some sections of the boardwalk had chairs lined up, stationary, against the railing. Those chairs were rented by the week or by the season to people who wanted to sit out in the evening and watch the boardwalk strollers. Friends sometimes rented adjoining chairs. It was a very social thing to do. The rolling chairs disappeared around 1955, though years later they would make a comeback.

If you look at those old grainy black-and-white photos of the strollers, you might notice that all the people are white. Where are the blacks, the Hispanics, the Asians, the American Indians? The answer is that there were none. Not on Atlantic City's boardwalk. Hispanics, Asians, and American Indians were rarities. You might not encounter one in months, anywhere. Blacks, on the other hand, were plentiful in Atlantic City but not on the boardwalk. They worked behind the scenes in every hotel and restaurant, out of sight, in the kitchens and the laundries and the basements. In 1939, they were "colored people" or "Negroes." They weren't "blacks" until thirty-five years later. Atlantic City was as segregated as any city in the Deep South, not by ordinance, but by practice.

A black person who strayed onto the boardwalk was soon hustled off by the boardwalk policemen. Blacks were not seen on the beach either, except on a one-block stretch of beach in front of Missouri Avenue next to Hamid's Million Dollar Pier, which was an amusement pier similar to the great Steel Pier, except smaller and not as popular.

The beach for blacks had a name, a derogatory one. It was called Chicken Bone Beach, so-called because blacks were not served in the restaurants, not even at the boardwalk hot dog and hamburger stands. They were not permitted on the boardwalk, not even long enough to buy a hot dog to eat elsewhere, not even in order to cross it to walk down the opposite steps to Chicken Bone Beach. Chicken Bone Beach was reached by walking *under* the boardwalk, where the sand was dug out to allow walking through without stooping. For blacks visiting the beach, box lunches of fried chicken were the order of the day; hence, the name. It is not one of Atlantic City's proudest memories.

Mr. Krilow owned a big gift and candy shop on the corner of Virginia Avenue and the boardwalk. The kitchen gadget booth was at the boardwalk end of the store. Being opposite Steel Pier, it was the center of the busiest part of the boardwalk, where there were always crowds of people.

The kitchen gadgets were a variety of small, inexpensive kitchen implements—a plastic grater, plastic knives, a curved grapefruit knife, plastic spoons and forks, a pushbutton bottle cap that made a carbonated soda bottle shoot out its contents in a frothy stream like an old-fashioned seltzer bottle, an egg poacher, a rotary potato peeler that carved a raw potato into a chain of thin slices, a juicer that plugged into an orange and let you squeeze out a glass of juice, and other cheap but handy items.

The gadgets were sold by a pitchman who stood behind the counter, right on the edge of the boardwalk, demonstrating the items. The pitchman stood on an eighteen-inch-high platform. The countertop was likewise elevated, giving the counter sort of a pulpit feeling. The pitchman gathered a crowd. He cried out, "Ladies, Gents, gather 'round. Step up for the next demonstration. You'll be entertained, you'll be educated! You ain't *never* seen anything like it. You won't find these things in any store! I'm gonna surprise you. It's a giveaway. And *it's all done to advertise.* Gather 'round. Yes, you, sir, step in a little closer. You, too, madam. Step right up" ... and on and on, until he had the nucleus of a crowd. A crowd is a magnet. It attracts just by being a crowd. The pitchman's performance makes it grow quicker and larger.

Krilow's employed a few pitchmen and a few shills. The shill's job was to stop in front of the booth and be the first spectator, help get a crowd formed. People rarely assembled unless someone was already standing there, looking interested. Nobody wants to be a pioneer. Nobody wants to go first.

The pitchmen were colorful, glib, entertaining. They had a personal magnetism that made them believable and effective. They all dressed the same way, sort of a pitchman's uniform: a blue-and-white striped shirt, with rolled-up sleeves, blue suspenders, a yellow necktie, and a white apron. They kept their arms clean shaven, their hands and nails manicured. The booth had pink lights above the counter, giving the pitchman and the vegetables a very attractive soft, rosy tint—clean, smooth-shaven rosy arms and rosy vegetables and rosy hands and immaculate fingernails. Only the headgear was not uniform. Some pitchmen wore a white chef's hat, others preferred a yellow straw skimmer.

The pitchman gave his pitch, demonstrating the gadgets, all the while keeping up a non-stop line of explanations, jokes, and quips that made the demonstration interesting and amusing.

"Now look at this handy grater. You'll never scrape your knuckles with this beauty. Don't serve your husband mashed potatoes laced with your scraped and bloody knuckles. Lady (looking earnestly into the eyes of one), I can tell that you are good in the kitchen … and I'll bet your husband finds you even better in other parts of the house!" The crowd laughs. The lady giggles. The pitchman holds up his palms. Big grin. "Did I say something wrong? Look here, you'll grate and shred carrots! Look, this side slices, this side grates! Look here, you'll shred lettuce; you'll shred cabbage! Look, you'll make coleslaw! You'll make hot slaw! Why, you'll use this little wonder so much, you'll wonder how you ever got along without it!"

Rosy arms and rosy hands in constant motion, shredding, grating, slicing, using a large kitchen knife to arrange the shredded and grated vegetables into a neat pile, always asking the audience to step in closer to see his handiwork. Then the big knife blade sweeps the vegetable parts into a hole in the counter into the container below. He dips the plastic grater in water to demonstrate how easily it was cleaned. Then on to a demonstration of the next item.

He demonstrates the bottle cap by holding a bottle of ginger ale with the cap on it and shooting a fizzy stream of ginger ale into a tumbler. The juicer was a plastic cylinder with a disc-shaped ring around the center. One end was serrated. The pitchman plunges the serrated end of the cylinder into the top of the orange as deep as the ring will let it go in. He holds the orange upside down. Effortlessly, with one hand, he squeezes out a glassful of juice. It was as easy as apple pie. The glass was a special glass with very thick walls. It didn't take much juice to fill it, but it looked like a lot of juice. The juicer seemed to release a fountain of juice with just a light squeeze of the orange. When the pitchman had the crowd won over, it was time for the sell.

"Now here's what I'm gonna do. Today. Just this once. Remember, it's all done to advertise. You're a good bunch." Holding open a brown paper bag, he drops in item after item. "I'm gonna give you the grater, a $1.98 value, folks, and I'm gonna give you the handy grapefruit knife. That's worth a quarter. And I'm gonna throw in the juicer. That's worth a couple of bucks, and I'm gonna let you have it all for … wait a moment. I'll throw in the bottle cap fizzer. You'll never have a bottle of soda go flat again, and all for … wait, what the devil. Look here, take the plastic knife, fork, and spoon … all of this for ONE DOLLAR! Look at this, you get the grater, the grapefruit knife, the juicer, the bottle cap, the knife, fork, and spoon. Altogether, a six dollar value! For this demonstration, ONE DOLLAR! *It's all done to advertise!*"

At this, the shill pushes forward, one hand raised, holding a dollar bill like a battle flag, yelling, "I'll take one!" That gets the crowd started. Everybody wants a bargain, but nobody wants to go first.

My job was pitchman's helper. I stood behind him in the booth. I kept the booth organized. I kept the merchandise arranged. I kept the booth clean. I replaced the container under the hole in the counter where the pitchman pushed the cut-up and grated vegetable parts. I ran back and forth to the second-floor storeroom to get more merchandise. I handed up the items as the pitchman needed them for the demonstration. When the selling began, I filled the bags and handed them up to the pitchman.

I liked to think I was a pitchman-in-training. But I was not. I was the gopher; I never made it to pitchman.

My favorite pitchman was a twenty-five-year-old charmer who called himself Benny James.

After I met him, my life was never the same.

10

Benny James

I'M SURE THAT wasn't his name. My guess is he adopted the names of two favorite big band leaders of the day, Benny Goodman and Harry James. Girls adored him. He was handsome. He had a million-dollar smile, dark curls, dancing blue eyes—a cavalier. Smooth as silk. Pleasant as sunshine. Everybody adored him. A good-looking girl was always waiting for him at the end of his shift; summertime girls in light cotton dresses, beautifully tanned, with smooth shoulders and bare legs and shining hair. For a fifteen-year-old boy, Benny's girls were an out-of-reach dream. How I envied him. Most times Benny showed up for his shift a little tipsy. He drank too much. He smoked incessantly. He was the best of the pitch-men. I don't know what he earned, but it must have been a lot. Benny must have been good for $75 or $80 a week. This was 1939, when a family of four could live on less than $30 a week, when $100 a week was affluence, when $200 a week was big time. I was earning fifteen cents an hour.

After I had been working at Krilow's for two weeks, I decided to bring a bag of gadgets home to mom. Our gadgets were really nifty. During a lunch break, I ran up to the second-floor storeroom and asked the bookkeeper, Mrs. Adler, if I could buy a one dollar bag. I told her that I wanted to give it to my mom. Mrs. Adler looked at me strangely.

"Why don't you just take a bag, Jack?"

"Mrs. Adler, I want to *buy* a bag."

"Just take one, Jack," she said. "A bagful of the stuff only costs us thirty-five cents, including the bag."

"Can't I *buy* a bag, Mrs. Adler?" I asked. Why didn't Mrs. Adler understand me? After looking at me searchingly, without speaking, for about ten seconds, she said, "OK, Jack, but take two. You're entitled to an employee discount."

Mom was delighted with my gift. I felt grown-up. I spent about seven hours' wages. It was worth it to buy a gift with money that I earned myself.

Most of the shills were drunks who managed to pull themselves together long enough to make it through a demonstration. They probably collected $1.50 for their dollar when they turned in the brown bag they pretended to buy. The pitchman was at the top of the pecking order. He was respected by all—the folks in the store-room on the second floor, the bookkeeper. Even Mr. Krilow was deferential to the pitchmen, and especially to Benny James.

When Benny demonstrated the bottle cap, he held the bottle a full two feet away from the tumbler and shot the soda into the tumbler. It was Benny's special trick. I tried to do it. The best I could do, like the other pitchmen, was to start out a few inches away and draw back slowly, after making sure I was in the target.

Benny was my hero. He was everything a fifteen-year-old boy wants to be. And, he liked me. "Jack, you're a good kid. I'm gonna teach you. Wanna try a pitch?" Sure, I wanted to, but I couldn't. I could croak out the first "Step right up, folks," but if anybody did, I froze. "You'll get the hang of it, Jack." Between demonstrations, he told me one story after another about his adventures and his women. He was the most exciting, most glamorous guy I had ever known.

Benny shared some of his wisdoms with me: "Treat girls tough, Jack; they love it." "If you want to know how a guy is doing, look at his shoes and cuffs; they tell you everything." "Jack, when you're in trouble, laugh; when you're in big trouble, laugh big." "Don't stay in one place too long; your ass will grow roots." "Don't be afraid of the boss, Jack; make him afraid of you!" "Jack, be a little nuts; people are careful how they behave with a nut." "Dress sharp, Jack, look like a winner; nobody likes a loser."

"What happens after Labor Day, Benny?" I asked one day.

"This town dies after Labor Day. I follow the action. I work the circuit. Kitchen gadgets, auto wax, miracle cleaners. I work the fairs, the carnivals, the resorts. Lots of girls and lots of money. I keep moving."

"Will you be back in Atlantic City next summer?"

"Maybe yes and maybe no. Depends what I find and where."

I adored him. When he showed up a half-hour late for his shift, a little wobbly, and gave me a big wink and said, "Whatta girl!" I would dissolve into wanting to be like him. Whatta guy!

11

Suppers With My Father

Working at Krilow's was good for me. I thought less and less about the beating that Tom Mackey gave me in May on Atlantic Avenue. I worked late. I got home late. I began to wait for supper until my father got home. He never had supper before ten. We ate together, exchanging news of the day. I started to feel close to him. I started to feel grown up.

One night at supper, I asked him how much rent we paid. Mom told me that was not my affair. Dad disagreed. He saw no reason why I shouldn't know the family's finances. So he told me everything. The rent, the phone, the gas, the groceries, the clothing—*everything*. And he told me how much he was bringing home and how much mom was making from envelope stuffing.

I was impressed that my parents were so solid and steady and how much work went into earning a tight-budgeted living for a family. I offered to contribute my salary to the pool. They would not hear of it.

"No deal, supporting this family is our job, not yours. You save your money. We want you to know how to handle money."

So I kept two dollars a week for myself to spend, and I put the rest in a handkerchief box that I kept under the top bunk bed mattress in Evie's room.

Those were my first real conversations with my father. We were fellow wage earners. He was earning $30 a week. I was earning $7. We talked about lots of things. We talked about his work and what made a business work. I even got him to tell me some stories of his service in the Army in the World War. He was nineteen when the United States entered the War. He enlisted and ended up as an infantryman in the American Expeditionary Force. He said it was a miracle that he survived six months of trench warfare without a scratch, while half of his company got killed or maimed or died from the flu. He was short on details. I pieced together something of the ugliness and horror. He drew a curtain over it, merely saying, "It was real bad, son. I pray you will never have to do it. I'm afraid another war is going to break out in Europe. This time Roosevelt will keep us out of it."

To a teenage boy, a father is an enigma. A boy wants his father to be a hero, to be wise and strong and all-knowing. Some fathers are always in disguise, behind an image of what they think they should be, careful to conceal anything that might mar the image, cheating both father and son by hiding the flaws of humanity in a failed attempt to project perfection. I only began to know my father that summer when he began to lower his guard over our late suppers.

Getting to know him brought an appreciation of his qualities. I had thought of him as a quiet and passive man. I was amazed that time when he punched out the truck driver who insulted Mom. I marked it up to a moment of bravado because he didn't want me or mom to think he was a coward. At the time, I thought the incident was out of character for him. I admired what he did. I thought maybe he didn't even realize what he had done. Later, I came to understand that his quiet reserve came from self-assuredness, not from feelings of inferiority as I had once thought, and that he would rather die than submit to insult or humiliation. All of that made it even tougher for me to bear the humiliation of the Tom Mackey beating without avenging it.

Working for Krilow's threw me together with men. I drew closer to my dad, and there was Benny James and another man who influenced me, the Amazing Roland.

12

Roland

Mr. Krilow also owned the Vi-de-lan Studio a few doors away from the kitchen gadget booth, near Pennsylvania Avenue.

The Vi-de-lan Studio sold a hair preparation made from combing out the natural oil in sheep's wool. It was called lanolin. The lanolin was processed into a smooth pale amber cream. According to the Vi-de-lan folks, it thickened, strengthened, lengthened, and generally beautified your hair. It made your hair healthier, too, and it stopped hair loss dead-in-its-tracks, and sometimes it even grew new hair on bald heads.

The Vi-de-lan Studio did not have a storefront. It was a small theater without seats that opened onto the boardwalk. Popular music of the day poured out of it from an amplified phonograph machine; favorites like *String of Pearls, Bei Meir Bist Du Schoen, Song of India, Pennsylvania Six-Five Thousand*, and *Sing, Sing, Sing*, and the big band sounds of the Dorseys, Glen Miller, Benny Goodman, Woody Herman, Harry James, and Glen Gray. The interior was shaped like a quarter sphere, like a miniature Hollywood Bowl. The floor was red quarry tile. The dome-like curve of the bowl was smooth ivory-colored stucco. There was a stage across the rear of the theater, concealed by a red-and-gold velvet curtain.

At the entrance was a large easel. A sign rested on it, four feet wide and more than six feet tall. The sign was pale ivory with bright red letters. It proclaimed:

VI-DE-LAN Studio

presents

ROLAND

THE INCREDIBLE MECHANICAL MAN!

$100 reward!

If you can make him speak or smile!

NEXT PERFORMANCE IS AT

Below the last line of text a clock face with movable hands pointed to the time of the next performance. The bright red text was superimposed on a pale, sepia-toned, life-sized, full-figured picture of Roland.

A few people attracted by the music and the sign drifted into the theater in anticipation of the performance. At the appointed time, the red-and-gold velvet curtain parted to reveal Roland. The audience grew. He was alone on the stage, standing perfectly still, at attention. The backdrop was a Parisian mural. It was painted from an impossible point of view from which, miraculously, you could see the Notre Dame Cathedral, the Arc de Triomphe, the Opera

House, the Eiffel Tower, Les Invalides, and Montmartre. Even Sacre Coeur was there in the background.

Roland was dressed as a Parisian boulevardier, like Maurice Chevalier. He wore a navy linen double-breasted jacket with a gold-embroidered crest on the breast pocket and white trousers. His shirt had blue-and-white stripes with a high white starched collar with rounded collar points, like an old-fashioned 1890s high celluloid collar. He wore a bright, wide red-and-gold necktie. A silk red-and-gold handkerchief peeked out of the breast pocket and above that was a tricolor campaign ribbon. His shoes were yellow, half covered by white laced canvas spats. He wore white gloves. The outfit was topped off with a round, flat-topped, yellow straw hat, a skimmer, with a red, white, and blue band.

Roland's left hand rested on the ivory cap of an ebony walking stick. He stood motionless, for fifteen seconds. Was it a person? Or a doll? You could not tell. Then, his head began to turn to the left, slowly, ever so slowly, with a series of minute motions, almost a smooth motion, but ever so slightly a tiny bit stiff and jerky, like a very well-crafted robot. The audience grew larger as passers-by stopped to watch. He lifted and moved his right arm and slowly, slowly, rotated his right wrist and hand. The fingers moved into a cupped position. Every motion was perfect. Just the faint hint of a mechanism, no movement perfectly smooth. He tilted his head up, down, turned it to one side, then to the other. He turned his torso, moved his arms, hands, even raised and lowered the walking stick. You thought, "It must be a doll. A man could not move like that."

What really captured your attention—and held it—was Roland's face. The straw hat was tilted rakishly to the right, revealing glossy, raven hair, luxurious, brushed straight back, covering the upper half-inch of his ears. The sideburns were perfect, an inch-and-a-half long and a half-inch thick. Was it a man's face? Or polished maplewood—absolutely smooth, with a circle of rouge on each cheek? Perfect black eyebrows, slightly arched, gave him a slightly quizzical expression. The eyes were deep-set and dark. They never moved. They stared straight ahead, motionless. *He never blinked!*

His lips were chiseled, outlined and touched with a pale red gloss, corners upturned ever so slightly, fixed in the faintest of smiles, a wooden doll-like smile. He had a thin, black pencil-line of a moustache, split in the center.

To add to the artificial look, Roland wore a gold-rimmed monocle in his left eye. Nobody wore monocles any longer. You saw them in movies about England in Victorian times, and one American actor, Charles Coburn, wore a monocle, sort of as a parody of an English country squire. All together, Roland was a handsome fellow. His expression suggested a thoroughly agreeable personality beneath the stiffness of the carved wooden features.

Slowly, Roland moved his arms and hands. Slowly, he turned this way and that, one motion at a time. At the end of each movement, there was an almost imperceptible quiver, as if the mechanism was stopping abruptly. He was able to take a few steps in exquisite slow motion. How could he do it? He had superhuman control.

Some in the audience made noises, called out, waved their arms, contorted their faces, spread their mouths open and wide with the forefingers of each hand, poked out their tongues. *$100 reward if you can make him speak or smile!* Roland's expression never changed. The dark eyes never wavered. As his head rotated, his eyes stared straight into the eyes of one audience member after another, piercing. When his eyes fixed on you for those few seconds, you had to look away.

All the while, a whisper of a whirring sound came from somewhere inside Roland's chest, the sound of well-oiled machinery, elegant, so smooth and quiet that the sound was barely audible.

Roland's performance lasted four minutes. Then, suddenly, he snapped to attention, thumped the walking stick, and breaking into a broad smile, swept off the straw hat and half bowed to the applause of his audience. At that moment, a door opened in the mural behind him and an attractive girl emerged onto the stage. She hooked her arm in Roland's and called out, "Ro*land*, ladies and gentlemen, the great Ro*land*! A big hand for Ro*land*." She pronounced the name with the emphasis on the second syllable, a broad "A," like *roLAHND*. She clapped her hands. The audience applauded again. "Before Ro*land* leaves us," she called out, "I want you to look at his hair." His hair *was* remarkable. It was thick, black as his ebony walking stick, gleaming, combed and brushed straight back, the richness of it sweeping around and over his head and across the tips of his ears, and full-bodied behind his head, ending in a thick sharp curving line across the bottom of his neck. "Now, look at *my* hair," she said. "Come closer. Look at my hair. You, sir, would you like to feel … my hair?" A chuckle and a broad smile. Her hair was long, full-bodied, shining, the color of old gold, full of highlights. "This is Vi-de-lan hair. Roland's hair is Vi-de-lan hair." Roland backed away, smiling and saluting to right and left, through the open door in the mural while the girl began her demonstration.

An assistant came on stage. He carried a tall table and a jar of Vi-de-lan. The girl demonstrated how to use Vi-de-lan. She lifted some from the jar, delicately, with the third and fourth fingers of her right hand. She stroked it into her hair. She brushed it in. She stroked in more and more, and brushed and brushed, long, languid strokes. She turned her head from side to side. The hair cascaded across her shoulders, a waterfall of golden richness, then across and to the other side and another golden waterfall. The long brush strokes showed off its marvelous shine and body.

As she brushed, she extolled Vi-de-lan: "Vi-de-lan is made from lanolin. Do you know what lanolin is? It is the oil that is impregnated in natural sheep's wool. You never saw a sheep go bald. You never saw a sheep with thinning wool. That thickness, that strength, that beauty comes from that special oil of the sheep. The lanolin saturates the wool and keeps it strong and healthy and thick. It waterproofs. A sheep can stand in rain for hours, days even, and the rainwater never penetrates the wool. It is the sheep's natural hair treatment. It preserves, it protects. It will do the same for you. Do you want hair like mine? Like Roland's? Sure, you do!"

Her demonstration went on for about five minutes. Then, the sales pitch, "Ladies and Gentlemen, you cannot buy Vi-de-lan in any store. This is the only place where you can purchase it. Only Vi-de-lan uses the natural sheep's lanolin. The price, it's only one dollar and fifty cents. This is a four-ounce jar. If you use it every day the way I showed you, it will last three months. So, if you are not going to be returning to Atlantic City any time soon, I suggest you buy several jars."

The assistant emerged again. Now he has a wheelbarrow. It is filled with jars of Vi-de-lan. A shill pushes forward, "I'll take two." That starts the buying.

I liked to watch the show during my lunch break. Roland fascinated me. Sometimes I practiced his movements, always in front of a mirror. I could almost get a few of the movements, but only fleetingly. The slow-motion walk was impossible. What control he had. And strength. Try it yourself. The slow-motion walk was excruciatingly slow. The rear leg has to lift up onto its toes slowly, ever so slowly, and he has to maintain balance, as the other leg slowly swings forward. It is impossible.

One day, Mr. Krilow called me up from the kitchen gadget booth to his office on the second floor. He asked me if I knew the assistant's job at the Vi-de-lan Studio. I told him I'd seen the show. I knew the assistant's job. It wasn't much. "Go over there now, Jack, they need an assistant. The boy didn't show up today. Work a few shows over there. I'll get someone to cover the booth here. Go around the back. There is a door back there."

I ran around the block to the alleyway behind the stores. I was excited. I was going to meet Roland.

13

Meeting Roland

ICOUNTED THAT the Vi-de-lan store was the fourth one from Pennsylvania Avenue. Then, in the rear alleyway, I counted the fourth door from the end. It was unmarked. I tried it. It was locked. I knocked. "Wait a moment," I heard. Then the sound of a lock turning and the door opened. It was a man, about forty years old, and more, mostly bald, wearing thick horn-rimmed glasses. "I'm from the kitchen booth," I said. "Mr. Krilow sent me to be the assistant."

"Come in. What's your name, son?"

I told him.

"You're a little early, Jack; we don't need you until I go off."

"Go off where?"

"I mean, finish my gig."

"What gig? Who are you?"

"I'm Roland, kid."

It couldn't be! This old man, Roland?

"Yes, yes, come in; you can watch me get ready."

There was a small dressing room. The man invited me in. "Sit down, young fella, make yourself comfortable. And watch me turn into Roland."

He took off his shirt. He was wearing an armless undershirt. I could see that he was well built except for a slight paunch, but sort of old and balding, and his face was kind of craggy. He covered his shoulders with a large terrycloth towel and seated himself on a folding chair in front of a counter with a large mirror against the

wall, brightly lit by a row of hooded bulbs across the top. The
counter was lined with tubes and jars and pencils and brushes.

He removed his glasses, dipped into a jar, and covered his face
with a pale coat of some kind of cream. "This is called basecoat,
Jack. It smoothes out my face. I have a problem making up
because I can't see worth a damn without my glasses. This part is
easy. The eyebrows and lips are hard because I can barely see what
I'm doing."

He took up a brush, dipped it in a powder, and powdered his
entire face. He rubbed in the powder. Then he rubbed in another
layer of a different cream. His face became smooth, every line and
wrinkle gone. He leaned forward to within six inches of the mirror,
squinting. With a stick of reddish gloss, he outlined his lips carefully and then filled in the outline. He used a black pencil to draw
the fine mustache right above the upper lip and then the slightly
arched eyebrows.

"You see, young fella, I'm becoming Roland!"

On the counter was a black wig resting on a figure of a woman's
head. He pulled on the wig. He turned to face me. "By the way,
Jack, my name is Morris, but see, now I'm Roland. Did Krilow
explain that you are not to talk about me, *ever*? Only a few people
know who I am. Roland has to be mysterious. Get it? You'll be
working with us from time to time. But you can't talk about me or
Roland or *anything*, get it? You don't even know who Roland is. You
only see him on the stage. Get it? OK, young fella? This is important. Don't forget. Roland is a man of mystery." He bent his head
and looked up at me from under his brow, "Mystery," he repeated,
"don't forget."

Carefully, he put on the heavy glasses. He stood up and shook
out the towel. Then he produced a girdle-like band, six inches

wide. He strapped it around his waist and tugged at it until it was tight. The band had three hooks, which found their way into three grommet holes. Gone was the paunch. He reached for his shirt. On it went, and then the tie and then the blue blazer. He slipped off the old khaki pants he was wearing, pulled on the white trousers and the yellow shoes. He laced on the white canvas spats. He removed the heavy glasses. From his left pocket, he lifted out the monocle and placed it under his left eyelid. He pulled on his gloves. The transformation was complete. He reached for the walking stick standing in the corner.

"Now, Jack, give me a hand onto the stage. It's dark. I can hardly see where I'm stepping. I can't see a damn thing without my glasses. Actually, it helps me because I can't see their faces. They are all a blur. When I tell you, you open the curtain. Ah, here comes Anne Marie, right on time. The curtain pull is over there. Then start loading the wheelbarrow. Hi, Annie, how's it going? Anne Marie will show you what to do. Your job is easy. When she is ready, help her hand out the jars and collect the money. After the show, sweep up. There will be cigarettes and candy wrappers all over the floor. OK? Any questions?"

"How do you keep from blinking?"

He laughed, "It's an illusion, Jack. When I pass my hand over my face and turn my head at the same time, I blink. It goes unnoticed. Annie, this is Jack. Say hello to Jack."

"Hello, Anne Marie." I offered my hand.

"Hi, Jack," she smiled. "Don't worry, I'll tell you what to do. You'll be fine."

Roland took a small round silvery metal device from his pocket. It was flat on the bottom with a shallow domed top. It had a hinged butterfly-shaped piece lying flat against the bottom of the device.

He raised the hinged piece so it became perpendicular to the flat bottom. He wound it several times. The device began to give off a low, whirring sound, the robot's motor. Roland slipped it into an inside pocket of his jacket. "This runs four minutes, Jack. When it stops, so do I."

"OK," said Roland/Morris, "let's do it!" He assumed his position. He nodded to me to pull on the curtain ropes. The ropes parted to reveal Roland, motionless, the mechanical man.

14

Letter from Eddie

Coshocton, Ohio
Sunday, July 9, 1939

Dear Jack:

Well, here I am on Uncle Ted's farm. He calls it Vilnius Farm. Vilnius is the city in Lithuania that he and my father came from. It is eight miles from the nearest town, which is called Coshocton, population 2,400. We work hard. We have fifteen acres of corn, twenty acres of tomatoes, seventeen acres of soybeans, and about fifty acres of grazing for the cows. We have twelve milking cows. We have a bull. We are raising twenty steers. They will go to the slaughterhouse in October. We have a mating pair of hogs and six hogs we are raising for slaughter. We have one horse and about fifty chickens. We have two farmhands and their wives. One couple lives with us in the main house. Another couple lives in a little house that my uncle and my cousin Boris built last year. Boris is seventeen. My cousin Nina is sixteen.

Uncle Ted has a beat-up seven-year-old Ford stake body truck. It was in terrible shape. I did a lot of work on it. Now it runs smooth. Uncle Ted could not get over it. He calls me *the mechanic*. Boris says he has to paint the truck to make it look as good as it runs.

Boris is a great guy. He is big and powerful. He was the starting fullback for Coshocton High last year. They won seven, tied one. When he goes back to school he will be a senior and about fifteen pounds bigger than last year. He is hoping for a football scholarship to Ohio State plus a living allowance. Everybody around here thinks he will get it because he is a really great fullback. Boris calls himself *Boris Dunn*. I think I'm going to be *Eddie Dunn* when I start high school. Dunauskas is such a mouthful. I hope my father doesn't go nuts when I tell him.

Cousin Nina is real good-looking. She looks like a picture of the All-American farm girl. She is blonde with blue eyes and a GREAT build. I could go for her if she wasn't my cousin. But I would have to fight off four farm boys from nearby farms. And they are BIG! The boys around here are all big. And strong. They toss around hundred-pound sacks of feed like you and me toss a football. Working on a farm is like working out twelve hours a day.

We all work real hard, seven days a week. Sunday morning we all drive into town for church then back to work. We get up at five every morning and work two hours until seven. Then we stop for breakfast at seven. Then we work until lunch at two, then we work until supper at eight. There are a few chores after dinner. When work is over, I go right to sleep. No radio. No reading. I am dead tired at the end of the day. I can't get over it that my uncle and his kids work like this all the time. And my aunt works the hardest. She gets up at four to start her chores. And when I flop into bed at nine, she is still downstairs cleaning up after supper and starting to get ready for tomorrow's breakfast. I guess I'll make it through the summer but full time of this, no thanks. I don't even want to go into town Saturday night. Too pooped. Uncle Ted is paying me ten dollars a week! I will save up $100 by the time I come home.

And listen to this. I built a pump, without electricity, to draw water up out of an old well. The well is about a hundred yards away from the house, on the other side of the barn. It is a good place for a well because it saves us going back to the house for buckets of water. There is a well under the kitchen. The house was built that way. Whoever built the house, they first dug a well under where the kitchen was going to be. Then they put an upside-down iron funnel into the water with a long iron pipe that goes all the way up into where they built the kitchen. Then they built the sink and the kitchen counter so the iron pipe comes up through the counter-top. They put a leather cone-shaped cup on the end of a long rod into the pipe, open end up, with a small hole at the pointed end, attached to a two-foot long pump handle. They cut an iron spout into the tube, and there, you got water at the sink. It's cold water. When we want hot water, we heat it on the stove.

Anyway, there is this old well near the barn. When I saw it, I asked Uncle Ted why he doesn't use it. He said the well was all clogged up twenty years ago when he bought the farm and he never tried to clean it out and anyway, it is easier to walk back to the house for water than to drop a bucket into the well or build a turnhandle.

I thought about it a lot. I figured out how to make an automatic well using a circular wind vane, like those miniature windmill vanes that you see in the movies out west where they use the wind vane to turn a generator to make electricity. Me and my cousin Boris cleaned out the well. There must have been twenty-five years accumulation of junk down there. And the smell! It could kill you. And it was black sludge. What a mess. I washed myself for hours afterward. I built my pump so the wind vane is lifting a rod inside a long tube down into the well. The rod has a leather cone-shaped cup, like inside the kitchen pump. The cup draws the water up the tube. I cut a spout into the tube. The water pours out of the spout. When the well is not being used, the up-and-down rod can be unhooked from the wind vane. When you want to draw water, you hook on the rod and the rod starts to move up and down. On the upstroke, it pulls the water up the tube until it runs out of the spout. The wind vane is fifteen feet in the air, on a tripod we built out of wood.

Sometimes there is not enough wind, so I built a hook on one of the vanes opposite the other hook that drives the up-and-down rod, and I have a long wooden rod, it's actually three broom handles lashed together, with an iron ring on the end. You reach up and put the ring over the hook. Then you can make the vane go around as fast as you want by pulling up and down on the rod. It works. We all use it. Uncle Ted said I am not only an auto mechanic, I am also a natural engineer. It was a great project. It made me feel real good because I improved the farm. A couple of neighboring farmers want me to build one for them. I told them to just copy what I did. I don't want to build the same thing. I am trying to figure out how to electrify my well without buying a generator and a motor. They cost too much. What I built was all from junk lying around the farm. For the vanes, I used the slats from a tomato bushel. They are one-quarter inch thick by two inches wide by eighteen inches long. Perfect. Uncle Ted never throws away anything. There are piles of pieces of lumber, wooden crates, bricks, stones, wrapping paper, barrels, string, bottles, cans, pieces of hose, rope—you name it. Nothing ever leaves this farm except the produce we sell. We don't have an indoor toilet even. We use the privy. So even our shit doesn't leave the farm. Whatever comes here stays here, except the crops. And me. I came in June and I'm leaving in September.

I been thinking about you and Tom Mackey. I got an idea. I'll tell you when I get home. I saw that girl I told you about from last Christmas. She got bigger. She wanted to talk to me but I said I'm too busy—ugh!

Hope you and Evie are OK. Hope you like working at Krilow's. It sure beats what I'm doing. My father said that when I get home after Labor Day, Dunauskas Delicatessen is gonna look real good to me.

Write to me.

Your best friend,
Eddie

15

Morris

AFTER MY FIRST experience at the Vi-de-lan Studio, Mr. Krilow made me the regular assistant for the 4:00 Vi-de-lan demonstration, every day except Tuesday, which was my one day off. I didn't have to arrive at the studio until 4:10, after Roland performed, but I tried to arrive at 3:45, to watch Morris turn into Roland. After the sales pitch, if the kitchen gadget place was still on break, I liked to watch Roland turn back into Morris; everything in reverse. Off monocle, off black wig, off navy blazer and white pants, off necktie, shirt, and collar. He used a cleansing cream to remove the makeup, and then lots of soap and water and vigorous towel work.

He liked to talk to me while he was dressing up or dressing down. I learned that he was in his twentieth year as Roland at Vi-de-lan. Atlantic City was his home. He was born here. He rarely left Atlantic City, even for a day, except when he was drafted during the World War. He lived alone in one room at Mrs. Ormont's boarding house on South Carolina Avenue above Arctic Avenue. Mrs. Ormont used to be Mrs. Goldberg, but after her husband died, one of her boarders translated her name into French. Morris was one of six boarders. It was a sort of seedy place in a seedy neighborhood, but clean. Mrs. Ormont served good meals, breakfast and supper every day.

Morris was a watercolor artist. He painted three to five watercolors every week. All were scenes of Atlantic City. He signed them

Morris. A boardwalk art gallery carried his watercolors on consignment. He priced his works at $2, $3, or $5, depending on how much he liked each piece. The gallery took 40 percent commission.

During the season, the gallery sold about ten pieces a week. For the rest of the year, maybe five pieces a month, so Morris's inventory was always growing. That summer, he had more than 200 pieces. The gallery would not stock more than twenty-five at a time. Morris kept the rest in a number of portfolios in his room. He searched through them every week to replace what the gallery sold.

Once every year in the spring and once in the fall, there was a two-day arts and crafts show on the boardwalk. Morris always participated, one of about a hundred artists, displaying their work along the boardwalk railing from Mississippi Avenue to Kentucky Avenue. Morris usually sold fifteen to twenty paintings during each boardwalk show.

Morris told me that he had a girlfriend once, when he was twenty-four. She turned out to be a disappointment, but he never told me how or why. He told me that he was in the American Expeditionary Force in France during the World War, but that was it. He never elaborated. I told him my father was in the AEF also. Morris merely grunted.

He was frugal. He preached the virtue of thrift. He was proud to tell me that he had almost $6,000 in a passbook account at the Boardwalk National Bank. That was serious money in 1939.

Morris had no close friends. Just a few casual acquaintances. Benny James was closer to him than anyone else. Once or twice a season, Morris bought a ticket to watch a minor league baseball game at the stadium on Albany Avenue. He read a lot. Serious stuff, like Joseph Conrad, Sinclair Lewis, Ernest Hemingway. He listened to the radio a lot. He liked to walk on the beach along the water's edge. He liked dogs, but the boarding house did not allow dogs.

He paid Mrs. Ormont fifteen dollars a week for room and board, and that included having his laundry done and clean sheets and pillowcases every ten days. He did not own a car. He got around on a bicycle, like my father did, like I did.

Morris led a solitary life. He certainly was not Roland, the boulevardier. He told me that sometimes he could go a whole day without speaking more than fifty words: fifteen at breakfast, fifteen at dinner, and twenty scattered throughout the day. That was the way he was; precise about everything. Not *a few words* at breakfast. No. *Fifteen* words at breakfast. His act was exactly *four* minutes long. During his act, he took a total of *six* steps, *two* at a time: *two* at Minute One, *two* at Minute Two, the final *two* steps at Minute Three. He said the slow-motion steps were so arduous that he could not manage more than two at a time, and he needed the minute interval to prepare for the next two steps.

Morris was my introduction to literature. He told me once that Joseph Conrad was the greatest writer who ever lived.

"Imagine, Jack, here is a guy, born in Poland; uneducated; middle of the nineteenth century; a stevedore and a sailor. Learned French and then English because he worked on French ships and then on English ships. And he wrote in English! Imagine, to write in a language that is not yours. And his command of English, the nuances of the language. Like no other. He is the greatest."

Morris loaned me some Conrad short stories. I read *Typhoon, The Secret Sharer, Heart of Darkness, Youth.* I loved Conrad. I still do. Then he brought me some novels, *The Nigger of the "Narcisses"* and *Lord Jim.* I devoured them.

He loaned me Harold Lamb's *The Crusades: Iron Horses and Iron Men.* It was my first exposure to history outside of junior high school textbooks. What an awakening! My appetite for history and biographies began with that book.

Morris made me a gift of Conrad's novel *Victory.* Since then, I guess I read just about all of the rest of Conrad's short stories and the rest of his novels, too.

Once a week, Morris ate at the lunch counter at the Waldorf Grille, on the boardwalk near Missouri Avenue, ten blocks down-beach of the Vi-de-lan Studio. He liked a particular waitress there. The rest of the time he brought a sandwich to work, with a thermos of milk and an apple or a pear. Sometimes Mr. Krilow would toss me an orange as I was about to start out for my shift at Vi-de-lan. "Catch, Jack; give it to Roland."

Morris spoke slowly, quietly. His voice was a low rumble, almost monotone; it hovered around E below Middle C. He seemed neither happy nor sad with his life. There was a serenity about him. He troubled no one. No one troubled him.

He was a pleasant enough looking man, although his eyes were magnified behind the thick eyeglasses, so that his face seemed to be all eyes. He wore a perpetual half-smile, as if sharing an amusing secret with himself. I liked him. I liked him about as much as I liked Benny James, even though two people could not be more different. Benny was so alive and energetic and voluble. Morris was slow-moving and lethargic and quiet. Benny was young and handsome. Morris was only in his forties, but he looked and acted like an old man. I wanted to be like Benny, but I liked being with Morris just as much.

The girls all adored Benny, but none ever noticed Morris. He was so nondescript, so ordinary-looking. Unless you knew him, he seemed to be without any personality at all. So it was no surprise that although he had a boyish crush on Gracie, she never knew it.

16

Gracie

ONE DAY, BENNY invited me to lunch at the Waldorf Grille. "C'mon, Jack, I'm springing today. We'll pick up Morris and take him with us. I'm springing for him, too."

"Gee, thanks, Benny," I said. I was glad to be part of such a threesome.

"And remember, Jack, only a few Krilow people know Morris is Roland. Remember that. Don't spill the beans!"

"Not me, Benny."

As we approached the pavilion at South Carolina Avenue, where we were meeting Morris, Benny whispered, conspiratorially, "Jack, you'll see that Morris has a thing for the waitress who works the lunch counter. Gracie is her name. Watch how he behaves. It's cute."

We met Morris. "Hey, Morris, how's it going?" Benny sang out.

"Good, good, Benny. Hello, Jack."

I was proud to be one of the guys. I was tall for my age, about five feet ten inches. I noticed that we were all close to the same height. It was good to be in their company.

"Benny, did you listen to the game last night?" Morris asked.

"No, I was otherwise occupied." Benny grinned as he threw his arm around Morris's shoulder. "Morris, there's something better than listening to baseball."

"Sure, Benny," Morris went on, "but it was a good game. DiMaggio is having a great season."

"Who cares, Morris, *Benny* is having a great season!"

We paused at the door to the Waldorf Grille to study the three lunch specials at 35 cents each. Benny nudged me with his elbow, alerting me to what he was about to say, and gave me a sidewise grin. "Morris," he said, "let's get a table so we don't have to sit on those damn stools."

"Benny, I really like the counter. The service is better."

"Yeah, yeah, Morris, the service is better." He nudged me again. "All right, you're my guest. We'll go with the counter."

Again, the elbow nudged me, "Look, Gracie is working the counter. Hey, Gracie, how's it going?"

"Hello, Gracie," Morris rumbled.

"Hello, boys. Who is this?" Gracie indicated me with an upturned palm aimed in my direction. She was about thirty, I guessed. She had kind of a pretty face in a halo of light brown curls. By today's tastes in slender women you would say that Gracie was a bit heavy, but by the standards of those days she was just about right. Her arms were full and looked strong. She had broad shoulders and capable-looking hands.

"This is Jack. He works for me," said Benny. "He's a good kid. I hope you'll be careful with your language today, Gracie, because Jack doesn't know any bad words."

"He'll learn soon enough, hanging around with you," Gracie replied, smiling.

"How are you today, Gracie?" Morris asked, earnestly. He really wanted to know. "Everything OK?"

"Sure, Morris, everything's great, as usual. I'm making a living and I am not supporting a man." She laughed. An infectious laugh. A great laugh. You wanted her to laugh again.

She looked familiar. Yes, I had seen her in the Vi-de-lan Studio. More than once. I guessed that she was intrigued by Roland, like I had been.

"Well, Morris," she asked, "sell any paintings this week? I don't know how you make a living selling those $2 paintings. You must have a secret job. Or is some waitress keeping you?"

Morris studied the silverware. He moved the fork to be certain it was exactly parallel to the knife and spoon. He looked like he was going to blush.

"Lay off, Gracie," Benny said, coming to the rescue. "Morris is the secret heir to a big fortune. He doesn't have to work. You ought to get next to him."

Morris bent his head even lower. He rearranged the silverware. "I manage," he said.

Gracie became all business. "OK, guys, whatlyahave?"

During the meal, Benny and Morris talked about the big bands and the movies that were playing at Steel Pier, and Benny told Morris that it was looking like a real good season. "Money's good this year," Benny said.

Morris agreed. Then he shifted the conversation. "Benny, do you pay attention to what is going on in Europe? Do you think there is going to be a war?"

"I think so," Benny surmised. "Hitler gets everything he wants. Why shouldn't he want more? But he will overplay his hand."

"You think Hitler will take on England and France?" Morris asked.

"He won't have to. He picks up what he wants, a piece at a time. Look, last year, that *schmuck* Chamberlain gave away part of Czechoslovakia. That was last September. Feed the beast. Keep him quiet. It don't work. Six months later, Hitler takes over the rest of Czechoslovakia. I never even heard of Czechoslovakia until last year."

Benny continued, "Hitler figures his next grab is Poland and he figures the English and French won't do anything about it except make some speeches."

"I was in the last war," Morris said. "I don't ever want to see us in another one."

"You're too old, Morris. They won't take you. They'll take me," Benny said.

"If it comes to that," Morris said, "don't go. Disappear. Run away. You don't want to see what I saw. I was one of the lucky ones. The guys who got killed were almost as lucky as me. The guys who lost arms and legs and eyes, they were the unlucky ones."

"Forget that stuff, Morris," Benny said. "Let's talk about something else."

So they talked baseball. They talked about the four leading hitters in the American League: Ted Williams, Bill Dicky, Joe DiMaggio, and Hank Greenberg. They talked about cars. They discussed the relative merits of Cadillac, Packard, and Chrysler.

Then Morris changed the subject again. "There's a demonstration of something called *television* at Convention Hall. Did you read about it?"

"What is it?" Benny asked.

"Not sure, exactly. Live pictures on a screen coming through a radio. Something like that."

"Whaddyamean?" Benny asked.

"The article said you can see something that is happening a hundred miles away, while it is happening," Morris explained.

"How can that be? Do you believe it?" Benny was incredulous.

"I don't know. That's what the article said," Morris said.

Morris cleared his throat. "Hey, Gracie, wanna go to see the television demonstration?"

"Do I have to buy a ticket?" she asked.

"No, Gracie. I'll buy the tickets; they're only twenty-five cents."

She leaned on the counter and smiled at him. "Would you invite me if the tickets were a buck?"

Benny intervened. "C'mon, Gracie, give the guy a break. Go or don't go, but cut out the smart-ass stuff."

Morris shrunk, telescoping his neck into his shell. He looked miserable.

Gracie laughed, again that great laugh. "C'mon, Morris, lighten up, guy. Sure, I'll go. You know you're my favorite customer. I'll even put on high heels for you. But Morris, you gotta dress nice. This is a date … wait a minute. What night?"

"It's all week."

"OK, Morris, let's go Saturday night."

Morris brightened. Saturday night! He cleared his throat again. "That's swell, Gracie. That's swell. Saturday, hey? OK, good."

***

Benny took me out for lunch at the Waldorf Grille several times. He always took Morris along. I liked Gracie. She was like Ann Sheridan. She had an easy way about her. The customers liked her. She was fast and she didn't make mistakes and she was quick to fetch the mustard or ketchup or another glass of water. She had a quick tongue, but never mean. You knew she was good-hearted. "A waitress like Gracie can make good money," observed Benny. "I'll bet she's good for ten dollars a day in tips."

"Probably," Morris agreed, "but in the winter, she probably doesn't make half that. Like me. Krilow cuts me in half from Labor Day to Memorial Day."

"You and Gracie ought to get together," Benny declared. "Two can live as cheap, you know."

"She's got a boyfriend," Morris said, wistfully. "She told me about him when we went to the television thing. Some guy named Barry Zoll. I don't know him."

Benny said, "You've seen him around, Morris. Nice looking guy. Dresses nice."

One day at lunch, Benny asked Gracie about Barry Zoll. "What does Barry Zoll do, Gracie?"

"He's a salesman. He sells drug store stuff, like toothpaste and hair dressings and cosmetics."

"Who does he work for?" asked Benny.

"I think it's Colgate or Proctor & Gamble, or one of those. A big company. His territory is Philadelphia and South Jersey."

"Where does he live?" Benny inquired.

"He lives in Philly. He's here Tuesday and Thursday."

"How did you meet him?" Benny wanted to know.

"He was a customer here."

"How long do you know him?"

"Coupla months."

"Well, he's a lucky guy," Morris said, intent on smoothing out the creases on a paper napkin.

"He's pretty terrific," Gracie beamed. "And soon, he's going to change around his schedule so we can be together."

Benny raised his eyebrows. "You only see him on Tuesday and Thursday?" Gracie laughed, an embarrassed laugh. "Well, he works the shore those days."

Benny would not give it up. "Well, when do you see him? After your dinner shift? Does he stay over?"

"Forget it, Benny." She turned red. "Pretty soon, he'll be here full time."

As Gracie hurried away to another customer, Benny turned to me. With his right forefinger, he pulled down the lower corner of his right eye, exposing the pink inside of the lower eyelid. I knew the gesture. It was pure Italian. I knew it from the Italian kids at school. But why was it relevant? I looked at Morris. He looked crushed. Addressing his plate, he whispered, "This hamburger steak is pretty good."

17

Rhoda

Blinky showed up at Krilow's one Monday. It was his day off from his job at Michaelson's Bakery. I saw him in the crowd during the 1:00 demonstration. After the demonstration, he approached the counter.

"Hey, Jack," he said, squinting. "I've got a couple of real good ham and cheese sandwiches and a couple of Michaelson's Danish. I came to have lunch with you. Whaddya say?"

Since Tom Mackey gave me that beating, I was not close to Blinky like before. I knew that Blinky was ashamed that he and Bernie let me and Eddie get beat up and didn't try to help. We didn't talk about it. What good would it do? It would be good if things were the way they used to be. They couldn't be. That beating changed everything.

"Sure, Blinky," I answered. "I have a break coming after the next pitch. Stick around and watch. It's gonna be Benny James who I told you about … here's Benny coming now. See him, there?" I pointed down toward Pennsylvania Avenue. "The guy with the straw skimmer. With the good-looking blonde."

Benny arrived with a girl on his arm. They were a handsome couple. I was used to admiring the Benny James girls. Blinky was getting his first look. The girl was a beauty. She looked like a state fair beauty queen, wholesome and blonde and tanned, a pink sun splash across her upper cheeks over the smooth tan. The hint of pink highlight on her cheeks lit up her face and showed off her blue eyes.

"This is Anna," Benny introduced her, hugging her to him by her shoulder, "from Easton, Pennsylvania. She is waiting tables at the Dennis this summer. Anna, say hello to my pal, Jack, and ..." he indicated Blinky, with a questioning look.

"Blinky," I said. "My friend, Blinky."

"... and Blinky," Benny completed the introduction with that graceful style he had.

"Hi, Blinky," he shook hands with Blinky. "Glad to know you, Blinky. Any friend of Jack's ... you know." Benny gave Anna another hug and a peck on her cheek. "Bye, Anna. See you later. Time for me to *do it.*"

Benny hopped onto the counter, clapped his hands, vigorously, and sang out, "OK, OK, right here, everybody. This is it. This is what you came to see. C'mon. C'mon ..."

After Benny's pitch, I bought two Cokes and steered Blinky to the pavilion at South Carolina Avenue. We sat on my favorite bench, facing the ocean. Blinky pulled out the sandwiches. They were good.

"How's it going at Michaelson's?" I asked.

"It's good, Jack. It's clean work, and it always smells so good. And Rhoda is a doll. And Mr. Michaelson likes me. He taught me to make the croissants." He pronounced it *cross-ants*. Blinky continued, "But, Jack, I got nothing to do at night, and I'm off on Monday. Nobody is around. Bernie is away. Eddie is away. You're never around. And I know you're still mad at me for the Tom Mackey thing." He blinked three times, "Even though you said forget it, I know you're mad at me. I wish everything was like it used to be."

"Forget about the Mackey thing," I said. "It happened. It's done. It's over. You're still my friend."

"But the Mackey thing ain't over, is it, Jack? It can't stay like this. How will it be over?"

"Don't know, Blinky, I haven't figured out what to do. You're right; I can't leave it like this, afraid to walk down to Annapolis Avenue. Always looking out for him. I'm gonna have to do something. I don't know what. And I ain't going to apologize like you wanted me to do. No. That prick needs a lesson."

"Well, anyway, Jack," Blinky said, his mouth full of sandwich, "I thought it would be a good idea if you and me went to see *Pygmalion*. It's at the Warner. You could ask Rhoda."

"Why would I ask Rhoda? If you and me are going, why would I ask Rhoda? Anyway, she won't go with me. She goes with older guys."

"I thought if you go with Rhoda, I could ask Evie."

"EVIE! Are you nuts!? She's thirteen. She doesn't go on dates. What's wrong with you, Blinky?"

He stammered and blinked furiously. "I ... I ... don't mean like a date. I just thought it would be real nice. The four of us. Just to go to the movies. What's wrong with that?"

"Blinky," I asked, suspiciously. "Do you have ideas about Evie?"

"What are you getting so excited about, Jack? It's a little thing. We could walk up the boardwalk together, see the movie, and then maybe an ice-cream soda at the Sodamat. Then, we walk home. What's wrong with that? You and me hardly talk anymore. This would be good. We could stop thinking about Tom Mackey for one night."

I pondered that. He was right. But Rhoda wasn't going to go with me.

"Blinky, OK, but what makes you think Rhoda will go?"

"I think she will, Jack."

"Why? Did you say something to her?"

"No, only I said I was going to see *Pygmalion* with you, and she said she wants to see it."

"Yeah, but not with me."

"What can you lose, Jack? Ask her."

It turned out just like Blinky said. I stopped in the bakery the next day because it was Tuesday, my day off. I stood in line at the donut counter where she was working. She was in constant motion; when she was not packing the donuts for a customer, she was refilling the trays in the display booth, and walking back and forth to the kitchen. She wore a white apron over a white man's shirt, and a white paper cap. There was a spot of white powdered sugar on her cheek. I stammered and mumbled my way through a clumsy invitation, ending with "I'm paying."

Without stopping her work, she said, "Sure, Jack. Love to join you," like it was an everyday thing. She barely looked at me, just kept working. "I'll pay my own way, Jack. But it was sweet of you to offer."

Then I ran upstairs and told Evie that she was coming with us and she squealed, excitedly. So we went to the 6:30 show the next Monday. Benny got me off at 4:00 so I could get home in time to meet up with everybody. We met in front of Michaelson's at 4:30. Blinky and the girls were there. The girls were dressed alike. Each wore a light-colored skirt, and a colorful blouse. They wore white socks—*bobby socks*, they were called—and white-and-brown saddle shoes. Each had a light cotton sweater draped over her shoulders. It was almost a teenage girl's uniform those days. They were bronzed from the summer sun. Two good-looking girls.

We walked the twenty-five blocks uptown on the boardwalk to the Warner Theater, walking four abreast. Rhoda even took my arm and walked in step with me. I felt I was holding something fragile and precious. I kept my left arm crooked just so. I measured the length and pace of every step just so. I had difficulty making conversation. It was like being with a celebrity. She was worldly wise and mature. I felt like a child. It took over an hour to reach the Warner. By the time we got there, I knew that Rhoda was not out on a date. She was just going to the movies with the neighbor's kid from upstairs.

I told her about my friend, Morris, and about how I was reading Joseph Conrad. She was impressed that I read stuff like that. She said she didn't find time to read. What with schoolwork and helping out in the bakery and cheerleading. She wanted to know how I know Morris. I couldn't tell her about Roland so I just said he is a friend of Benny James. I told her about Benny, describing him in glowing terms. She was intrigued that he was a pitchman. "I'd love to see him in action," Rhoda said.

Evie squeeked, "Can I come too?"

"Tell you what," I said, "the movie will let out around eight. We'll watch his last pitch, around 8 or 8:30."

"Oh, great idea," Rhoda said, excitedly. She squeezed my arm.

The Warner Theater was one of those grand movie houses that was built in the late twenties and early thirties. It had a big lobby, done in red velvet and gold. Twin ornate gilded stairways at each side of the lobby swept up in a half-circle to another lobby on the balcony level, where people gathered along a gilded railing capped with red velvet to look down on the main lobby and the streams of people entering the theater. In the theater itself, the walls were decorated three-dimensionally, with gilt carvings and ornate balconies, mosques and parapets, in the style of an Arabian palace. The ceiling was a dark blue sky illuminated with a moon and a thousand stars, pinpoints of light, some brighter, some blinking. Pale indirect lighting from behind the structures along the walls threw a romantic and mysterious half-light onto the sky. The feeling was of being in the open-air courtyard of a magical palace, at dusk. When the curtain parted for the movie to begin, the sky darkened, but the moon and stars continued to shine. The lights behind the parapets and balconies dimmed. They cast a pale light onto the edges of the sky during the movie.

Protected by the darkness of the theater, I leaned toward Rhoda. Her scent was delicate, hardly noticeable. It aroused me. I leaned, slowly, a fraction of an inch at a time. My arm touched hers. Would she move away? She didn't. I sat absolutely still, not wanting to spoil the moment. She was absorbed in the movie. I could hardly concentrate on it. And then, a miracle. When Wendy Hiller made her appearance at the Duchess's Ball at the head of the great stairway in that satin gown, Rhoda covered my hand, and gave a quick squeeze before she withdrew.

All the while, I kept an eye on Blinky. He wasn't fooling me. He wanted to touch Evie, but he didn't. He and Evie sat straight up in their seats, like soldiers. Blinky was behaving. For Evie, it was just a night at the movies, not a date. She was unconscious about how her body was developing. I looked at her through Blinky's eyes. Damn. She was actually pretty. I was going to have to watch out for her.

The movie over, we walked on the boardwalk the few blocks to Virginia Avenue to Krilow's. Benny was nearing the end of a demonstration. I took Rhoda's arm and drew her into the center of the crowd. Benny spotted me. As he came to the end of his pitch, his eyes rested on me for a split second, and he worked into his patter these words: "Now, spring!" Those were the code words to prompt the shill to holler "I'll buy one!" because half the time the shills were too drunk to know when to spring unless they heard the signal.

I saw that Benny was working without a shill in the crowd, so I pushed forward, a dollar bill held high. It was important to hold the money high so everyone saw it. I cried out, "I'll take one!" Lots of buyers joined us.

After the crowd dispersed, I introduced Benny to Rhoda and Evie. He acknowledged that he already knew Blinky. He told everyone that I'm a good kid. Then, he said, "C'mon, sodas are on me!" and off we went to the Sodamat. On the way, he dropped back with me and whispered, "Hey, Jack, your girlfriend's a looker! You're OK!"

"She isn't my girlfriend," I answered. "I wish she was. She's my neighbor."

"Who says your neighbor can't be your girlfriend?"

Benny was such a good host. That easy manner. He sure knew how to talk to girls.

"Rhoda," he said, looking her squarely in the face, "do you know that the shape of your face is what the cosmeticians call a perfect asymmetric oval? Here," he said, running his index finger lightly around her face. "You see, here, between your eyes and your upper lip, this perfect fullness of your cheek, but here, below the cheek, the line straightens, only for an inch. Then the curve of the two join, sort of Eastern European, like the Khazars, or maybe even a hint of Tartar. Are your folks Hungarians or Russians?" She blushed as she leaned forward. "My dad's parents came from Austria; my mom's came from Belgium. No Hungarians. And anyway, Benny, you must have picked up that line from the movie we just saw, *Pygmalion*. Did you?"

"Well, maybe a little." They laughed together. He continued. "You're a good-looking gal, Rhoda. Real good-looking. Tell you what. I'll bet you are musical. I see it in your eyes. Do you play an instrument? The flute, maybe. Your lips are perfect for the way the flute players purse their lips when they pour that little air stream into the mouthpiece."

"No, again, Benny," she laughed. "The closest I get to music is turning on the Victrola. I suspect you are a fraud, Mr. James."

We all laughed. Benny laughed the heartiest.

"Hey, Jack," he chuckled, "this Rhoda is a great gal. Hang on to her."

He leaned to Rhoda and said, in a stage whisper, "Jack is good stuff. Don't lose him. He's a winner. And Rhoda, I love the way you walk. You have this wonderful stride. Forthright, I would call it. Not stuck-up or pretentious. Direct. Purposeful. Like you know who you are and you know where you are headed."

It was Rhoda's turn to say, looking squarely at Benny as she spoke, "Jack, I like your friend. But I think he is a menace to girls. He is irresistible." Benny laughed.

Rhoda looked and carried herself like a young lady. She was poised and self-assured. Only fifteen, she could have passed for twenty. I watched her interchanges with Benny with wonder. She spoke and acted like his contemporary, not like a fifteen-year-old kid struggling to make conversation with a man ten years older.

Benny was still chuckling as he focused on Evie. You were in a warm spotlight when Benny focused on you. Evie felt the beam. She sat more erect, expectantly.

"Evie," Benny smiled, "let me tell you something. I see a beautiful young woman developing. You have a winning smile. Don't be afraid to show it, often. You are going to be a tall, willowy beauty. You have good shoulders and good legs. Try to hold yourself more erect, like Rhoda. Pretend someone, like a puppeteer, up above, has a string tied to your head and he keeps it firm. So you have to keep your neck stretched and your body straight. Try it. It will improve your posture. It will make you look like a great lady. Slouching becomes a way of life. If your body slouches, so does your mind and your character."

He reached forward with his index finger and touched the small of Evie's neck, the V between the collarbones. Blinky squeezed his eyes a half-dozen times.

"Here's a bit of perfection," Benny murmured. "And I'll bet you don't have one bad habit or one wicked thought. You're like a flower, just starting to open. All is perfection ... so far."

Evie was hypnotized. All she could say was, "Oh, Benny. Thank you."

And so it went. Benny was a charmer. He knew it. But he kept his charm in check. He praised me as a quick study, and reliable, and honest. He said I had the makings of a good pitchman, but that I was cut out for better things. He put everyone at ease. He demonstrated a few sleight-of-hand tricks. He kept us entertained and laughing. The perfect cap to a great evening. But what was this peculiar unease I felt? Jealousy? I was jealous of Benny? I saw the way Rhoda looked at him. He just about had her on his hook, but she was too young a catch, so he tossed her back in the water. It was as though he was practicing. I didn't like him any less. I admired him even more.

On the walk home, I was more at ease, because I accepted my relationship to Rhoda: the friendly kid upstairs. Having accepted that, I could relax, because there was no way Rhoda would become my girlfriend, so I needn't try. When we arrived at Michaelson's, Blinky said good night to us all, and Evie ran into the narrow apartment stairway. Rhoda gave me a quick kiss on the cheek and darted into the building.

I was left standing on the sidewalk, full of feelings for Rhoda and my own feelings of inferiority. What turmoil.

18

Zena

Zᴇɴᴀ ʜᴀᴅ ᴀ tiny bit of a storefront on the boardwalk, between Missouri and Columbia avenues. A sign mounted on her easel read:

ZENA
OCCULT READER
Know Your Future
Readings, $1.00

Zena usually kept the door open, but a thick black curtain hung at one side of the entrance. She drew it closed when she had a customer, and she hung a sign that said *Please wait. Reading in progress.* Inside, her little space was furnished as a parlor. She had a small sofa, a colorful Oriental rug, and a round table where a smoky glass ball rested on a carved dark wooden base. The walls were waves of dark blue, maroon, and deep purple and covered with mystical symbols and heavenly objects. On one wall, a pale sun shone through a gray mist. On another wall was a full moon, half hidden behind dark clouds, a beam of its moonlight drawing a silver bead across a black ocean. Some of the better-known constellations covered a midnight blue ceiling. Strange circles and geometric shapes were everywhere. A painted eye decorated the center of the back wall. A flush door was cut into the back wall, painted as part of the wall, so that when the door closed, it almost disappeared, becoming part of the wall.

Behind the door were Zena's living quarters, consisting of her bedroom, a bathroom, and an efficiency kitchen. At the back of the parlor was a large, ornate silver and brass samovar, standing on a corner table, surrounded by a fine china tea service. When the samovar was in use, it gave off a pleasing aroma of fresh tea to the accompaniment of a deep baritone *bloop, bloop, bloop* every few seconds. There were three embroidered chairs around the round table. Zena did her readings at the table, but while waiting for a customer she reclined on the sofa, smoking a cigarette in a long cigarette holder, and reading a newspaper.

Zena was a handsome fifty-year-old woman. She wore a colorful silk robe with huge sleeves, and a silk shawl and several silk scarves. Her robe had a heavy silk, rope-like belt with enormous golden tassels. She wore a multicolored turban with a large eye-shaped red stone set in the center. Full white silk trousers and full white silk sleeves peeked out from under the robe.

Her hair was black, long, and straight, gathered into a braided ponytail. Her face was swarthy. Only her pale green eyes betrayed that her deep coloring washed off every night and was reapplied every day.

Benny James took me to Zena one day. He wanted her to give me a reading. "Hi, Zena," Benny said. "This is Jack. He's a good kid. Give him a reading."

Zena studied me for a few moments while she shuffled a deck of tarot cards, slowly. Looking into her eerie pale green eyes, I believed she really *knew* things.

"I will do it, Benny, because I see much in this boy," she spoke in a low whisper. There was a hint of Slavic heaviness in her voice.

"Keep your money, Benny. This boy interests me." I shivered with the mystery of it. Benny left. Zena closed the curtain. We sat at the round table. The glass ball lit up. She took my hand.

When the reading was over, I was convinced that Zena *knew*. She read my thoughts. She embarrassed me by telling me my secret yearnings. She ended with predictions of a good life. When she drew open the curtain to dismiss me, she cupped the side of my chin in her right hand and smiled at me, "God bless you, Jack. Good fortune will follow you."

Boy, oh boy! Was I a lucky guy. Zena *knew*. I knew she knew.

Benny returned for me. Before we left, Zena spoke to him, very seriously. "Benny," she said, "a strange man came in here the other day. I think he's a kook. He wanted to talk about cocoa beans. He thinks I know something that he wants to know. He made me nervous. I don't know what to do if he comes back."

"Forget it, Zena. He's probably a tourist from Oshkosh. You'll never see him again."

He was the cocoa man.

19

Letter to Eddie, July 22

Atlantic City, New Jersey
Saturday, July 22, 1939

Dear Eddie:

Thanks for the letter. You know what they say about hard work never hurting anybody. You will be so tough by Labor Day, maybe you and me will take on the Mackeys. You will have to do most of the work but I will help if Tom Mackey does not grab me first.

My job is great. I am the gopher for the pitchmen at Krilow's. The work is easy. The pay is good. I am getting fifteen cents an hour. I work six days. Tuesday is my day off.

I met two great guys. One is Benny James, the top pitchman. He is a terrific guy. You would like him. It would take twenty pages for me to tell you about him. He treats me like a grown-up. The other guy is Benny's friend. His name is Morris. He introduced me to a writer named Joseph Conrad. When you come home I am going to give you something to read by Joseph Conrad. You will like it as much as I do.

Benny says he will most likely take off after Labor Day. I hope he will stay around for a little while. Maybe until after the Miss America contest. Because there is still some action on the boardwalk until the pageant is over. If he does you will meet him. And you will meet Morris, who is also a great guy, but in a different way from Benny. I can't tell you much about Morris until you get home. Something I am not allowed to tell you. Sounds mysterious, hey?

The big news. I took out Rhoda.

Yes, Rhoda and me and Blinky and Evie. We went to the movies together. Blinky set it up. Evie looked so grown-up. I think Blinky has the hots for her. But he must know I will kill him if he tries anything. Rhoda looked great as usual. After the movie I took them all to see Benny give a pitch. Then Benny took us out for a soda. I had a good time. And so did Blinky and Evie and Rhoda.

I know Rhoda thinks of me only as the kid upstairs. And really, that is what I am. She is all grown-up. She fits right in with older guys. Even a guy like Benny, who is ten years older.

But I am depressed. Yesterday I asked Rhoda to go to the movies with me tonight. She said "gee Jack I would love to, but I have a date." I said "sure Rhoda maybe next week." She said "no, not next week, but maybe later." I guess it's the brush-off for sure, not that I really thought I had a chance with her.

I have to stop thinking about her. When you get back, let's you and me start dating some of the girls that hang out at Frederick's Drug Store.

When school starts I am going to work afternoons and Saturdays. I like having money to spend. I saved up

$25 so far. By Labor Day I figure to have almost ONE HUNDRED, like you!

Congrats on building the automatic well. I am so impressed with you. What a project. It looks like you are going to get some real benefit from this summer. You are doing man's work. My job is kid stuff.

I keep thinking about the Mackeys. They are my only problem. Everything would be wonderful except for them. I do not know what to do about it. I want to get advice from Benny, but I am ashamed to tell him how I got beat up. He will think I really am just a kid. Any ideas?

Your best friend,
Jack

20

The Rescue

EARLY MORNING, JUST after sunrise, is a magical time at the shore. The ocean sparkles. The air is clear. Everything is fresh and cool before the midsummer heat rolls in from the mainland.

One of Morris's favorite painting places was on the pavilion on the boardwalk at South Carolina Avenue in the early morning, a strategic point from which he could face the boardwalk to do scenes of the grand hotels, or the shops, or the passers-by. Or he could point his easel at the ocean for seascapes, sunrises, and beach scenes. The ocean was his favorite subject.

Since my shift at Krilow's Kitchen Gadgets did not begin until noon, I came to watch him often, in the morning. He liked my company. He encouraged me to watch him work.

"The ocean is never the same two days in a row, or two hours in a row," he told me, "and it is every color of the rainbow, depending on when you look at it. Look, Jack, now it is silver over there, and gray over there. Tonight, at 8:00, if there are no clouds, it will be all gold. Yesterday morning, the sky was red, rain coming. Do you know the rhyme?"

> *Red sky at night,*
> *sailor's delight.*
> *Red sky in the morning,*
> *sailor take warning.*

"*Take warning*," he repeated, theatrically.

"Is that for real?" I asked.

"Oh, yes. You can rely on it."

"Why is that?" I asked.

"Well, it works like this: The prevailing winds along the Northeast coast are easterlies. That means that most of the time, the wind is coming from the east. If there is rain in the west, it is the sunset that comes through the moisture. The water acts like a prism, breaking down the light into the yellow end of the spectrum. Reds and golds and oranges come through and paint the sky. When you see that at sunset, rain or moisture is in the West, and the easterly wind is taking it away from us; so, red sky at night is a sailor's delight tomorrow. But if the rain is out there," he pointed to the east, to the ocean horizon, "the sunrise coming through the moisture makes the sky all red and angry in the east, and the east wind is bringing the rain here. So red sky in the morning means rain or a storm coming."

One day, on a typical beautiful morning, I was watching Morris paint a beach scene; perfect sky, calm sea, the sun was already halfway up. The beach was empty except for a young mother and child. The mother smoothed out an oversized beach towel. The little boy, maybe a year and a half old, squatted alongside, digging in the sand. The young woman stretched out on the towel. She had a book, but it soon fell from her hands as sleep overcame her.

Morris was accomplished with watercolors. You have to be precise with watercolors because the colors will run into each other if you give them the chance. So each brushstroke has to be planned. You can't correct it once it is on the paper.

The scene took shape on his easel. The robin's-egg blue of the morning sky, the white line of surf rolling in to the silver beach at the water's edge. Deft strokes began to capture the girl, the beach towel, the squatting baby.

The baby stood up. He was barely able to toddle. He took a few steps and fell, then struggled up for another few steps before falling again. His mother was asleep. Oh my God! The baby was heading for the water! I ran to the end of the pavilion, flipped over the rail and began running toward the baby, shouting, "Lady! Lady! Lady!"

The water's edge was about seventy-five yards away, about three-quarters of a football field. Running on the soft sand is hard. Your legs are churning away, but you feel that you are in slow motion.

"Lady! Lady! Lady!" I cried as I ran.

I tried to make my legs churn faster. Running on soft sand is like running in glue. As I got closer to the water, I came to where the receding tide had left a swath of hard-packed beach. The running became easier and faster. I was more than halfway to the baby when the woman stirred, aroused by my shouts. She sat up, looked about, wildly. She jumped up and started to run to the child, that funny way that women used to run. Today they run like men.

"Billy! Billy! Stop! Billy!" she shrieked.

Behind me, Morris reached the beach after running off the pavilion onto the boardwalk and to the nearest flight of steps down to the beach. I heard his bullhorn cry, "Baby! Stop baby! Baby! Baby!"

The woman and I reached the child at the same time, just as a small wave struck him and tumbled him into the surf. The undertow was already beginning to drag him seaward as we scooped him up together. His diaper washed away. He sucked in his breath, shocked and surprised. Then the wailing began; great, frightened, ear-splitting wailing. The woman cried and hugged me, and cried some more.

Morris, seeing that all was well, stopped running and headed back to the pavilion. He was still panting when I returned. "Good job, Jack," he panted. A crowd had gathered at the railing, attracted by the shouting. A few men had even started to run for the steps to the beach, but the incident was over before anyone got very far. I got a few congratulations and congratulatory handshakes. It was embarrassing.

Morris returned to the easel; I resumed my observer's seat. When finished, the watercolor was a study in serenity. A young mother, asleep on her stomach on a colorful beach towel, her head resting on her arm. Morris gave her long blond hair, and he also gave her a better figure. The baby squatting alongside, pushing sand into a tin bucket, a low ripple at the water's edge, benign and inviting, long early morning shadows, all under a cloudless sky.

"This is a five dollar painting," Morris declared.

21

Reading Gracie

PEOPLE OFTEN GATHERED to watch Morris at work on the pavilion. Sometimes Benny stopped by on his way home from a night of adventure. Gracie sometimes looked in on Morris at 10:00 or 10:30. Her workday began at 11:00 with the early lunchers at the Waldorf Grille. Morris was something of a regular tourist attraction.

I was at the pavilion one morning when Gracie came to visit. Morris was doing a black-and-white line drawing of Steel Pier while Gracie chattered on about everything. She seemed to think that she and Morris were having a conversation because Morris responded with a word now and again and an occasional grunt. She talked about her job, her customers, a new Philco radio she wanted to buy, the movies, John Garfield, Bette Davis, Ida Lupino. Ida Lupino was her favorite. I thought her favorite ought to be Ann Sheridan. She told Morris about a car that her boss just bought for his nineteen-year-old son. A cream-colored convertible Plymouth, three years old, with a *rumbleseat*. What a car! She allowed as how that car must have set her boss back at least $400. And over and over she talked about Barry Zoll while Morris grunted occasionally to show he was listening.

A nice-looking older woman approached. "Hello, Morris. Hello, Gracie," she called out. She noticed me, sitting with my back toward the boardwalk, facing the ocean, absorbed in Morris's latest loaner, Stefan Zweig's *Napoleon*.

"Hello, Jack," she called to me. I turned. Who was she?

"Hi, Zena," Morris and Gracie said in unison. Zena? It sure didn't look like Zena. She was wearing a nice-looking dress, and high-heeled shoes, and white gloves. Her coloring was fair. The pale green eyes looked fine in that setting. She did not look at all mysterious. Just a pleasant-looking older woman.

"How are things, Morris, Gracie?" Zena asked.

"Much the same, much the same," replied Morris.

"I've got a boyfriend!" Gracie sang out. "That's what's new!" Her face lit up as she gave Zena the good news about Barry Zoll.

"Well, well," Zena sounded happy for Gracie. "That *is* good news. Tell me about him."

Gracie did, in a torrent of adulation. Her face glowed. *How wonderful,* I thought, *to be adored by a girl like Gracie. Barry Zoll is a lucky guy!*

I wondered if Zena knew that Morris is Roland. It was a close-kept secret. But Zena knew things. She had to know about Roland. I thought that she must be one of the secret sharers. Could she tell by studying me that I was another of the secret sharers?

"It is *such* a nice morning," Zena observed. "I am going to relax here for a while before I open the parlor. And I need your advice, Morris, about something strange."

She told Morris about the strange man who wanted to know about cocoa beans. She said that she told Benny, and Benny said she would probably never see him again. But he was back, not interested in any of the usual stuff. He wanted to know just one thing—cocoa futures. Were they headed up or down? Zena told us that she did not know what a cocoa future is, so she did some mumbo-jumbo and spoke in metaphors and dealt out the tarot cards. It was her stock in trade. The listener interprets the metaphor himself and believes that Zena *knows*.

"I told him that prices rise and prices fall, just as summer follows spring, like rainbows following storms. I gave him the mysterious look into his eyes. I told him that he was *right*, that he *knew,* and that I knew that he knew. You know, Morris, a typical spiel. He lit up like a light bulb. He thanked me over and over, and he practically floated out of my parlor. Well, a week later, here comes this guy again. He is excited. 'Zena!' he says, 'you were right! I went long twenty contracts. I made eight hundred dollars! In four days! I want another reading.'

"That made me nervous. I told him I would try. I was scared I might hurt the guy, so I did some murmuring and I looked into the globe and then I told him that a veil was drawn. I told him that happens sometimes. I told him I could not see anything.

"He was disappointed. He says he'll come back. When should he come back, he wants to know. He is anxious, and I tell him it is hard to tell. I tell him to try again in three days. Maybe the veil will lift.

"Then I went to the library. Do you know what a cocoa future is, Morris? No, I didn't think so."

She explained what commodities are. She explained futures contracts. She explained margins. She explained how, because of margin leveraging, you could make big money on a small investment, quickly. Or you could lose your money just as fast, and maybe lose more than you invested to start with.

It was pretty complicated. Morris caught on right away. Gracie and I were groping. I almost understood, for a moment, then it slipped away.

"Morris, what should I do?" Zena was worried. "He'll be back in three days."

"Best thing is to tell him you are a fake. Don't lead him on. You might hurt him."

Zena straightened. She lifted her jaw, majestically. "I am *not* a fake, Morris. Shame on you. I thought you were my friend."

"Sorry, Zena. You know I love you. But come on. This is *me*, Morris. Just tell the guy that you can sense things about a person, but your gift does not extend to reading next month's *Wall Street Journal*. Tell him you see prosperity in his future, but you don't know why. Tell him you can't tell if his prosperity will come from cocoa or from something else; you know, the usual."

"You are no help, Morris," Zena said. "No help at all. This guy is a nut. Please, Morris, try to think of something."

Morris said she should talk to Benny again. Benny would know what to do.

"Good idea," said Zena. "He brushed it off the first time I told him about this man, but now this is a real problem." She turned to Gracie. "Anyway, I am real happy for you, Gracie. It is about time you met the right man."

Gracie held out her hand. "Read my palm, Zena. Please. Give me a reading, right now. I'll pay."

"C'mon, Gracie, you know it is not real. Did you hear Morris? He called me a fake!"

"It *is* real," Gracie argued. "You have a gift, Zena. You don't even know it. But you do. I have seen it. Please, read me."

Reluctantly, and with a sigh, Zena took Gracie's hand. She turned serious. Her eyes narrowed. A faraway look of oneness with the occult came over her. Slowly, she traced the creases on Gracie's palm with her little finger. "This is your Life Line, Gracie. It is long and strong. And this is your Heart Line. It begins late. See here. Some Heart Lines begin all the way up here near the first finger. Yours starts down here, just about right now, I would say. But look how deep and long it runs. A good line. Here is your Head Line. You have a good head and good brains and good thoughts, but your head is dominated by your Heart Line." Zena touched Gracie's palm in the rounded area below Gracie's thumb. "This is called the Mound of Venus. It shows you have a great capacity for love. And this is your Fate Line. I see prosperity coming. I see happiness, Gracie. A child … a good man. Your long waiting is almost over."

Gracie threw her arms around Zena. "Oh, Zena, you're wonderful!"

I got to meet Barry Zoll on a Friday morning, a week and a half after the baby rescue.

22

Barry Zoll

I WENT TO the South Carolina Avenue pavilion at 7:30, hoping that Morris would be there. He was not, so I sat facing the ocean and opened up *Lord Jim*. Morris had loaned it to me recently. I was nearing the end of it. I was afraid that Lord Jim was going to let his faith in the inherent goodness of people prevail over the reality that Brown was an unreformed killer. I was sure that Lord Jim was making a bad mistake by not finishing off Brown when he had the chance. Jim was such a good guy. He wanted to believe that honor was in everyone. *Be careful, Jim*, I thought. *Do him in. He will do* you *in if he has the chance.*

Morning reading on the pavilion was a favorite thing. I loved to face the ocean, feel the warmth of the sun as it climbed out of the ocean. Breathe the salty air; smell the freshness. The sandpipers raced back and forth at the water's edge in a pack. How did they know to turn as a unit, as if following a drillmaster? *Left flank, run in unison, right flank, wheel to the left, about face.* All together, like one consciousness. I didn't understand it then, and I don't understand it today.

The boardwalk stretched off into the distance, as far as the eye could see. The boards glistened with early morning dew, not yet evaporated by the rising sun. Gulls circled and whirled above. A soft sound came from the low early morning waves barely breaking as they rolled in to the shore. The gulls called *Cah! Cah! Cah!*

111

Good to be alive. I felt vigorous. And still awed by my recent introduction to Conrad.

At age fifteen, the future spreads out, endlessly, its mysteries hidden. I could see the future but could not make out details. The future was a vast sunlit plane: visibility good and skies clear, but the details were missing, just the blurred shapes of hopes and plans, but nothing clear or in focus. I guess some youngsters see the future being bright, as I did, but without the details, while others see the future as bleak, littered with indistinct troubles and dangers. I believed in my good fortune, even though I couldn't see how or why. I believed that hard work pays off. I believed that honesty and loyalty are returned in kind. I had the wonderful feeling of good health and vigor and a strong and obedient body. There is that smoothness and suppleness of youth that feels eternal. Some days I never thought of Tom Mackey. This was such a day.

The country was in an economic funk. Our family was just about getting by. Money was precious. We had no frills. My parents were happy that I was working for the summer. My friends' families were in similar circumstances. I knew that times were tough. I heard that there was going to be a war and that we would be dragged into it. There was already a war going on in China. The newspapers and radios told of atrocities by the Japanese. But that summer of 1939 was for me a time of optimism, a feeling that I would be OK. That everything would be OK. That I would succeed. I didn't know at what or how, but I believed that good fortune was going to be mine.

Morris showed up at 9:00, easel and artist pad under his left arm, carrying his two-foot-square paint box by its handle, like a briefcase, a businessman arriving at the office.

"Good morning, Jack," he greeted me. "Nice day. Ah, *Lord Jim*, I see. Looks like you're about through it. Take it easy, Jack. There's only so much Conrad. Ration it. There's no more where that came from."

"What are you gonna paint today, Morris?"

"The Traymore. Look at it, Jack. Look how the sun lights up this side. And the gold trim under the arches. And the shadows. I better get started. I want the long morning shadows."

In a few minutes, the easel was up. A 12″ x 18″ sheet of artist paper was pinned to a 3/8-inch sheet of plywood, portrait style, leaning on the easel. Morris extended his arms forward, stiffly. He formed his hands into an open rectangle, framing the scene he was about to capture. He began—a careful vertical stroke became the far corner of the Traymore.

While I watched the scene take shape, Morris told me some of the history of the boardwalk. "This is the fifth boardwalk, Jack. Some were too close to the water. Some got blown down in storms. Boardwalk number four was too narrow. This present one was finished around 1900. I remember when the Traymore got built. All those beauties over there," he pointed his brush, "the Shelburne, the Marlborough-Blenheim, the Traymore, the Dennis, they all got built around the same time, in the twenties. Aren't they grand? And over there … hey, look, there's Benny!"

Benny approached, one arm around the waist of a good-looking girl. She looked to be about twenty, a Benny James girl, pretty and blonde, and tanned, bare-legged, wearing open sandals.

"Hi, Morris. Hi, Jack. Say hello to Gwen."

"Nice to meet you, Morris," she said, smiling. "And you, too, Jack." The girl turned to Benny and excused herself. "I best be going, Benny. I don't want to be late for work." She kissed Benny's cheek. "Will I see you tonight, Benny?"

"Not tonight, Gwen, but I'll meet you after work tomorrow. We'll go to the Pier. I want to see Glenn Miller."

"OK, Benny. See you tomorrow." She smiled at us before turning away. She had a lively bounce in her stride, her long hair swinging from side to side.

"Great gal," Benny addressed her back as she strode away, then he turned to us.

"I'm going to sit here for a few minutes, fellas." Benny sat on a bench, facing the ocean, his arms spread out along the top of the bench. "I'm tired. Busy night. Maybe I'll just catch a little snooze. Nice day." He tilted his head back. "Aah, that sun feels good."

Benny was facing away from us, but he spoke to us, addressing his remarks to the beach and ocean. "Y'know, fellas, my social agenda is getting too crowded. Maybe I'll stick to one girl for a while. Like Gwen. She's great. Isn't she pretty? And sweet, too. Sort of innocent. I almost feel like a cad." He turned to face us. "Almost, I said," he laughed. He turned back and spoke to the ocean again. "It's a great life. Great. I love it. I love Gwen. But I love Gloria, too. And Anna. And Carol. They're all great!" he sighed. "But Gwen— she *is* special!"

Morris spoke in his deep monotone, as he added a stroke to his painting, facing the boardwalk, his back to Benny, "You're no good, Benny. You know that, don't you? I don't know why I even like you. Jack, why do we like Benny? We *know* he is no good."

I would like to have answered with a wisecrack, but I didn't know how.

I spotted Gracie. "Hey, Morris. Look, there's Gracie!"

"Oh, yes," observed Morris, "and that guy must be Barry Zoll."

"Gracie," Benny called.

Gracie and Barry were strolling, slowly, coming from the down-beach direction, stepping in unison. Barry's left arm was right-angled across his waist. Gracie was holding his upper arm with both hands, her head leaning against his shoulder. Her eyes were half-closed, dreamy-like. A peaceful smile illuminated her face. "Gracie," Morris called in his foghorn voice, "Gracie." Benny rose. "Hey, Gracie," he chimed in. She saw us. She waved and gave us the big smile. She directed Barry into a half-right turn. They headed toward us.

It was the first time I saw Gracie out of her waitress uniform. She was pretty. She was wearing a sleeveless, light blue, flowered cotton dress, down to mid-calf, and white high-heeled shoes. A white lacy-looking cotton sweater was draped over her shoulders, and a white handbag hung by a white strap from the crook of her angled left arm. She looked terrific. Move over, Ann Sheridan.

Barry Zoll was a good-looking man. Tanned. Crisp-looking. I guessed him to be only a little younger than Morris, but he had a youthful buoyancy. He was wearing a brown-and-white striped seersucker suit, with a white button-down shirt and a handsome brown and yellow floral necktie with a matching breast pocket handkerchief. He wore a smart cocoa-colored straw hat, shaped like a snap-brimmed fedora. His shoes were white with brown wingtips. He carried an overnight bag in his right hand. He was a handsome package.

"Hi Morris, hi Jack, hi Benny," Gracie sang out. "Morris, this is Barry Zoll, who I told you about. And Barry, this is Jack, and Morris, and Benny James."

"Hello, Jack," Barry offered his hand. "I heard about you. You're a hero. The baby rescue …" He spoke with an even quietness. His smile was genuine. An attractive man.

Benny gave Gracie a big hug. "Hiya Gracie, hi Barry," Barry and Benny shook hands. Barry turned to Morris.

"Morris," Gracie said, wanting to make a proper introduction. "I don't even know your last name."

"It's Rubens," Morris said.

"Glad to know you, Morris," Barry smiled. A generous smile. Good teeth. He shook Morris's hand vigorously. "Rubens, hey. How do you spell Rubens, Morris?"

Morris spelled his name. R-U-B-E-N-S.

"Like the Belgian painter?" Barry asked.

"Actually, he was Dutch," Morris said, "but, yes, that's the name."

Barry told Gracie about Rubens. "Rubens was quite a guy. He was a diplomat and a very rich businessman, besides being a painter. He liked to paint *zoftik* naked women."

"What is *zoftik*?" asked Gracie.

"Full bodied, full breasted," explained Barry. "Plump, maybe beyond plump."

"I see you know something about painting," Morris ventured.

"Just a little. I like art. I hear you're a pretty good artist, Morris. I see what you're doing right now. You have a good eye for perspective. That hotel is a tough subject with all those angles and columns and gingerbread. You're good."

"Do you paint, Barry?" Morris asked.

"No, I picked up some pointers from my sister-in-law. She paints, mostly in oils; sells a few things now and then, but she earns a living as a schoolteacher."

"Painting is a tough way to make a living," Morris agreed.

Benny spoke up. "How about you, Barry? How do you make out? Gracie told me you work for Colgate and Ivory Soap."

"No, Benny," Barry laughed, a good laugh, like Gracie's. "I work for a distributor. We carry a full line of drugstore and health products, and beauty aid products. All the major brands. Soaps, cosmetics, lotions, deodorants, hair dressings, shampoos, mouth washes, first-aid stuff, like mercurochrome, Band-Aids. No stationery, no greeting cards, no tobacco, no housewares. Company's name is Nelson and Lorch. Here's my card." Morris returned to his painting.

"Who are your customers?" Benny inquired, still studying Barry's business card.

Barry explained, expansively, "Just about every independent drug store in South Jersey and Wilmington. The City of Wilmington is mine. And South Jersey from Trenton down, but I don't have Trenton."

I ought to explain that in 1939 almost all the drugstores were independent. There were hardly any chains, only a handful of small drugstore chains that were struggling to gain customer acceptance. Names that are long gone, like Sun Ray and Nevins. Walgreens was around, and is still with us, but then it was a small chain, struggling to make good.

Benny slipped Barry's card into his pocket. "How about Philadelphia?" Benny asked. "Is that your territory?"

"No, I live in Philly, but it is not my territory."

"Are you going to move to New Jersey?"

"Oh, yes," he squeezed Gracie and kissed her cheek.

"Good," Benny said. "We'll be glad to have you. How many customers do you have?"

"About two hundred."

"Two hundred!" Benny was surprised. "How can you cover so many?"

It was plain that Barry Zoll liked to talk about his business. He explained, "I break them down into three kinds: weekly stops, twice-a-month stops, and once-a-month stops. It works out to about twenty stops a day. I average about three stops an hour. It keeps me moving. It's a lot of work, but I like it. What about you, Benny? Gracie tells me you're the king of the boardwalk pitchmen."

"I ain't bad," agreed Benny, "but you. You are *something*. Two hundred stops. Wow. How many are weekly stops? How do you cover so many?"

"Are you really interested?" Barry smiled. "Because if you are, I can bore you for hours about my business."

"Yes, Barry. This stuff interests me. I love business. Tell me."

"Well, I have thirty weekly stops. They are my best customers. I see them once a week. Then, there are about seventy that I see twice a month. They are sort of average customers. And I have about a hundred that I only go to once a month. They are my smallest customers. But I love them all, Benny," he laughed. "Every one is precious. In between, I do prospecting for new customers. I try to see one prospect every day."

"Do you work every day?"

"Pretty much. I work hard."

"Weekends?"

"Well, sometimes … most times."

I was a little embarrassed for Benny. All those questions. Barry didn't mind. He seemed to enjoy talking about his business. And I believe he might have told us much more, except that Gracie tugged at him.

"Barry, dear, we ought to be on our way."

"Sure, Gracie. Benny, Jack, Morris, nice to see you all. Hope to see you all again." Goodbyes all around. As Gracie and Barry moved off, Benny called out. "Hey, Barry, do you have a younger brother name of Walter? Sells cars in Asbury Park?"

"No, Benny. No brothers, no sisters. See you guys."

"That Barry is a nice guy," I observed.

"Yes," Morris growled. "You can see why Gracie likes him. Lots of personality."

Benny caught my eye. He gave me a very sober look. He did the Italian thing on his right eye. Again that gesture. What was I missing?

23

Truth

THAT SAME DAY, at Krilow's, during the break following Benny's noon pitch, I asked Benny, "Benny, what is with this?" I did the Italian thing on my right eye.

"What does it mean, Jack? Do you know?" Benny asked.

"Sure. It means '*That's a lie.*'"

"Right. It means, '*What a load of bullshit!*' That's what it means, right?"

"Right."

"OK, then you *do* know, Jack."

"*What* do I know, Benny? What is the bullshit?"

He motioned me to a bench. "Sit down, kid. Here, have an orange. Now, listen: I'm gonna teach you something. Tell me what you think of Barry Zoll."

"He looks like a nice guy to me. Friendly. Works hard. Looks like he's doing OK."

"And Gracie likes him, right? He must be a good guy, right?"

"Sure, Benny, why? What's wrong with him?"

"Here is the lesson. It's about truth."

Benny leaned back. His expression became serious. He made his eyes level with mine. "Truth is perfect," he said. "It is like a perfect piece of engineering. It is perfect from every angle. Everything about it fits. Everything works. Nothing is out of place. The truth doesn't have any flaws or anything that doesn't fit. Sometimes the truth is not pretty. Sometimes it gets ugly, but it is always perfect."

He paused. He raised a finger. "If *one* thing doesn't fit—just *one* *thing*—then it is not truth. Because truth is perfect. In truth, everything fits perfectly. One lie, and the whole thing is a lie. Because there are no lies in truth. That is why I never lie."

"Never, Benny?"

"No, never, unless I have to." He laughed.

Then I asked, "What is the lie, Benny?"

"OK, follow me. Number one: Barry Zoll is here only Tuesdays and Thursdays. He stays over with Gracie on Tuesday night and Thursday night. Never on weekends. What's wrong with this picture?"

I shrugged my shoulders.

"C'mon, Jack, *think*. What is wrong with that picture? He is never here on weekends. Why not?"

"I don't know," I answered. "Why isn't he here on weekends?"

Benny didn't answer. He continued. "Number two: Barry only has to work five days a week to cover his territory. Follow the arithmetic: He has thirty once-a-week stops. He has seventy twice-a-month stops. He has a hundred once-a-month stops. How many stops is that each week?"

I was bewildered. "I don't know, Benny, how many?"

"I'll tell you. Thirty once-a-weekers, plus thirty-five a week for the seventy twice-a-monthers, plus twenty-five a week for the hundred once-a-monthers. That is thirty plus thirty-five plus twenty-five. Total, ninety stops a week, or eighteen a day for a *five-day week*! He covers about three stops an hour. That is twenty-four a day! In five days, he can cover 120 stops! In *five days*! That covers the ninety stops and leaves plenty of time for prospecting and lunches and fooling around."

"So?" I asked. I couldn't follow the numbers.

"So! *So*, you say. So, *he does not work weekends*! That's what is so! So where is he on Saturday and Sunday? Where is he, Jack?"

Benny knitted his brows. He peered into my eyes. His eyes were points of blue ice. "Next case, Jack. Solve this puzzle. How can a man have a sister-in-law, but no brother?"

"What do you mean, Benny?"

"Barry has a sister-in-law. Remember? She is a schoolteacher and a painter. But Barry does not have a brother. Remember? I asked him about Walter Zoll. There ain't no Walter Zoll. I just asked that to find out if Barry has a brother. He doesn't."

"I don't get it, Benny."

"What don't you get, Jack? Barry is *married*! His *wife* has a *sister*! That's how come Barry has a sister-in-law."

"How can you be so sure, Benny?"

"Because the truth works. It is perfect. The truth explains everything. Lies don't work. The truth is what I said. He is a married man! He spends Monday night, Wednesday night, Friday night, and weekends, *at home*. And poor dumb Gracie." He made a double-thrusting motion with his right fist. "She gets *shtupped* every Tuesday and Thursday night, and she thinks she is in love."

Benny did the eye thing. I was horrified.

"Should we tell her?" I asked.

"I have to think about that, Jack. I don't like to butt in where nobody asked me."

"But, Benny, it's Gracie!"

"I'll think about it. Meanwhile, mum's the word. OK, Jack?"

"Sure, Benny."

"How about Morris?" I asked.

"Believe me, Jack. Morris has it all figured out. You don't have to educate Morris."

Benny started to walk away.

"Wait a minute," I called after him.

He returned.

"Benny," I asked, "how did you do all those calculations so fast? I couldn't follow you."

He repeated the numbers slowly. "Do you follow me?" he asked. "Just about," I replied. He produced a pencil from behind the counter and a brown bag.

"Here, Jack," he said, handing me the pencil and the brown bag, "write down about six or seven numbers, three-digit numbers, like 246, 834, you know. Don't let me see them. Write them in a column. Go ahead. Turn away and write them. Don't show them to me. Write big and neat."

I turned away and carefully wrote a list of numbers:

247
186
465
352
678
921

"OK, Benny, I wrote them."

"Draw a line under them."

I did.

"Now," said Benny, "turn the bag so the numbers are facing you. I want to see them upside down. I won't look at them until they are in position."

He turned away.

"Tell me when you're ready," he said.

I turned back and laid the bag on the counter, the numbers facing me, away from Benny. "OK, Benny," I said.

He turned. He glanced at the upside-down column of figures, for two seconds. Then he turned away again.

"Write down this number: 2,849."

I did.

"Now add the numbers. See if I'm correct."

I added them, carefully, slowly. His total was correct.

"How did you do that?" I was astonished.

"It's a thing I have for numbers. It's a gift, I guess. I can't explain it. I see the numbers and the total is in my head, like I have an adding machine in my brain. I don't have to add them, like seven and six is thirteen and five is eighteen. The total is just there. I been able to do that since I was twelve."

"You are a genius, Benny." I was in awe of him.

He laughed. "Jack, it don't mean a thing. There's nothing I can do that a forty-dollar Burroughs adding machine can't do. If I had Miss Alper's job, I could shave off about fifteen minutes a day from what she does. So what? No big deal. If you figure out a way for me to get some mileage out of it, let me know."

"There must be something. Maybe like a magic show. Can you do division and multiplication the same way?"

"Nope, just adding. I'm OK with multiplication and all that, but I do it like you do. It's work. The adding is a strange gift. But it's completely useless. About as useless as tits on a boar."

24

Letter from Bernie

Asbury Park, New Jersey
August 2, 1939

Dear Jack:

I did not know what hard work means until I came to this place. That is all we do. Work. Seven days a week. The diner opens at six in the morning and stays open until midnight. My uncle and my aunt are here together from when we open until eight at night. Then one of them goes home. I work from six in the morning to nine at night six days, which includes Saturdays and Sundays. On Thursday, I get off at two o'clock after lunch. That's my big day off.

They want me to live with them when I graduate high school and someday they will give me the diner. My aunt does not have any relatives. Her parents are both dead. She never had a brother or sister or even an aunt or uncle. My uncle is my father's brother and he doesn't have any relatives either except my father and me. He calls me *Son*. He is a swell guy, but he and my aunt do not have a life. Do I want that?

I did not meet any fellows up here. There is a girl who works in the kitchen. She is fourteen. We go swimming at night sometimes. She is OK, but my uncle warned me not to mess with the help.

See you soon. I will be glad to get home. I feel like I will be five years older. Work. Work. Work.

Hope everything is OK with you.

Your friend,
Bernie

25

Awkwardness

I NEVER DISCUSSED the Barry Zoll thing with Morris. It was a dirty thing. I wanted to bury it. Morris must have felt the same. But the Barry Zoll thing was there, like foul air. It made us both uncomfortable. Conversation with Morris became stilted. The Barry Zoll thing clouded everything. It would have been better if we acknowledged it and shared our anger and sadness. But foolishly, we submerged it, except it did not stay down. After a while, we hardly spoke. There was some comfort in just being together, even if our conversations shrank into meaningless pleasantries and foolish and irrelevant observations. The Barry Zoll thing was with us in Roland's dressing room and on the pavilion. I didn't carry it with me all the time. Only when I was with Morris. But I think Morris carried it with him always and everywhere. He stopped going to the Waldorf Grille. So did Benny. So did I. It was hard to see Gracie, bubbling about her good fortune, knowing that she was being had.

I really liked Morris. I wanted to be with him. But the silences became longer and awkward and painful. I started to avoid him.

I tried to replace Morris's friendship with Benny's. It didn't work. I adored Benny, but friendship with him was difficult. He was clever, brittle, world wise, cynical. No easygoing leisurely shmoozing with Benny. With Benny, everything was quick and sharp. Benny was a great guy, and I thought he could be a good and loyal friend, if needed. But he was a whirlwind. There was nothing relaxing or peaceful about Benny. No one could get a lot of Benny's time. You picked up the bright pieces that he scattered, but you did *not* get Benny.

I thought about something I read about John D. Rockefeller. He scattered newly minted dimes when he walked from his office to his limousine. Children waited for him. They swirled around him, scrambling for the dimes he tossed about. Rockefeller scattered dimes; Benny scattered something better—pieces of wit and good humor.

I would soon see another side of Benny. We were about to meet Alan Goren, the cocoa man.

26

Alan Goren

O N MONDAY, A few days after I met Barry Zoll, Zena showed up at the kitchen gadget booth. I spotted her in the crowd for the 2:00 demonstration. Benny was giving the pitch.

When it was time for the sell, Zena jumped in ahead of the shill. She had a clear, rich voice. It carried. "I'll buy a bag," she called out, holding up her dollar bill. She knew the drill.

Afterward, when she turned in her bag and collected her dollar, she again told Benny about the cocoa man, and that she asked Morris to help her, but Morris said he didn't know what to do.

"Morris said I should ask you to help me," she said, "and he was right. The cocoa man will listen to you. You know how to talk to people. You are persuasive. How about it? Give me a hand. He will be at my place tomorrow morning at 10:00. I don't want to be alone with him. He is a screwball. I tried to give him the brush-off, but he won't leave me alone. He says I *know* things even if I don't know that I know. He said he made another seven hundred dollars after his last reading. And I never told him anything that last time. I was afraid to say anything. But he thinks I told him something. I tell you, he is a nut."

"What's with the cocoa?" Benny asked.

Zena told him everything she knew. She explained it to Benny the same way she explained it to Morris. Benny was intrigued.

Benny said OK. "Jack," he said, "how about you come, too? We're both off tomorrow. We'll help Zena and maybe we'll learn something about cocoa futures. Listen, the guy might be a nut, but if he could make seven hundred bucks in four days, I wanna know how. I gotta work a lot of weeks to make seven hundred bucks."

"Thanks, Benny," Zena said, relieved that Benny was going to help her. "You're a friend. And you, too, Jack, you are a good boy."

"Jack *is* a good kid," Benny agreed.

"I feel better," Zena smiled, as she backed away. "See you fellows tomorrow."

Back to work. Benny clapped his hands, as he sang out. "Yes! Yes! Yes! Yes! OK, folks, watch this! Step right up. Hey, look a' here. Look! Look! Look here!"

The great Benny James at work. He was *The Greatest*.

***

The next morning, Benny and I went to Zena's parlor to meet the cocoa man. We showed up before he did. We waited. Zena let him in. I recognized him. He was the man in the gray suit who looked so out of place in the Memorial Day Parade, marching in one of the three World War platoons. When he saw us, he turned to leave, a startled look on his face. "What is this?" he said. Benny grabbed his elbow. "Whoa, fellow," Benny said, softly. "It's OK. We're here to help you and Zena."

The man pulled free. "Let … me … go!" He headed for the door. Zena stood in his way. "Please, it's OK," she said, soothingly. "Please, relax. These are my friends. Nothing is wrong. We all want to help you. I don't want you to lose money on account of me. I'm afraid you are going to misinterpret something and get hurt. Please calm down. Relax. Everything will be OK. Come, sit down. We'll all sit down. I'll pour some tea. We will talk this out."

The stranger hung back. "Zena," he said, "how could you do this? I mind my own business. Nobody knows my business. This is gangster stuff. Please step aside. Let me go." It took some coaxing, but after a few minutes, he calmed down enough that Zena could lead him to the round table. Benny and I sat on the sofa.

"I saw you in the Memorial Day Parade," I said. "You were in the middle platoon. My father was in the front platoon."

He nodded in agreement. "That's right," he said, "I march with the boys every year."

"Now, look, Mr. ..." Zena said. "I don't even know your name. If you invest your money on what I tell you, or what you *think* I tell you, you are going to lose your money. Do you understand? I can't see the future. I don't even know what a cocoa future is except what I read in the library after you came here."

Benny joined in. "If Zena could read tomorrow's paper, we would all get rich on the horses. We wouldn't have to mess around with cocoa. Me and Jack came to convince you. We know Zena. She's a *fake*." Benny ignored the way Zena bristled and shot him a dirty look at that word. He continued, "Now, look here, mister. You look like a sensible guy. You gotta know nobody can do what you want. If you made a score, believe us, it was an accident. Take your profit and quit while you're ahead. What is your name, anyway? I'm Benny James. This here is my friend, Jack."

"Listen to Benny," Zena said. "That is what I've been telling you. Take your profit. Don't count on me. Whatever you think I said or whatever happened, it was just plain luck or coincidence."

The cocoa man relaxed a little. "Zena," he said, "I *will* have some tea, if you don't mind."

"Just take it easy," Zena said quietly. "Relax. We are your friends."

While Zena prepared and poured tea for all of us, the cocoa man loosened up and told us something about himself and the cocoa futures. His name was Alan Goren. He looked to be about fifty. He was completely nondescript. He was medium height, medium weight. Everything about him was gray. His face had hardly any color. He was balding. His thinning hair was pale gray. His eyes were gray. He wore steel-rimmed glasses. He wore a dove-gray suit, a white handkerchief in his breast pocket, a white shirt, a solid gray necktie. He had a soft gray felt hat. When he reached for his teacup, he revealed French cuffs with silver cufflinks. Everything about him was neat. His clothing seemed of good quality. Yet the overall impression of him was somewhat unkempt and slightly in need of a pressing. It was the grayness. No color in him anywhere. The only spot of color was a military button on his lapel.

He told us that he lived at the end of Atlantic City, near Ventnor, that he was in real estate, that commodities were sort of a hobby, and he did pretty good at it. "I know," he said, "that nobody can read the future. I came to Zena just for fun. But then she told me what to do, and *it worked!*"

Zena interrupted. "I did not tell you *anything*, Mr. Goren. I just gave you my standard spiel. You made the decision. You made the right guess."

He became animated. "It was *not* a guess! I figured it out. I took everything into consideration. I figured it out that cocoa prices have to go up. Here is why." He held up his fingers as he explained. "Number one: Ninety percent of the world's supply of cocoa beans comes from Brazil, and the number of Brazilian acres planted in cocoa is less than last year. Liberia is starting to export, but their exports are all within Africa. Number two: Worldwide per capita consumption of chocolate and other cocoa products is rising. It rises every year. Number three: I plot the price movement of cocoa by price and volume. I spend a lot of time doing my charts. My chart shows a strong bottom formed two months ago. The dynamics are pushing the price line higher. Number four: There is going to be a war in Europe soon. Demand will surge. Shipping will be disrupted. The price of delivered beans in New York will climb like crazy. Surpluses will develop in Brazil because there will be a shipping shortage. In Brazil, beans will be cheap but in New York they will be in short supply."

Benny asked, "Mr. Goren, if it is that easy to figure out, why is there any risk at all?"

Goren replied, "There are other factors to consider. If you want to make out a case for lower prices."

"Like what?" Benny asked.

Again, Goren recited, using his fingers for emphasis.

"One: There could be a bumper crop. Even with fewer acres in production, there could be more beans available than last year. Farming techniques and fertilization get better every year. Two: Chamberlain—the British Prime Minister—and Daladier—the French Premier—will give Hitler whatever he wants. There may not be a war. No war, no shortage. Three: The British are the biggest market for cocoa. Their per capita consumption is the highest in the world. And they are starting to add more milk to their chocolate and less cocoa. They call it *British chocolate*. Their demand for beans could drop even if their consumption of chocolate goes up. Four: A lot of traders are long already because they figure a war is coming. Every time peace is in the air, the price drops."

Benny frowned. "It sounds more to me that prices are going down. The *down* story sounds better than the *up* story."

Goren explained. "There is always a conflict between higher prices and lower prices. It is like two almost equal forces pushing against each other. When the forces are equal, the price stays stable. Sometimes weeks go by with hardly any change in the price. There are so many factors when it comes to commodities. And I didn't even mention the possibility of poor crop results because of weather. In Brazil, the weather is pretty reliable, but you never know. Too much rain can ruin a crop. Not enough rain can kill a crop. There could be a disease that destroys the crop. If it were easy, there would not be a futures market."

Benny had a puzzled expression. "What does *futures* mean?"

Goren sipped at his tea. "This is excellent tea, Zena," he said. He now seemed at ease. He answered Benny like a professor giving a lecture on the economics of cocoa beans.

"If you are a processor, and you are going to need a few thousand tons of the beans every month to keep your plant going and to satisfy your customers' delivery schedules, you want to know where you are going to get what you need next month, and the following month, and the month after that and so forth. And you want to know what it will cost. You know today's price. That is called the *spot* price. But, how about six months from now? Your big customers want to fix the prices now for their deliveries in the future. So you have to know what you will pay for the beans in the future. You could make agreements with some growers to take their future crops and fix the prices now. And lots of big users do that. Or you can hedge your price by buying futures contracts. On the New York Board of Trade, you can buy a contract for delivery as far out as nine months from now. That is called 'going long.' That is a futures contract. It takes the guesswork out of what you will pay for the beans in the future, when you need them."

"Who sells you the contract?" asked Benny.

"It could be a grower," Goren explained. "He might want to fix the price for his future crop, or fix a price for part of it. He might want to know now what his crop will bring, or part of it, instead of taking his chances on what will be the spot price when he is ready to ship. Or it could be somebody like me. I buy contracts and I sell contracts."

"But you are not a user or a grower. How can you buy the stuff? Or sell the stuff?"

"I don't have to be a user or a grower. I can buy a contract of cocoa beans for September delivery or December delivery or next March delivery. Before then, before the month arrives, I have to sell my contract. Otherwise, I will have to take delivery."

"How can you take delivery?" Benny was listening intently, leaning forward. He was getting interested. "Are they going to bring it to your house?"

Goren smiled for the first time. "Hardly. A contract is ten tons of beans. In a public warehouse in New York, ten tons of beans would get marked mine, and I have to pay for them, and I have to pay storage. I never want to take delivery. That is a disaster."

"Suppose you *do* take delivery," Benny persisted. "Suppose you can't sell the contract before the month arrives, and you have to take delivery. What then? Do you kill yourself?"

"No," was Goren's reply, again with a smile. "It's very costly. I would have to sell the beans on the spot market. I would pay commission, storage charges, insurance, and if the spot price falls down, I could lose a *lot* of money."

"Alan—may I call you Alan?" Benny asked. "Suppose you think prices are going to drop. What then?"

"Ah, if I think prices are going down, I can sell a contract. That is called *selling short.* I could sell September cocoa or December or March. But before the month comes, I have to buy it in. I have to buy back a contract, because I am not a grower and I can't deliver. I have to *cover my short.*"

"Who would buy a contract from you? You can't deliver."

"I *can* deliver. All I have to do is buy a contract. I cover my short by buying it in, by going long. I deliver my long position. I don't actually deliver the beans."

"Does the buyer know you can't deliver the beans and that you have to deliver a contract instead?"

Goren sipped at his tea again. He set down the cup. He was thoroughly into his lecture.

"No, the buyer does not know me. The buyer buys through the New York Board of Trade just like I buy or sell through the New York Board of Trade. When the delivery month arrives, the contracts of the speculative buyers and sellers all get cancelled by each other, and what is left are the real users and the real sellers—processors, growers, jobbers, importers, exporters."

"Wow," said Benny. "I still don't get it. But I get the drift. You're a gambler. You're a crapshooter. You bet right, that the price will go up. Or else you bet wrong, that the price will drop. That's about it, isn't it?"

Goren was insulted. "No. I am *not* a gambler. Maybe you could say I am a speculator, but I am not shooting crap. There is no rhyme or reason for dice to do anything. Dice is purely chance. Commodities prices are affected by things that we know—demand, supply, weather, size of the crop, all things that I study. And they tell me a story. They tell me where prices are headed.

What I do is a discipline, like mathematics, or physics. I know the causes and the effects. I analyze them.

"I reach a disciplined result. Once I go long, or short, I continue to analyze all the data. If I see the data is changing, I change. If I am long and a factor changes, I am ready to sell, or maybe sell and go short. And vice versa. I can make money on the long side or on the short side. If I conclude that the factors are negative, I go short and buy it back at a lower price."

"What if you go short and you don't deliver?"

"Ah, there is a rhyme for that:

> *He who sells what isn't his'n,*
> *must buy it back or go to pris'n."*

Benny shrugged. "This is too much for me to understand. Let's get some lunch."

Then after a moment, Benny said, "Hey, Alan, do you really know what you're doing? Should I give you a coupla hundred to invest for me?"

Before Goren could respond, Benny stood up and said, "C'mon, Alan, lunch is on me. C'mon, Jack, Zena."

Zena declined. She wanted to open her parlor. Goren hesitated, but that great Benny James smile hooked him. It was easy to be drawn to Benny. And Goren seemed to be enjoying his role as teacher. Benny had that gleam in his eye, like a big win was coming his way. Labor Day was coming. Business dies in Atlantic City after Labor Day. Maybe this year Benny would not have to go on the circuit.

That's how we met Alan Goren. Our lives would be changed forever.

27

Lunch With Goren

W E WENT OUT to lunch. Not to the Waldorf Grille. Benny and I were still avoiding having to see Gracie.

Benny and Goren talked about the commodities market. Benny was full of questions.

"How many pounds of cocoa beans did you say are in a contract?" Benny asked.

"Ten tons," said Goren.

"*Ten tons!*" Benny was amazed. "Twenty thousand pounds. What does a ton of cocoa beans cost? How much is the down payment?"

"It's not called a down payment," Goren explained. "It's called the *margin*. You need ten percent margin. Think of it like this. Suppose you bought a contract of cocoa; that's called *going long*, that's ten tons of beans. Say you bought it for September delivery. Say that somebody loaned you ninety percent of the contract and you put up ten percent."

"What's the price of the cocoa beans?" Benny asked.

"Today, the September beans are 4.08 cents per pound."

Benny was quick. "That's $816 for a ten-ton contract—the ninety-percent loan is about $735, ten percent is $81.60. I need $81.60 to buy a ten-ton contract. If the price goes up a penny a pound, my contract is worth $1,016, but my loan stays at $735. My contract is worth $281. I put up $81. My profit is $200 on my contract if the price goes up a penny. Pretty nifty. Cocoa goes up a penny; I make $200 on an investment of $81. Is that correct?"

"You understand, Benny," Goren nodded. "You are remarkably quick with the numbers. Except the ninety percent is not a loan. Remember, this is only a contract to buy the cocoa anytime it is delivered to you after September 1. If you have to take delivery, because you didn't sell your contract, then you have to pay the full price. If you bought the contract at 4.08 cents a pound, you owe $816, less the ten percent margin you paid when you bought the contract. If you want to figure out how you're doing, you don't need to value the entire contract and subtract the ninety percent. It's easier to know that your contract is ten tons. If the price goes up a penny a pound, you made $200 dollars. But a penny is a big move. In either direction."

"What if the price drops?" Benny asked.

"That's where the margin rule comes in. You have to maintain ten percent margin. So if the price drops a quarter of a cent, to 3.83 cents, let's say, the broker wants you to put up another fifty dollars. Unless you have money on deposit with him, or equity in other contracts."

"What if I don't put up the fifty dollars?" Benny asked.

"The broker will sell you out. He wants to get your additional margin fast, or else sell you out fast, because he doesn't want you to lose more than the ten percent you put up. If you do, he may have trouble collecting from you."

"How many contracts do you own, Alan?"

"Right now, I am long twenty contracts."

"Wow! A one cent increase is a four-thousand dollar profit!"

"That's right, Benny. You understand how it works. You're a quick study. In the last six trading days, I made a thousand dollars. Cocoa was up a quarter of a penny a pound."

"Why don't you sell? Why don't you cash in?"

"I think cocoa has another penny to go. I am going to go long thirty more contracts today. I don't have to put up any money. I have enough equity in the twenty contracts I already own. But I'm not going to buy the September beans. I'm going to buy the Decembers. They're selling for 4.12 cents. I will have a longer ride with the Decembers. My plan is to sell the September beans on September 1 and roll the money over into December beans, or maybe I'll go out to March. Right now I don't see anything in sight to stop cocoa from going to five cents a pound."

"Maybe I'll get in on it," said Benny. "I have a few bucks."

"Tell you what," Goren said. "After lunch, I'll take you to my broker, Krieger and Son. You'll see how it works."

28

Bobo Truck and the
Arithmetic Contest

THE OFFICE OF Krieger and Son was on Central Pier, opposite St. James Place. Benny, Goren, and I headed there. On the way, we passed Royce's Shooting Gallery, near Kentucky Avenue: *Ten Shots, 25 Cents, Win a Prize*. Goren wanted to stop there. "What for, Alan?" Benny asked.

"You'll see," was Goren's reply. The shooting gallery was a small open storefront with a counter across the front. There were six .22 caliber rifles chained to the counter. The chains were attached to the muzzle end of the rifle, just long enough to let the shooter raise, aim, and shoot into the gallery, but for safety's sake, too short to allow the rifle to be pointed away from the gallery's interior. Otherwise some crazy might shoot people on the boardwalk. The rear wall of the gallery was covered with targets—wheels, bells, flags, and, most inviting, a continuous line of steel ducks, moving from right to left. The ducks were mounted on hinges. When a duck was struck, it fell down, with a satisfying *clang*. The ducks traveled on an oval track that went across the front of the gallery, then around behind the rear wall, where the knocked-down ducks stood up again, automatically, by passing over a wedge-shaped device alongside the track. They were standing again when they next appeared rounding the curve.

Two shooters were at the counter, firing away. *Bam, clang! Bam, bam, clang! Clang!* Pale blue smoke and the acrid scent of gunpowder filled the air.

Goren directed us to a door that opened into a narrow corridor along the left side of the gallery. We entered and walked twenty feet to a closed door. Goren tapped, two shorts, one long, two shorts. *Tap tap, tap, tap tap.* A small panel opened in the door. Somebody's eyes appeared. Goren announced himself.

"It's me, Alan Goren."

"Who's with you?"

"This is my good friend, Benny James, and this is my nephew, Jack."

The panel closed. The door opened in. We entered a smoke-filled room twenty feet square. There was a counter across the rear with an elevated platform behind it. The center of the room was a seating area—five rows of leather easy chairs, four chairs in each row. Four men stood behind the counter, each with a clipboard and an open cash box. About twenty men lounged in the easy chairs or stood at the counter. The men behind the counter wore radio headsets wired to small radios. The radios seemed to be silent, but evidently the headsets were active. The countermen alternated between taking money, writing on the clipboards, and turning to chalk in numbers on four blackboards across on the wall behind the counter. At the top of each blackboard was a name—Delaware, Suffolk Downs, Arlington, Aqueduct. Each blackboard held rows of chalked numbers, like this:

Delaware

1:	5-2-4	$11.40	$9.70
2:	1-3-5	$8.20	$7.00
3:	2-4-3	$12.30	$10.50

Along the left wall was a buffet table with a coffee urn, three large platters of sandwiches, and three large platters of small cakes and cookies. Two cops in uniform leaned against the wall, coolly, arms folded across their chests, studying us through watchful eyes. The floor was heavily carpeted. The sounds of the boardwalk and the shooting gallery were audible, but muffled. All the men in the room spoke softly. The room was filled with the low murmuring sound of hushed conversations.

"What is this place?" I asked.

Benny answered me. "It's a bookie joint. Those blackboards are the four tracks running today. The first is Delaware. The first three races are over. In the first race, the Number 5 horse won, the Number 2 horse placed. That means it came in second. The Number 4 horse showed. That means it came in third. The winning horse paid $11.40 for a two-dollar bet. This joint paid $9.70. Looks like they discount about fifteen percent. Evidently, this joint does not take place and show bets."

"These men," he indicated the twenty or so men seated or milling about the center of the room, "are customers. The cops are … cops. I guess this is the place where all the numbers money is collected, too."

"What are the numbers?" I asked.

"Tell you later."

Goren picked up one of the racing forms that were stacked at the end of the counter. He eased into one of the leather easy chairs to study the form.

A door opened behind the counter. Two men emerged. One was carrying a heavy adding machine, which he set down at the left end of the counter. The other man was obviously someone of importance. All who were seated rose out of their chairs, as if a

judge entered a courtroom, as if someone called out *All rise.*
Everyone greeted him. A chorus of *Hello, Bobo.* Bobo was a big
man; he looked powerful. He had slicked-back jet-black hair, dark
eyes, smooth face, rosy cheeks. He wore white trousers and a colorful long-sleeved silk shirt, open down to the third button. He
had a massive neck, with a thick gold chain and a heavy gold cross.
He smiled and raised his right hand in greeting. "Hello, fellas."

He spread the fingers on his raised hand and slowly lowered his
arm, like a prince, signifying it was OK to be seated in his presence. He addressed the two cops specifically. "Hello, boys. How's
everything?"

"OK, Bobo," they responded.

"Good. Good. Don't forget to give my regards to the
Lieutenant."

"Sure, Bobo."

Bobo's eyes swept the room. He nodded to each customer and
murmured his name. "Rudy," he nodded. "Fred, Jim." Each customer replied with a smile. "Hello, Bobo."

Bobo acknowledged Goren. "Hello, Alan."

Goren responded, "Hello, Bobo."

Bobo's eyes stopped at me and Benny. "And these fellows over
here?" he asked, to no one in particular, without taking his eyes
from us.

Goren rose out of his chair and came to us. "They are with me,
Bobo," he said. "This is my good friend, Benny James, and this is
my nephew, Jack."

"*Tch, tch*, Alan," Bobo shook his head, negatively, side to side.
"This over here is not a place to bring guests. Don't do it again."

"They're OK, Bobo," Goren apologized.

"OK, Alan," Bobo clapped Goren on his upper arm, twice, with a wide smile. "OK for now, but no more. Unless," he said, looking at Benny, "you want some action."

"Sure, Bobo. Can I buy a number?"

"Not in here, Benny. They's places outside for that."

"OK, Bobo, I'll try the next race at Aqueduct."

"Right over there, Benny," Bobo put his arm around Benny and pointed to the Aqueduct blackboard. "I'm Bobo Truck, Benny. Nice to meet you."

"A pleasure, Bobo," Benny gave Bobo the big Benny James grin. You could see its effect on Bobo. He smiled back at Benny.

"See ya 'round, Benny James." He was committing the name and face to memory.

Benny left us to pick up a racing form. He went to consult with Goren.

Bobo addressed me. "And what do you do, Jack?"

"I work for Mr. Krilow. I help the demonstrators. Benny is one of my bosses."

"How old are you, son?"

"I'm fifteen."

"Go to school, do you?"

"I'm starting high school in September."

"Good. Good. Get an education." He started to turn away.

At that moment, the man who brought in the adding machine took off one of the pages from the Delaware clipboard and began to add the numbers. He was fast on the machine. *Plink, plink, crank! Plink, plink, crank! Plink, plink, crank!*

Bobo half-turned, half-faced me, "See that, Jack?" Bobo said. "That is Sammy Beck over here. He is the fastest man on an adding machine in this town, maybe in the whole country. Look at him go."

Sammy Beck sure was fast. His right hand flew, up the keyboard, then *crank*! He never looked at the machine. His eyes were fixed on the rows of numbers on the paper. His left hand went down the column, number by number as he entered each into the machine, and then cranked.

The 1939 state-of-the-art adding machine was a Burroughs hand-cranked machine with vertical banks of keys and a printout adding machine tape. Each bank had ten keys, numbered from bottom to top from 0 through 9. The number of banks of keys determined the size (in digits) of the individual numbers that could be added, and the number of digits in the total. For example, in a machine with eight banks of keys, you could input a number as large as 999,999.99 and receive a printout on the adding machine tape up to a total of one additional digit, like 9,999,999.99.

As with any machine, practice and training improved the performance of the operator. A skillful operator, like a skillful typist, could operate the adding machine rapidly, without concentrating on the keyboard. And, unlike an ordinary user, a really skilled operator worked his way up the banks of keys from the lowest individual digit to the highest individual digit, while the ordinary user worked the keyboard from left to right, regardless of the size of the individual digits.

For example, inputting the number $814.73: The ordinary user punches in, from left to right, an 8, a 1, a 4, a 7, and lastly, a 3, then *cranks*. The skilled operator, on the other hand, punches in the digits, from lowest to highest, in their respective banks, first the 1 in the fourth bank from the right, then the 3 in the first bank on the right, then the 4 in the third bank, then the 7 in the second bank, lastly the 8 in the fifth bank, then *cranks*. The skilled operator's hand moves less, because his hand moves up the keyboard once for each number entered while the ordinary operator's hand moves up and down the keyboard, from left to right, seeking out the digit that belongs in each bank.

A good operator not only moves up the keyboard from the lowest digit to the highest digit, he does it without looking at the keyboard. A really good operator is many times faster than an ordinary user. Regular use of the machine makes for speed and accuracy. The occasional user is somewhat of a groper. It is like the difference between an excellent touch-typist whose fingers fly over the keys without looking versus a hunt-and-peck typist who has to look and find each letter.

"I bet Benny is faster," I said, only half-aloud. I was really talking to myself.

Bobo turned back to me.

"What's that, son?"

Uh-oh. I didn't even realize I had spoken.

"What did you say, Jack?" He asked again.

"Nothing … really," I stammered.

"Yes, you did. You said you bet Benny is faster on the machine than Sammy over here."

"No, Mr. Truck. I said I bet Benny is faster. He doesn't need the machine."

Bobo pulled back in surprise. "What are you saying, son? That your Benny could add up that whole page of numbers without a machine? Faster than Sammy over here?"

Boy, was I in it. A few men overheard Bobo and drifted toward us. Goren approached.

"What is happening, Jack?" he asked.

"I didn't mean anything," I said. "I was talking to myself. I said Benny could add faster than that man with the machine."

Bobo called to Benny. "Hey, Benny James, c'meah. Didja hear what your pal Jack over here said about you?"

Benny smiled, "What? That I'm great with the girls?"

"Well, I can believe that. You're a good-looking dude, that's for sure." Bobo laughed and slapped Benny's back. "No, Benny," he said. "Your friend over here said, to use his exact words, he *bet* you are faster *without a machine* than Sammy over here. He used the word *bet*. The magic word. He didn't say maybe you're as fast, or he thinks you *might be* as fast. He said he *bet* you're as fast."

Benny turned to study Sammy Beck. He studied him the way a prizefighter studies his opponent in action. Sammy Beck was really fast. I felt terrible. What kind of a mess did I make? Benny asked if he could see a sheet. Bobo moved to the counter. He picked up a clipboard, removed a sheet, and handed it to Benny. There were about sixty numbers on the sheet, in a column—mostly two-digit numbers, like $36, $74, a few three-digit numbers, like $150. They were all whole dollar amounts, no pennies.

Benny closed his eyes. He was counting Sammy's cranks. After about twenty seconds, he opened his eyes, and looked at me. "Jack," he said, with his biggest grin, "you are going to get me in trouble. This guy is really fast! I don't know. He is fast!"

"OK, Benny, forget it. I'm sorry," I said. I addressed Bobo. "I didn't mean anything, Mr. Truck. I've seen Benny add numbers. He *is* fast. I was just wondering out loud, that's all."

Benny interrupted me. "Wait a second, Jack." He turned to Bobo. "Tell you what, Bobo. I'll bet ten bucks. What'll you lay me? How about 5–1? Your man is *real* fast."

"No odds, Benny James," Bobo said with a smile. "But I'll tell you what. If you win, I'll buy you and your friends dinner at Trucci's. That's my place."

"It's a deal," Benny offered his hand on it. Bobo grasped it and pumped it vigorously.

Goren spoke up to the crowd that had gathered around. "I've got twenty bucks here on Benny. Anybody want it?" Five men said *yes* in unison. "Tell you what," Goren said. "I'll lay you each ten. OK?"

Benny drew Goren aside. "Alan, you don't even know me. What are you doing?"

"I have a good feeling about this," was Goren's reply. I had suspected Goren was a mystic. Now I knew I was right.

"All right, now," Bobo called out. "Bets go over here on that counter. Sammy, finish off that sheet. Don't start another until I tell you. Benny, I have a stopwatch here. Do you want to go first?"

Benny answered, "You don't need the stopwatch. I see there is a carbon paper and a carbon copy sheet. I'll take the carbon copy. Sammy can have the original. We'll start together. Whoever finishes first."

"Are you sure you wanna do it that way?" Bobo asked.

"Yes, Bobo. Just as long as the carbon copy is clear."

"OK, Benny, you get up behind the counter, next to Sammy over here, and I'll check out the carbon copy for you."

So Bobo arranged the match. It was obvious he was enjoying himself. He cleared away about six feet of the left side of the counter. "You will stand here, Sammy. Benny, you over here. Here, I put the sheets over here face down on the counter. When I say *start,* you guys will turn over your sheets and start adding. OK?"

"I need a pencil," Benny said.

One of the men behind the counter handed Benny a yellow pencil.

"Do you want to try it out?" Bobo laughed. He was having such a good time.

Benny laughed at Bobo's joke. It looked like Benny was also having a good time.

Bobo spread his arms, his back to the counter. He walked toward the crowd. By now, everyone in the room was pressing forward to watch the contest.

"Everybody back," Bobo said, "give them room." He cleared away a ten-foot space in front of the counter. "You guys," he said to the other men behind the counter. "Come on out from behind."

"But, Bobo, we'll miss the results."

"OK, then," Bobo said. "You're right. You fellows move all the way to the right. Write the results on a piece of paper. Don't put them on the board until this is over. We don't want to distract the … the … *contestants* over here!" He laughed again. Bobo went to the clipboard at the right end. He opened it and took out the bottom two sheets—the original and the carbon copy. He studied the carbon copy.

"Benny James," he said, "I'm lookin' to see that the carbon is clear. I don't want you hollerin' *foul* that the numbers are too faint or anythin'. It looks OK to me. Do you wanna see a different carbon sheet? I don't want you bellyachin' later on over here."

"If you say it's OK, that's good enough for me." Again, the big grin. Benny looked just like when he is about to start a demonstration. I half-expected him to clap his hands and call out, "OK, folks, step right up here. This is gonna be somethin' to see!" He didn't look anxious at all. I, on the other hand, was pretty near trembling with apprehension that Benny should be shamed and all because of me.

Bobo arranged the pages, face down. He stood back. "I'm gonna count down from ten. Then, I will say *start*. That's when you pick up the papers over here. If either of you jump the gun, you lose automatically. Agreed?"

"Yes, Bobo," Sammy said. It was the first time he'd spoken.

"Sure, Bobo," Benny said, completely relaxed, his hands resting easily, face down on the counter.

Bobo started the count. "Ten. Nine. Eight." The room became silent. The only sound was the distant sound of the shooting gallery, muffled by the walls in between.

"Two. One. *START!*"

The contestants reached for the papers and turned them over. Sammy began to work the machine. He was a wonder. *Plink, plink, crank! Plink, plink, plink, crank!* His right hand flew up the keys and to the crank, then up the keys again and to the crank. Watching Sammy Beck was like watching an engine at work.

Benny held his right hand palm down, on the paper. His hand moved down the paper, smoothly. I measured Benny's progress down the paper against Sammy's. Benny was going down the paper faster! Much faster! Almost twice as fast. He was doing it effortlessly. He looked at ease. He wore a half-smile. He might just as well have been reading the morning paper. Oh, boy! Benny is doing it! I couldn't believe it, how fast he went down that column of numbers. He was at the bottom! Sammy's left hand was only three-quarters down the page, his right hand still flying over the keys and crank. Benny picked up the pencil and wrote down a number. He set down the pencil. He won! I was elated. But wait! He started over. He placed his palm down at the top of the page again and started down the column a second time. What was he doing? Checking his answer? He went down the page much quicker this time. Benny reached the bottom a second time. He picked up the pencil and as he started to write again, Sammy shouted, "Done! I'm done!"

Benny finished writing a second later.

"Wait a second, Bobo," Benny said, "I had the answer before Sammy hollered *done*. All I was doing was writing it down."

"You lose, Benny James," Bobo said. "Good show, but you lose. Sammy over here edged you out by a half a second."

"Well, I don't agree," Benny's smile was a little thin, "but you're making the rules, Bobo. OK, I concede."

As everyone crowded forward to congratulate Sammy, Benny suddenly clapped his hands. Two quick claps. "Wait up, everybody. Let's compare the answers. Here's mine: 3,176. What's yours, Sammy?"

"I get 3,212."

"Hold everything," Benny sang out. "If Sammy's answer is wrong, he can't be the winner."

Silence for a moment.

Bobo spoke up. "Of course. The answer has to be right. Maybe yours is wrong, Benny James."

"Maybe they're both wrong," somebody in the crowd called out.

"Tell you what," Benny said. "I'll bet a hundred bucks I'm right and he's wrong."

Like a shock wave, silence fell on the room. Bobo studied Benny through narrowed eyes. When he narrowed his eyes that way, his expression lost that look of good-natured openness. A shadow of menace passed over his face, only for a second. Then the smile returned. You could see that he smelled a scam. But he dismissed the idea almost as quickly as it came.

Bobo was first to speak. "Benny," he said, "you are *somethin'*! You're on."

"How 'bout some odds, Bobo?" Benny asked with that innocent grin.

"No odds, Benny James. If you win a hundred from me, you'll be a celebrity in this town. That's enough."

"A hundred and ten, Bobo. Don't forget the first ten bucks."

Bobo laughed again, "Sure, Benny, a hundred and ten. I'll tell you what. I like your style. Dinner at Trucci's on me, win or lose. With your friends." Another vigorous handshake. "Now then," said Bobo, "how do we do this?"

Goren spoke up. "Hold it, Bobo. I'll put another hundred on Benny. Anybody?"

Bobo answered before anyone could speak up. "Me, Alan, I cover you," he said with a broad smile.

"OK," Bobo repeated himself, "now how we gonna do this?"

"Easy," said Benny. "Let somebody read off the numbers and you check them on the adding machine tape."

So Bobo called over one of the cops and handed him the paper. The cop read out the numbers while Bobo checked them off on the adding machine tape. Halfway down the cop called out 137.

Bobo said, "Stop. The tape says 173."

"That's the mistake," Benny said. "A difference of thirty-six dollars. I am right. Sammy's tape is thirty-six dollars too much. I win."

Bobo was puzzled. He picked up a pencil and paper. Laboriously, he wrote and calculated. He struggled for almost five minutes. Finally, he looked up. "Benny James is right. Benny is the winner!"

Pandemonium! Everybody in the room was talking at the same time, and all moving toward Benny. I was so excited, I thought I was going to cry. Benny came to me and threw his arms around me. He hugged me.

"Why did you add it twice?" I asked. "Were you checking your answer?"

"Not at all, Jack. The first time, I only added the first two digits columns on the right, like fifty-three and twelve and thirty-eight. The second time, I added the hundreds column. There weren't many of them. Then I added them together."

Here came Alan Goren. "I knew it was good luck when I met Zena and you guys. Benny, you are a genius! I can't believe what you did. How did you do it? You have to teach me. We are going to make a fortune in cocoa."

Bobo approached. "Here's your money, Benny James. And yours, Alan. This is the first bet I ever lost that I didn't mind to lose. You're some guy. We are gonna do somethin' together over here. Meanwhile, you three are my guests at Trucci's. C'mere, Georgie," he called to the doorman. "I'll let you know when. Georgie here will tell you when. Where will he find you?"

"At Krilow's Kitchen Gadgets," Benny said.

"Kitchen Gadgets? Whattaya do there? The boy says you are a demonstrator. Are you a pitchman?"

"Yep, that's what I do."

"You can do better. You'll hear from me."

I picked up the paper that Bobo used to find out if Benny's answer was correct. Here is what it said, after a number of false starts and cross-outs:

```
right number        137
Sammy's tape        173
Sammy too much       36
_____

Sammy's total       3212
Sammy's mistake      -36
Benny's number      3176  ok
```

I folded it and slipped it into my pocket. I kept it as a souvenir. I still have it.

As we turned to leave, Benny waved to the room. "So long, everybody. Come see me at Krilow's on Virginia Avenue," he laughed.

"So long, Benny. Take it easy, Benny. You're something, Benny." A chorus of good-byes.

We were almost at the door when the Aqueduct man called out, "Hey, Goren, Alan Goren. Hey, Benny James, wait a second. Your horse won at Aqueduct!" Benny had backed Goren's pick.

"Is this something, or what!" exclaimed Goren. "I haven't had a winner in this place since March. Benny, you are my lucky piece. Tell me how you did that trick."

"It ain't me, Alan. I don't *do* anything. The numbers come into my head by themselves. It's a gift," Benny laughed. He threw his arm around my neck and pulled me to him. "It's Jack. He's the lucky one."

29

Krieger and Son

W<small>E HEADED FOR</small> Central Pier to the Krieger and Son office. The Bobo Truck adventure drew us together. Now we were three friends. Goren's early suspicions were gone, blown away in the excitement of the arithmetic contest.

"Benny," he said, as we walked toward Central Pier, "I tell you, something good is going on. I feel good luck. I feel like I'm wrapped in good luck. Like an energy. First, I met Zena, now you. I feel a big score coming. You should get on it, Benny. Buy a couple of contracts."

"Maybe, Alan. I'm not a gambler. But maybe you know what you're doing. Cocoa sounds awful cheap, only four cents a pound. I guess I can spring for about six hundred dollars. That will buy me what, seven contracts?"

Benny turned to me. "Jack, you are part of this deal. I want you to buy a couple of contracts."

"Benny, that's about $170. I don't have $170."

"How much do you have?"

"When I get paid this week, I'll have $30."

Benny addressed Goren. "Alan, you and me will lend Jack enough to buy a coupla contracts, OK?"

"But I can't pay you guys back if I lose the money. I can't do it."

"Don't worry about it, Jack," Goren said. "You're not going to lose anything."

"I can't do it, Mr. Goren. If I lose the money, I'll be in debt. I can't do that. It is against my family's rules."

"Well, this is a dilemma," Benny murmured, thoughtfully. "I agree, no debt is the way to live. I don't owe anybody anything. How 'bout you, Alan?"

"You're right, Jack," Goren agreed. "And I'm like you, Benny. I don't owe anybody."

Benny brightened, "Tell you what, Jack. Between the horse and the arithmetic, I won over two hundred bucks. How about you, Alan?"

Goren made a quick mental calculation. "I did better than you, Benny. I had fifty on the first arithmetic bet. I guess I won two hundred and forty."

"Let's divide our winnings three ways," Benny said. "We're partners, ain't we, sort of?"

"Good deal," Goren answered.

"OK," said Benny. "My $200, your $240; $440 all together, $146.66 apiece. Call it $147. Jack, I owe you $53.33, call it $54. Alan, you owe $93. Jack, you won $147. With your $30, you have enough for two contracts."

"Thanks, fellows, but I can't accept it. You put up the money. You won it. If you lost, you wouldn't be asking me to give you money."

Benny stopped. We all stopped. Benny placed both hands on my shoulders and gave me that level-eye look, his face perfectly serious, almost grim. His smile was put aside. "Let me teach you something, Jack. Your principles are good. I ain't knockin' 'em. But there is something else you gotta learn. It's about gift-giving and gift-receiving. A gift out of friendship is a beautiful thing. Being on the receiving end is also a beautiful thing if the receiver feels the same friendship and the gift is pure, no strings. It takes a good man to stand by your principles. But also it takes a good man to know how and when to accept a gift. Besides, you earned this. If you didn't tell Bobo about me, there would'na been a bet. And anyway, it wasn't a fair contest. I watched Sammy. I knew I would win. I even went slower just to be sure. I coulda eyeballed the column without passing my hand down the list. I wanted to be a thousand percent sure and I thought it added some theater to my performance, didn't it? But it don't matter. I woulda had the answer in one-half the time just by looking down the column; it was a sucker bet. No way I could lose."

"You could have come up with the wrong answer," Goren observed.

"No way, Alan. I don't add the numbers. All I have to do is look at 'em and there's the answer in my head. Like I have an adding machine up there. But my machine never makes a mistake. OK, then, it's done. Jack, you have enough to buy two contracts."

I was embarrassed. I can't even describe the feelings I had for Benny. And for Goren. He was a pretty nifty guy. Sort of strange. A little bit like Morris in being a loner. But Morris was the same from outside all the way in. Goren fooled you. He looked like a stone face and a cold fish, and sort of detached from everything, and suspicious of people. But he was a gambler! I started to understand him. He was full of superstitions. And he bet on hunches. I liked him, but I feared he would come to no good. Benny hit the nail on the head when he heard Goren's analysis of the future of cocoa prices. Benny said Goren was just a gambler. The opposite point of view, that the price of cocoa was headed down, sounded just as realistic as Goren's reasons for cocoa to go up in price.

I must have turned beet-red as I stammered, "I don't know how to thank you guys. Except to say *thanks* and ... and ..."

Benny cut me off. "Forget it, Jack," he said. "It's nothing."

Central Pier was a short pier opposite St. James Place. Unlike Steel Pier, which went more than a quarter mile out to sea, and Million Dollar Pier, which was almost as long as Steel Pier, Central Pier was almost entirely above the beach. It barely reached the surf. It was primarily a two-story commercial building. The lower level was even with the boardwalk. A half-dozen amusements were in the center of the pier. Both sides of the lower level were lined with stores. Several flights of wide stairways led to an upper level, open in the center where a wide, oval-shaped balcony circled the building. Offices and stores lined the outside of the balcony. The central area of the pier was open all the way to a glass roof, giving the entire pier a feeling of outdoors. Today you would call it an atrium. In 1939, it was just called a glass roof. When you stood on the second floor balcony, you looked down on what was doing on the lower level.

Central Pier was home to a few insurance companies, a couple of bank branches, a dozen upscale stores, some brokerage firm branches, some law offices, and several restaurants. A pair of heavily paneled oak double doors on the downbeach side of the second floor displayed the name, *Krieger and Son, Commodities Specialists since 1897*. Beneath the sign were the names *Carl Krieger, Carl Krieger, Jr.*

The offices of Krieger and Son were furnished in the handsome richness of polished cherry woods, with soft indirect lighting, gleaming brass, mellow leathers, and luxurious carpeting. A projected image of a ticker tape moved across a screen at the front of the main seating area, where a half-dozen clients lounged in the rich-looking red leather armchairs. The similarity with Bobo's joint struck me. Were Bobo Truck's gamblers any different from the commodity speculators at Krieger and Son? Krieger and Son was elegant, quiet, polite, hushed. Goren looked at home there, just as he looked at home at Bobo's.

Goren pointed us to the receptionist. She knew him. "Hello, Mr. Goren, how are you today?" She looked thirtyish, very professional, very attractive. She wore her hair pulled back tight in a bun.

"Hello, Beatrice, can I see Mr. Krieger, Junior? Is he available?"

"I'm sure he will have time for you, Mr. Goren." She pressed a buzzer on the intercom machine on her desk.

"Yes, Beatrice?" A man's voice came from the intercom box.

"Mr. Goren is here to see you, Mr. Krieger. Can you see him?" she asked.

"I'll be right out," answered the box.

Junior emerged from one of the offices, wearing a broad smile. He was a man in his mid-forties. His face was tanned to perfection, the color of soft sandalwood. He looked as though Hollywood's central casting supplied him for the role of a successful broker. He had a head of silvery hair, blue eyes behind silver spectacles, attractive squint lines alongside his eyes. His tailoring was a study in crisp perfection. He wore a double-breasted pin-stripe dark navy suit. It looked like flannel. Obviously, Mr. Krieger, Jr., believed in proper dress even in the heat of summer. This was 1939. Air-conditioned offices were about ten years in the future.

A half-dozen ceiling fans moved the air around. Several open windows let in a ghost of a breeze, enough to put a belly in the lace curtains. That was the state of the art for cooling an office in 1939.

Junior's shirt was white as fresh snow. His collar was slightly spread, well-starched. It lay perfectly over a red, blue, and gold diagonally striped necktie. An inch and a half of starched French cuffs showed beyond his jacket sleeves. His black shoes gleamed. They looked brand new. When he sat and crossed his legs, you saw that the *soles* and *heels* of his shoes were polished mahogany-colored leather. Later, I observed that Junior's shoes always had polished leather soles and heels. Did he only walk on carpets? I figured it out later. He kept the new shoes in the office. The out-of-the-office shoes were like anybody else's: good shoes with gray soles and gray heels, the new mahogany finish worn off on concrete side-walks. Junior sported a white silk handkerchief in his breast pocket. It was another piece of perfection. The three points of the handkerchief drooped, ever so slightly, the sign of expensive silk rather than good cotton. Everything about him was crisp, unwrin-kled, tailored to perfection. I wondered how he managed to sit without wrinkling his jacket or pants.

Junior carried a file in his left hand. He was happy to see Goren. He approached with his right hand extended for a warm hand-shake. "Hello, Alan, glad to see you. Alan, you are doing very well with your cocoa. The beans are at 4.11 cents. Here, let's sit at this table. I'll go over your account with you."

He seemed to notice Benny and me for the first time. "Who are your friends?"

Benny was introduced as Goren's friend. I was again introduced as the nephew. Junior invited us to join him and Goren at a small conference table where he opened Goren's file.

"Here is your account, Alan. You are long twenty September cocoas, five February soybeans, and three December pork bellies. Your cash credit is $2,347. Your unrealized gains, as of last night's closing prices, are $3,487 on the cocoas, $235 on the soybeans. You have an unrealized loss on the bellies, $812. All together, your account is worth $5,257. That is marvelous, Alan. Your account was only worth $2,500 at the end of June. You really struck it rich on the cocoas. Are you going to sell any?"

"No, Junior, I think I have enough equity for another thirty cocoas. I want the Decembers."

"Let me figure it out," Junior said. "I'll give it to the margin clerk." He picked up the file and disappeared into one of the offices, which said *Krieger Personnel Only*.

Benny, looking about at the richness of his surroundings, said "Alan, I'm gonna open an account. Will they open one for me with only $600? And how about Jack? He has $177. Enough for two contracts."

Junior returned to tell Goren that he could buy thirty December cocoas. "December is going for 4.11. You need $2,466 for thirty more contracts. You have enough. You could buy as many as forty Decembers."

"No, I'll just do thirty for now. And Junior, before you go to fill my order, let me ask you about Benny and Jack. Benny wants to open an account with $600. He wants to buy seven December cocoas. And Jack wants to buy two. He has $177. What say, Junior?"

Junior stood. He looked at Benny, then at me.

"All right, Alan, I'll do it for you. Normally we don't open an account with less than a thousand dollars, but I'll do it for your friends. I will go and execute your orders; thirty Decembers for you, seven Decembers for Benny, and two Decembers for Jack. Benny and Jack, why don't you fill out some new account applications while I execute the orders."

"Wait a minute, Junior," Benny said. "Jack and I don't have our money with us."

"Not a problem," said Junior with a smile. "Bring it in tomorrow. The trades settle in five business days. Meanwhile, Alan will guarantee you. All right, Alan?"

Goren said that was all right.

Before we left, Goren wanted us to meet the senior Carl Krieger. He was a twenty-five-year-older version of Junior. Same silver hair, silver spectacles, pin-stripe suit, same everything, except for the necktie. Senior's stripes were navy and silver. He had the same graciousness and elegance as Junior, and a slow courtliness that made him seem to belong to an earlier age.

Goren and Benny and I agreed to meet on the South Carolina Avenue pavilion at 8:00 the next morning. Benny and I would bring our money, and we would talk strategy.

This was real excitement. I didn't fully understand it, the way Benny and Goren did. What I understood was that somehow I owned twenty tons of cocoa beans, forty thousand pounds, and that the beans were selling for a little over four cents a pound. And Goren. He owned fifty contracts! That was five hundred tons of beans, a million pounds of beans!

And I was working at Krilow's for fifteen cents an hour. It didn't figure.

30

Benny's Research

THE NEXT MORNING, Goren and Benny were already on the South Carolina pavilion when I arrived on my bike at ten minutes before eight. I always tried to be early. I wasn't surprised to find Goren was there before me. I sort of knew that Goren would always be prompt. Everything about him suggested he wouldn't want anyone to be discomfited by waiting for him, just as he wouldn't want to be discomfited by waiting. Benny was another story. I never saw him pay attention to promptness, so I was surprised to find Benny was already there. They were sitting on a bench, facing the ocean. Both had their hats tilted forward and low to shield their eyes from the fireball that was climbing out of the ocean. Benny held a book in his lap and a pad of ruled writing paper. He was writing with a mechanical pencil as I approached.

They greeted me and shoved over, inviting me to join them on the bench. I preferred to sit on the railing, facing them.

"Got your money, Jack?" Benny asked.

"Right here, Benny," I answered, handing over my $30.

"Good," Benny said. "I have my six hundred, and Alan and I have your 147 bucks right here in this envelope." He opened an envelope marked *Jack* and added my thirty dollars. On the outside, he added the amount, *$177.00.*

"Thanks again, Benny, Mr. Goren," I said. "I know you said it is a gift, but I call it a loan. I will pay it back, $54 to you, Benny, and $93 to you, Mr. Goren."

Benny waved my comment away, as if erasing my words.

"Forget it," Benny said. "Let's talk business. I went to the library last night. See this book? It's called *How to Trade Commodities Futures*. I stayed up until three in the morning reading it. I think I understand everything. Not good as you, Alan," he said to Goren, "but I got a good feel for it." Benny was animated. His words came tumbling out. His thoughts were racing ahead of his words. I had never seen him like that. "But I tell you what, Alan," he continued. "I think you're missin' the boat. I studied the charts and how to keep 'em and how to read 'em. *You* go long and stay long until you're ready to sell. Or maybe you sell short until you're ready to cover. I think there's more to be made by trading. In and out. Go long. Sell when you see a top forming on the chart. Go short. When you see a bottom forming, cover, and go long again. What about it, Alan?"

Goren was listening carefully. He responded, slowly, choosing his words carefully, "Benny, what you are talking about is a dangerous game. If you go long and jump out with a small profit, you may miss the biggest part of a run-up. Or vice versa, if you sell short and cover too soon. I used to do what you are talking about. I found that if I jumped out too soon, I missed the big profit. And if I was wrong to begin with, if I was long and the price dropped, or if I was short and there was a run-up, I tended to stay too long. So what happened was that I made lots of small profits by jumping out quickly, but when it went against me, I took big losses."

Goren continued. "Now, I play it this way. I analyze all the news about the crops and the weather and demand and acres planted. I form an opinion about the trend for the next four to six months. And I stay on course. Sure, I am wrong sometimes. When it goes against me, I try to get out fast with a small loss. My game today is to take small losses, let the gains run. What you want to do, Benny, I am afraid, is the opposite; take small profits, but get hurt bad when you are wrong."

"I'll tell you what, Alan," Benny said. "I am going to sit in the library with six months of old *Wall Street Journals*. I'll do point and figure charts starting six months ago, and each day I will make a hypothetical decision—to buy, sell, or hold. I won't know if I was right until I look at the next day's paper. I'll do it for six months. Let's see if the point and figure chart works. According to this book," he tapped the book with his forefinger, "it works. And I'll tell you why I think it works."

Benny went on, "Who are the big buyers and sellers of cocoa futures? Not little guys like us. It is the big users and the big growers. They *know*, or they *should* know. I say *they* should make the best guess where prices are headed. They read all the farm journals and the commodities newsletters and they have agents in the field and they know what they themselves are doing. Their guess is the best informed. You or me can't hope to understand even a tiny pimple of what they know. I mean big companies like Hershey or Nestlé or Tobler or the big English and French and German chocolate outfits, and the growers' combines. They are the big buyers and sellers. If they don't know what is happening, how can you and me know?

"Now here's the whole secret. The *collective* opinion of all the big guys is right there to be seen. Point and figure charts tell the story. The Hershey trader goes long the December beans if he believes the price in December will be higher than today's spot price. The grower shorts the December beans if he thinks today's price is better than what he will get in December.

"Now, you have dozens or maybe hundreds of guys buying and selling. Their *collective* opinions are going to push up or push down prices. I'd rather follow those guys than try to dope it out myself."

"What you are talking about," Goren said, "is chart theory. You think the charts can tell you the future. They can't. They are only reciting history. Don't be like one of those roulette junkies who write down every number that comes up on the wheel. As if the wheel knows. As if a number *has* to come up because it's due to come up. The wheel does not know. The chart does not know. Only a smart analysis of the real facts can tell you what is going to happen. Stick with me, Benny. I know what I am doing. And Zena, even if she doesn't believe it, Zena *sees* things. It is her gift. Just like adding numbers is your gift. Between me and Zena, we are going to hit it big."

"All right, Alan," Benny said. "I'll play it your way, for the most part. But I'm gonna to do the six months' study and if it works, I'll try the in-and-out deal with a couple of contracts, on my own."

"Fair enough," Goren said. "I'll be curious to see how you make out."

Goren turned to me, "How about you, Jack? What is your game plan? Are you sticking with me or are you going to follow Benny?"

Benny answered for me. "He better play it your way, Alan. I think your way is safer."

I understood most of the conversation. I was glad Benny answered for me. I didn't know how to answer.

Benny said he was going to the library to get started. He gave Goren his money and mine and started off. As he was leaving, we saw Morris arrive, with his painter's box and easel under his arm.

We exchanged greetings. Morris asked what kind of plot we were cooking up. He said we looked like three anarchists planning a revolution.

Benny introduced Morris to Goren. Benny said he had to leave, but Goren could tell Morris what we are doing. That is if Goren wanted to. Benny said he left it to Goren. Benny also told Goren that Morris is a good friend and also a good friend of Zena. With that, Benny took off.

"What is it all about?" Morris asked.

Goren explained. Morris knew about Goren from Zena. Morris said he was glad to meet Goren and see that he seemed to have both feet on the ground, except that maybe Goren should not put too much stock in Zena's visions. In response to Goren's invitation to join us in our cocoa adventure, Morris declined, gracefully.

"I am afraid," Morris explained, "that if I lose, I will feel like a fool. And if I win a few hundred dollars, it won't affect my life style. I am all right the way I am. I don't want to adopt something else to have to think about. But thanks for inviting me in. And I wish you fellows good luck."

***

On Monday morning, Benny told us that he spent the whole weekend studying. He called off his Saturday night date with Gwen and his Sunday night date with Anna. He stayed in the library until it closed, doing his point and figure charts starting with the beginning of February. He went at it methodically, never looking at the next day until he wrote down what action he took. Then the next day's paper told him if he had been right or wrong. He didn't buy or sell every day, only when his chart told him to. From February 1 to August 4, he made twenty-five hypothetical trades, an average of about one per week. Not regular though; sometimes no trades for a while, sometimes three in one week. Starting with a hypothetical six hundred dollars, he was up to fifteen hundred. And he was long fifteen contracts, so his wins were getting bigger. He had some losses along the way, but he was able to keep them small. He showed his work to Goren. Goren had trouble believing that Benny wasn't looking ahead.

"It's as though you can see the next few days' papers, Benny. This is remarkable. You wouldn't fool me, would you?"

"C'mon, Alan, what would be the point? I'm going to play this with my own money. I would be a *schmuck* to kid myself. No, I read each day's papers. I did the points and figures each day. I made a decision each day to buy more or sell or go short or stand pat. I wrote down what I did and calculated the value of my positions every day. Next day's paper told me if I was right or wrong. Most days, nothing happens strong enough to give me a signal. But when I get the signal, it is almost always right."

"Tell you what, Alan, let's try it my way for a couple of weeks. If it don't work, we'll let you run the show. But I'll tell you every time I'm gonna make a trade. You don't have to go along. You can do it your own way, any time you want."

"I'll give it a try," Goren said. "Let's see what happens. But I might want to cut my losses and bail out if it's not going our way."

"Good enough," Benny replied. Then he turned to me. "Jack," Benny said, "I'll trade your account for you. OK?"

"Sure, Benny." I barely understood what he was talking about.

"You know what else," Benny mused. "I'll bet if I was sitting in Krieger's place all day, I could do even better. Every hour is a trend. When I did the six-month study, I only saw the results once a day."

31

Errand for Bobo

L ATER THAT DAY I had a visitor at the Vi-de-lan Studio after
Roland's 4:00 performance. It was Georgie, Bobo's man. I recognized him in the audience. When the sales pitch was over and all
the audience left, he approached me while I was sweeping up the
cigarette butts and candy wrappers.

"Jack, isn't it?" he said. "I'm Georgie. They told me at Krilow's I
could find you here."

"Hello, Georgie. I recognize you from Mr. Truck's place."

"That's right, Jack. Bobo sent me to ask you to do an errand for
him. Will you?"

"Sure thing. What is it?"

"Now, listen careful. I don't want you to write down what I tell
you. Keep it in your head. OK?"

"OK."

"You go to a candy store at 2615 Arctic Avenue. That's between
Texas and California. Exactly at 9:00 tonight. Knock on the door. It
will be closed and locked. Knock four times, two shorts and two
shorts, like this."

He rapped on the wall, knock-knock, knock-knock. "Got it? Two
double knocks."

"I got it."

"Before the door opens, you'll hear somebody say *Give me your
number*. You'll say *4578*. The door will open. You'll be given a box.
Take it immediately to the back door of the shooting gallery. Three

double knocks. You'll be asked for your number. You'll say *8754*. The door will open and let you in to deliver the box."

"Is that it?" I asked. "What's in the box?"

"Never mind. Don't open it. Just do what I said, OK?"

"Sure, it's easy."

"What is the number?"

"4578. Then backwards, 8754."

"You caught that. Good boy. See ya 'round."

I went to the candy store on my bike that evening. I got there at five minutes before nine. I waited until exactly nine. As the big church bell on Pacific Avenue began to strike, I did the two double-knocks. It happened like Georgie said. The box was an ordinary shoebox. The candy store man said to hold it upright. I held it with both hands. It weighed about a pound. It was not tied. The lid seemed a little loose. I wondered what was in it. All I had to do to find out was lift the lid and look: easy. The lid was loose. The box was untied. But the instruction was that I was not to open it. So I didn't.

I strapped the box onto the carrier on the back of my bike. I rode, carefully, to the alley behind the shooting gallery, and I did the three double-knocks and recited the number. The door opened, and I was motioned to enter. It was an office. It was the room behind the back wall of Bobo's bookie joint. Inside were Bobo, Georgie, and another man.

"Jack, this is Frankie over here," Bobo introduced me, "and you know Georgie."

"Hello, Frankie. Hello, Georgie. Hello, Mr. Truck."

"Hand over the box, Jack," Bobo held out his hand.

I handed it to him, holding it with both hands. Bobo took it from me. He looked in my eyes. "Did you look in the box, Jack?"

"No, Mr. Truck."

"Look at me. Look in my eyes. *Did you look in the box?*"

I tried to hold my eyes steady. I looked at Bobo's eyes. They were dark brown, almost black, expressionless. Why was I scared? I hadn't looked in the box. What expression should I wear to make him believe me?

"Honest, Mr. Truck. I didn't open the box."

"Come with me over here," he said.

He led me into the alley. Georgie and Frankie followed. I was getting really scared. I didn't understand any of it. How could I convince Bobo that I didn't open the box?

"Now take the box, Jack, and open it."

"You want me to take off the lid?"

"That's right. Take off the lid."

I lifted the lid. A cloud of white talcum powder flew up and out of the box. It covered me all over—my clothes, my face, it climbed up my nose. Bobo, Georgie, and Frankie exploded into huge laughter. They doubled over with laughter. They roared with laughter.

I looked at the lid. There was a stiff wire taped to the underside of the lid. The wire was welded or soldered into the inside of a tin cup. The box was still half-filled with talcum powder that the tin cup didn't pull out. The box had been filled. When the lid was closed, the cup buried itself in the powder. Lifting the lid pulled the cup out of the powder, sending the powder flying in the cloud that covered me. It was a trick. I was angry.

"Hey, Bobo," I blurted out. "What's the big idea? Is this your idea of a joke? Well, it ain't funny."

Bobo laughed. He poked Georgie in the ribs. "So now, I'm Bobo. What happened to *Mr. Truck*? That's OK. I want you to call me *Bobo* like all my boys do over here. I wanted to know if you were going to open the box after Georgie told you not to. You're a good boy, Jack. Forgive the test. I wanted to try you out."

Bobo had taken me into the alley because he didn't want to get the powder all over his office. Bobo took back the box. Georgie handed me a damp towel. While I tried to clean up, Bobo emptied the rest of the powder, carefully, into a trashcan. At the bottom of the box was an envelope. Bobo opened it and counted the money that was in it. It was two hundred dollars.

"Jack," Bobo said, "you are a good boy. You did real well over here. You didn't write anything down, did you?"

"No, Mr. Truck, Georgie said to keep it in my head."

"And you did. And you did everything right. And you didn't open the box. Good boy. And drop the *Mr. Truck*. The name is *Bobo*." He slapped me on the back. His backslaps were hearty. This one pitched me forward.

"Clean yourself up and go home, Jack. You're a good boy. You will hear from me. I can use a good boy. A good boy like you can do things over here that a man can't."

I brushed myself off as best I could. I wiped my face. I took off my cap. I blew my nose a half-dozen times. My hair was full of powder. I brushed it off. I felt silly and foolish and angry at being the butt of the joke. *Ohmigosh*, I thought, suddenly. *Suppose I had opened the box? What then?* I didn't want to think about that one.

I rode home. I was so puzzled. What did Bobo have in mind for me? Should I get involved with him? He was dangerous, I was sure. But he was excitement and … opportunity?

When I got home, it was almost 11:00. I tried to slip in and head straight for the bathroom.

"Jack, is that you?" My father called from the parlor. "Where were you? Mother and I were worried."

I headed for the bathroom. Once inside, I opened the door and called out, "I had to do an errand, Dad. Sorry I'm so late."

As I closed the bathroom door and began to wash up, I heard him whisper to Mom, "I wonder where he was?"

32

Dinner With Bobo

Bobo's dinner invitation came a week after the arithmetic contest. Benny, Goren, and I presented ourselves at Trucci's on Arctic Avenue near Georgia Avenue. I wore my one white dress shirt and my camelhair blazer and one of my father's neckties, and my one pair of dress shoes, dark brown leather wingtips. I wore them so seldom that I was a little unsteady in them. They were stiff and the soles kept slipping off my bicycle pedals.

Goren seemed to own only one suit. That soft gray flannel one he wore when Benny and I first met him. I learned later that he owned several suits that looked the same, some lighter or heavier in weight, but all the same color and all with the same three-button single-breasted tailoring.

Benny was crisp and beautiful. He wore a tan polished-cotton summer suit, a pale blue dress shirt with French cuffs, a flowered yellow-and-white necktie and breast pocket handkerchief to match, a cocoa straw hat, and white-and-brown wingtips. His blue eyes sparkled. The midsummer tan added to his good looks.

Atlantic City's two most popular restaurant clubs were The 500 Club and Trucci's. They were both on Arctic Avenue, within a block of each other. The clubs were the hangouts for celebrities and Atlantic City's prominent and for tourists who came to see the celebrities. The clubs had live entertainment, usually a pianist or a singer, sometimes a small band or an instrumental ensemble.

Well-known performers, like Louie Armstrong, Billy Holiday, Dizzy Gillespie, Cab Calloway, and Carmen Caballero, appeared from time to time. Most often, however, the dinner patrons were entertained by an unknown piano soloist and a singer who never made it big.

Trucci's was bright enough to be seen from six blocks away. Moving lights circled its marquee around the word *Trucci's*, formed out of light bulbs that blinked on and off every half-second. Searchlights threw moving crisscrosses of light beams across the sky. A row of bright goose-necked lights mounted on the roof parapet shone down on the pavement below. A tall Negro uniformed doorman stood outside, dressed in an ornate long military coat with broad lapels, lots of gold buttons, heavy gold-braided trim, and handsome epaulets. A steady stream of expensive cars pulled up to the curb, discharging well-dressed men and attractive women, while valet parkers whisked away the cars. Before allowing us to enter, the doorman stepped inside the vestibule to ask someone about us. It was Benny James's name that gained us admission.

Benny started to repeat his name to the *maitre d'*. Before he even got to *James*, Bobo came up behind us. He slapped Benny's back and shook hands with Goren and me and motioned to us to follow him. The entrance to the dining room was through the bar, all polished cherry wood with paneled walls. Behind the bar was a wall of smoked glass, reflecting the good-looking women sitting on the high bar stools in their little black dresses, revealing lovely arms and legs, and the self-assured men who stood at their elbows. The bar was dark. It opened into a brightly lit dining room. We followed Bobo to a table set for seven in the center of the dining room.

This night, Trucci's featured a young pianist who played mostly soft dinner music and an occasional jazz piece, or ragtime, played quietly. The singer was a good-looking girl with a pleasant but unexciting voice. The dining room was full of well-dressed diners. All the men wore suits or expensive sport coats and dress shirts and neckties. The women wore evening dresses. Jewelry glittered.

The circling lights were silver and crystal globes made of hundreds of small facets. Light danced and sparkled from them, making the entire dining room seem in motion. The table linen was pure white; a live floral arrangement was centered on each table. The air was filled with laughter and the babble of a hundred conversations and the smoke from dozens of cigarettes and cigars.

Bobo introduced us to the three other guests at our table: Georgie, Frankie, and a good-looking woman. The men stood up as we approached. The woman remained seated. Bobo and Georgie looked like they came from the same cutout. They were the same height, about six feet. They looked like weightlifters, all muscle. They had huge necks, as wide as their heads, widening into shoulders that looked like football padding. They had big smooth hands, with manicured fingernails and ruddy cheeks. They wore their hair slicked back. They wore dark double-breasted suits with white cuff-linked shirts. In silhouette, you could not have told them apart.

Frankie was two inches shorter, not as broad, with something of a paunch. He wasn't as muscular as Bobo and Georgie, but he projected the same kind of power.

Bobo made the introductions. "This is Georgie over here. You know Georgie already, from back of Royce's. Georgie, you know these boys, Alan, Benny, Jack, and this is Frankie. Jack and Frankie know each other." Frankie waved and said hello. "And, boys, this is my friend, Loretta. Loretta, say hello to my friends."

Loretta was a black-haired beauty. She looked to be in her early thirties. She wore a low-cut, white silk sleeveless blouse that revealed perfect shoulders and arms and a tantalizing look at the inner edges of the smooth globes of her breasts. Her necklace was made of flat silver bars, suspended, Egyptian-style, from a silver circle. It was studded with diamonds and emeralds. She wore a heavy silver bracelet covered in diamonds. Her broad smile showed perfect white teeth framed in bright red lips.

Girls' eyes usually lingered on Benny. But not Loretta's eyes. It occurred to me that Loretta knew better than to rest admiring eyes on any man except Bobo.

"Hello, fellows," she smiled. She remained seated, extending her hand for a firm handshake. I was not used to girls shaking hands. It was a handsome thing the way Loretta did it. She held her arm out straight, her elbow locked. Her hand was soft, but her grip was firm.

"Loretta, Frankie, these are the fellows I told you about. What a time we had the other day. Benny James over here is a mathematical genius, and cool as a lemon sherbet. And Alan Goren. He's a cool one, too. Never cracks a smile. He's all business." He motioned us all into our chairs and signaled for a waiter. "Boys," he said, "can I order for you?"

"Sure, Bobo," Benny answered.

"Please do," said Goren.

"Sure, Mr. Truck," I said, glad that I would not have to struggle with the right way to order and the right things to choose.

"Nick," Bobo addressed the waiter, "start us off with a big antipasto over here. And bring some of the big peeled shrimp and some backfin lump crabmeat. And bring some melted butter and some fresh white horseradish. And bring some raw broccoli and some raw cauliflower. Then bring us a tureen of minestrone. I'll ladle it out. For the main course, bring us each a small filet, medium, pink, and baked potatoes and stewed tomatoes and fried string beans and almonds."

He turned to us and asked, "Is that OK, fellows?"

Goren and I nodded and murmured, "OK."

Only Benny answered, "Please make my filet well done."

"OK, Nick, that's the order," Bobo said.

"Yes, sir, Mr. Truck."

"Nick, how many times over here did I tell you to call me *Bobo*?"

"Yes, Mr. Truck. I mean, yes, Bobo."

You knew that Nick was never going to be able to call him *Bobo*.

"And, Nick, bring us a couple bottles of Chianti."

"Yes, Mr. Truck."

"He is hopeless," said Bobo.

Bobo rested his arms on the table and leaned toward us.

"So, fellows, tell me what you guys are up to."

"Nothing special," Goren said.

"What do you do, Alan?" asked Bobo.

"I do some real estate."

"Tell him about the commodities, Alan," Benny said.

"There is not much to tell," Goren answered.

"C'mon, Alan, tell him about commodities. Tell him how it works," Benny insisted.

"Really, Benny," Goren said, "I don't want to bore Bobo. He is our host. We should not bore him about commodities."

"What about commodities?" Bobo wanted to know.

Goren was disturbed. I saw that he just didn't want to talk about commodities. But Benny was relentless.

"Go ahead, Alan, tell him what you do. Tell him what we are doing."

Goren hesitated. Then he said, sort of dismissing the thing, "It is a little like buying stocks, Bobo, except it is buying commodities, like wheat, like corn, or copper, coffee. Things that get bought and sold in big amounts. When the price goes up, you sell it and make a profit."

"How 'bout when the price goes down. You lose, right?"

"That's right, Bobo, when the price goes down, you lose money."

"Sounds like gambling to me," Bobo observed. "By the way, what's that ribbon you wear? It looks like the silver star. Is it? Were you in the war?"

"I was," Goren admitted. "I was at a place called Chateau-Thierry."

"Hey!" Bobo said. "I know where that was. You musta been there in May '18, right? I was at a godforsaken fuckin' hellhole called the St. Mihiel salient, in the Argonne, in July. Yeah, the St. Mihiel salient." Bobo pronounced it the *San Milly Sally*. "That's near Chateau-Thierry," or as Bobo pronounced it, *Shattoo Terry*. "Maybe twenty, thirty miles, right? I was a supply sergeant. I was supposed to rest my ass in a supply depot, but they put me in a fuckin' trench. I was one of the lucky ones. That fuckin' butcher, Pershing. They gave him medals. They shoulda cut off his balls for what he done. How about you? How'd you get the medal?"

"I didn't deserve it," was Goren's reply. His tone made it clear he didn't want to elaborate. Bobo left it alone.

Before a silence could develop, Benny returned to the commodities discussion. "Bobo," Benny said, "commodities are a great game. You get great leverage. A buck does the work of ten. And Alan knows his stuff. He really has the *feel* of it. He has got me into it. And even Jack. We're making pretty good money."

"Please, Benny," Goren said, quietly, "don't bother Bobo with this. It is not for him."

The waiter brought our antipasto, and shrimp and crabmeat, and hot Italian rolls, and a deep dish of melted butter, and the wine. Bobo opened a bottle and poured. "Salut," he raised his glass. Everyone raised a glass and responded in unison, "Salut."

I sipped the wine. It was my first taste of wine. It was sort of bitter. But sweet. I drank a little. The warmth flowed through me. It was good. I tried to pretend that drinking wine was not a new experience. I drank some more.

"Now, Alan," Bobo smiled, glass in hand. "Tell me about it. How can I back this commodity game over here?"

"You can't back it, Bobo," Goren answered. "There are thousands of buyers and sellers buying and selling on the New York Board of Trade and the Chicago Mercantile Exchange and the Chicago Board of Trade. A buyer and seller don't know each other. One buys, one sells, that's it."

"Who is the middleman?" Bobo figured that there has to be a middleman. Somebody has to make money on the transactions, regardless of which way the price goes.

"Well, there is a commission on each trade."

"Ah-ha," said Bobo. "Who makes the commission over here?"

"The broker, but it's small money."

"How small?"

"Real small, only two or three dollars on a contract."

"How much is a contract?" Bobo wanted all the details.

Goren answered, "The margin money on cocoa, for example, is about eighty-five dollars a contract."

"How many contracts do you buy at a time, Alan?"

"Maybe five, maybe ten."

"The commission is peanuts," Bobo observed. "Where's the money in it for the broker?"

"The broker has lots of customers," answered Goren. "The broker might be doing twenty or thirty tickets a day. Some are five contracts, some are ten or twenty. I guess an average ticket has about ten dollars commission."

"Well, that's real money," Bobo said.

"But Bobo, the broker has expenses: an office, and traders and secretaries, and margin clerks and big telephone bills, and a ticker service. It costs a lot to run a broker's office." Goren wanted to end the discussion. "Real estate," Goren went on, "is a better investment. I know listings right now that can bring fifteen to twenty percent returns. And the bricks and mortar are there, solid. They are not going to go away or expire in a couple of months."

"I know all about real estate," Bobo said. "And I know about stocks. I even have some. I have Johns Manville, Bethlehem Steel, Pennsylvania Railroad, Western Union. Stuff like that. My broker says they are solid, safe, *blue chips* he calls them. But they ain't done a thing for me. Tell me all about commodities. Sounds like there's action in it."

So Goren started to explain commodities. He said that it's a high-leverage speculation. He said it about a half-dozen times. I understood that Goren did not want to be the cause for Bobo to get involved in commodities.

Bobo dropped the subject. The conversation turned to other things. I sipped at the wine some more. I was liking it a lot. Benny wanted to know about Bobo's business. Bobo laughed and waved him off. It was not for discussion.

Throughout our dinner, people approached our table to greet Bobo. Bobo had a smile and a warm handshake for everyone who approached. You could tell the standing of each person who approached by Bobo's greeting. I observed that Bobo practiced at least three levels of greetings. Level One was Bobo seated, offering a smile and a handshake. A Level Two person rated a stand-up by Bobo, same smile and handshake. A Level Three greeting had Bobo standing, smiling, and administering a bear hug. Maybe there was a Level Four greeting, but I didn't see one that night.

I learned about Bobo later on. His name was Benno Trucci. Bobo was his nickname from childhood, but he dropped the *Trucci* in favor of *Truck* when he was in his late teens. He began to build his empire in 1919, after being discharged from the Army after the World War. A lot of the men I knew in 1939 were veterans of the World War—Morris, my father, Goren, Bobo, even Mr. Krilow, who was almost sixty. Mr. Krilow had been a Major. He manned an intelligence desk in Washington during the War.

Bobo was the Boss of Atlantic City. He controlled every form of gambling: the numbers, bookmaking on horses, on football, on baseball and basketball games, on prizefights. He liked to brag that there were no drugs in his town, and that prostitution was confined to the big hotels. He operated like one of today's franchisors. He had the city divided into territories, geographically. In addition to the geographic territories, each big hotel was a territory unto itself. Some of the big hotels had gaming rooms, complete with crap tables, blackjack, roulette, and baccarat. While the small hotels didn't have such facilities, every small hotel had someone who would cover your number or a bet on a ball game, but no girls. They were confined to the big hotels only. And no drugs, absolutely none, anywhere.

Every territory had a franchisee. Bobo didn't call them *franchisees*. That word wasn't around in 1939. He called them his *piedi*, his *mani*, his *diti*, the Italian words for *feet, hands, fingers*. He gave out rights in a territory like one of today's franchisors. Every territory had a *piede*, who had the rights to write numbers in that territory. Every territory had a *mano*, who had the rights to bookmaking in that territory. Every big hotel had a *piede* with rights to write numbers, a *mano* with rights to bookmaking and gaming, and a *dite* with rights to prostitution.

Sometimes one *uomo* (man) had more than one set of rights. Sometimes one *uomo* had rights in two territories. Many of the *uomi* held down regular jobs besides being a *piede*, or a *mano*, or a *dite*, regular jobs, such as barbers, bartenders, desk clerks. Some were small businessmen, shopkeepers, owners of small restaurants, grocery stores, delicatessens. Bobo's network was big; some four hundred men were in his organization.

Bobo's bookie joint behind Royce's Shooting Gallery was the one hands-on operation that he ran. He didn't want any more.

Every *piede, mano,* and *dite* paid Bobo a weekly royalty. Bobo called it the dues, from as little as $10 a week to as much as $200. It depended on Bobo's evaluation of how profitable was the territory.

In Bobo's office on the second floor, above Trucci's, which I got to visit many times, there was an 8′ x 3′ map of Atlantic City mounted on the wall. The territories were outlined and numbered and showed the name of the man who operated each territory.

Altogether there were sixty territories, including the hotels. The territories were grouped into five districts. Each district had a district boss. They were Bobo's *capi*, which is the Italian word for

heads. The *capi* were on Bobo's payroll. Bobo also had twenty soldiers to help him keep the peace. Bobo protected his people by
taking care of the police, the district attorney, the county
Prosecutor, and a few judges; he was always trying but couldn't get
them all. The chief of police was on his payroll. So were a half-
dozen police lieutenants and a dozen policemen.

If somebody tried to muscle in on one of Bobo's people, Bobo's
man had only to report it to his *capo*. Usually the *capo* sent an invitation to the intruder for a meeting. That one meeting was usually
enough to convince the intruder to seek another means of liveli-
hood. The intruder would receive a warning, nothing physical. If
an intruder failed to heed a warning, something bad happened to
him, such as a broken arm or a few loose teeth. That was the second warning. If the second warning did not convince the intruder
to keep out, the problem was erased. There was hardly ever a need
to go beyond a second warning.

Bobo's soldiers were his police force. They were his *soldati*.
Georgie and Frankie were his two trusted generals and body-
guards. They ran the army. They ran the *capi*. They noticed everything. When they were with Bobo, their eyes were in constant
motion, scanning the room or the street, watchful for any stranger
or any suspicious motion. They knew everything that happened in
Atlantic City. They guarded Bobo the way the Secret Service guards
the president.

***

Dinner at Trucci's that night was special. I never ate such food.
We hardly ever ate meat at home. It was a treat for special occa-
sions, and when we did it was not like Trucci's filets, which were

like nothing I had ever eaten before. A Trucci filet covered with Trucci's lemon butter–horseradish sauce was indescribable.

At one point, the *maitre d'* approached our table. He asked Bobo if everything was satisfactory.

Bobo said, "Yes, the food is great, as usual, but tell me, when did you get the nigger out front? He's new."

The *maitre d'* said that the last left town in a hurry unexpectedly. This one came from an employment agency.

"Get rid of him," Bobo said. "He's not black enough. Get us a real black nigger. That one looks like a big Jew with a suntan." He smiled at us, pleased with his joke. "None of you guys Jews, are you?" he questioned.

Goren said, "If that's your idea of something cute, Bobo, let me tell you, it isn't."

"I'm sorry," Bobo apologized. "Sorry, Alan." He held up his hands, palms out, surrendering for his poor manners. "I didn't know you're a Jew, Alan. You don't look like a Jew over here, Alan. That's the trouble with you Jews. You look like everybody else."

"I'm not Jewish," Goren said. "I just don't like that kind of talk. And I don't call colored people *niggers*. That stinks."

Bobo glared at Goren for a moment. For a second, that dangerous look. Goren sat still, composed. He returned Bobo's look with an emotionless steadiness. Bobo smiled. "Alan, you're a terrific guy. You say what's on your mind. Forgive me. Forgive me for embarrassing you. I didn't mean nothin' by it. I got nothin' against Jews. I like 'em. Hell, one a my lawyers is a Jew. So's my accountant."

"OK, Bobo," Goren said. "Let it go. No damage."

Then Benny spoke. He had been listening to the exchange between Bobo and Goren with his eyes closed, as if in a reverie.

"I'm a Jew," he said quietly. "At least that's what my mom was. She's been dead since I was twelve. I been on my own since then. My old man was an Irish drunk. He used to like to beat up on my mom. What a pathetic loser he was. He disappeared two years before mom died. I don't practice any religion, never did. Bobo, I been listenin' to your kind of insults all my life. When I was a kid, I used to get in fights about it. Now, I don't even bother. I hear that shit all the time. It sickens me. Coming from you, Bobo, it's a real disappointment. I can't pick a fight with you because I value my health. So give me a suggestion, Bobo. What do I do? Get up and leave? Keep quiet? Laugh along with you? What? Alan here didn't even know that I'm a Jew. He's some guy. He stood up for me and didn't even know it. And by the way, Bobo, I don't like that word you used about the doorman. I have trouble even saying it." He raised his eyebrows and opened his hands in a questioning gesture. "Tell me what to do. Should I leave? Should I check up on my health and accident insurance? What?"

Again that look of menace from Bobo. It chilled me every time I saw it. He stared at Benny with dark expressionless eyes. A shark's eyes. Benny tried to be calm and cool, but he wasn't like Goren. Goren could sit quiet and still for however long it took for Bobo to speak. But Benny needed Bobo to say something. Benny couldn't wait it out like Goren. Benny spoke first. "Well, Bobo, whattya say?"

Bobo looked at Frankie, then at Georgie. At last he spoke, "Did you ever see guys like these two over here? What balls." He glanced at Loretta and apologized for his language. "I don't know whether to throw them out onto Arctic Avenue so's they'd get hit by a cab, or offer 'em jobs over here. I never seen such balls."

He made up his mind quickly. He stood and raised his wine-glass. "Here's to Alan Goren and Benny James. They say it like it is. Everybody take a lesson from these two. Alan, Benny, take my hand. I respect you guys. I apologize for anything I said what offended you."

Handshakes. Then everybody drank to Bobo's toast. It seemed that the toast was going to be followed by an awkward silence, but before that could happen, Goren steered the conversation to current events. He asked Bobo's thoughts on Danzig. It was in the newspapers every day. Danzig was a free city, a major port for Poland on the Baltic, in the Polish Corridor, which separated Germany from East Prussia. Hitler wanted to reconnect East Prussia to Germany. He wanted to annex Danzig and the Polish Corridor. That would reunite East Prussia with Germany. The British and French were committed by a treaty to join Poland if war broke out between Germany and the Poles.

Goren asked everybody's views about Danzig. Goren was convinced that war was imminent. War would mean a sharp increase in commodities prices. His analysis of the pros and cons of the forces at work on cocoa prices included a heavy dose of believing in a coming war. That tipped his analysis in favor of higher cocoa prices.

Bobo was not much interested in Danzig. He said *yeah, he heard about it.* He thought Hitler would take whatever he wanted. Just like he took Austria and part of Czechoslovakia and then all of Czechoslovakia. Whatever or wherever Danzig was, Bobo thought Hitler will take it if he wants it.

But Bobo didn't believe a war would start over Danzig or Poland. "The English and the French," he snorted. "Don't make me laugh over here. They'll sell their own kids to keep peace. I served with them in the War. They were rotten soldiers then and now all they want is peace. Didn't you hear that Chamberlain guy when he gave Czechoslovakia to Hitler? *Peace in our time,* he said. He ain't gone to war over Polacks."

Goren said, "Don't forget how England, France, Germany, Austria, Russia, Italy all blundered into the World War. Nobody wanted it. Nobody even knew what anybody was fighting for. It was a case of everybody miscalculating. And that is what's going on now. Hitler doesn't expect a war. He expects to get what he wants, for free."

Benny ventured an opinion. "It's an old story. The grabber gets away with it, once, twice, three times, maybe. He starts to think he can get away with anything. Meanwhile, the other guy comes to know that he has to stop it. Or else, the grabber will grab everything. The English don't want a war. The French don't want a war. They ain't recovered from the last war. But they can't be pushed forever. They miscalculated by giving up Czechoslovakia. They know now they made a bad mistake. Now Hitler is miscalculating. He thinks he can get away with anything. He is wrong. I read the papers every day. The other day, I read what Lord Halifax said. He is the English something-or-other big shot. He said that *force will be met with force.* Hitler laughed at him. That was a mistake. Big government leaders are no different from you and me. Lord Halifax ain't gonna take an insult and do nothing about it. Hitler screwed up. Maybe he would get want he wants like he did three or four times before, if he *negotiated* like before. This time, he's too cocky. Now, even Chamberlain is warning Hitler. But Hitler will laugh at him, too. And the French guy, Edouard Daladier. He said that Hitler has to stop or be stopped. My sense is there's going to be a war. Hitler will make a grab at Danzig. He thinks he'll get it for free. He's wrong. There's gonna be a war."

"Why do you guys care?" asked Loretta.

"Yeah," Bobo repeated, "why do you guys care? We won't get in it. I was in it the last time. We ain't gettin' in it this time over here. The country won't go for it. Roosevelt knows that. If he tries to get us in it, somebody will kill him. America first, that's what I want. Let 'em kill each other in Europe. We are gonna stay out of it. Anyway, what do you care?"

Benny answered, "I don't want to see a war. But I know it's coming. And I aim to cash in on it."

"How you gonna do that?" asked Georgie.

Benny leveled his eyes at Bobo. "I am going to make a *big* score in commodities when the war begins."

"Hey, hold on," said Bobo. "You best tell me about this."

I went at the wine again. Finished the glass. Bobo gave me a refill. "Hey, Jack, you like the *vino*. Why not?" he said as he poured.

Goren tried again to steer the conversation away from commodities. But Benny kept on. He explained everything to Bobo, slowly, patiently. He asked for a pencil and paper. Georgie had a mechanical pencil in his shirt pocket. He handed it to Benny.

"Write on the tablecloth, Benny," Bobo said. "It will wash out."

By the time Benny finished, the tablecloth was covered with numbers and arrows and circled prices. Finally, he handed the mechanical pencil back to Georgie.

"Get it?" he asked.

"Not a word of it," said Bobo.

Goren spoke. "It is not for you, Bobo. I knew you would say it is not for you." He sounded relieved.

"Wait up," said Bobo. "Alan, how much money do you have in this cocoa deal?"

Goren hesitated. "Really, Bobo, do you want to know? It is a private matter."

"OK, Alan, I respect that. How 'bout you, Benny James?" Benny did not hesitate. "I don't have much money, Bobo. I put in six hundred just a week ago. It's worth about $680 today. But the big move is coming. War is coming. The price is going to shoot up like a rocket. I expect I'll make ten grand soon. I think the war is only weeks away. I even got Jack, here, into it for a couple hundred."

"Who's your broker?" Bobo asked. "I use that Merrill Lynch Pierce Fenner and somebody outfit. They have an office in Central Pier."

Benny answered, "We use Krieger and Son. They're also in Central Pier."

"Never hearda them," Bobo said. "Tell you what, Benny. I'm gonna give you five grand. Invest it for me."

"Thanks for your confidence in me," Benny said, "but no, thanks. I don't want the responsibility. I'll take a chance with my own money. Not with yours."

Goren added his reluctance. "Please, Bobo. Don't do it. Benny relies on me. He just started trading, but I am still responsible for deciding the long-term trend. I don't want the responsibility of handling your money. You could lose it all. This is a very speculative game. I have been doing it for almost twenty years. I made a few bucks here and there, but never a big hit. And Benny is a wild man compared to me. He's making me to be like him. I used to take a position and stay with it a while. He has me in and out every day or two. He gets out for a quarter of a penny a pound. He goes short just as easy as going long. You don't want Benny handling your account. He is dangerous."

"You know, you guys," Bobo mused. "You could be the world's slickest con-men over here. The way you are begging me to stay out. What a con!"

Goren stood up. "This is no con, Bobo. You are insulting me. I don't want you in this business. I am glad you are staying out. If you think it is a con, I am insulted, but if that is what it takes to keep you out, I am satisfied. Good night, thank you for an excellent dinner. Good night, everybody."

He turned and walked away. I stood to leave. So did Benny.

"Bring him back, Georgie," Bobo said. "Jack, Benny, sit down."

Goren returned, reluctantly.

"Sit down, Alan," Bobo said. "I'm sorry if you think I insulted you. No such thing. I would trust you three guys with anything. I know quality guys when I see 'em. Now, relax over here, and let's have some dessert."

Bobo turned to me. "Jack, you are a good kid, just like Benny says. I never paid you for that errand. Here's a twenty."

"Oh, no, Mr. Truck. That was a favor. I was glad to do it. Please, don't embarrass me."

"You *are* a good kid, Jack. I like you. I want to do something for you. Tell me, do you have a girlfriend?"

"No. There's a girl but she treats me like a kid. I guess that's because I am, compared to her."

"Why, how old is she?"

"She's fifteen, same as me. But she is all grown-up like an adult. I feel like a little boy when I am with her."

"Little boy, huh. What do you think, Loretta? Does Jack here look like a little boy?"

Loretta gave me a steady look. I wanted to look away. She did not speak for about eight seconds. I focused on my napkin. I folded it and refolded it.

"Did you ever kiss this girl?" Loretta asked.

I felt my ears go on fire. "No, ma'am." Boy, was I embarrassed.

"Know what I think, Bobo," she said, keeping her eyes fixed on me. "I think that Jack here is a *virgin!*"

I wanted to slip under the table. My head was burning with embarrassment. I twisted the napkin violently. I stared at my half-eaten dessert. How could I escape?

Bobo stroked his chin, thoughtfully, "How about it, Jack, are you? Don't be embarrassed. We're all friends over here."

"Hey, Bobo, leave the kid alone," said Benny. "Can't you see how embarrassed he is."

"I don't want to embarrass the boy, Benny. OK, Jack, I'll leave it alone. But let me introduce you to a real nice gal. See that little blonde girl over by the second bar. Her name is Patti. Georgie, bring Patti over here."

Patti was pretty enough to be a Benny James girl. She had a generous smile and a pretty upturned nose. I guessed she was about twenty. What was Bobo up to?

"Hi, Mr. Truck," Patti smiled. "Nice to see you here. What can I do for you?"

"This here is Jack. He's my friend. I want you to take him out of here. Take him to a store. You'll know where. Let him have anything he wants. Go on, Jack, go with Patti. I'm gonna do some business with Alan and Benny. You go on. Thanks for coming to dinner. You're a good boy. See you again, soon."

He stood and put his arm around me. "Go on, Jack. I owe you a gift. Let Patti pick one out."

I felt a little lightheaded. I had almost two big glasses of wine. I wasn't used to it. And the terrible heat of embarrassment from Loretta still had me feeling flushed and shaky. I didn't know what to make of Bobo's offer of a gift or of Patti. I was bewildered.

Patti took my hand. "Come with me, Jack. My, you're tall. Wait here for me, by the service bar. I'll only be a minute." I followed, docilely.

She returned in less than a minute. She had removed her apron and white sneaks. She was wearing white high-heeled shoes and carrying a handbag over her shoulder. She gave me a big smile and took my arm.

"OK, Jack," she said. "Let's go."

33

Patti

WHEN PATTI LED me out of Trucci's, I was still wobbly from the wine and the way Loretta embarrassed me. The cool evening air helped. Patti led the way. She held on to my arm, but she was leading. I felt her body against mine. It felt very nice. I tried to think about the movie date with Rhoda, when Rhoda took my arm. That was good, but not like Patti. Rhoda hung on like a pal. Patti's contact was sensuous. Her hip rubbed against me every few steps. I felt her body, satin-like and smooth through her yellow cotton dress. She had great legs. The white pumps accentuated them.

I didn't know what to say or talk about. The whole thing was so crazy. What was it Bobo told her? *Let him have anything he wants.* What did I want?

"Where're we going, Patti?" I asked.

"We're headed for the Claridge."

"What's there?"

I always admired the Claridge. It was at the center of the six grandest hotels, set back from the boardwalk with a park in-between. The park was circled by a line of ornamental trees and planted with thousands of colorful flowers and shrubs. A 50-foot wide oval of groomed shrubs spelled out *Claridge* on an incline, which made the letters easier to read from the boardwalk. Behind the shrubs a great fountain threw columns of water sixty feet into the air. The water was bathed in light by a circle of colored lights at the base. The pillar of water changed color gradually, from red to orange to yellow to green to blue and so on through the entire spectrum of colors.

The boardwalk had an extra railing in front of the Claridge, on the land side. At that point, the boardwalk was about twenty feet higher than the Claridge's park. At night, the Claridge park railing was always lined with people watching the changing lights and colors of the Claridge fountain.

"What's at the Claridge?" I repeated.

"Well," she said, "there's the English Shop for men's clothing. And there is the Hollywood Shop for women's sportswear. Maybe I could pick something out for you, or for your girlfriend. We'll see."

By the time we arrived at the Claridge, my head was almost all cleared. My footing was steady again. Patti's body brushed against me, arousing me. My blood got hot. This was bad. I was afraid I would have a big hard-on as we entered the Claridge. I tried to wish it down, but it only got bigger.

Patti noticed. "Hey, Jack, whatcha got there? I think we'll skip the shopping." She reached over and felt it. Oh, boy! It was bursting my pants. I tried to walk bent over. That corrected the problem, partially, but made me look deformed. Patti led me through the big revolving doors and through the big, elegantly furnished lobby to the elevator corridor. I felt a hundred eyes on us. The bellboys and the bell captain and the concierge all followed us with their eyes. So did most of the guests, especially a few old ladies who looked at me admiringly, as if they wanted to feel it themselves. The men paid attention, but not to me—to Patti's great legs, clicking across the marble floor in her white pumps. Patti's legs were bare. They shone with a golden tan. They put Betty Grable's to shame.

Patti hustled me into an elevator and out onto the fifteenth floor and down the corridor to Room 1508. Once inside, I straightened up, the huge thing pressing against my pants so hard it hurt. I tried to put it down, along my left leg. It wouldn't budge.

"I'm so embarrassed, Patti," I said. "I don't know what to do with this thing."

"You don't," she laughed. "Here, let me show you," she said as she kicked off her shoes and unbuttoned her yellow dress. "Get those pants off, Jack. Let the tiger out!"

Oh, yeah!

***

The experience is hard to describe. She threw me on the bed; a flagpole rose up from between my legs, so swollen that it felt like it would burst. She slipped a rubber on it. The touch of her hands brought me to the edge. She pulled off her white panties and lubricated herself with some kind of creamy lotion. I never felt anything like the passion I was feeling. I wanted to shout, to laugh. It was ecstasy. She climbed on. She inserted me. As she started to lower herself, I exploded. She lowered herself the rest of the way as I shot off another explosion. Ohmigod! What a feeling. I wanted to scream. I stiffened my back and thrust into her. I convulsed in ecstasy. Then I collapsed. I never felt so weak or tired. I covered my eyes with my right arm. I didn't want to look at her. I was ashamed. She climbed off.

Room 1508 was a small suite. In addition to the bedroom and oversized bathroom, there was a living room and a miniature kitchen with a pass-through bar and four bar stools. After Patti gave me my first lesson and I lay exhausted on the bed, she slipped on a silk robe and went to the little kitchen. She returned after a few minutes with a silver tray. It held two tall glasses of orange juice, two cups of black coffee, and a dish of cookies. She sat on the edge of the bed and set the tray on the bed. I observed that she was blonde all over.

"Here, Jack." She offered the refreshments. "Drink the orange juice. Relax, have some cookies. You have to get your strength back. That was too quick. It was your first time, wasn't it? You came before you were all the way in. Relax, maybe take a nap. I'll put on the radio. Next time will be better. You'll see."

"Hey, Patti," I said, red-faced with embarrassment, "this is a swell place you have. It must cost a lot. I'll bet this is a hundred dollars a week."

"You're about right, Jack," she agreed. "But I can manage. I do OK."

"Patti," I apologized, "I am so sorry. I am so ashamed. I lost control."

She removed my arm from across my eyes and made me look at her. She smiled. "It's all right, Jack. You were fine. Don't worry. And boy, do you have a cannon! Now tell me the truth, Jack, was that your first time?"

I nodded.

"No wonder. You need some practice. Just you wait and see. You will be great. You have the equipment. We'll do it again in a half hour."

"Patti, I don't even think I'll be able to stand up in a half an hour. I'm shot. I have no strength left."

She laughed and kissed my cheek. "We'll see, Tiger."

She gave me two more lessons that night. Lesson Two was about forty-five minutes later. She was right. I was a man by then. Then we slept. I awoke at 2:00 AM. The flagpole was back. Lesson Three was long and slow and full of surprises and wonder.

"Congratulations, Jack," she said afterward. "You're terrific and you'll get even better with practice. Rest up for a little while. Then it's time for you to shower and be on your way."

"Can't I stay, Patti?" I loved her.

"No, afraid not, Jack. I have some things to do." What could she have to do at two in the morning? I didn't ask. As I was about to leave, I tried to kiss her. She turned away and said, "Don't, Jack." She touched my cheek, gently.

"Can I see you again, Patti?" I implored.

"Sure, Jack. Anytime. This one was a gift from Bobo. Next time, it's twenty-five bucks for one hop, seventy-five for an hour, two hundred for the full course."

34

After Patti

I DIDN'T SLEEP much that night. I lay awake half the night, reliving each moment of the Patti experience. Everything felt different. My body felt different. In a half-sleep, I was conscious of my body in a new way. I lay on my back, my hand on my heart, feeling the solid beat of its rhythm. I caressed my chest and stomach and thighs. I felt the smoothness and muscle of my arms. I felt so alive, so strong. I marveled at the miracle of sex. I had moved on from childhood to manhood, like a chrysalis that sheds its old skin and grows a new, larger one.

I was only half-asleep when my father shook me awake at 6:30.

"Yes, Dad," I said, lifting myself onto one elbow. "What's wrong?"

"Where were you last night, Son?" he asked in a stern voice. He wore an angry look. "I *know* you weren't here at two. What time did you come home? Where were you?"

I was prepared. On the way home, I knew that I was going to have to explain being out almost all night. Mom knew I was going out to dinner. She admired the way I looked and picked out my father's tie for me. I told her that Benny James was giving a party. My father and mother knew all about Benny because I was always talking about him. I never told them about Goren or Bobo. Bobo was notorious. My father would have forbidden me to get any-where near Bobo. So I decided that my description of the make-believe party would omit Bobo and Goren. I said the party was for

Benny's friends, all adults. I was the only boy. I admitted to drinking two full glasses of wine. I said that the wine knocked me out, that I fell asleep on a sofa and Benny let me sleep until the party broke up.

My father frowned as he looked into my eyes from under knitted eyebrows. He didn't speak for a few seconds. I managed to return his stare. I raised my eyebrows a little. I thought that would add an air of innocence.

When he spoke, it was with a sadness and skepticism in his voice. I had lied, and he knew it. I felt terrible and ashamed. "All right, Son," he said quietly as he backed away. "We'll leave it at that. Go back to sleep. I have to get ready for work."

35

In Business With Bobo

THE NEXT DAY I told Benny about Patti. "Tell me everything," Benny said. I did. He listened intently. Then he punched me on my shoulder and said, "Welcome, Jack. Ain't it great? What an invention!"

I said I wanted to thank Bobo for Patti. I asked Benny if he took Bobo's five thousand dollars. Benny said *no*. He realized he talked too much about the cocoa to Bobo. He didn't want the responsibility. Losing Bobo's money could have serious consequences. I said I would go over to Royce's at lunch break. Maybe Bobo will be there. Benny said he'll tag along, maybe bet on a horse. So we walked to Royce's and Georgie let us in, but Bobo wasn't there. Georgie phoned Trucci's. That's where Bobo's main office was, on the second floor. Georgie said Benny and I are asking to see Bobo. Bobo said we should come to Trucci's. So we did.

Bobo's office was furnished more like a gentlemen's club than an office. He had a huge desk made of polished cherry wood. His chair was a soft red-leather judge's chair, a high-backed swivel chair. He had thick carpets and thick drapes, pulled open so the windows could be open to let in the breeze. Two ceiling fans kept the air moving. He had a big red leather sofa and four red-leather chairs and a huge radio set, about five feet tall and almost three feet wide. Off to one side was an oval-shaped cherry wood conference table and eight high-backed wooden chairs, also cherry wood. A full-size Wurlitzer jukebox played soft, popular ballads and quiet Italian melodies.

The walls were of satiny walnut paneling so highly polished that you could almost see yourself reflected in them. Set into the paneling were prominent raised millwork squares framed in two-inch molding. A wide mill-worked chair rail circled the room. A life-size painting of Pope Pius XII in a heavy gilt museum frame hung on one wall, facing a large crucifix on the opposite wall. The 8′ x 3′ map of Atlantic City was mounted on another wall, with the territories outlined on it.

Frankie answered our knock and let us in. Then he sat and opened a newspaper. Bobo greeted us, "Hey, you guys, c'mon over here. I'm glad to see you guys. I was going to call you, Benny James. And you, Jack, how ya feelin' these days?"

I stammered, unsure of how to thank Bobo. "I ... I ... want to thank you, Mr. Truck, ... er ... Bobo."

"What for?" he asked, with a big grin.

"Well, you know, Mr. Truck, for ... for Patti."

"Ah, yes," Bobo grinned some more. "Patti. Ain't she somethin'? Forget it, son. I owed you. But don't look for a replay. You'll have to find your own. Patti is major league. You got to start in the minors, and work your way up."

He turned to Benny. "Sit down over here, Benny," he said, indicating the leather sofa. He sat next to Benny on the sofa, leaning toward him, one arm across the back of the sofa. "I been meanin' to talk to you some more about the cocoa business. I don't unnerstan' it, but I think you're a lucky guy. I want you to invest five grand for me."

Benny did not look happy about the idea.

"I don't know, Bobo," Benny said, with a negative head shake. "This is not a sure thing. Not by any means. I don't mind speculating with my own money, but to be responsible to you, for your money, that's heavy. And five grand! That's big money to me, Bobo. I only started with six hundred."

"When did you put it in?"

"Let's see. The exact date was the day I met you behind Royce's. The day we had the arithmetic contest. That was twelve days ago."

"And how are ya doing? Last night, you told me your six hundred was up to 680, in a week. Is that right?" Bobo remembered.

"An hour ago, my account was worth about seven-twenty."

"Not bad. Not bad. I want you to open an account in the name of Loretta Mauriello with five grand I'm gonna give you. I trust you. If you guess wrong, how much can I lose?"

"You could lose all of it. Maybe even more."

"How could I lose more than the five?"

"It's leverage, Bobo. If I invest the whole five, you will have fifty thousand dollars worth of cocoa beans. You will owe forty-five thousand. If there is a sharp drop, say fifteen percent, and you get sold out, you lose seventy-five hundred. You only put up five thou. You will lose the five thou you invested and still owe another twenty-five hundred. It is too big a chance for me to take. I don't ever want to be on your wrong side."

The conversation continued. Bobo promised he would not hold it against Benny if Bobo took a loss. I saw that Benny was torn between the excitement of handling Bobo's money and his fear of having Bobo turn on him if he lost any. I knew that Goren didn't want us to take Bobo's money. I didn't want to either. I was scared.

In the end, Bobo prevailed. Benny tried to put on the big smile. It didn't look real. Bobo put his arm around Benny and pulled him close.

"Stop worrying, Benny," he smiled. "It's only five grand. No big deal. One thing I know. You will do the best what you can. You will take care of my money over here like it was your own. Better than your own, right?"

"You bet, Bobo," Benny relaxed a little.

"We're gonna do good," Bobo said. "I got a good feelin'. Stop worrying. Keep me informed. Frankie, give Benny five grand."

I was real scared. I think so was Benny.

***

The following Monday, August 14, Benny opened a new account at Krieger and Son in the name of Loretta Mauriello. Goren surprisingly was not as negative as I thought he would be. He even encouraged Benny. He said if he had his way, Bobo would not have given us the money. "But," said Goren, "what's done is done. I'm not worried. We are going to make a lot of money for ourselves and for Bobo. I watched your trades last week. You have a gift for this. My account is up almost four hundred dollars. Yours is up a hundred and change. And Jack's $177 is now about $210. I am going to sit at Krieger's all day. If I see us taking a hit, I'll get us out real fast. Is that OK with you, Benny? I may have to override you, but unless you are there all day, you won't spot a turnaround until it's too late."

So that's how we worked. Benny ran to the Krieger and Son office in Central Pier after every one of his demonstrations. Goren sat there the entire day, from 10:00, which was when the New York Board of Trade Exchange opened, until 4:00, when the Exchange closed.

It worked. Benny called the turns. Goren did the paperwork. He started a journal and recorded the value of our accounts every day. All of our accounts grew. Benny put all the profits back into bigger positions. By August 18, Goren's account was up to $6,276. Bobo's was $5,567, Benny's was $824, and mine was $241! Why was I working for fifteen cents an hour? Benny said he was ready to quit Krilow's. He was going to ask Mr. Krilow to look for another pitchman.

"This is foolish, me working here," Benny said to me. "I can make a few hundred *a day* if I sit there all day. Alan is terrific. He is precise and he's great with the paperwork. But he is slow. I am quicker than him. If I was there, I wouldn't need him to tell me what is happening. I could do the points and figures every few minutes. I would have the pulse of it. Alan could turn in the orders and do the paperwork. He wouldn't have to do the charts; I'll do them. We would be a great team. Yeah, I have to quit Krilow's. I'll give him a week's notice."

GOREN'S JOURNAL

Date	Price	Alan	Benny	Jack	Bobo	Contracts				Trades
8/4	¢ .0411	$ 5257	$ 600	$ 177		50	7	2		1
8/7	.0415	5417	656	193		50	7	2		0
8/8	.0420	5617	726	213		50	7	2		2
8/9	.0415	5417	656	193		50	7	2		2
8/10	.0417	5497	684	201		50	7	2		2
8/11	.0420	5617	726	213		50	8	2		3
8/14	.0421	5637	740	217	$ 5000	55	8	2	30	4
8/15	.0418	5665	744	218	5025	55	8	2	30	6
8/16	.0420	5948	781	229	5276	55	8	2	30	8
8/17	.0422	6245	870	240	5540	55	9	2	30	8
8/18	.0420	6276	824	241	5567	55	9	2	30	8

36

Letter to Eddie, August 19

August 19, 1939

Dear Eddie:

I have to tell you what happened to me last week.

First I went to dinner with Bobo Truck. Did you ever hear of him? I never did until a couple of weeks ago. He is a big shot. My friend Benny James told me that Bobo controls the numbers and the bookmakers in the whole city. Bobo has a bookie joint behind Royce's Shooting Gallery on the boardwalk near Kentucky Avenue. I was in Bobo's bookie joint about a week ago with Benny and a new friend. Benny got into an arithmetic contest and beat Bobo's man. Benny added up a row of about sixty numbers in his head. Can you imagine that? In his head! Bobo's man added them on an adding machine. And Benny won! It was unbelievable.

My new friend is Alan Goren. I will tell you about him later and about cocoa. A lot of exciting stuff is going on. All my new friends this summer are adults. I like hanging around with them. There is Morris and Benny and Gracie and Goren and Zena. And even Bobo, I guess, although I'm not sure I can say he is a friend. But for sure you don't want Bobo as an enemy.

I ran an errand for Bobo, so he invites me and Benny and Goren to dinner at his restaurant, which is Trucci's on Pacific Avenue near Georgia Avenue. Anyway, after dinner, Bobo fixes me up with this beautiful girl, Patti. She takes me to her room, more like an apartment, at the Claridge.

AND I GOT LAID!!!! Boy, did I!!! She was really something. It was so terrific, I can't even describe it. And she is beautiful and she has a great bod, smooth as silk. She is a professional. I'll never be able to afford to go back. That one was on Bobo.

I told Benny what happened. He laughed and said, "Ain't it great, Jack, that's what it's all about, good times, pretty girls, great sex." He said, "Jack, you even look different. Now you're a man."

I feel different. I feel like I have a sign over my head that says *this boy got laid.* I wonder if I look different like Benny says.

I am going to ask Rhoda to go out with me again. One last try. They are giving free big band concerts on Garden Pier. Tommy Dorsey is here this week. Woody Herman was here last week. If Rhoda says no, I am going to ask Alice Keever. I see her hanging around Frederick's soda fountain. You know who she is. I guess she is fourteen. The right age. And she does not act like a big shot.

The cocoa thing is so damn complicated, I can't tell you about it in a letter. What an education I am getting.

Everything here is great. Hope you are doing good.

Your best pal,
Jack, ex-virgin

37

Alice Keever

O<small>N</small> S<small>UNDAY</small> <small>AFTERNOON</small>, ten days after Patti, I worked up the courage again to ask Rhoda for a date. I waited for Sunday, when Blinky was off. If I was going to be turned down again, I didn't need Blinky to witness it. I went into the bakery and waited for a moment when there were no customers. She saw me waiting and smiled at me as she went about her work. I studied her as she moved about. I admired the smooth slenderness of her arms and legs and the grace of her movements. What must her body feel like? I tried to imagine it. A sudden warm wave of desire flooded over me as I remembered the satiny feel of Patti, the incredible smoothness of her breasts and the feel of my palm stroking her inner thigh. I wanted Rhoda. I wanted her with a painful intensity. If only I could tell her about my entry into manhood. I wondered if she was *experienced*. I was sure that she let her dates go beyond kissing in cars. How much beyond? I realized that being sexually active did not show. She could be the most promiscuous girl in Atlantic City and nothing would show. Her reputation was clean. But so what? Had she experienced the wonder of sex?

"Hi, Jack," she called to me. She leaned forward on the counter, hands resting on the bleached white oak counter. Everything about her was clean, white, pure. The white paper cap, the white apron, the white blouse under the apron, the white pleated skirt and white socks and white sneakers. A sprinkling of powdered sugar added whiteness to the bleached oak counter. Her dark hair and rosy complexion stood out like jewels. "Can I get you something?" she asked.

I was surprised at how easily my invitation came. No groping or stammering. "Hi, Rhoda, I'd like to take you to Garden Pier Tuesday night. Tommy Dorsey is gonna be there with that new singer, Frank Sinatra. They say he's terrific. The girls love him. How about it?"

She studied me for a moment. "Gee, I'm sorry, Jack. I'm busy. There's a frat social. Maybe another time." She turned away to go back to her work. Then she turned back. "Jack, you look different. What is it?"

"I don't know, Rhoda, is it a good different?"

"Yes, you look … more … more … *mature*. That's it! Like you grew up some—more mature," she laughed. "Please ask me again, Jack, in a couple of weeks. See you."

I was dismissed. I left with an aching heart. Love, jealousy, sexual desire, a longing to be a man. These are the precious longings of healthy fifteen-year-old boys. I wanted to tell her my manly activities. About Bobo and Benny and Goren and the cocoa business. And Patti. No way to do that. I left, trying for a casual attitude. "So long, Rhoda. See ya 'round." I gave her a broad smile, a half salute, and left the bakery.

Once outside, I headed for Frederick's Pharmacy. Maybe I would find Alice Keever there. Thinking about Patti and imagining Rhoda had worked me up. I wanted a girl. I *needed* a girl.

Alice Keever was there. The drugstore was the neighborhood hangout for lots of kids aged fourteen to eighteen. The five round white porcelain tables were just about all occupied. So were the eight stools at the marble-topped soda fountain counter. The jukebox was playing *String of Pearls*. The central area of the drugstore was the dance floor for three or four jitterbugging couples. The white-and-black marble tiles made a good dance floor.

Alice was at a table with a couple of her girlfriends, sipping at a milkshake.

"Hey, Alice, howya doin'?" I asked, cheerfully.

"Jack. Hi, Jack. Nice to see you. How are you? Nobody sees you around anymore since you started working for Krilow's. I guess it keeps you busy."

"Yeah, pretty much so. But I have a little time for myself. In fact, I came looking for you. I want to take you to Garden Pier. Tommy Dorsey is there. And that new singer, Frank Sinatra."

She lit up. "No kidding, Jack. Sure, I would *love* to go. When?"

"Let's go tonight," I said. "It's not like there's school tomorrow."

"You bet," she said. "This is great. Anybody else going?"

"My friends are not around, Alice. I guess it's just you and me. OK?"

"You bet it's OK." She turned to her girlfriends. "Hey, girls. Whyncha get dates and come with us?" She looked back at me. "If that's all right with you, Jack."

"Sure," I said, "absolutely," hoping that no one would join us.

Alice was not a beauty. She had plainness all over her, and a touch of horsiness in her face, but she had a beautiful complexion and a nice figure, and she was always smiling, a wide generous smile. She was pretty when she smiled. And she loved to talk, and she laughed easily. There were no awkward silences with Alice. She bubbled with stories, gossip, and news. I knew I would be at ease with her.

For our date, Alice wore a light cotton dress and white socks and brown-and-white saddle shoes, the teenage girl's uniform. She didn't wear makeup.

Admission to Garden Pier was free. There was a stage at the ocean end of the pier, covered by an open quarter dome. The spectator area was a large open dance floor. No seats. The spectators pressed up to the stage or danced. Tommy Dorsey played the trombone. His orchestra specialized in vigorous swing music, although they could, like all the big bands of those days, deliver all the popular ballads and the slow romantic numbers.

I was not a good dancer. Alice was pretty good. She sort of steered me around the slow numbers and fox trots. When the orchestra belted out a jitterbug number, she held me by one arm while she twisted and circled, tugging me into a semblance of dancing with her. Pretty soon, I dropped my inhibitions and did everything; not pretty or graceful I am sure, but once I felt the rhythm, I was able to stomp and swing and perform a reasonable facsimile of jitterbugging. And I liked it. And I liked the slow numbers, too. I liked holding Alice. I liked pressing her to me with my hand at her waist. And I liked the way she felt against my chest; and I liked her big smile and the way her eyes brightened during the jitterbug numbers. She was a lot of fun.

She looked hypnotized when Frank Sinatra sang *You Go to My Head, And the Angels Sing, I've Got a Crush on You, Deep Purple,* and *Moonlight Becomes You.* She swayed to his ballads. She squealed, delightedly, with all the other girls. "I love him. I love him," she cried. I even got jealous. Sinatra didn't look like much of a prize to me. He was so skinny, and he had a face like a skeleton. I thought Bing Crosby had it all over him.

After the concert, I bought ice-cream cones. We licked them as we walked the boardwalk toward home. I was aroused from all the touching and closeness of the dancing. Now that I was paying attention to girls' bodies in addition to their faces, I noted with some appreciation that Alice's body was first rate. During the jitter-bug numbers, her dress would swirl up around her thighs, reveal-ing legs as good as they get. And once I got a peek at her white panties as her skirt flew up.

When we approached Maryland Avenue, I said I wanted to show her something. It was the rolling chair storage shed. I knew the place. Benny showed it to me. Sometimes Benny slept in a rolling chair after a late date. Sometimes I slipped into a chair for a quick catnap during a work break.

"What is this place, Jack?" Alice asked.

"It's where the rolling chairs come to sleep. C'mon in. Sometimes I take a snooze in one."

I led her to the rear of the shed. It was dark inside. We climbed and groped our way over the chairs until we were deep in the heart of the shed. I picked out a chair with a roof and a half front and I pulled her into it. We were enveloped in darkness. In the closeness of the rolling chair, I smelled her soap-scrubbed cleanness.

"Here, Alice, this is where I come for a snooze sometimes." I put my arm around her and pulled her to me. She moved into my embrace. Her skin was smooth and cool. We kissed. Long, sensu-ous kisses. She giggled. She was an eager partner. My ardor increased. Kisses were not enough. I touched her breast. It was in early development, nice. I cupped my hand around its gentle swelling. She offered no resistance. None. More kisses. A quick flash of her tongue. I loved it. More pressing against her. More touching. My passion rose. I rested my palm on her knee, under her skirt. I felt myself getting hard. She threw her arms around me and pressed me down and back. She was almost climbing on top of me. I moved my hand along her leg, up, higher, reveling in the smoothness of her thigh. All the way. I touched her panties. She opened her legs. I pressed my hand against her. She groaned. She pressed my hand tighter into her, against the panties. Through the panties, she was damp. I tugged at the panties, trying to pull them down. She moved my hand away.

"No," she panted. "This is enough."

"Alice," I moaned, my erection bursting. "Alice, yes. Please, Alice."

"No, Jack. No. That's enough."

"My God, Alice, look at me," I said. My pants were a tent from the pressure of my swollen erection.

"I can fix that," she whispered. She grabbed me through my pants and rubbed, saying "yes, yes." She rubbed and rubbed until I came, with a mighty groan, in my pants.

"There," she laughed, "feel better?"

Feel better? I felt terrible. The passion subsided instantly. All I was left with was a mess inside my pants and the nasty prospect of having to walk two miles with it.

38

Trouble With Gracie

ONE MORNING, A few days later, I went to my favorite pavilion, on South Carolina Avenue, half hoping that Morris would not be there and half hoping he would be. I missed him. I missed the easy camaraderie we had established before it was spoiled by the Barry Zoll thing. I saw him every day when I worked the 4:00 performance at the Vi-de-lan Studio, but we hardly spoke.

Morris was not on the pavilion. Good. I sat facing the ocean and turned to my reading. It was a book about the Last Crusade. I was reading about Richard the Lionheart and his great adversary, Saladin. Their story was beyond imagination. Could there have been such men? The story fired my imagination. I wanted to see the places where they made war. Places like Jerusalem and Caesarea and Acre. I didn't believe I would ever see these places. I did, twenty-five years later, when the world got smaller and New York to Jerusalem was fifteen hours by jet. In 1939, the trip was fifteen days by ship. I found myself more attracted to Saladin than to Richard. I felt guilty about that. I was sure that I should favor the English King, not the Muslim.

I was immersed in the twelfth century when Morris's "Hello there, Jack," brought me back into the present.

"Morris, hi." It was good to see him. He gave me a big smile and put his hand on my shoulder. "Good to see you, Jack. I'll go over there and do a beach scene. I won't disturb you."

So I continued to read and Morris started a beach scene. I was so aware that we were not communicating that I could not concentrate on Richard and Saladin. I read the same paragraphs over and over, concentrating on our silence and not on the book. It was very uncomfortable.

After awhile, I thought I must leave. It was too uncomfortable to remain, surrounded by the pained silence. I closed the book and started to stand when I heard Gracie. She had come onto the pavilion, apparently in search of Morris.

"Morris," she called. "Oh, Morris!"

"Gracie." Morris was surprised to see her. "How are you, Gracie?"

"Morris, can I talk to you?"

They looked at me, together. "Jack, would you excuse us, please?" Morris asked, more politely than necessary.

"Sure," I moved away, to the other side of the pavilion. I tried not to watch, but I couldn't take my eyes away. They stood close, whispering. I couldn't hear them, but I saw that Gracie was distraught. She was wearing her waitress uniform, clutching her apron and twisting it. She was trembling. Morris was uncomfortable. He wanted to look in her eyes but couldn't. He looked away and then back to her and then away again. He looked like he wanted to reach out and embrace her. His open hands moved toward her, but he arrested them. Gracie was talking fast, animated, her features distorted by held-back tears, a dam about to burst. She sobbed. She shook with sobbing. Then she fainted or collapsed into Morris's arms. Poor Morris. People were looking. Two men approached offering assistance, which Morris declined. I ran to Morris. I helped to set Gracie onto a bench.

"It's OK," Morris said to the curious onlookers. "She's OK, just a little faint."

"Jack," he said, "please hand me my thermos."

Morris held the thermos to her lips. She stirred.

"Milk!" she laughed, a hysterical laugh. "Milk! Boy, oh boy, is that ever you, Morris. Milk." She laughed again, this time more controlled, as if she really found it funny.

"Should I go and get something?" I asked.

"It's OK, Jack," Gracie said. "I'm OK now. Just got a little nervous. I'm OK now."

The few onlookers moved away, looking backward at Gracie, curiously, until Morris's level gaze caused everyone to leave.

"I'll leave, too," I volunteered.

"No, Jack," Gracie said. "Stay. It's all right for you to hear this. Is that OK, Morris?"

Morris cleared his throat. "If you say so, Gracie," he said. His voice was raspy, choked with emotion.

Gracie composed herself. The sobbing stopped. She sat up erect. She dabbed at her eyes and runny eye makeup with a sodden handkerchief, which she then crumpled into a ball and squeezed continually as she spoke.

"Morris, I didn't know who to turn to. I hardly know you, but I think you are a friend and a good man. I guess I don't have any real friends. And I can't go to my mother with this. My dad died four years ago. I have a sister out in Cleveland. Haven't seen her in ten years. We were never close anyway."

Her story was brief and terrible. She was pregnant by Barry Zoll. When she realized it, her first reaction was joy. Barry had led her to believe they were headed for marriage. Gracie was thirty-two years old. She had just about given up the hope of having children.

Suddenly, it seemed that all her hopes were going to be realized. Marriage, to a wonderful man, and motherhood. Last night, she told Barry the wonderful news.

"Morris, he is married!" she whispered. "Married! He has two children!"

She collapsed again. Morris, sitting alongside, caught her as she slumped into his arms. But she straightened up after a moment, and forced a wry smile. "Don't give me more milk, Morris," she giggled. She even gave us, briefly, that great smile.

"Oh, Morris, this is so horrible," she said. "My happiest day turned into the worst day of my life."

"It's OK, Gracie," Morris whispered in her ear. He drew her close, a protective bear hug around her shoulders. "It will be OK."

"How can it be OK?" she sobbed. "I have to get an abortion. I need money. I am so embarrassed, Morris. I don't have the money. I am asking you for a loan. You're the only one I can ask."

"You can have whatever you need, Gracie."

Gracie became matter-of-fact. "There's a woman on Baltic Avenue," she said. "She wants three hundred dollars. Can I borrow two hundred? I will pay you back, Morris. I can pay you twenty dollars a week."

"Are you sure you want to do that?" Morris asked, worried, frowning. "Who is this woman? Is it safe? People die from botched abortions."

"Morris, I don't have a choice. This woman is a nurse. She knows what she's doing. She does a sterile job. Oh, I am so embarrassed. I am so stupid." She began to cry again.

"Please don't cry, Gracie. There must be something else you can do. How about an adoption?"

This was 1939, when abortion was a dirty, secret thing done in back alleys with a wire coat hanger. Performing an abortion was a serious crime. The terms "right-to-life" and "women's choice" did not exist. Abortion was a sacrilege and a crime. An unmarried woman who got pregnant became a social outcast. There was no Mothers' Assistance or Welfare Agency to help. A woman became a disgrace to herself and her family and an economic burden besides.

"Morris," she choked back the tears, "I have to be realistic. I will start showing in another four or six weeks. I won't be able to work. I have to get rid of it."

I was embarrassed to be there. I was too embarrassed even to say that I wanted to leave and not hear any more.

"Gracie," Morris said, "won't you ever want a child? You might never have a baby if you don't have this one."

"I know," she began to cry again. "I gave up on it. And then there was Barry. It was an accident. We got careless. I loved him. I thought my dreams were coming true. What a laugh!" She fell on Morris's shoulder again. "Last night, I wanted to kill myself. My life stinks. I'll get rid of this thing and things will be like before, only worse."

They spoke some more. Gradually, Gracie gained her composure, and Morris restored his no-emotion mask. The conversation became businesslike: when to do it, how to assemble the money, would Gracie be able to work the next day. Morris said he would go to the Boardwalk National Bank and draw out two hundred dollars. Gracie threw her arms around Morris. She turned on the great Ann Sheridan smile. "Morris, how can I thank you? You are so wonderful, and you hardly even know me." She kissed him, soundly, on his cheek. The mascara left a mark. Solicitously, she brushed it off with her fingers. Morris turned red. "It's nothing," he mumbled. They departed—Gracie to make arrangements, Morris to draw out two hundred dollars from the Boardwalk National Bank. They arranged to meet on the pavilion tomorrow morning at 8:00. "You, too, Jack; you are part of this."

Their parting words were to me, "Jack, this is between the three of us, OK? Nobody else." I since learned that the correct grammar was *among* the three of us.

39

The Plan

GRACIE, MORRIS, AND I assembled on the pavilion the next day at 8:00 AM. All the passion was spent. Morris gave her the money. It was like arranging a minor social event. Gracie told Morris that the thing was set for 9:00 that night. She gave him the address. She wanted Morris to come with her. Morris stammered. I knew that Roland's last performance was at 10:00 PM. "I … I … I can't go," he said, his impassive mask firmly in place. I wondered if he didn't *want* to go with Gracie or if it was the 10:00 performance. I couldn't tell. Gracie was disappointed. She sagged. Clearly, she needed support and had expected Morris to provide it.

"That's OK," she said, trying to put on a smile. "I'll be OK. Thanks for everything, Morris. You are a good friend. I'll be all right. And I'll repay the loan; twenty dollars every week. You can count on it."

"I'll go with you, Gracie," I volunteered.

"Not necessary, Jack," she said. She got up on her toes and kissed me on my forehead. "But thanks, anyway."

Morris said, "That's a good idea, Gracie. Somebody ought to be with you." She looked at him, curiously. I could see that she was puzzled and disappointed that Morris was abandoning her. Somehow, it made it worse that he offered me instead.

"Yes, Gracie," I pleaded, "let me come. You can't tell. Maybe you will need me. I don't mind. I'll feel better if you're not alone."

"You are a dear," she said. "Sure, I need you. How about I meet you here at quarter after eight? I finish my shift at eight."

"OK," I agreed. "I get off at eight, too."

Morris said, "Good. It's all arranged then. Good luck, Gracie." He turned away and left without another word or a backward look.

"I'm going, Jack," Gracie said. "I have things to take care of. See you at quarter after. And, Jack … thanks!"

40

The Abortionist

I MET GRACIE at 8:15 PM. She had changed into street clothes. We barely spoke. Our destination was about fifteen blocks away. We walked briskly, not wanting to be late. Gracie knew our destination. It was an ordinary house in a black neighborhood. A *colored* neighborhood, as we said in those days. An old black woman answered the door. She was expecting us. She invited us in and asked us to make ourselves comfortable in the parlor. It was her daughter who was the nurse. The daughter would be home soon; she was still at work, at Atlantic City General Hospital. Would we like some tea? We declined.

It was the first time I was ever in a black person's home. It made me uncomfortable. I had no contact with colored people. I was not sure if I was uncomfortable being in a colored home or because I was in an abortion place. I sat stiffly in a high-backed chair and studied the pictures on the wall. A drawn curtain closed off the rest of the house from the parlor.

Gracie spoke. "Jack, I'm really scared." She began to cry. I moved next to her on the sofa. I didn't know what to do with my hands, but I thought I had to do or say something comforting. So I took her hand and said, "You'll be OK, Gracie."

She repeated, "I'm so scared. If there was some other way. I'm so scared." She dabbed at her eyes. "I'm so glad you're here." She closed her eyes, as in a reverie. After a few minutes, she spoke again, quietly, dream-like. "I don't know what happened to my life.

It just passed by. I was a pretty girl. Boys liked me. I was popular in high school. What happened? I was sure I was going to marry a nice boy and have a home and a family. I've been a waitress since I was sixteen, part-time and summers until I got out of high school. I went to Atlantic City High School. After that, I started waiting tables full time. It was a temporary thing, waiting tables. I thought I would go to college at night, or meet the right fellow, or look for some other kind of job. Being a waitress was just temporary, until something better. Ha, temporary, for fourteen years. That's my problem. I was always busy trying to make a living and pay my rent. I never had time to think about changing things."

Her words made an impression on me. I remembered them years later, when I observed that most people postpone doing the really important things, because the really important things do not have to be done today. Today, one has to attend to today's things: work the job, clear up the paperwork, answer the mail, serve the customer, return the phone calls, rearrange the stockroom … The important things, the things that could improve your life—looking for a better job, or learning a new skill, or searching for a new product line, or getting serious about training an employee to take over some of your less important tasks, or maybe taking off a week to spend with your wife and children—they get pushed to tomorrow because you are too busy today. And life slips away and tomorrow never comes.

"Where do you live, Gracie?" I asked.

"I rent a one-bedroom apartment on Texas Avenue. Same place for the last ten years. I get by. I ought to have some money saved up, but I don't. I don't even know where it goes. I make decent money, about fifty dollars a week in season, about twenty-five the rest of the year. There was a boy when I was twenty-five; he was a nice boy. He was a bookkeeper for a furniture store on Atlantic Avenue. He wanted us to get married. He was such a nice boy. But dull. I couldn't marry him. I thought I would go nuts from boredom. I guess I should have. He married one of my classmates. They bought a house in Pleasantville. They have two children. Their life is dull, dull, dull." She paused, took a deep breath. "I wish I had it.

"There were a few other fellows, nothing serious. Mostly wise guys trying to get into my pants. Did I ever meet a real gentleman? I don't think so. The years slip away. You stop looking. And then Barry came along. He was so wonderful. He was fun. And he was alive. And romantic. I fell for him like a ton of bricks. Rotten son-of-a-bitch! Now what do I have to look forward to? Nothing. Worse than before. Everybody knows I was screwed. And somehow, the word will get out about the abortion. Happy endings are for fairy tales."

She asked me about myself and my family. I told her about my friends, about my work at Krilow's, about my work at Vi-de-lan.

"Oh, yes, Jack," she said. "I've seen you at the Vi-de-lan place. Hey, tell me about Roland."

"What about Roland?"

"Who is he? Do you know him? What is he like?"

Morris and I had a canned reply for such questions. The secret of Roland's identity was carefully guarded.

"He doesn't talk to me," I said. "I only work one show. He comes and does his act, and then he goes."

I started to tell her about Goren when the curtain moved aside and a black girl entered the room. I guessed she was about the same age as Gracie. She wore a nurse's uniform. She looked nervous.

"Who is this?" she asked, indicating me with a nod of her head in my direction. "I wanted you to come alone."

"He is my nephew. I asked him to keep me company. I might need some help when this is over."

"All right, all right. We ought to get started." There was no warmth in her voice or her manner. "Do you have the money?"

"Yes, right here," Gracie reached into a pocket in her skirt and took out the folded bills.

"Let's count it," said the nurse.

Gracie smoothed out the bills. The first hundred was mostly ones and a few fives, Gracie's money. Morris's two hundred was all twenties.

"OK, let's get started," said the nurse, businesslike. She moved aside the curtain. "Come with me," she said to Gracie. "You stay here," she told me. Gracie squeezed my hand.

They disappeared behind the curtain. A few minutes passed. From behind the curtain, I heard a piece of furniture being dragged. I heard voices, but they were distant, as if several rooms away. I tried to imagine what was happening. Then I stopped trying. I didn't want to know.

***

I was startled by the doorbell ringing. A long ring. Loud. Then a pounding on the door. *Thump! Thump! Thump!* There was something chilling about that sound. It made the whole house vibrate. Twenty years later I heard that sound again, in the fourth act of *Don Giovanni,* when the statue of the Commendatore came to dine with the Don. Again, *Thump! Thump! Thump!* The bell rang again. The pounding continued. The old woman appeared. She was frightened. She motioned me to go through the curtain. She held a trembling finger to her lips, commanding me to silence.

Behind the curtain, I found myself alone in a dining room. Another curtain closed off the dining room from the next room. I heard the latch turn in the front door. I heard the front door open.

"I'm looking for Gracie!" boomed the foghorn voice. Morris!

I came out into the parlor. "Morris, what are you doing here?" I was thrilled to see him.

"Where is she? Gracie! Gracie!" he boomed.

The nurse emerged. "Who–who are you?" her lips quivered. "What do you want?"

Gracie appeared. She was shaking. "Morris! What are you doing here?"

"Did you do it?" Morris growled. "Am I too late?"

"Too late? Too late for what, Morris?"

He took her by the shoulders. "Did you do it?" he whispered. "I came to stop you."

"No, Morris, we were just getting started."

"Well, you are not going to do it!"

"Morris, what …"

"Leave us alone, please," Morris ordered the two black women away.

"Marry me, Gracie. We'll be good together. Everything will be good, you'll see."

"Morris, you must be crazy. Or else you are feeling very sorry for me."

He pulled her close. "Gracie, I'm crazy about you. I always have been. I know you don't have any feelings for me, but Gracie, this is right. This is probably the last chance for both of us. And we'll have a baby. We'll be happy. I promise."

"You *are* nuts, Morris. I don't know the first thing about you. You don't even have a job. How could you support a family? With those two-dollar paintings? When I get married, it won't be so I can support a man."

"I *do* have a job, Gracie. And I have money saved up."

"Really. Doing what?"

"I'm Roland, the Mechanical Man."

She stared at him. Then she laughed near hysteria. "You, Roland? Is this a joke?"

"Yes, Gracie, he's Roland!" I chimed in.

"Yes, Gracie, I *am* Roland."

She sat on the sofa. Or rather, she fell into it. She was shaking. She held her face in her hands.

"I don't believe this," she sobbed. "This is crazy."

"How about it, Gracie?" Morris knelt and took her hands, "And I have money, Gracie. I have six thousand dollars in the Boardwalk National Bank. I'm not rich, but we'll be fine."

In 1939, six thousand dollars was three or four years' income for an average family.

"I can't do this to you, Morris," Gracie said. "You are the nicest, kindest man. I should have paid more attention to you. But I can't accept this. It is a kind of charity. I always thought I would marry for love."

"If you turn me down, then I am giving you three thousand dollars. Half of what I have. You can go away somewhere! Have the baby. Nobody has to know you are not married. Make up a story. You'll say your husband died. Don't say no. I'll give you the money tomorrow. Let's get out of this place."

He lifted her to her feet. She was limp. She fell against him.

"Oh, Morris," she sobbed, burying her head in his chest. "Yes, I'll marry you. I only hope I can be good enough for you."

He embraced her, "Oh, Gracie, Gracie, Gracie. It will be good! You'll see!"

"Hey, congratulations, you two."

"Thanks, Jack."

"Thanks, Jack."

Morris embraced me. Gracie embraced me and kissed my cheek.

"C'mon, let's go," said Morris. He was grinning so hard, it didn't even look like him.

He took her arm and steered her to the door.

"Hey," he said. "Gracie, dear, I don't even know your name."

"It's McGlynn," she smiled, looking up at him, hanging on to him with both arms, that great smile. Her eyes glistened. Was that a tear on her cheek? "But you can call me Mrs. Rubens!"

***

Morris and Gracie left town a few days later. They came to say goodbye to me at Krilow's. They wanted to leave before anyone suspected that Gracie was pregnant. Their story was that Morris had a good job offer in Virginia Beach and that Morris and Gracie were going to get married. The marriage announcement took everyone by surprise, but everyone wished them well. Mr. Krilow gave them his best wishes and even gave Morris a $200 present, although he grumbled about losing Roland mid-season. Morris spent a few hours with Anne Marie, teaching her how to be the mechanical man. She caught on pretty good, but she couldn't manage the slow motion walk. She quickly mastered dressing as

Roland—same clothing, make-up, even the same moustache and monocle. Only the long blonde hair was different, and her bosom. She looked even better than Morris. And a girl in a man's clothing was pretty startling and revolutionary, especially with the moustache and monocle. Mr. Krilow loved it.

Gracie's boss said he was sorry to lose her, but he was happy for her and Morris. He gave Gracie a $100 wedding gift.

Gracie hugged and kissed me; Morris gave me a manly handshake. He held my hand for an extra moment, then he embraced me in a bear hug. "God bless you, Jack," he said. "I love you." Then he turned away, embarrassed by his words.

I lost track of them during the war. The last I knew, they had opened a small restaurant on the boardwalk in Rehoboth Beach, Delaware. They called it *Gracie's*. They were getting on just fine. Morris was doing Roland atop the lunch counter a couple of times a week.

The baby was a girl. They named her Jackie. A brother came along within a year. His name was Roland!

41

Goren and Zena

G OREN STARTED TO spend time with Zena. At least once a week and every Sunday, they went to dinner and then returned to Zena's parlor. Sometimes Benny joined them. Sometimes they asked me along. The four of us met at Zena's parlor regularly to review our trading posture and to plan future strategies. Benny and Goren tried to persuade Zena to join us in the cocoa business right from the beginning. She declined. She said she had no interest in it. And she was not going to have Goren pumping her for insights. She warned us not to read anything into whatever she said on any subject. Despite Zena's warnings, Goren listened to her every word and read revelations into things she said. I think Goren believed that spirits spoke to him through Zena. Like one time when Goren arrived at Zena's parlor moments after the start of a summer shower.

The sun was shining even as a soft rain began. "It just started to rain," Goren said, brushing off the raindrops from his hat and shoulders as he entered the parlor, "and the sun is out. You don't see that often."

Zena, looking out at the sky, replied, "Yes, the sun is out, but look over there," she pointed. "That dark cloud coming. This is just a sprinkle, but it looks like a downpour is coming."

Goren straightened. He stopped brushing off the raindrops and said, "Zena, listen to what you said. A dark cloud coming. And you said *a downpour is coming*. You sounded so strange. *This is just a sprinkle,* you said. *A dark cloud is coming. A DOWN-pour. Down!* You are getting a message. Sit. Concentrate. Think about cocoa. What is happening? Does the *down* mean the price of cocoa? Or does the *dark cloud coming* mean war? Which is it?"

"Stop it, Alan," she said, sharply. "You are doing it again. I can't just talk to you anymore. I have to choose my words so you don't think I'm giving you a signal. I like you, but you're a nutcase and you'll make me one. Now stop it."

"OK," Goren said, reluctantly. "No metaphysics. I like your company just like this. And that is a strange thing for me. I've been solitary for so many years, avoided getting close to people. I built a wall around me. When people get close, it always spells trouble. Now I have a confession to make." He paused. He sure caught our attention.

"Are you going to confess that you're a wanted man, Alan?" asked Zena with a big smile.

"No, my confession is just this. Lately, I find that I want company. You guys broke into my wall. Now the wall is down. All of a sudden I don't like solitude. I used to enjoy it. Being alone was a pleasure, with a book or a commodities newsletter, and a brandy and some good music or the Victrola. That's all I needed. Now I need company."

"Well, isn't this better, Alan?" Zena smiled. She had a pretty smile.

"I don't know, Zena," Goren answered. "You don't get disappointed in people when you keep them out of your life."

"That's horrible," Zena protested. "To deny yourself friendship and good company because *maybe* you'll be handed a disappointment."

"Yeah, Alan," Benny added. "You understand the arithmetic. You give up a thousand good experiences because maybe you avoid one bad one. What's the percentage?"

"It's not a matter of percentage," Goren replied. "It's a matter of relative value. How many ordinary, uninteresting, or even wasted hours or years of socializing does it take to balance one minute of insult or betrayal?"

"Boy, are you a cynic," Zena said. "Somebody must have wounded you really deep."

"As a matter of fact, that's not so," Goren answered. "I figured it out the way I said, long ago, so I never got wounded. Nobody ever was close enough to me to disappoint me. Maybe I was ripe for letting somebody in. You guys. I hardly just met you, and you were under my skin that fast. It's a big surprise to me."

"We'll try not to disappoint you," Benny said, "but if we do, so what? Onward and upward. No looking back. Keep moving. Something new and better is around every corner."

"We couldn't be more different, Benny," Goren said. "You pick up people easily, and you discard them just as easy. People are attracted to you. You're young and good-looking, and you're a charmer."

"You're right, Alan," Benny replied. "Especially the girls … I have a hundred friends, and I don't really have any … except you three. What am I saying? I don't talk like this. You guys are affecting me."

"Let's drop the philosophy," Zena said. "Even metaphysics and cocoa are better than philosophy."

So the talk turned to everything in the world except cocoa. Lots of talk about politics, about the lousy economy, about Hitler and Mussolini and Roosevelt and Stalin and Chamberlain and

Daladier. And Father Coughlin. And whether Tom Dewey or Bob Taft was going to be the next president, because no American president was ever going to be elected for a third term. Goren, who read the *New York Times* every day from cover to cover, told us about a man named Wendell Wilkie. One columnist called him *the darkest of dark horses* but the best man the Republicans could nominate to beat Roosevelt in 1940.

They talked about Charles Lindbergh's admiration for Hitler. They talked about Paul Muni and George Raft and the movie *Lost Horizon* and Ronald Coleman and Madeleine Carroll and Joe Louis and "Wrong Way" Corrigan, who started out on a solo flight from New York to California and ended up in England. And Amelia Earhart and the Marx Brothers and Bing Crosby and all the big bands and the New York Yankees and the Brooklyn Dodgers and Sigmund Freud and Albert Einstein. Goren must have read just about everything ever written; Zena, too, even more than Goren. When one of them made a literary allusion, the other understood it. Not me. Not Benny. For example, Goren, talking about war, said "Like Stephen Crane's poem …"

"Yes," responded Zena, "*War Is Kind.*"

Benny and I looked at each other. I was embarrassed at my ignorance. Not Benny.

"What are you guys talking about?" Benny asked. "Talk plain English. Jack and me are uneducated."

"Sorry," Zena said. "Listen to this. About war." She recited, somberly:

> *Do not weep, maiden, for war is kind.*
> *Because your lover threw wild hands toward the sky*
> *And the affrighted steed ran on alone,*

> *Do not weep.*
> *War is kind.*

Goren finished:

> *Mother, whose heart hung humble as a button*
> *On the bright splendid shroud of your son,*
> *Do not weep.*
> *War is kind.*

Although I did not understand it, the rhythm and the dark words touched me. That and Zena's solemn tone and the way she looked off into the distance through half-closed eyes.

Benny, ever the Philistine, spoke up, "Great performance, Zena. Great performance, Alan. You guys are good. But what does it have to do with the price of beans?"

"No talk of cocoa, Benny," Zena said.

"But it's everything about cocoa," replied Benny. "War is the wild card to my charts. Is there is or is there ain't gonna be a war?"

42

Goren at Chateau-Thierry

ONE DAY, GOREN told me about the military boutonnière he wore. He was a West Point graduate, Class of 1911. He served in the World War as an infantry Captain. He was decorated for bravery, but he said he was anything but brave.

"It was at Chateau-Thierry," he said. "June 2, 1918. I was in the 28th Division, the 12th regiment. I was a Company Commander. My company was Baker Company. We were in the trenches. The Battalion Commander ordered me to have my company take a hill that was about a hundred and fifty yards in front and looking down on the right side of my line. Charlie Company was in trenches off to our right. The hill was in front of us and between us. A German rifle company was on that hill. They had a couple of mortars and four machine guns. They were firing down on our right flank and on Charlie Company's left flank. We had to retreat out of there, or else take the hill. Charlie Company was supposed to charge the hill from the other side. The idea was to make the Germans deal with simultaneous charges on their left and on their right. I knew the statistics for charges like that. For a successful attack of a position defended by a rifle company with hand grenades and a couple of mortars, the attacker will lose ten men for every defender. If the defenders are in machine gun nests and the charge is over open ground, the attackers will lose just about everyone, and of course, the attack will fail.

"When the time came, I blew my whistle to start the charge. I was the first one over the top. I was more scared than I can describe. I peed in my pants as I climbed out of the trench. I hollered over my shoulder, *Follow me! Follow me!* I planned our charge in a left half-circle, so we would hit the hill from the Germans' right, near their rear, from their three o'clock to five o'clock positions. Charlie Company would do the same maneuver on the other side, so they would hit the hill at the seven o'clock to nine o'clock positions. The only thing that got me out of that trench was embarrassment not to do it. I had two of my lieutenants come out of the trench last. Their job was to keep the boys moving. The boys will want to find cover and lie down. What keeps them moving are officers in front and rear. I showed the way. The lieutenants in the rear kept them moving. I ran as fast as I could. The faster you cover the ground, the better your chance to get close before you get killed. We were lucky. The Germans had their four machine guns in nests, dug in and fortified. Two guns faced Charlie Company. Two faced us. One was at one o'clock and one was at two o'clock. The two o'clock gun jammed. The one o'clock gun could only hit the right end of my charge.

"Charlie Company did their job. They got mowed down like hay. None of them even got to within fifty yards of the hill.

"We hit the hill at the Germans' four and five o'clock. We didn't stop to fire until we were on the hill. The hill was wooded. Once we were on the hill, the odds were evened. I kept our boys running through the trees until we were on top. It was almost all hand-to-hand. I killed four Germans with my revolver. I thought we were all going to be killed. Suddenly, I heard a shout, *Kammerad! Kammerad!* That means *surrender* in German. What a surprise!

"There is a lesson. When you are in the middle of a struggle and you don't think you can carry on, remember the other guy also might be ready to quit. Winning, sometimes, is just the other guy quitting a minute before you are ready to quit. Anyway, I lost half of my men, almost fifty men. I got a bullet in my left leg, inside the thigh. It grazed my thighbone, just missed my balls. I didn't even know I was hit until the action stopped. It was a million-dollar wound. It got me out of action and got me sent home.

"My Colonel, the Battalion Commander, visited me in the hospital before I got sent home. He said, *Chrissake, Captain, what the hell were you doing leading the charge? Don't you understand 'command'? You're a West Pointer. Didn't they teach you how to command? You belonged in your bunker, with your staff. I understand you put everybody on your staff into the charge. What were you thinking? We can't afford to lose officers.*

"I said I was sorry. I guess I was not a good officer. Maybe that's why I got passed over for promotion. According to seniority, I should have been a Major. The Colonel said I was a sorry excuse for a Company Commander, but he was going to have to recommend me for a Silver Star. He said what I really should get is a dumbness award. So … I was decorated. What a joke. The guys behind me who saw guys getting killed, and kept on running—they were the heroes. I was in front. I didn't see my guys getting killed. I just kept on running. Pride, ashamed to be a coward, peeing all the way. They ought to have a medal for *Peeing in Action.*

"When I got mustered out, I didn't know what to do with myself. I got a job with a big brokerage firm, Bache and Company. They liked the idea that I was a West Pointer, an infantry Captain, decorated. They sent me to a course on stocks and bonds. They gave me a small roster of clients. They even introduced me to a few blue-blooded girls.

"They predicted big things for me. They told me to leak out my war story to my clients. *Leak it out slowly*, they said, *in pieces, make them drag it out of you.* Modesty, you know. I was to be a self-effacing hero, reluctant to talk about my exploits. I was the perfect candidate for a promising young broker."

"Didn't you like the brokerage business, Mr. Goren?" I asked. "Sounds pretty good to me. You were like the Kriegers."

"I couldn't take it, Jack," Goren said. "Leading men to get killed changes you. And almost catching it yourself. You never get over it. After that, it's hard to put up with phonies and put-on airs. And I found that I couldn't take orders any more. My tolerance level for bullshit was too low. I had to be on my own.

"I figured that it was my time that day at Chateau-Thierry. An accident of fate spared me. Every day since then is an extra that isn't due me. I'm getting extra innings. It could stop any time when fate realizes it made a mistake. I was supposed to be lying face down in the mud with those boys who bought it that day. Those boys were certainly as worthy as me. I have no business being here twenty-one years later."

"What exactly do you do?" I asked. I knew he didn't work. To my way of thinking, work meant going to a job every day, for eight or ten or twelve hours, and doing it again the next day and every day. Like my father. Like the Michaelsons. Like Eddie's parents. Like Mr. Geek with his debit route. Goren seemed to be adrift.

"I had a few bucks," he said. "So I moved here. I like the air and the ocean and the boardwalk. The town is small enough that I can manage without a car. I decided to try some small real estate spec-ulation. And I got turned on to commodities. So between doing a few houses a year and doing commodities, I managed to be pretty comfortable all these years. It's twenty-one years since I got mustered out of the Army. It's nineteen years since I left Bache and Company. I've been on my own for nineteen years. No bosses, no customers, no overhead. I live in a one-bedroom apartment on Montgomery Avenue, thirty dollars a month rent. I get along fine. I have a few bucks. I've done OK. Now that I ran into Zena, and Benny, I expect I'm going to do a whole lot better."

43

Benny Quits Krilow's

BENNY GAVE KRILOW a week's notice on August 22. Mr. Krilow didn't understand. He said, "Benny, it's only a couple of weeks to Labor Day. After that, you'll take off anyway. What's the rush that you can't finish out the season? I can't find a pitchman for a couple of weeks' work. I'll have to ask the other fellows to pick up your schedule. I hope they will cover me."

Benny said, "Sorry, Mr. Krilow. I hate to let you down but I can't stay on. I need the time for something that I have to do. It's very important."

Mr. Krilow nodded sadly and said, "All right, Benny, I respect whatever it is you have to do. I'll give you your bonus anyhow. You did a fine job this summer. Mrs. Adler kept count of your pluses. I think you have about four thousand up to now. That's two hundred dollars for you, five percent."

A plus was awarded for every dollar taken in above the take for the same demonstration of a year ago, not by dates, but by the days of the week. The season was broken down into fourteen calendar weeks, beginning with the first Monday in June and ending with the last Sunday following Labor Day. Monday of Week Two, Demonstration No. 3, was measured against 1938's Monday of Week Two, Demonstration No. 3, and so on. Benny's demonstrations took in four thousand dollars more than the same demonstrations in 1938. Two hundred dollars was serious money. That was almost seven weeks' salary for my father, and I wouldn't earn half that much for the ten weeks of the season that I was working, from June 26 to Labor Day, which was September 4. School started the day after Labor Day.

Benny fidgeted for two days. His demonstrations suffered. He ran to Krieger's four and five times a day. He ate lunch there. Goren always had a sandwich waiting for him. He spent almost every night in the library, which was open weeknights until 9:00. When he was not working or not at Krieger's, he studied his charts.

Benny was making money for us. He showed me his charts. "See here, Jack," he pointed, "these points are the prices of the last trade. I connect them into this line on the chart. These vertical bars at the bottom are how many contracts traded at that price before the price changed. That is the volume indicator. When the price changes, I mark the new price with a point in the next column. If the price remains for a long while, the volume column goes way up, like the reading on a thermometer.

"What it tells me is this: Heavy volume on an up-tick is bullish. It means that a lot of buyers jumped in at that price. If the volume is light, it is a neutral indicator regardless if it is an up-tick or a down-tick. Heavy volume tells me something. Heavy volume on a down-tick is bearish. It tells me that the sellers are dominant. But sometimes the down signal is false. I can't describe how I know it. Something about the trend and the volumes *feels* like the price is getting ready for an up-tick. I can't explain it. I feel it. I tried showing it to Alan. He doesn't see what I see. If I sit at Krieger's all day, I'll spot more turns. Sometimes there's four or five in a single day. I miss most of them. They're gone by the time I get to chart them. Don't forget, I'm trying to work three months at a time. Right now, I have a chart for September, one for December, and one for March 1940. I'm buying and selling in all three months, wherever the action is. The beauty part of what I do is that the whole market-place is doing my work for me. All those buyers and all those sellers, they're telling me what to do. They know. They study all the things that Alan studies, like crops, politics, weather. I don't have to do any of that. Collectively, they are always right. Just the fact that more buyers come into the market is enough to push prices up. It's like a self-fulfilling prophecy. And I know how to read it."

He covered part of a chart with the blank side of another chart. "Look here," he said, as he moved the top paper slowly to the right, stopping briefly at each column. He stopped at a column with a particularly high volume. "Do you see the tension building to this point? Something is about to happen. Do you see it? Is it going to break out higher or lower?"

I could not see or feel anything. "Do you see it, Jack? Look at the tension at this price. It can't hold. A down-tick is coming." He moved the top paper one more column to the right. "There, you see, *down*! It's clear as day that it was coming. I saw this move. I got us out here," he pointed, "and we went short here." He pointed again.

Whatever it was he was doing, Benny was doing it right. All of our accounts were growing. Goren was up to $6,622. Benny was at $869. I was up to $254, and Bobo's $5,000 was worth $5,873.

The cocoa business was changing Benny. Now he was always tense. The Benny James smile rarely was seen. His kitchen gadget demonstrations lost their sparkle. I noticed even that sometimes his audience thinned before the sales pitch. That never used to happen. His audiences always used to get bigger during the demonstration. His sales slipped badly. And I didn't see any of his girls coming around any more. Benny seemed to have lost his interest in everything except cocoa and his charts.

Benny quit two days after he gave Mr. Krilow his notice. Benny said he was sorry he could not stay any longer. Mr. Krilow said it was just as well. "Benny," he said, "I don't know what is eating at you. It must be bad. You are not the same. Forget the business and the customers. I will get your spots covered. It's you I'm worried about. Is there something wrong? Something I can help you with?"

"You're an OK guy, Mr. Krilow," Benny said, flashing the old grin for just a moment. "Sorry to let you down. It's something I have to do, and I can't keep my mind on anything else."

"How about you, Jack?" Mr. Krilow asked me. "Are you taking off with Benny?"

"No, Mr. Krilow, I'm staying 'til Labor Day, like you hired me. I'm sorry I can't do Benny's job. If there's anything else I can do for you, tell me. I'll do it."

He cupped the back of my head and smiled. "You *are* a good boy, Jack. Keep up the good work. Next summer, I'll find a more important job for you."

Benny's total immersion into cocoa futures continued to take a toll on him, until one day, he exploded.

Date	Price	Alan	Benny	Jack	Bobo	Contracts				Trades
8/4	$.0411	$5257	$600	$177		50	7	2		1
8/7	.0415	5417	656	193		50	7	2		0
8/8	.0420	5617	726	213		50	7	2		2
8/9	.0415	5417	656	193		50	7	2		2
8/10	.0417	5497	684	201		50	7	2		2
8/11	.0420	5617	726	213		50	8	2		3
8/14	.0421	5637	740	217	$5000	55	8	2	30	4
8/15	.0418	5665	744	218	5025	55	8	2	30	6
8/16	.0420	5948	781	229	5276	55	8	2	30	8
8/17	.0422	6245	870	240	5540	55	9	2	30	8
8/18	.0420	6276	824	241	5567	55	9	2	30	8
8/21	.0418	6307	828	242	5594	55	9	2	30	3
8/22	.0420	6622	869	254	5873	55	9	2	30	2

44

Benny Blows Up

GOREN AND BENNY met every weekday morning at 8:00 on the South Carolina pavilion so Benny could show Goren the charts that he worked on the night before. Benny was tense all the time. As the days passed, Benny grew short-tempered. He started to speak so rapidly that sometimes it was hard to understand him. His thoughts raced ahead, faster than he could get them out. There was no more easy banter, no quips, no girls, not even any admiring looks at the girls. It was a long time since I saw a Benny James girl, or heard him talk about one, or heard him talk about anything, for that matter, except cocoa.

One morning I joined them and found Benny talking, rapid-fire, to Goren, his finger pointing and jabbing at one chart after another. I could barely gather in his words. For sure I couldn't digest them. Goren was frowning. I thought Benny was getting to be too much for Goren.

Benny spat out the words, like a machine gun. "Here you see this movement and this confirmation, and look back here, the last time there was a structure like this it was followed *immediately* by this up-tick, see it and see here you could spot that this up-tick couldn't hold, it was almost played out before it started. See I spotted it. I jumped in here, I jumped out here, I shorted it here, I covered it here, I see it again right here. I'm going long on the opening today big time, ten contracts for me, sixty for you, and forty for Bobo. And Jack, too, three for him. And I bet I'll pick up a tenth of a cent in a half hour and I'll be out, and I got a feeling I'll go short within an hour after that. I see it, Alan, do you see it like I do? Here, here," he pointed and drew his finger up and to the right, tracing the imaginary line that he saw, that *only* he saw.

Goren spoke slowly. "Benny, I can barely follow you any more. I read a crop report last night and …"

"Fuck the crop report!" Benny's voice rose. "I don't give two shits about all the crop reports and weather forecasts and consumption estimates. They are all *bullshit*. This here," he jabbed again and again, his index finger stabbing at the charts. "Here is the story, the whole fuckin' story. You been pissin' away your life with those fuckin' crop reports. You don't even know whatchyer reading. Look at you! I made you more money in three fuckin' weeks than you made in twenty years!"

Goren lowered his head, as if he'd been struck. He started to stand up. Before he could rise, Benny held him down with a hand on his shoulder.

"Alan," Benny said, soberly, "forgive me." He hesitated, then slowly, almost a whisper, "I don't know what's wrong with me, to talk to you like that. I'm so fuckin' wound up all the time. And I *see* things in the charts. Like they light up to tell me something. Please, Alan, forgive that outburst. I got all wound up last night when I saw that this configuration was repeating."

"Benny," Goren said, earnestly, frowning, looking directly into Benny's eyes, "Benny, Benny, ease up. This is no good. The money is *nothing*. Where did *you* get to? Where is Benny James? What happened to him? I'm ready to give it up. I am worried about you. You look all worn out. I don't think you are eating right. You are not getting enough sleep."

Benny sighed, "You're a good friend, Alan. I appreciate that you are concerned. Don't worry. I'm okay. You're right. I am taking this too serious. I'll ease up."

Benny flashed the big smile. Like the sun came out. "You, too, Jack. I see that you're worrying, too. Well, you guys, stop the worryin'. Maybe I'll stick to one trade every other day. We'll see."

"Yes, Benny," Goren said, skeptically, "we'll see. Meanwhile, here are the numbers at yesterday's close. My account, $7,151; yours, Benny, $938; Jack, $274; Bobo, $6,342. Like I said, it's all right with me if we bail out right now. I never expected to have this much money. Benny, you are a genius, but hell with that. You're worth more to me than the money you made for me. I don't know what to do for you. You need help. You're going to make yourself sick. Too much pressure. And for what? For money? Forget it. Go back to being a pitchman. You used to enjoy life. Where are the girls, Benny? Where did all the good times disappear to?"

"You know something, Alan?" Benny said. "I think you're the best friend I ever had. And I don't even *know* you!" he laughed, a big Benny James laugh. Like old times. "C'mon," said Benny, the old Benny, at least for the moment, "enough of this lovemaking. Let's go to work!"

45

Thursday Night, August 24

W E MET AT Zena's. There was stunning news that day. The Germans and Russians signed a non-aggression pact. It would leave the way clear for Germany to invade Poland without the fear of Russian intervention on the side of the Poles. This was the background: For a year, the Russians were urging a mutual defense pact with France and Britain. The Russian foreign minister was a Jew named Maxim Litvinov, a man who hated Hitler and who struggled unsuccessfully to fashion mutual defense agreements with France and Britain. The Russians knew Hitler's aggressive intentions to expand. Litvinov pledged to the French and Britons that the Russians had no wish or intention to export Communism. He argued that Germany was the only threat to peace in Europe. "One only has to read Hitler's memoirs," said Litvinov, "to know Hitler's plans. Read *Mein Kampf.*" Hitler's plans were all there, in the biggest selling book of the decade: Eastern expansion. Enslave the Poles, the Hungarians, the Rumanians, the Russians. Enslave all the Slavs; they are lesser creatures. Eradicate the Jews and Gypsies; they are subhuman. Take over all the oil fields in Eastern Europe and Russia. Feed Germany from the Ukraine. It was all there, in print. Why didn't world leaders believe it?

The Russian design was for a British–French–Russian alliance, pledged to come to Poland's aid and to each other's in the event of German aggression. That would stop Hitler, whose tactics depended on taking one bite at a time, without resistance. Hitler would not take on such an alliance. That was Litvinov's story. He tried to sell it in London and Paris. He didn't make the sale. It probably didn't help him that he was a Jew.

The trouble was that there were too many conservative French and British who were more frightened of Communism than of Hitler and the Nazis. There were French and British Nazi sympathizers, too many, including the British monarch himself, Edward VIII, who saw Hitler as a champion, holding back the red tide of Communism. It was good for the civilized world that Edward VIII abdicated to marry Wallis Simpson. If he remained King, he might have changed the course of history for the worse. He was a pathetic little man, sexually enslaved by his domineering American-born wife. He admired and was awed by Hitler. He was at the head of a coterie of British and French Nazi sympathizers who had a good solution for Europe's tensions: Hitler should be encouraged to conquer Russia, wipe out Communism, and be satisfied with digesting all of Eastern Europe; make the world safe for British and French capitalists and landed gentry.

The world was still in the Great Depression. Nothing seemed to work to end it. Socialism was a powerful force in Britain and France. The Depression fueled it. So far, the British and French brand of Socialism didn't seem a serious threat to the wealthy. But the British and French upper classes worried that it's only a quick sidestep from Socialism to Communism. The Russian Revolution, only twenty-two years earlier, frightened Europe's wealthy; it even frightened the entrepreneurial middle class. So the Litvinov solution to contain Hitler was ignored. The British and French upper classes were not about to get into bed with Communists. *You can do business with Hitler*. That's what they thought.

Hitler read the signals correctly. The Russians would fail to get an alliance with Britain and France. He saw that Neville Chamberlain's England and Edouard Daladier's France felt more threatened by Communism than by Hitler and the Nazis. Here was an opportunity! Hitler made a brilliant decision. He sent the German foreign minister, Joachim Von Ribbentrop, to Moscow, where an anxious Joseph Stalin, unable to ally Russia with England and France, was only too willing to sign a non-aggression pact with Germany. Stalin understood that the British and French wanted to feed Russia to Hitler in hopes of filling his appetite for more land and more grain and more oil. At the stroke of a pen, on August 24, Russia and Germany were allied. Litvinov, the Jew, was fired. The new Russian foreign minister was Vyacheslav Molotov, a sour, humorless Bolshevik, no friend to the West. Russia no longer had to seek protection from Germany through an alliance with England and France, and Hitler no longer had to worry about a two-front war when he was ready to make his next move. What a turnaround. Nazis allied with Communists, an unholy alliance of Nazi black and Communist red. Hitler came to power on fear of the growing strength of German Communists and, once in power, he destroyed them. Now deadly enemies became partners. In the United States, the German-American Bund and the American Communist Party, bitter enemies, became friends and partners overnight. What cynicism. They didn't even seem embarrassed. If there were ever any doubts about where their marching orders came from, the way they reversed their field and marched to a new line put to rest such doubts.

Benny said, "War is any day now. Hitler has a free hand."

Goren said, "Maybe not. With Russia neutralized, Hitler can pick off Poland whenever he wants. The British and French won't

THE HITLER-STALIN PACT, AUGUST 24, 1939

do anything about it. It will be just like when he took over Austria and the Sudetenland and then all of Czechoslovakia. Nobody will do anything about it. No war. Commodity prices are not going to be affected by this news. That's what I think. Zena?"

Zena shook her head, negatively. "I don't understand any of it," she said. "And if I did, I wouldn't say anything for fear you'll *think* I saw something. Leave me out of your calculations. Anyhow, how much are your accounts worth?"

Goren took out his journal page:

Alan	*$7,866*
Benny	*$1,031*
Jack	*$301*
Bobo	*$6,976*

"Pretty good," she said. "Benny, you're good at this."

"I keep telling you to get on me, Zena," Benny said.

"That's OK, Benny," she answered. "I'm doing all right without it. If I lost any money, I would feel very, very stupid. I'll be happy to see you fellows make a lot of money. I don't have the stomach for risk."

Goren turned to me. "How about you, Jack," he asked, "any thoughts?"

"My dad says a big war is coming. He says it's a good thing I'm too young to go."

Benny said, "OK, let's sort of stand pat. I been makin' us a few bucks every day on tiny changes. The beans are trending up. But I'm goin' long and then short. I make money both ways. I'm hitting the tops and selling and goin' short. I'm coverin' at the troughs and goin' long. It's brutal—a lotta work—a lotta small profits. I know the breakout is coming. War will do it. Meanwhile, I am goin' home *long* every night. If war starts, we're in the right posture."

"Come everybody," said Goren. "Dinner at the Waldorf Grille, on me."

Date	Price	Alan	Benny	Jack	Bobo	Contracts				Trades
	¢	$	$	$	$					
8/4	.0411	5257	600	177		50	7	2		1
8/7	.0415	5417	656	193		50	7	2		0
8/8	.0420	5617	726	213		50	7	2		2
8/9	.0415	5417	656	193		50	7	2		2
8/10	.0417	5497	684	201		50	7	2		2
8/11	.0420	5617	726	213		50	8	2		3
8/14	.0421	5637	740	217	5000	55	8	2	30	4
8/15	.0418	5665	744	218	5025	55	8	2	30	6
8/16	.0420	5948	781	229	5276	55	8	2	30	8
8/17	.0422	6245	870	240	5540	55	9	2	30	8
8/18	.0420	6276	824	241	5567	55	9	2	30	8
8/21	.0418	6307	828	242	5594	55	9	2	30	3
8/22	.0420	6622	869	254	5873	55	9	2	30	2
8/23	.0423	7151	938	274	6342	60	10	3	40	4
8/24	.0428	7866	1031	301	6976	60	10	3	40	2

46

Another Letter from Bernie

Asbury Park, August 28, 1939

Dear Jack:

Life stinks. My uncle is dead. He fell down behind the counter in the diner ten days ago. Just like that. One minute, he was serving up a hot roast turkey platter and the next minute he was on the floor. A heart attack. An ambulance came with a doctor. He said it was a massive heart attack. He said my uncle was probably dead by the time he hit the floor.

My aunt got crazy. She screamed and screamed. The doctor gave her a shot to put her to sleep.

My folks came up here for the funeral. Maybe they told you already. Or maybe somebody else told you.

Anyway, here's the shitty deal. I have to stay up here for a while. I have to help my aunt run this place until she can sell it. She don't have anybody else she can count on. So I am it.

My dad is pulling me out of school for the fall term. Maybe we'll get lucky and sell this place in a couple months. If that happens, I will come back to ACHS and they will either put me back in our class, or put me back a half-year. It depends how long I am away. If I get back in our class I have to make up the time in summer school. Meanwhile I am just about running this place. My aunt ain't worth diddly. She cries all the time. I have to keep her in the kitchen. She is no good out front. She makes the customers depressed.

I am managing to keep the thing going. I got some extra help. They are not much good but they are extra hands. I have to do just about everything my uncle did, including the money and the bank and pay the bills and the help. This is not a bad business. But the work. It's murder. That's all I do is work. I thought it was hard before. Now it's impossible. And my aunt can't even keep house. She just sits and listens to the radio. I don't even think she listens. She just sits there. I have to tell her it is time to go to sleep. I have to make the beds. Do the wash. Clean the house. What a life. But there is nobody else to do it.

I hope you and everybody are OK. I am going to miss you guys. Let me hear from you.

Your friend,
Bernie

47

Getting Hired After Labor Day

BENNY ASKED ME if I told my father about the cocoa. I told him
no. I didn't tell anyone. No one. I was wondering if I should tell
my best friend, Eddie. I said I mentioned it in a letter to Eddie, but
I didn't know if I was going to tell him about it.

"You're like me, Jack," Benny said. "I ain't told a soul. But you're
different. You have parents. You live with them. Why're you keeping it a secret?"

"Benny," I answered, "my father and mother work real hard.
They're always working. And for what? Some days I make as much
money in a day as the two of them earn together in a week. I'm
embarrassed to tell them how easy it is. And anyway, our profits
could evaporate overnight. We don't have any money. All we have
is what Mr. Goren calls our *unrealized gains*."

"On the other hand," Benny said, "I can close the accounts in
five minutes and the money is ours."

"Maybe we should do that, Benny."

"Hey, Jack, I'm just getting the hang of this. Like Al Jolson says,
you ain't seen nothin' yet."

"I been thinkin', Benny," I said. "School starts the day after
Labor Day, my first year at Atlantic City High. That will be
September 5. My father fixed me up with a job at his store for after
school and Saturdays—stockboy and general gopher. Twenty
cents an hour. I don't want to do it. I want to be available for you
and Mr. Goren if you need me. Errands and stuff. So I want to tell

my father that Mr. Goren wants me to work for him, as his assistant and runner, for twenty-five cents an hour. That's more than I would make at the Nu-Enamel store. I figure I can take a little money out of my boodle," I said, using a word I learned from Benny, "every week, like five dollars, so I'll have the money I'm supposed to be earning."

"No, you won't, Jack," Benny said, sternly. "You are not gonna tell your father a lie. Forget it; no lies, ever."

"But Benny, I can't be in school and at the paint store all day and out of touch with you and Mr. Goren and out of touch on Saturday. You guys might need me. Bobo might need me. I'm not trying to be a big shot. It's not that I don't want to work for twenty cents an hour. It wouldn't matter if I was earning a *dollar* an hour. I just don't want to be away from you and Mr. Goren. Maybe you'll want me to run to the library for you, or bring you guys lunch. I could save us a lot of money if I did stuff so you didn't have to do it yourself."

"What time do you get out of school?" Benny asked.

"I'm not sure. Probably 2:00 or 2:15."

"You know something? I think you're right," Benny mused. "Tell you what, Jack, I'll get Alan to hire you for him and me for a quarter an hour. For real. He will pay you every week. For real. You're right. We need you around. You'll meet us at Krieger's every day. You'll ride your bike direct from school. And you'll bring us sandwiches and the early editions of the *Philadelphia Evening Ledger* and the *Evening Bulletin*. Good idea."

"You don't have to pay me, Benny. I have money. I'm a partner."

"No lies, Jack. We'll pay you. Just like you'll tell it."

48

War!

O<small>N</small> A<small>UGUST</small> 27, the last Sunday in August, Benny called for a meeting. We met at Zena's at 7:30 in the evening. She hung out the *Closed* sign. There was not much business on Sunday evenings, anyway. Sunday is when the one-week tourists and the weekend tourists check out and head for home. The new arrivals are not yet fully installed, so Sunday evening is sort of quiet. Benny said this was an important meeting. He asked Zena to close early so we would not be disturbed.

Zena was out of costume. She greeted us in the ordinary dress of a non-mystical middle-aged woman. Her face was scrubbed clean of the dark gypsy stain. Her hair was pulled back and tied behind. She had brewed a dark, rich, fragrant tea for our meeting. Its aroma filled the parlor. She sat at her round table. Goren and I sat opposite her. Benny relaxed on the sofa.

"Fellows," Benny said from the sofa, "this is an important meeting. I have a big decision to make. I don't wanna make it alone."

The big decision was that Benny believed a war in Europe would break out over Danzig and the Polish Corridor within the next two days.

Benny explained: "For weeks, I been reading every word in every paper. I been listening to every news program and every commentator. I even been hanging around the Associated Press office, and I been reading everything that comes in from their correspondents from London, from Paris, from Berlin, Rome, Warsaw,

Danzig, Moscow. They have a real big short-wave radio there. I listen to the BBC to get the British slant on the situation. Some of the people in the Associated Press office know German. They listen to Radio Berlin and translate as they listen. Now here's what I am thinking. The Germans made that alliance with Russia three days ago, on the 24th. It gives the Germans a free hand in Poland. The Russians won't help the Poles. Probably the Russians will grab a piece of Poland for themselves. The Germans will invade Poland, maybe tomorrow, maybe even tonight. At most, in two or three days. They are not gonna walk in and be cheered by the crowds, like in Austria. They are not gonna walk in to quiet grumbling, like in Czechoslovakia. The Poles will go to war. They are mobilized. It's gonna be a war, and here's the most important part: The English and the French are gonna declare war on Germany! That's what I believe. It's gonna be the World War all over again.

"And commodities are gonna go up through the roof. Cocoa will go up a cent in the first hour. That's $200 on a contract! Alan, you can have a hundred contracts. You can make *twenty thousand dollars* in the first hour! I intend to up my position to eleven contracts. That's every penny I have at Krieger's. I'll make over *two grand* in the first hour! Jack, you have enough for another contract. That'll bring you to four. You'll make over eight hundred bucks. Tell me what you think."

Goren rubbed his chin, thoughtfully. "Benny," he said, "cocoa has been inching up for a few weeks. Your charts show what's happening. The beans go up a little, then down a little less, then up to a new high, then they back off and give up half the gain. Then another run up. Another new high. The charts are predicting war. There is nothing in the crop reports to suggest higher prices. If there is no war, cocoa will *drop* a half-penny overnight. That's a hundred dollars a contract. Maybe we should go light."

"That's why we're here, Alan," Benny said. "Whatever we do, it's gotta be a unanimous decision. As for Bobo, whatever you do, I'm gonna do for him. I don't want to put his whole boodle on the line. Now, OK, let's talk about it. What it hangs on is whether or not there's a war coming next week. If it isn't next week, say by next Sunday night, I don't think there will be a war. Hitler will make a grab in the next day or two, I'm a thousand percent sure of it. The question is will the Brits and the French tell the Poles to lie down. Or will they go to war? What's your guess? Jack, you're part of this, do you have an opinion?"

"No, Benny," I stammered. "I rely on you. My father says war is coming, but he don't say when."

"Alan?" Benny raised his eyebrows questioningly.

"Big decision," Goren answered. "Zena, what do you think?"

Zena shrank from the question. "Don't ask me, Alan," she said. "I don't want you reading anything into what I say. I *cannot* see the future." She was fidgeting nervously, trying to keep all expression out of her face, like somebody at an auction who is afraid even to wipe his nose for fear it will be taken for a bid. Her hand rested on the table. Accidentally, she must have touched the light switch for her globe. It lit up. A milky cloud swirled about in it. Zena's eyes were drawn to the globe. The light from below cast an eerie shadow on her face. She held her hands over the globe, her palms formed into a half dome. She moved her hands around the globe, not touching it, only several inches away from the surface of the globe. She stared into it. She became motionless, trancelike—the Occult Reader.

Goren whispered, "Zena, what's happening? What do you see?"

She did not speak. She stared into the globe. About ten seconds passed in silence. Then she sighed, a long, sorrowful sigh. She pursed her lips. "War," she whispered, so quietly, almost inaudibly. She closed her eyes.

Benny was on his feet. He kneeled beside her and put his arm around her shoulders, his face almost touching hers. "Here, Zena," he said, "take a sip of this tea. What's wrong? Are you OK?"

She opened her eyes. She straightened. She took the teacup from Benny and drank.

"I'm OK," she said. "I don't know what happened. I must have passed out for a moment. What happened?"

"Zena," Goren said, "do you know what you saw? Do you know what you said?"

"Alan, I told you," she said. "Don't pay attention to me. Sometimes I see what I hope for. Sometimes I see what I fear. I don't see the future. Believe me. What I see are my own thoughts. My own hopes. My own fears. Did I say I saw a war? That's what I saw. A war. A terrible war. But that is my fear manifesting. *Remember*, I can't see the future. Don't pay attention to me. If you bet on me, you'll be making a mistake. You might just as well ask my cat."

Goren and Benny were always half-convinced that Zena was a clairvoyant, despite her protestations. Now, they looked at each other as if acknowledging what they already believed: Zena *knew*.

"That's it," Benny said, soberly. "There's going to be a war. I knew it. I felt it in my bones."

Goren said, "Let's pray we stay out of it. Benny, you're the right age. If we get dragged in, you're going to go. God forbid. I know war. I hope you and Jack never have to know it."

We sat in silence as if we just heard a radio announcement that the war had started. It seemed so real, the way Zena stared into the globe.

Benny was the first to speak. "Let the politicians make wars. We'll make money. Alan, let's see our accounts. Zena, you really should get in on this. It's gonna be easy money."

Zena declined, again. Over the past several weeks, Benny and Goren must have tried to persuade her a dozen times. She was steadfast. I think she thought there was something immoral about it.

Goren pulled out a sheet of paper and unfolded it. It was the daily record of our accounts.

Alan	*$8,259*
Benny	*$1,082*
Jack	*$316*
Bobo	*$7,324*

He had been listing them every day since Benny and I opened our accounts at Krieger and Son. He smoothed out the sheet on Zena's round table. "I have enough equity for ninety-six contracts," he said. "That's too close. I'll go for seventy."

Benny studied the sheet. He produced a pencil and a small-ringed notebook. He did some calculations.

"Alan," he said, "first thing Monday, on the opening, you go long an additional ten Decembers. That'll bring you up to seventy contracts. I have ten Decembers. Buy me one more. Jack has three Decembers. Buy him one more. I'm going easy with Bobo. He's long forty Decembers. Buy him ten more. Put the orders in before the opening. We want to be buying at the opening. They're gonna move up tomorrow. Get us in early. All right, Alan? All right, Jack? We're going for a big score."

Benny clapped his hands. The pitchman. His eyes lit up with excitement. "OK, guys. Great. This time next week, we'll all be a lot richer."

World War II started five days later. The Germans invaded Poland on Friday, September 1, 1939. That day, cocoa ran up from 4.65 to 5.45 cents, $160 on a contract. Goren was long eighty contracts. His account jumped over $12,000 that day; Benny's moved up $2,700; mine, $1,100; Bobo's, $9,600. By the end of the day, our accounts were:

Alan	*$27,444*
Benny	*$4,848*
Jack	*$1,708*
Bobo	*$21,556*

Britain and France declared war two days later. Hitler misjudged. He thought Poland was going to be a free lunch, like Czechoslovakia.

In Britain, a humiliated Neville Chamberlain resigned as Prime Minister. He and Edouard Daladier of France were the architects of the infamous Munich Agreement in 1938, which gave away part of Czechoslovakia to Germany, the Sudetenland, as it was called, the areas of Czechoslovakia bordering Germany.

Chamberlain was Hitler's dupe. He tried to buy peace with appeasement. The new Prime Minister was Winston Churchill, a bulldog, a determined enemy of Hitler and Nazi-ism. It was Churchill who said of Chamberlain after Munich, "He had to choose between war and dishonor. He chose dishonor. He shall

Date	Price	Alan $	Bunny $	Jack $	Bobo $	Contracts				Trades
8/4	.0411	5257	600	177		50	7	2		1
8/7	.0415	5417	656	193		50	7	2		0
8/8	.0420	5617	726	213		50	7	2		2
8/9	.0415	5417	656	193		50	7	2		2
8/10	.0417	5497	684	201		50	7	2		2
8/11	.0420	5617	726	213		50	8	2		3
8/14	.0421	5637	740	217	5000 $	55	8	2	30	4
8/15	.0418	5665	744	218	5025	55	8	2	30	6
8/16	.0420	5948	781	229	5276	55	8	2	30	8
8/17	.0422	6245	870	240	5540	55	9	2	30	8
8/18	.0420	6276	824	241	5567	55	9	2	30	8
8/21	.0418	6307	828	242	5594	55	9	2	30	3
8/22	.0420	6622	869	254	5873	55	9	2	30	2
8/23	.0423	7151	938	274	6342	60	10	3	40	4
8/24	.0428	7866	1031	301	6976	60	10	3	40	2
8/25	.0430	8259	1082	316	7324	60	10	3	40	5
8/28	.0440	9562	1304	403	8222	70	11	4	50	4
8/29	.0435	9611	1312	406	8259	70	11	4	50	2
8/30	.0431	9572	1307	403	8227	70	11	4	50	3
8/31	.0465	14,334	2131	684	11,734	80	15	6	60	2
9/1			WAR !							
9/1	.0545	27,444 $	848	1708	21,556	100	30	12	80	2

CONTINUE ———

have war as well." With Churchill as Prime Minister, it was clear that the war would be real.

My father was worried. "We'll be dragged in," he said at dinner that night. "I pray it's over quick, before they come for you, Son."

The United States Ambassador to England was Joseph Kennedy, who made his fortune as a prohibition-days bootlegger, and whose son became the 35th President twenty-one years later. Kennedy was what the British termed a *defeatist*. He believed Germany would win the war. Before the war began, his sentiments clearly had been on the side of Germany. He didn't try to conceal his bias. The beginning of the war made him an embarrassment to President Roosevelt, who asked for, and received, Kennedy's resignation.

It is an irony that Kennedy's oldest son, Joseph, Jr., an American B-24 bomber pilot flying combat missions with the British Naval Command, was killed in action on a special mission in August 1944. It was a high-risk mission, for which he volunteered, aimed at the German Peenemunde Factory, on the German island of Wolgast in the Baltic Sea, which turned out the V-2 rockets.

49

September 3

EDDIE CAME HOME on the Sunday before Labor Day. Mr. Dunauskas and I were waiting at the terminal when the bus arrived and Eddie swung off the bus. His father embraced him. I thought I spotted a tear in Mr. Dunauskas's eye. "Welcome home, Eddie," he murmured. "We missed you."

"Me, too, Pop," Eddie said. I heard a choke in his voice.

I went to shake hands. Eddie ignored my outstretched hand. He slipped one arm under mine and the other around my neck. "Eddie, it's so good to see you," I said, as we pounded each other's back.

"I missed you, Jack," he said.

"Let me see you," we said in unison as we stepped back from the embrace. We laughed.

"There's a war in Europe, Eddie," Mr. Dunauskas said. "Did you know that?"

"Yeah, Pop," Eddie said. "I heard it on the radio. Uncle Ted explained it to us. He said it has nothing to do with us. Is he right, Pop?"

"I hope so, Eddie," Mr. Dunauskas said soberly. "I hope it's over quick. You'll be old enough for them to take you if it goes on three years and we get dragged in like the last time."

Three years. That's an eternity for a fifteen-year-old. Eddie wasn't worried. Me neither. That sure turned out to be wrong.

Eddie was deeply tanned. His arms looked bigger. His neck was thicker.

"Eddie, you got bigger," I said admiringly.

"You, too, Jack. Looks like you put on a few pounds. And maybe a half-inch."

I couldn't wait to tell Eddie everything that happened during the summer. About Benny and Morris and Gracie and Joseph Conrad and Goren and Bobo and Patti. And Alice Keever. I told him about Goren and Benny's cocoa trading. I left out that I also had an account and that I was worth $1,708. A staggering amount. It was more than a year's salary for my father.

"Did you run into the Mackeys?" he asked. That sobered me. I hadn't thought about them in a long time. I was so involved in the cocoa business that the Mackeys problem hadn't switched on in my mind for a couple of weeks. I dismissed Eddie's question with a backhanded wave of my hand.

"I'll get around to that now that summer's over," I said. Not that I had any ideas about how or when.

"Yeah, Jack," Eddie grinned. "We'll figure out something. Maybe I could take one of them. I'm feeling mighty strong."

It was great to have him back.

"Boy, did I miss you," I said.

50

Labor Day, September 4

Heavy black headlines that day told us that a British passenger ship, the *Athenia*, was sunk by a German U-boat, with 292 Americans aboard. The first ship sunk in the war.

A smaller headline reported a speech by Fritz Kuhn, head of the German-American Bund. He shouted at a Bund rally in Madison Square Garden, "Hitler and Germany can lick the world!" The United States was neutral, but I assumed that everybody here wanted the Allies to win. I didn't understand how Fritz Kuhn could get away with it.

That day, I asked Benny and Goren if I could take $177 out of my Krieger and Son account, so I could repay what I borrowed from Benny and Goren to open the account.

Goren said that was a good idea. "In fact," he said, "it's a good idea for all of us to take some money off the table." Benny agreed.

The next day, Goren withdrew $5,000 from Loretta Mauriello's account, $5,000 from his own account, $1,000 from Benny's account, and $300 from mine. I paid off my loans, $93 to Goren and $54 to Benny, and I still had $153 in my pocket of which only $30 was my original investment. It was more money than I earned for the entire summer working at Krilow's. I felt some guilt at so much easy money. I thought of my parents working so hard for so many years and my father so proud to have saved up $1,720.86 in his passbook at the Boardwalk National Bank.

I asked Benny if he thought it was time I should tell my father about the cocoa. Benny said no. At least not yet. "Jack," he said, "I don't figure the money's ours until we close out our accounts and cash in. When it's in our hands, then it's ours. The cocoa could go against us. I'm no wizard. I could make a bad call. We're playing with a lot of contracts. One bad mistake could eat up half of what we've made. In a day! That's the high-roller thing about what we're doing. I love it. All that leverage. A buck does the work of ten. When I bet a buck and I'm right, I win ten or maybe twenty. I only made a couple of mistakes so far, but I quick reversed field. I only got us nicked a tiny bit. I'm worth almost *five grand*. I can't hardly believe it."

"Jack," he went on, "I got a gift for this thing. I can't explain it. The trend jumps out of the chart and hits me in the eye. I show it to Alan. He doesn't see it. He still plays with the crop reports and the processors' reports and the commodity newsletters. All that is bullshit! I hit it big because I saw the war coming. That's the only thing I got out of my head and not out of the charts.

"And, Jack, here's what I'm trying to dope out now. Is it a real war? Or a phony war? Forget about Poland. They're finished. Are the Brits and the French gonna do nothing? They might say they did their bit. They declared war. Big deal. And let it go at that. If there ain't gonna be a real war, cocoa is gonna slide back to four and a half cents, and we better get out right now. *But*, and this is what keeps me up all night: If it looks like there is gonna be a real war, then watch out. The beans will shoot up past six cents and we'll make a bundle."

"Well, which is it, Benny?" I asked. "My father says this war is for real. He says Winston Churchill is not gonna let Hitler off the hook."

"Ah, if only I knew for sure," he sighed. "Right now, I'm keeping us long, but you notice I'm only buying about half as many contracts as what I could buy with the equity I have. But stay tuned. It will come to me.

"Meanwhile, you should keep quiet. Don't tell your folks. Don't tell your friends. Don't tell your girlfriend. And don't talk in your sleep!"

51

My New Job

W HEN SCHOOL STARTED the day after Labor Day, my new job
began—general gopher for Goren and Benny, every day
after school and Saturday morning. On school days, I rode my bike
to school and locked it in the bike rack. As soon as school was over,
I got on my bike and rode to Krieger's to put myself at the disposal
of Benny and Goren. I ran out for their sandwiches, coffee, and
donuts. I brought them the early editions of the evening papers. I
ran their personal errands, shopped for them at the grocery and
the drugstore. I took care of their shirts and laundry. I took their
clothes to the cleaner. The idea was for me to relieve them of personal chores so they could devote themselves entirely to our cocoa
business.

One of my regular duties was to take a report to Bobo, just about
every other day. Goren would write a few words on a small note
pad:

Loretta Mauriello	*9/8/39, Close*
Long	*130 December*
Equity	*$41,755*

Goren would place the note in an envelope and seal it. I delivered it to Bobo's office on the second floor of Trucci's. Usually, I
handed it to Frankie or Georgie through a half-opened door.
Sometimes, I was invited in and Bobo would exchange a few words
with me, like *How's everything, Jack? Are you OK? Need anything?*

Sometimes, he gave me a message to deliver. Usually an invitation for Benny and Goren to come to his office at a particular time, always after the trading day. Bobo didn't want to distract them while the commodities markets were open.

Benny kept up his miraculous performance. Our accounts kept getting bigger. By the end of the first week after Labor Day, cocoa was up to 6.55 cents per pound. Our accounts were:

Alan	*$53,179 after pulling out $5,000*
Benny	*$14,369 after pulling out $1,000*
Jack	*$5,461 after pulling out $300*
Bobo	*$41,755 after pulling out $5,000*

Unbelievable! Could they keep it up?

Date	Price	Alan	Benny	Jack	Bobo	Contracts	Trades
—CONTINUED							
9/4	LABOR DAY - CLOSED						
9/5	CASH OUT →	(5000)	(1000)	(300)	(5000)	WITHDRAW CASH	
9/5	.0566	26583	5172	1950	20075	120 40 15 100	4
9/6	.0595	33977	7633	2870	26125	150 50 18 120	2
9/7	.0620	41653	10363	3835	32371	160 55 22 130	3
9/8	.0655	53179	14369	5461	41755	160 65 25 130	3

52

Back to School

For Atlantic City High School kids, back to school in September is a good time of year. The weather is perfect; crisp mornings give way to warm, sunny days under cloudless skies. The rich blue skies of summertime are gone, and gone also are summer's cotton clouds. September and October are the months with the fewest clouds. Sometimes days pass without even a solitary cloud marring the perfection of the day. These are the months of solid blue skies, a paler blue than summer, a last show of color before surrendering to winter's grayness.

Atlantic City's distinctive salty tang is in the air, more pronounced at this time of year; mild breezes so clean and fresh, coming in off the ocean, filling the air, air so delicious you want to bottle it.

The students are glad to be back at school, even though grumbling about it is the rule. No one says it's great to be back in school. That would not be hip, as we called it in those days. That was the new word in vogue. Bellyaching is the order of the day—complaining about summer's farewell and the return to the discipline of high school.

Everyone talks about their summer adventures, enlarged and embellished in the telling. The boys form recess teams for stickball, two-hand touch, and buck-buck. And they study the girls—which ones developed over the summer, who are this semester's lookers. The girls gather in small clusters. They rank the boys—who are this semester's best-looking, most desirable?

It is football season. The varsity players wear their white varsity sweaters with the big blue chenille AC on the chest. They are the school's royalty, adored by the girls, admired jealously by the boys. What is it about the football players? Neither the springtime baseball team nor the mid-winter basketballers get the same respect as the footballers. The wrestlers, boxers, and track-and-fielders go largely unnoticed.

The school day ends at 2:15. The students pour out of the big front doors on Albany Avenue, a colorful parade. They stream down the wide polished granite steps. Half the student body heads to the athletic field to watch the football team practice, to watch the cheerleaders rehearse and the marching band go through maneuvers and formations. Track-and-field meets aren't 'til the spring, but good September weather brings out a handful of track-and-fielders who train throughout the fall and winter. A few wiry track team members run around the oval. On the far side of the field, lean, muscular track-and-fielders practice sprints, hurdles, pole vaults, and broad jumps, while some powerfully built team members hurl the discus and javelin and put the shot.

Some of the students who don't head for the athletic field make their way to one of several nearby drugstores, like Frederick's, which is sort of a teenager's after-school clubhouse where the kids gather for sodas, dancing, gossip, and reading the latest comic books.

The kids who worked after school didn't get to enjoy any of these after-school activities. Eddie returned to his job at the gas station. Business at Mr. Dunauskas's Polish Delicatessen slowed down after Labor Day. He didn't need Eddie in the store in the off-season. He told Eddie, however, that next summer he wanted Eddie to work in the store. My afternoons belonged to Benny James and Alan Goren. When the final period bell rang, Eddie and I and other kids who worked after school joined the stream of kids coming out of the big front doors and down the steps. But only briefly. Instead of heading for the athletic field, or one of the drugstores, or to some other social activity, we headed for work.

I found myself regarding the other students as children. Even the seniors. Even the footballers. They all seemed immature. My summertime exposure to adults and adult things made me feel apart from the other kids. Their preoccupation with social activities and fun and gossip seemed shallow. I saw Rhoda on the arm of a senior fraternity president. They made a handsome couple. Not that I imagined myself a grown-up, but having spent time with the likes of Morris, Benny, Goren, Bobo, and Georgie, Atlantic City High School's prominent students looked to me like children pretending to be grown-ups.

What did the frat president talk about? I overheard a fragment of one conversation. He told Rhoda about a new hazing game he was going to work on this year's pledges. He grinned at its cleverness. Rhoda looked at him admiringly, as though he just invented the telephone.

C'mon, Rhoda, I thought. *You're better than that. He's a kid playing grown-up—and a sadistic one at that.*

It was like the Garden of Eden and the apple. I had a taste of adult life and now the world and everything in it was different. The genie was out of the bottle, and it wasn't going back in.

I started to teach Evie how to play Pinochle. With Bernie away, we needed a fourth. She was pretty smart. Then I asked Blinky to teach her. He started hanging around our house whenever Evie was available for a lesson. We played our first game of four-handed Auction Pinochle with Evie as the fourth. She was terrible. But she got better. By the end of the game, she moved up from terrible to very, very bad. We were determined to keep trying. We needed a fourth.

I had long talks with Eddie. I couldn't spend as much time with him as we used to. I had to scoot down to Krieger's after school and Saturday mornings, and Eddie to his job at the gas station. We spent as much time as we could during the school-day breaks and in the evenings and Sundays. I told him every detail about all that happened in the summer. He wanted to know if I was stuck on Alice. I brushed off the question. "Naw, are you kidding? She's a lot of fun, but that's it." I wasn't about to admit that maybe I was getting soft on a fourteen-year-old girl who was still in Junior High. I described the cocoa business in more detail, but I continued to omit that I was a player. I resolved to tell about my good fortune only after we cashed in. The money that I pulled out so far was in currency, carefully hidden away in a handkerchief box, deep inside the mattress of the upper bunk of the two-tiered bunk bed in Evie's room.

Eddie's summer had been very physical. Hard work, some fooling around with local girls, camaraderie with his cousins. He never read a book all summer or talked about anything but girls, work, and sports. He described in detail how he built the wind-driven well. I was in awe of his accomplishment. He knew there was a war in Europe. He could find Danzig and Austria and Czechoslovakia on the map. To him, the war was a faraway thing. It had no bearing on him or on our country. When I said that Uncle Ted's produce would bring higher prices this harvest season because the war was pushing up the prices of all commodities, he asked, even after I described how the cocoa futures work, "What is a commodity and what does a war in Europe have to do with the price of Uncle Ted's corn and tomatoes?" It was that summer when I first understood that people generally don't realize their own limitations. It's because a person sees and understands everything within the boundaries of what he knows. He sees into the farthest corner of the world he knows. So he thinks that he knows everything that he ought to know. That there is a universe outside the world he knows is an abstraction. Something is out there, beyond. He knows that. But so what? He can't see it or grasp it. It does not affect the daily life of living within the world he knows, so it is unimportant, of no consequence in his life.

A mediocre businessman, for example, thinks he understands everything there is to know about the business he is in. But what he understands maybe is only a small sphere inside the much-larger sphere of what his biggest competitor knows and understands. Inside the smaller sphere, he sees, knows, and understands everything. He can't comprehend how much more his chief competitor knows, only that the competitor knows more, but the *more* is an abstraction, since he doesn't know one iota of the *more*.

My own life used to be complete without knowing Joseph Conrad or Harold Lamb. Morris pushed my boundaries out. I never knew there could be a guy like Benny. He pushed my boundaries out farther. And Goren! He must have doubled the size of my world. He showed me things I never could have imagined. He pointed to things that were still covered and left it to me to learn to peel back the covers. And Bobo. Through his eyes, I saw a different world altogether, the world as a jungle. In Bobo's world, predators roamed and prey had to be ever vigilant.

I tried to explain these things to Eddie. He listened. He questioned me. He absorbed some of what I was saying. Most of it he didn't, because while my ability to describe events was good enough for a simple account of what happened, I tried but only succeeded in a limited way to describe the reasons for things. How could I when most of what I saw that summer was over my head?

There was a change in the relationship between Eddie and me. I used to look to Eddie for leadership in all things. Now it seemed our roles were reversing. He was seeing me as a reservoir of experience and understanding. The cocoa story really grabbed him. He couldn't get over the amount of money that could be made on a one cent a pound increase in the price of the beans. I went through the arithmetic with him several times: a penny a pound means twenty dollars a ton. A contract is ten tons. So a penny a pound means two hundred dollars a contract.

When Eddie heard what Goren and Benny had earned on September 1—the day the war began—his awestruck comment was, "I work at the garage for twenty cents an hour! Your dad probably makes thirty or forty bucks a week. What is wrong with this picture?"

How about me? I worked at Krilow's for $1.05 a day. The day the war started, I made $1,024 with cocoa. *In one day!* A week later, on September 8, I made $1,626. *In one day!* I couldn't tell that to Eddie. Not yet. Not until I cashed in.

***

I took Alice to the movies on Friday night. We saw *The Man in the Iron Mask*, with Louis Hayward and Joan Bennett. What a movie! The mask itself was a grim and cruel iron helmet. It covered the entire head and locked at the neck. Alice buried her head in my shoulder and shuddered whenever the fearsome thing came on screen. That loathsome mask was in my dreams for months. Louis Hayward as the good twin was so handsome, so brave, so good. Joan Bennett was so beautiful, equally brave and good. Louis Hayward as the bad twin was evil, unspeakably so, but splendid in his rich satin coats and handsome plumage.

Before the movie, there was a Pathe newsreel about the war in Europe, still in its first month. The newsreel showed the massive gun emplacements on the French Maginot Line and the intricate system of underground bunkers and passageways. "An impenetrable defensive line," as the narrator called it. Then the newsreel showed the German Siegfried Line, similar to the Maginot Line but, according to the narrator, not as sophisticated as the Maginot Line, and incomplete in some sections. The front was quiet, with only sporadic firing as patrols probed at each other. The two defensive lines were admirably suited for the World War of 1914–1918.

There was footage of scores of merchant ships being sunk, gray ships bellowing black smoke, the newsreel flickering and jumping as one ship after another was shown sinking beneath dark water. Some ships were the victims of U-boats; some were sunk by German surface raiders. Most notorious of the surface raiders was *Graf Spee*, the mysterious pocket battleship, a ghostly warship that could track a convoy from a distance of ten miles and fire its eleven-inch guns at its targets at will. A typical convoy was escorted by several British destroyers and light cruisers, which were powerless to engage *Graf Spee*, as the range of their guns was only three or four miles for a destroyer's four-inch guns, and only five or six miles for a light cruiser's six-inch guns.

The newsreel's most dramatic shots were of the German war machine in Poland, racing, almost unimpeded, toward Warsaw. Stuka dive-bombers dropped their charges on Polish military and civilian targets with impunity. The Stuka had strategically placed air vents in its wings, designed to create a terrifying whine as the plane went into its dive to deliver its bombs. There was no Polish Air Force. Messerschmitts and Stukas bombed and strafed Polish army units without interference. German mechanized columns rolled over the Polish landscape, meeting no resistance.

There was one scene that haunts me to this day. It was a Polish cavalry charge, flags and sabres held aloft, with all the pomp and splendor of a nineteenth-century Warner Bros. epic. They charged a phalanx of German tanks and armored cars, which cut down the riders like straw. While the British and French were going to try to fight the Great War all over again, the Poles were trying to fight the Crimean.

53

Letter to Bernie

Atlantic City

September 9, 1939

Dear Bernie:

I am so sorry about your uncle. And I am so sorry for you. What a rotten break. I hope you can get away from there soon enough to get back in our class. It won't be the same without you.

So much happened to me this summer, I don't know how to begin to tell you. Too much to write. It will have to keep until we meet, which I hope will be soon.

I can say this much. I never had such a summer. I been spending time with adults all summer. Eddie was away. I saw Blinky only once in a while, but mostly I was with one of the guys I worked with, a guy named Benny James, and some of his friends. He is twenty-five. His friends are all older. So I been with all these adults all summer most of the time. They treat me like a grown-up. It's great. They expect me to act like an adult and do things like an adult so I do my best. I feel like I went from being fifteen to being twenty-five in ten weeks. You wouldn't believe some of the things that happened this summer. I hardly believe it myself. Wait 'til we get together. What stories I have to tell you.

School started Tuesday. It seems so tame. All the guys and girls seem so immature. I don't have a swelled head or anything; it's just that I've been involved in grown-up things.

Take Rhoda, for example. She looks at me like a kid, but I look at her like a kid. Even the frat guys she goes with, they look like kids to me. They smoke and drink beer and think they are cool. But to me, they are children playing at being grown up.

We're going to miss you for the Pinochle game. Me and Blinky are teaching Evie to play. I did not have trouble getting Blinky to teach her. He likes her, and he knows the game the best, but I told him to keep hands off. I guess we are better with a rotten fourth than no fourth at all.

Eddie grew more than an inch. Working at his uncle's farm was like working out all day long. He looks fantastic. He is hard as a rock. I put on a few pounds. Maybe grew a half-inch. Feeling good. Now that summer is over, I been thinking about the Mackeys again. Have not run into them because I stay away from Annapolis Avenue. Don't know what to do. Eddie and me talk about it but we don't have a plan. Tell you what, though, you should see Eddie. I bet he could take Tom Mackey.

I hope you will be back here soon. We miss you.

Your friend,
Jack

54

Another Errand for Bobo

A FEW DAYS after Labor Day, Bobo sent Georgie to bring me to Bobo's office on the second floor of Trucci's. Bobo had another errand for me.

"I hope this isn't another joke, Mr. Truck," I said, respectfully.

"No, son," Bobo said, earnestly. "This is serious business, serious as it gets. You can help me. I don't know anybody else over here that could do it as good as I think you could."

What was the errand? Bobo explained.

The boss of Ventnor City, Bobo's counterpart in Ventnor, was a man named Sal DiMarco. It seemed that DiMarco wanted to try a grab at Bobo's territory from Albany Avenue to Montgomery Avenue. They are the last ten blocks in Atlantic City. Albany Avenue, where the Black Horse Pike enters Atlantic City, and where the World War monument stands on Atlantic Avenue, always seemed like the natural geographic boundary of Atlantic City and Ventnor. Instead, Atlantic City continues south, below Albany Avenue, for another ten blocks until it reaches the Ventnor City line at Jackson Avenue. On the map, it looks like Atlantic City's tail. It looks as if it ought to be detached from Atlantic City and given to Ventnor.

It was in this area, Atlantic City's tail, that I lived. Ventnor began eight blocks farther south.

One of Bobo's *mani* told Georgie that DiMarco arranged for a meeting and invited all of Bobo's *piedi* who worked that area. Bobo didn't think any of his men would go to such a meeting. Bobo thought DiMarco was foolish to try such a thing. Bobo said DiMarco should have propositioned Bobo's *piedi* one at a time. Bringing them together would be scary for Bobo's men. It was unlikely that any would be brave enough to come to such a meeting. Bobo was puzzled.

"I don't get it," Bobo mused. "DiMarco is not stupid. Does he think any of my boys will show up? They know better. It don't figure. Those territories are mine. I ain't gonna let any go. Any of my boys who tries to break away ... they know what happens. And DiMarco. What's his game? Is he lookin' for a war over here? Can't be. He is not nuts. He only has three or four soldiers. It won't be a war. It will be a massacre. And why does he proposition only the *piedi*? Why not the *mani* as well?"

Georgie thought he knew the answer: "Number one, Bobo, DiMarco must have propositioned each one of the boys, one at a time. This meeting is a show of strength that he's got a few of our boys in his pocket. Number two, DiMarco must have Chief Leonard's blessing for this [referring to Atlantic City's Police Chief]. He can't even think to operate in those territories without the Chief. It's still Atlantic City. It ain't Ventnor. Number three, DiMarco must be offering some months without any dues. Those guys pay us an average of about fifty bucks a week. And I bet he figures to offer our *piedi* the bookmaking on top of the numbers. He's gonna try to cut out our *mani* and give it to the *piedi*. That is an offer that our *piedi* will want, if any of 'em have the balls to join DiMarco, plus an introductory special to come with him, like four, five months no dues to pay, and he must be pitching them that he has the Chief, and they will be protected."

"That's crazy," Bobo said. "The Chief ain't goin' to double-cross me. He's mine. Him and the Lieutenant and the DA. Do they think I'm gonna sit still with my thumb up my ass while my territory gets broken off?"

"Money, Bobo," Georgie said, quietly. "I'm only guessing. But suppose DiMarco is laying heavy money on the Chief and the Lieutenant? And suppose you get a visit from the Chief and the Chief tells you to lay off DiMarco south of Albany Avenue. You ain't gonna argue with the Chief."

After relaying this conversation, Bobo turned to me, "You got the story, Jack? What I want is for you to check out this meeting. I want to know who comes and as much as you can hear what gets said."

"How about the man who told Georgie about it, Mr. Truck?" I questioned. "Why don't you tell him to go to the meeting and then tell you about it?"

"You're a hunnerd percent right over here," Bobo answered, "except my *mane* wasn't invited. He heard about it from his cousin. She's fuckin' one a DiMarco's boys, that dumb fuck, Vincent. I don't know why DiMarco keeps him, he's so fuckin' dumb. And he runs at the mouth." He looked at me with that shark dead-eye look. "Now look here, son. If I had anybody else what could do this ... but you're my best bet. I gotta know who shows up."

"How do you want me to do it, Mr. Truck? And when is it?"

The meeting was for the next evening at 8:00. Bobo and Georgie laid out the plan. Georgie made the arrangements.

***

So it was that the following evening, nervous and scared, dressed in a white waiter's jacket and black pants with satin stripes, wearing a white paper cap with blue piping and a pair of eyeglasses with plain glass lenses, I pushed a serving cart along the twentieth floor corridor of the Ambassador Hotel, headed for Room 2010. My cart held a variety of sandwiches, potato salad, a bowl of peeled hard-boiled eggs, macaroni salad, coleslaw, cookies, sodas, and a coffee urn. I had a room service order in my pocket. A man was seated on a wooden chair, tilted back against the wall of the corridor, near the door to Room 2010. He was reading a racing form and smoking a cigarette. He had a glass ashtray balanced on his knee, half-filled with cigarette butts. He looked up as I wheeled my cart past him and stopped in front of the door. I took the room service bill from my breast pocket and pretended to study it to be sure I was at the right door. Before I could knock, the man lowered the chair and said, "Hey, kid, whatcha doin'?"

"Room service," I said, "for Room 2010."

"Whatcha got?"

"Let's see," I said, studying the room service order, "six ham and cheese on rye, six bacon, lettuce, and tomato on white, six combo sliced turkey and roast beef on rye, two dozen Danish, assorted, two pounds potato salad, two ..."

"OK, OK. G'wan." He tilted back the chair and returned to his reading. "Wait a second, kid, gimme a sandwich, one of them combo sandwiches and a Coke."

"Yessir," I said. I handed him a sandwich and opened a Coke for him. *I'm lucky,* I thought. *This dope should have taken the cart from me and sent me away. He should never let me get to see the inside of the room. He's lazy and a dope.*

I knocked on the door. "Room service for Room 2010." I called it out vigorously, figuring I wouldn't sound so nervous if I put some spirit into my announcement. The door opened. A man looked out, "Where the fuck is Vincent? Vincent, whyn't ya get offa you ass? Hey, Sal," he called out over his shoulder, into the room, "it's the food cart. Did you order it?"

"No," answered the man called Sal. "Must be Pauli ordered it when he booked the room. C'mon in, kid."

Forty-five minutes later, I was in Bobo's office describing the adventure. I knew which one was Sal. I didn't have to describe him. I described the man in the hallway, Vincent. I described the man who opened the door. I said I knew he wasn't Pauli. Bobo and Georgie said in unison, "Little Tony and Gino." I described each of the other four men, as best as I could recall. Bobo and Georgie were able to identify three from my description, three of Bobo's *piedi*. The fourth man was a puzzle to them. They asked me to describe him again and again. I was afraid I missed something about him, but when I focused my mind's eye on him alone, and erased the others, I could see him clearly. I described his height, his build, his hair color, and the way he combed it. I said he had a mustache and he smoked a cigar.

"Describe the muzzy, Jack."

"It was thick, real black, like his hair, straight across, like a rectangle, solid. Wait a second," I said. "It's the Police Chief! I remember now. I saw him in the Memorial Day Parade. It was him, not in uniform, but it was him."

"*The fuckin' Chief,*" Bobo said, his face flushed. "You were right, Georgie. That prick. Workin' both sides."

Then to me, "Jack, did ya hear anything anybody said?"

"I wasn't there that long, Mr. Truck. I tried to hang around. That guy you said was Gino said *What are you waitin' for, kid*? I said I have to get the room service order signed. He grabbed it and looked for a pencil. That used up a little time. Then he gave it back to me with a five-dollar tip and told me I could go. Here's the five dollars, Mr. Truck."

"Did you hear anything at all?" Bobo asked, waving away my offer of the five-dollar bill.

"The guy you said was Little Tony, said *It's a big chance to take for fifty bucks a week*. Mr. DiMarco said *You are missing the main thing. Right now, you only got numbers. You can have everything in your territory. You get the horses, the games, the junk and the junkies and the whores. You get it all. It will cost you, but you're gonna milk your territory for a lot more than now*. That's all I heard."

"Jack, you did real good. You are a good boy. Here's fifty bucks. Keep the fiver. Thanks for what you did over here. This is between you and me and Georgie, OK? Not a word to *anybody*, not even Frankie. I'll tell Frankie if he needs to know. This is just between us. *Appena fra noi*. OK? Remember, you're mine now. You're one of us."

"Sure, Mr. Truck."

***

The next day, a car ran out of control and struck and killed Little Tony as he was stepping off the pavement to cross Ventnor Avenue. His girlfriend was with him. She survived, but she was badly crippled. It was a hit-and-run. The car was not identified.

Two days later, one of the other men from the meeting in Room 2010 was killed in a hunting accident. Another, who liked to cruise around the island in his Chris-Craft speedboat, died when the boat caught fire and exploded. Ten days later, soon after the Miss America Pageant, Chief Leonard's beautiful nineteen-year-old daughter, 1939's Miss Atlantic City, was raped, beaten, stripped naked, and left unconscious under the boardwalk at Michigan Avenue. The Atlantic City Police Department and detectives gave the case top priority.

Later on, I learned from Georgie that Bobo redistributed the territories of the three men who died. He gave the territories to *piedi* who had adjoining territories and did not go to the meeting in Room 2010. He told them to take care of their new territories and to *take good care of themselves.*

Georgie also told me that Bobo paid a call on Chief Leonard to express his sympathy for what happened to the Chief's daughter. Bobo offered to help search for the rapist. The Chief thanked him, but said the Atlantic City Detectives were hard at work and had a few leads.

Two weeks later, when the investigation was going nowhere, one of Bobo's men was fishing in the back bay and came across a body in the reeds and high grasses alongside one of the channels. It was a white male, mid-twenties, fair-haired, about five-foot eight-inches, 160 pounds. The body seemed to fit the description that the Chief's daughter gave of the rapist. She went to the morgue and identified him, more by his clothes and the tattoos on the back of his hands and on his arms than by his features, which were badly decomposed by then. The cause of death was a crushing blow to the back of the head.

The Chief couldn't get over it, that Bobo's man found the body. What a coincidence. The detectives had run out of leads. The Chief thought the rapist would never be found.

Benny said to me, "Pretty slick, Jack. Imagine you are the Chief. What would you be thinking?"

"Tell me, Benny," I asked. "What would I be thinking?"

"You would be thinking, *Maybe Bobo arranged for that tattooed drifter to rape the girl. A warning, you might say, for trying to double-cross Bobo, for planning to protect Sal DiMarco's grab at Bobo's territories south of Albany Avenue. The Chief would think Bobo could arrange the rape. Nobody could ever tie the rape to Bobo. Bobo could also arrange to do away with the rapist. But, on the other hand, maybe not. Maybe Bobo had nothing to do with the rape. Those three accidental deaths ... who can tell? That sure looks like Bobo's work, but who can tell? But why would Bobo come up with the rapist's body? Did Bobo kill the rapist? Was that how Bobo paid him off? Or did Bobo have nothing to do with the rape, but his men found the rapist and killed him as a favor to the Chief?* The Chief will never know, but he will never try to double-cross Bobo again. He'll stay in line from now on, either out of fear or out of gratitude. He won't take any chances."

Benny was right; it was complicated. I felt a chill from being so close to the action. Bobo frightened me. I wished I never met him.

55

Beach Party

IDATED ALICE Keever regularly after our first date. Sometimes we went to a movie; sometimes we went to Garden Pier; always we ended up in the rolling chair storage shed. Alice was sticking to her rules. She wouldn't let me go any further than on our first date. I was OK with that. She was only fourteen.

I rode my bike on our dates, with Alice perched on the top bar of the frame. She sat facing left, on the upper horizontal strut of the frame, between the handlebars and the seat. She sort of turned her body forward and gripped the handlebars. She steadied herself with her left foot on the diagonal bar that joins the handlebar stem to the pedal mechanism. She rested her right knee across the upper bar, the horizontal one. I thought she looked like an English horsewoman riding sidesaddle.

Riding my bike on our dates served more than one purpose: One, it was good transportation; two, I liked the feel of her back against my chest; and three, I didn't want to repeat the uncomfortable experience of our first date when I had to endure the embarrassment and discomfort of the long walk home with the wet aftermath of our petting congealing inside my pants.

The first time I dated her was in reaction to being rejected by Rhoda. I recall that I started looking at her body admiringly as that evening progressed. The fluidity of her dancing and the contact with her body aroused me until by the time the concert ended, I couldn't wait to get my hands on her.

I still admired Rhoda's beauty. Alice was an ordinary girl with a beautiful complexion and a nice shape who happened to be a lot of fun, but she didn't measure up to Rhoda in the beauty department. I was nervous on that first date about taking Alice into the rolling chair storage shed. Certainly she knew what I was after. I was surprised at her willingness and enthusiasm and even as I enjoyed her responsiveness, I wondered if she was an easy mark.

As I got to know her, the more I liked her. She was easy to be with. She was enthusiastic and upbeat about everything. We didn't talk about her other dates or experiences with boys. Sometimes I thought she never had any. I dismissed that notion as conceit. She never asked me about other girls. So we wondered about each other as we drew closer and more committed to each other.

Soon after school began, the fraternities planned an evening beach party bonfire and hot dog roast—open to all students, an Atlantic City High School September tradition. The fraternity houses chipped in to buy the soda, hot dogs, and marshmallows. Boys scavenged the beach and construction sites days in advance for driftwood and lumber, and they shaved long sticks into spears for hot dog and marshmallow roasting.

The day of the beach party was a warm September day with a pure blue sky that flamed into brilliant yellows and oranges at dusk when the sun started to drop behind the tree line on the mainland. The ocean takes all summer to warm up. By late August, it gets to a comfortable seventy degrees and stays that way well into September. It was ideal weather for the beach party.

We went in a group—Eddie and Blinky and me and Alice and two of her friends, Marilyn and Sandra. The girls brought blankets. The girls always think of such things. The boys brought big bath towels. We all wore swimsuits under our shorts and ACHS sweatshirts. A roaring bonfire was already lit. Flames reached high into the darkening sky. The fire crackled. Sparks flew upward. Off to one side there were open cartons of hot dogs and hot dog rolls and marshmallows and a metal trash can filled with ice and loaded with soda bottles. There was even a condiments table with pickles, relish, and mustard.

A radio stood on the condiments table with its cord stretched back fifty yards along the beach to an electrical outlet at the base of a boardwalk light pole. A few days before the beach party, the student body president asked Eddie if he could figure out how to get electricity for the radio. Last year, they strung together thirteen extension cords and ran them across the beach and up onto the boardwalk and into a store. Seven people walking on the boardwalk tripped over the extension cords. That was a problem. This year, the storeowner said it was dangerous and didn't want to be bothered. So Eddie borrowed some cable and a transformer and an electric socket from the electric shop teacher. There's an electric line that runs under the boardwalk to bring electricity to the light poles. Eddie spliced into it.

The radio filled the night with the music of the big bands. Boys and girls danced on the sand, dark figures silhouetted against the fire. Groups stood in small circles or sat or sprawled on the sand or on blankets. Dozens of kids squatted around the fire roasting speared hot dogs and marshmallows. Each fraternity formed its own big circle of blankets. Boys and girls leaned against one another or lay across laps, or danced in the center of their circle. In the undulating orange light, I caught a glimpse of Rhoda, lying on a blanket, the fraternity president seated at her side, leaning over her, their faces almost touching. The shadows made her even more beautiful. I was jealous of him and his good looks and easy manner.

Some twenty or thirty boys and girls were in the surf, carrying the sounds of the party into the ocean—laughter, singing, the hubbub of many voices trying to be heard above the general din. It was a perfect night for the party. The sun drew down its last fingers of light. Darkness fell. The early moon rose out of the ocean, big, pale yellow, accompanied by the evening star, low in the east.

Alice held my arm. "That is Venus," she said, pointing to the evening star. We could see one another's faces, red and dark, lit by the bonfire flames. "Sometimes it is the first star we see at night. Then sometimes, it is the morning star, and it's the last star to fade away in the morning. That's because it is really a planet, not a star. It moves across the sky. The stars don't move."

"I don't know the stars," I said. "Only the Big Dipper and the North Star."

She looked skyward. "I know some of the constellations," she said. There are more than a hundred. I knew a few. She held me closer and pointed skyward. "There is Capricorn. There is Gemini. There is Orion the Hunter. And there is Sirius, the Dog Star at the left of Orion's heel, and there is the Little Dipper, and there is Taurus the Bull, and there is Hydra the Serpent. I know a few more, but I can never find them."

I asked her how come she knew about the stars. She said she read lots of things, on all subjects. She said she had a particular interest in the history of the Earth and the planets. She said she wanted to study biology and geology and maybe anthropology. She said there's so much to know. How could she learn it all? She wanted to be a naturalist.

"I don't know what a naturalist is," I said.

"A naturalist studies animals, birds, plants, rock formations, land masses, weather," she explained. "Not very exciting to most people. But I like it."

"How does a naturalist earn a living?" I asked.

"Working for a research company," she explained, "or a college, or the government. Naturalists travel all over the world. They examine plants and animals. For example, in Australia, which is not connected to any other continent, the animals are not like anywhere else in the world. And the plants are different from anywhere else. It's like a different world. Everywhere else in the world, the dominant animal is a mammal. That includes us, human beings. But in Australia, the dominant animal is a marsupial, where the mother carries her babies in a pouch until they're ready to be on their own. The life forms on Australia followed a different evolutionary trail because it is a separate continent. Life forms from the other continents had no way to migrate to Australia. Don't you find that interesting?"

Yes, I did. Even more interesting was Alice herself. I had given up on Rhoda, who was beyond my reach. Was I *settling* for Alice?

We horsed around with Eddie and Blinky and the other girls. We ate at the bonfire. We danced. We played tag. We sprawled on the blankets.

The football team formed their own circle, filled with the entire 36-man squad and adoring girls. They sang all the college songs. They laughed, danced, tossed a football in the dim light. The first string formed up and ran plays on the sand, to the gleeful applause of the girls.

I saw Eddie grab a kiss from Sandra. She didn't respond, but she didn't shrink from it. It looked like a half-hearted effort by Eddie. I thought he was really not interested, just that he thought it was expected of him. Blinky tried to plant one on Marilyn, but she held him off and looked away.

"Everyone in the water!" Eddie shouted. "Last one in is a rusty mule." We stripped off our sweatshirts, shorts, and sneakers and away we raced into the surf, throwing ourselves into the first breaking wave. Alice's figure looked terrific in her black one-piece swimsuit.

The sea was calm. I asked Alice if she could swim. She could. We swam out beyond the breakers. The water was warm, black, with slow, easy, shallow swells, only a faint luminescence where our strokes broke the water into pale sparkles. Once out beyond the breakers, we treaded water, facing the beach, using slow rhythmic arm and leg movements under the water to keep afloat, not breaking the water's surface. The flames of the bonfire were reflected on the water, shimmers of orange and red dancing on the blackness of the ocean. Other heads bobbed in the water between us and the beach, black silhouettes. The distant flames and the pale moonlight let me make out Alice's features. Her wet hair hung about her face like an Egyptian headdress, a clean line of straight hair across her forehead, a shining headdress around her head and down and over her shoulders halfway down her back.

"Your hair is so long," I said.

"Because it's wet and it all fell down."

"I like it. You should always wear it that way."

"No way. Everybody would think I'm Sheena, the Jungle Girl."

"You'd be *my* jungle girl," I couldn't believe I said it. She swam toward me and kissed me, the salty water lending a briny pungency to her kiss. The water made her body feel slick and slippery. I palmed her breast. It was erotic, feeling her that way in the warm, dark water.

"Jack, I love you," she said.

I didn't have a response for that one. "Alice," I stammered, "that's ... that's ... You shouldn't say that. We're just kids. You don't mean that."

"I embarrassed you, didn't I?" she said. "That's all right. I don't expect you to say anything. It's just how I feel at this moment. I like to say what I feel." She laughed, that infectious laugh. "Maybe the feeling will pass. Don't worry." She clung to me, her face raised to me, her eyes shining.

"Are you sure you're fourteen?" I said, drawing her closer. "Sometimes you talk like you're thirty."

"I know I'll never get by on good looks," she said, "so I better be able to talk intelligently."

"You look pretty good to me," I said.

I remembered the way Gracie looked at Barry Zoll that day on the pavilion. I remembered thinking how wonderful it was to be adored by a girl like Gracie.

I threw my arms around her, and as we almost went under, I gurgled, "I love you, too, Alice."

She gurgled in response, "Don't worry, Jack. You don't have to love me tomorrow."

56

Monday, September 11

BENNY CALLED FOR a special meeting on Monday, September 11. We met at Zena's parlor at 7:30. As usual, she hung out the *Closed* sign and she brewed tea.

Benny wasted no time on niceties. He was flushed. He was disheveled. His shirt was stained with perspiration. He started right in. He stood. He paced. He never sat. He chain-smoked, not even finishing one cigarette before he lit another on it.

"Guys, I been walkin' and thinkin' since the market closed. The beans closed at 6.60 cents. We made a killing since the war started. Alan, how much are the accounts?"

Goren produced his chart:

Alan	*$54,999 after $5,000 withdrawn*
Benny	*$15,082 after $1,000 withdrawn*
Jack	*$5,743 after $300 withdrawn*
Bobo	*$43,139 after $5,000 withdrawn*

"Alan," Benny asked, "did you ever think you would be worth $60,000?"

"No, Benny," Goren said, "never. And I never would. It's you who did it. What now?"

"This is why I called this meeting." He blew a plume of smoke in the air. "Up to now, the market is saying this is a real war. Prices are up because war makes shortages. But here's what's come to me. I been studying everything and reading everything. This war is a *phony*!" He paced back and forth in the small parlor. He drove his fist into his palm. "Poland is finished," he said. "The Russians will move in from the East. Poland will be divided up between Hitler and Stalin. It's as good as over. Meanwhile, is anything going on between France and Germany? Nothing. Between England and Germany? Nothing. A few speeches. Some ships sunk. Some English soldiers heading for France. The Brits and the French are saving face. They ain't goin' to war. It's make pretend."

He continued to pace. He sought out our faces, one by one, with bloodshot eyes. "The war in Poland will be finished any day. Then what? You know what I think? Then *nothing*! The Germans and the English and the French, they'll sit on their asses for a while and then they'll make peace. That's what I think. I been thinkin' about this all day, tryin' to get a feel for it. Tryin' to read and listen." He sat. He paused. He blew more smoke. He leaned forward and spoke. Some of the agitation left him. "Today's chart told me higher prices are comin'. But for the first time, I don't believe the charts. They're all gonna be fooled. Any day now, they'll all see what I see. The war is a *phony*. Commodity prices are peaking *right here*! From now on, they're headed down, down, down. Back to where they were before the war started." He stood again and resumed pacing. "Zena, look in that goddamn ball and tell me if I'm right or wrong."

"Benny," she said, through carefully pursed lips, "I won't even take a breath or move a finger. You're not going to read anything into me tonight."

"Alan," Benny asked, "give me a hand here. What's happening?"

By now, the air was so thick with cigarette smoke, it was getting hard to breathe. Zena opened the door and pushed it back and forth like a fan to drive out some smoke.

Goren was silent for a few moments, collecting his thoughts, choosing his words. "I think this is a real war," Goren answered. "You are right about the British and French. They are not going to mount an offensive. What for? They can't save Poland." He paused. "And they don't know how tight the Russians are with Hitler. Last time the Russians were one of the Allies. Germany had to fight on two fronts. This time, the Russians are allies with Hitler. The German rear is safe. The English and French are hoping the war doesn't turn real. But they are wrong. Once Hitler gets tidied up in Poland, he's going to turn on France. It will be like the last time. The French will cave, but the English will prop them up. Don't forget, Hitler is facing Churchill now, not Chamberlain. Churchill means business. He has a hatred of Hitler and the Nazis and everything they stand for. It will turn into a real war. Last time, it took the French and English and Americans and Italians and Russians to bring down Germany. This time, we're staying out. So Hitler figures he is going to have an easy time of it. He figures to roll over France like he rolled over Poland. He is not looking to let the English and the French off the hook. I say this is a real war. Not only that, Benny, I'm afraid we're going to get dragged in."

"OK, Alan," Benny said, flopping into the sofa, "maybe you're right. But even so, look what you said. You said *Once Hitler gets tidied up in Poland*. That could be months. Meanwhile, the war will stagnate. Everybody will say it's a phony. Commodity prices will drop."

"So what do you want to do, Benny?" asked Goren.

"Big decision, guys. I want to sell out tomorrow *and go short!*"

"Benny, you're a wild man," Goren said.

Benny even looked wild. He was pacing again.

"Alan," he said, "if I'm right, the beans will drop a penny or penny and a half. Soon. That's two or three hundred bucks a contract. We can double what we have. I want to do it. I feel it. I know it's right. If you want to go light, you can, but I'm going to do it big. This is the chance of a lifetime. Just like I called the big run-up a few days before the war started. That's how I'm calling the top. What say? Zena, for Chrissake, give me a hand here. What do you say? Jack, speak up."

Zena was silent. So was I.

Goren broke the silence. "Benny, I pulled out five grand. That's about what I had when I met you. I'll pull out another five. You pull out $2,000. Jack, you pull out $1,000. I'll pull out another $5,000 for Bobo. I'm going to let the rest ride. I'll go short up to 160 contracts. I believe in you. You're a goddamn clairvoyant." He turned to Zena. "Sorry, Zena, I don't mean any disrespect. You're a clairvoyant too, but you seem to be closed for new business."

Benny turned to me. "Jack," he said, "I'm increasing my positions on the short side. I'm moving up to eighty contracts, short. I want to move you up with me. Are you game for it?"

I pondered that one for a bit. Should I cut down? I had about $246 in the mattress and about $5,700 at Krieger's. I had more than three times what my father accumulated from nineteen years' work. Benny was waiting, raised eyebrows making a question mark on his face. "I'm with you, Benny," I said. "Do for me what you're doing for yourself."

"Good boy," Benny said. "I'll get you up to fifty contracts in no time. You won't be sorry."

Date	Price	Alan	Benny	Jack	Bobo	Contracts	Trades
		——CONTINUED					
9/4	LABOR DAY - CLOSED						
9/5	CASH OUT ⟶	(5000)	(1000)	(300)	(5000)	WITHDRAW CASH	
9/5	.0566	26583	5172	1950	20075	120 40 15 100	4
9/6	.0595	33927	7633	2870	26125	150 50 18 120	2
9/7	.0620	41653	10363	3835	32371	160 55 22 130	3
9/8	.0655	53179	14369	5461	41755	160 65 25 130	3
9/11	.0660	54999	15082	5743	43139	160 65 25 130	2
9/11	SWITCH TO SHORT						

57

Miss America Parade

THE IDEA BEHIND Atlantic City's Annual Miss America Pageant was to keep the tourist season alive for ten days beyond Labor Day. The Monday after Labor Day is when the beauties started to arrive. The newspapers showed them arriving, splashing in the surf and gathering for the traditional group photo where the girls posed between the columns of the colonnade across the board-walk from Convention Hall. The preliminary contests started on Wednesday and went on during the week, followed by the final judging in Convention Hall on Saturday night.

On Friday evening, before the final day, the contestants were dis-played in a colorful boardwalk parade, complete with marching bands and open convertibles for the dignitaries. The contestants themselves rode on elaborate theme floats representing their states. The floats were quite marvelous. They were decorated with all kinds of imaginative features, such as a court of ladies-in-waiting, stair-ways, balconies, elevated thrones, canopies, arches, lots of flowers, statuary, and even working fountains, miniature waterfalls, and changing colored lights. The Miss America Parade was a major Atlantic City event. Like the Memorial Day Parade, the Miss America Parade brought out thousands of spectators who lined the boardwalk along the entire length of the parade. Finding a good observation point was a challenge.

I found a great spot for us. It was a one-story building not far from Royce's Shooting Gallery. The front of the building ended in a parapet, which extended two feet above the roof. I knew how to get onto the roof. There was an iron stepladder bolted to the rear wall in the alley behind the building.

I asked Alice to join Eddie, Blinky, and me. She said sure and asked to invite Marilyn and Sandra, which was OK with me. Then my mother said I had to take Evie and her friends. I didn't even grumble because I knew it wouldn't help. Evie was enthusiastic. She said she'd invite two friends. I groaned, just like Memorial Day. "No," Evie said, "I had *three* friends on Memorial Day."

So that was our group, all nine of us. The roof idea was great. We were only thirty feet away from the contestants. Both sides of the boardwalk were packed with spectators two and three deep, just like at the Memorial Day Parade. We sat on the parapet, our legs hanging over the ledge. I considered myself the sponsor of the event, so I felt it was my responsibility to caution everybody to sit still, no squirming or horseplay. I didn't want anyone falling off with me in charge.

Eddie sat on my right. Alice climbed on the parapet next to me on my left. She liked to hang on my left arm, which I didn't mind at all. Evie squeezed between me and Eddie. Eddie moved over to make room for her with a small grunt. It was obvious that Evie had a crush on Eddie and that it was unreciprocated.

The parade started at 7:00. It was dusk. I commented that only a few weeks ago, daylight was lasting until after 9:00. It was getting dark so early.

"Today is the fifteenth of the month," Alice said. "Next week will be the Autumnal Equinox. That day, we'll have twelve hours of daylight and twelve hours of darkness."

"Where did you learn that?" I asked her.

"We had that in eighth-grade science. Didn't you?"

I did. I remembered the term. I liked its sound. And I liked the sounds of the *Vernal Equinox,* the *Winter Solstice,* the *Summer Solstice.* I remembered what they were but not why they happened. Alice did. She explained about the Earth's axis being tilted and all that. The girl knew everything. Was I so dumb, or was she something special?

The parade began about a mile up-island of where we were. We saw it approaching. As usual, the Atlantic City High School Drum and Bugle Corps led the way. There were more than fifty floats. All the forty-eight states were represented plus a few cities and also Hawaii and Alaska, which weren't states in 1939. There was a Miss New York City, as well as a Miss New York State and a Miss Atlantic City, as well as a Miss New Jersey. Miss Atlantic City was Police Chief Leonard's daughter, who didn't make it as Miss New Jersey, but made a beautiful Miss Atlantic City. I thought she was better looking than Miss New Jersey.

Police Chief Leonard passed, relaxed, in full uniform, in the rear of an open convertible smoking a cigar. Another uniformed officer sat alongside. Chief Leonard was the man I identified a week earlier at the Sal DiMarco meeting. Not long after the pageant the Chief's daughter would be raped and beaten, but on this particular evening the Chief and Miss Atlantic City both were in fine form and good spirits.

The parade passed—floats, bands, drum majorettes. Music and drumbeats filled the air. The beauties smiled and waved. The ladies-in-waiting smiled and waved. The dignitaries in the open convertibles smiled and waved. There was a war in Europe. Not here. Here, things were looking up. The Depression was still with us, but already our economy was benefiting from the war in Europe. The Depression was losing its grip.

I thought of the contrast that here, with my friends, I was a fifteen-year-old boy doing the things that fifteen-year olds do, far removed from the cocoa business and Bobo. These people, my friends, could not imagine that other world I was in. Even when I told Eddie about Benny and Goren and cocoa, I held back about my own participation. Not even Eddie knew that I had an involvement with Bobo. Eddie would be stunned to hear that I had $1,200 hidden in Evie's bunk bed mattress and over seven thousand dollars in an account at Krieger and Son. This was 1939, when my father supported our family of four on a thirty-dollar-a-week job. I was rich. I remembered when Morris told Gracie that he had six thousand dollars in the bank. Gracie's eyes widened at that. She thought Morris was rich. So did I. What business did I have being worth more than eight thousand dollars?

Miss Georgia's float approached. Its theme was the *Peach State*. Miss Georgia had six ladies-in-waiting, all wearing peach-colored gowns. The float was covered in white- and peach-colored flowers and flower petals. In the center of the float there was a staircase leading to a canopy-covered platform and a white-petal-covered throne. There Miss Georgia stood, in front of her throne, wearing a white gown of lace and silk, waving and smiling. She wore a rhinestone tiara, and she held a rhinestone-studded scepter, which she set down every few blocks so she could raise the hem of her gown and throw her skirts in the air, revealing her perfect legs and peach-colored silk panties. Clearly, she was the crowd's favorite. A howl of male approval rose up every time she threw her skirts in the air. All the other girls just smiled and waved. Miss Georgia sure was my favorite, but she didn't win. The next day, we learned that the winner was the beauty from Michigan, Miss Patricia Donnelly.

I thought Rhoda was as good-looking as any of the contestants, including Patricia Donnelly, the new queen. The *Atlantic City Press* said she called herself *Patti*. That got me to thinking …

58

Patti Again

O N THE TUESDAY after the Miss America Parade, I rode my bike to Trucci's. I was all fired up for Patti. I parked in the rear alley some distance from the door that the employees used, but close enough to see everyone who came and went. It was a few minutes before six. I was waiting for Patti to show up. I figured she would arrive between 6:00 and 6:30 to work the dinner shift. Sure enough, at 6:20, I saw a dark maroon LaSalle sedan stop in the street at the end of the alley, and Patti climbed out. She was wearing her yellow waitress uniform. The car drove off. Patti slipped off her high-heeled shoes and replaced them with her white sneaks, which she was carrying in a shopping bag. As she started down the alley, I approached her.

"Jack," she said, surprised. "What are you doing here?"

"I want a date … er … you know," I stammered.

"Really?" she said with a smile. "You mean you want a professional appointment? Is that it?"

"Yes, that's it. I have twenty-five dollars. That's the right amount, right?"

"Did you tell Bobo you're going to do this?"

"No, do I have to?"

"It's best. Bobo likes to know everything. He won't object, but I better tell him. I'll see you at my apartment tonight at 10:30. If you see a *Do Not Disturb* sign hanging on the doorknob, that means Bobo said *no*. If the sign is there, go home; no appointment. OK?"

I was there at 10:30. No sign. I knocked. She let me in.

She was wearing only her silk robe, almost transparent, loosely drawn, half revealing her wonderful figure. I went to embrace her. She drew back and looked at her wristwatch, which was the only other thing she was wearing.

"Please put the money over here, Jack," she indicated the coffee table in her sitting room. I did. "Now, then, Jack, dear, come to me," she said, slipping off the silk robe. She allowed me to embrace her. Then she led me to the bed and helped me remove my clothes. "Leave your shoes and socks on," she said, as she pushed me down onto the bed. I was ready. She unrolled a condom onto me and climbed aboard.

Aah. That feeling. I ran my hands along her skin and creamy thighs and perfect legs. She leaned on my chest with her palms, arms straight, elbows locked. She rode me in slow motion, her head back, eyes closed. I thrust deeper, deeper, again and again, deep into her. My passion grew. I couldn't see her face because of the way she held her head back. So I fixed on her breasts and palmed them as she rode me up and down. This went on for some ten or fifteen minutes. I got hotter. She continued to ride me, slowly, detached, as if she were in an exercise class. It was very businesslike.

She looked at her watch. "What's wrong, Jack, can't you come?" she asked.

"I guess I'm not ready," I panted.

"Well, try, baby. Try hard."

So I pushed and thrust, but no climax.

"Get on top," she said.

We changed positions. She opened up and let me in. Now it was my turn. I plunged into her, deep, again and again. She still held her head back, eyes closed, as if she were not part of what we were doing. Her mind was miles away. She looked at her watch again. She thrust her hips, rhythmically. She knew how to make herself squeeze, relax, squeeze. It didn't take long. I came, violently, and collapsed onto her.

"You're heavy," she said, pushing to help me roll off. Again, she looked at her watch. "Jack, you're in the master class now. C'mon, I have to get you out of here. I have another appointment soon."

As I rode home, I examined my feelings. I didn't feel so great or elated. The whole thing was tawdry. I wanted to take a shower. Patti didn't seem so golden anymore. She sure was pretty, and what a body, and that squeezing trick, but she was just a whore, after all. And twenty-five bucks! That was almost four weeks' work at Krilow's.

I thought about Alice. I had cheated on her. I was ashamed. I made a vow that night to never do anything that would embarrass me if the whole world learned about it, a tough standard to live by, but worth it.

59

Wednesday, October 4

FROM SEPTEMBER 11, when Benny reversed himself and went short, until September 26, Benny's magic worked, better than ever. Goren's journal showed that our accounts reached their highs on the 26th:

Alan	*$75,183*
Benny	*$28,376*
Jack	*$10,791*
Bobo	*$58,912*

The amounts were stunning!

After September 26, we began to lose money. Benny's magic stopped working.

Goren called a meeting for Wednesday evening, October 4. As usual, we met at Zena's. Goren looked as if he'd been there for a while. He looked quite at home. He was not wearing the customary gray suit. He was dressed casually, a pair of khaki pants, a pullover sweater, gray ragg socks, and brown loafers. He was relaxed on the sofa with a cigarette, a part of the *New York Times* in his lap. Other parts of the paper, already read and disheveled, were lying on the floor.

I arrived before Benny. Zena poured a cup of tea for me. She inquired about my family and asked about school and who were my friends. I told her a little about Eddie. I told her that what I saw and learned in the summer from Morris and Benny and Goren made schoolwork seem like a waste of time and unimportant. She advised me not to get ahead of myself. "Sure," she said, "you were exposed to a lot of grown-up and serious things. Now don't start thinking that you outgrew schoolwork at your level. Your experiences ought to make schoolwork more meaningful because you've had a taste of the real thing. You have to learn everything, step by step, all in its time. You have to do and experience all the fifteen-year-old things. And the sixteen-year-old things and so on. Don't try to jump ahead too much. Tuck away what you've seen and learned. It will stand you in good stead when you need it." She studied me with those green eyes that drilled right into your head. "You're a good boy, Jack. I told you so. You're made of good stuff. You will be a successful person. Not just money. Real success in family and friends and children." It felt like a reading.

Goren put away the newspaper. He sat up and asked what I was reading these days other than schoolwork. I confessed that the last book I read was Stefan Zweig's *Napoleon*, which Morris gave me. I said I was so caught up in the cocoa and Bobo and school that I didn't have the time. And Morris used to select for me.

"Tell you what, Jack," Goren said, "do you mind if I take over for Morris? I have a lot of books. How about I bring you one? You should make reading a habit. Every night. The last half-hour before lights out. Worthwhile stuff."

"Like what, Mr. Goren?" I asked. "Morris gave me real good stuff. He gave me Joseph Conrad, and Harold Lamb, and Stefan Zweig."

"All good stuff, Jack," Goren said. "I'll try to pick out as well as Morris did. I lean toward histories and biographies. Ah, here's Benny."

Benny looked haggard and worn-out. He fell into the sofa. He rested his head against the back of the sofa.

"I ain't been doin' good, guys," he said. "Don't know what went wrong. But it's OK now. I'm back in sync again."

"That's why I called this meeting, Benny," Goren said. "But here, Benny, relax a little. Have some tea." Goren stood to pour a cup of tea. "Take it easy. Don't get down on yourself. You called the downturn in prices *to the day*." He handed Benny the cup and saucer and a sandwich still wrapped in deli paper. Prices have been headed down ever since. And you've been trading us short. Terrific. We made a ton. I never dreamed to make so much money. Now you're having a bad spell. Last six sessions. You're in a slump. Like a baseball player. You reversed yourself. I'm not sure why. Now you're trading long. But prices are still falling, just like you called it. I tried to talk to you about it, but we can't really talk at Krieger's. You're too absorbed in the charts, and I'm too busy doing the trading according to your instructions and making sure the executions are correct. By the time the trading day ends, you're fatigued. And me, too. So let's relax here, without any pressure, and talk about where we're headed."

"Fair enough, Alan," Benny said, unwrapping the sandwich. "Thanks for this. I ain't been eatin' regular. And I ain't been sleepin' much." He rose from the sofa and sat at the table. He composed himself. He spread out the deli paper and smoothed it with his palms, like a placemat. He ate while he spoke. "Last week, the 26th, Tuesday. I thought the downturn was over. I looked for confirmation in the chart, but I didn't see a signal. That was strange. I always got a signal. One way or another. At the end of the day, I still didn't see a signal. The beans closed at 5.95. Maybe you remember, Alan. I asked you to stick around a little longer and figure up our accounts. Here, I wrote them down."

Benny produced a small sheet of paper with his numbers, the same as Goren's for that day:

Alan	*$75,183*
Benny	*$28,376*
Jack	*$10,791*
Bobo	*$58,912*

He went on, "The next day, I decided that the downturn was over. The chart wasn't talking to me. I figured it out from the war news. The Germans are sinking twenty to thirty ships a week. And the number is climbing. Between the U-boat packs and the surface raiders, like the *Graf Spee* and *Prince Eugene,* transatlantic ocean traffic to England is being hurt bad. It can't go on like this. Something has got to change. And it ain't gonna be peace. This war is for real. Prices have to go up. So I went long the next morning, and it looked like the right move 'til about noon. Then I thought I spotted a short signal so I closed out our positions and went short. It was a mistake. They turned around on me and headed up. They closed at 6.01. We lost money that day.

"Next day, I covered our shorts and went long. It was a mistake. Since then, I been reversing myself almost every day. And I can't seem to get it right. I must have made twenty trades in the last six days. And I think I lost on almost every one. The trend is still down, and I've been trading us long."

He stopped to finish the sandwich and sip at the tea. "Alan, how much are our accounts today? I know we been hurt. I haven't wanted to look."

Goren produced his chart. Today's close was:

Alan	*$52,493*
Benny	*$12,873*
Jack	*$4,403*
Bobo	*$40,470*

"Wow!" exclaimed Benny. "It's worse than I thought. But late today, I caught a signal. Not from the chart. From my head. Like it used to be. Strong. Just like a couple of weeks ago. I have to go long. Big. Tomorrow I'm going long two hundred contracts for you, Alan. Jack and me are max'd out, we can't increase our positions. I'll go long 150 for Bobo. I'll make up the losses from the last six days. I'm back on the ball. The beans closed at 5.42. Tomorrow, they'll move right up to 5.49 real fast. By noon is my guess. I figure to be out and short by 12:15. And I'll cover by 1:00 at around 5.44. I see you making $4,000 to $5,000 on your two hundred contracts, Alan. I'll have you back up to $57,000 to $58,000 by the end of the day. Are you OK with that?"

Goren didn't answer Benny. He turned to me and asked if Bobo had anything to say when I delivered the envelope with last Friday's close. Bobo's account was worth $44,346, down from his September 26 high of $58,912. I said that I didn't see him open it. Georgie took it from me and sent me on my way. Today, I delivered the envelope with last night's value, $40,600, but no one answered so I shoved it under the door.

Goren turned back to Benny. "That's too much, Benny," Goren said. "Two hundred contracts is too much. It's too much. Listen, we've made fortunes. I'm satisfied to quit right now. If we stay in it, let's cut back. We made enough. We gave some back. So what? Let's not hurt ourselves by trying too hard. I say take it easy for a while

Date	Price	Alan	Bunny	Jack	Bobo	Contracts				Trades
—CONTINUED										
9/4	LABOR DAY - CLOSED									
9/5 CASH OUT →		(5000)	(1000)	(300)	(5000)	WITHDRAW CASH				
9/5	.0566	26 583	5172	1950	20 075	120	40	15	100	4
9/6	.0595	33 977	7633	2870	26 125	150	50	18	120	2
9/7	.0620	41 653	10 363	3835	32 371	160	55	22	130	3
9/8	.0655	53 179	14 369	5461	41 755	160	65	25	130	3
9/11	.0660	54 999	15 082	5743	43 139	160	65	25	130	2
9/11	SWITCH TO SHORT									
9/12 CASH OUT →		(5000)	(2000)	(1000)	(5000)					
9/12	.0651	52 739	14 645	5345	40 606	(160)	(85)	(33)	(130)	3
9/13	.0640	56 971	16 591	6119	43 678	(160)	(90)	(38)	(130)	5
9/14	.0625	61 391	19 347	7287	47 691	(160)	(100)	(42)	(130)	3
9/15	.0631	63 459	20 598	7320	49 395	(160)	(100)	(42)	(130)	1
9/18	.0618	67 787	23 271	8697	52 887	(160)	(110)	(45)	(130)	2
9/19	.0612	69 739	24 603	9245	54 468	(160)	(110)	(45)	(130)	2
9/20	.0615	68 779	23 943	8975	53 688	(160)	(110)	(45)	(130)	0
9/21	.0610	70 383	25 076	9441	55 012	(160)	(110)	(45)	(130)	1
9/22	.0604	72 303	26 396	9981	56 592	(160)	(110)	(45)	(130)	0
9/25	.0610	70 383	25 076	9441	55 012	(160)(110)(45)(130)				0
9/26	.0595	75 183	28 376	10791	58 912	(160)(110)(45)(130)				0
9/27	.0601	73 140	26 952	10205	57 242	(160)(110)(45)(130)				4
9/28	SWITCH BACK TO LONG									
9/28	.0575	64 575	21 169	7829	50 326	160	110	45	130	2
9/29	.0552	57 215	16 109	5759	44 346	160	110	45	130	4
10/2	.0558	58 655	17 099	6164	45 516	160	110	45	130	3
10/3	.0540	52 653	12 983	4448	40 600	160	110	45	130	4
10/4	.0542	52 493	12 873	4403	40 470	160	110	45	130	3

until we're sure you have your bearings again." Goren nodded his head, inviting Benny to do likewise.

"Sounds like good advice, Benny," Zena said. "You're a rich man now. Don't jeopardize it."

Benny stood up. He was agitated. Like that day on the pavilion. He leaned forward on the table. "You don't trust me, is that it? You think I lost it. Well, I'll tell you, I ain't lost nuthin'. I made you rich and I know what I'm doin' and I'm gonna get back every cent they took away from us. *That money is ours!* Those charts are trying to screw me up. Well, they ain't gonna. I still have it here." He tapped his head with his forefinger. "I don't even need the goddamn chart anymore. It's all right here." He tapped his head again. Then his belligerence faded. He sat down again. He looked tired, all washed out.

"C'mon, Benny," Goren said quietly, "don't get so agitated. What's our hurry? The market will be there next week, next month. Let's back off a little. I'm with you. Take it easy. Let's lighten up. You'll do better without having so much at stake all the time. You won't be on edge all the time."

Zena added her opinion again, urging Benny to take some profits, lower the amount at risk.

The discussion went on for a while. Benny calmed down. His belligerence was gone. He looked beaten. He agreed to cut back.

"But I'm not going back to twenty contracts for you, Alan, and ten for me. Might as well be playing Parcheesi. No, we'll go with a hundred and twenty for you, and a hundred for Bobo, fifty for me and twenty for Jack. You watch me. Tomorrow, I'll pick up seven hundredths on the way up. Then five-hundredths on the way down. Twelve hundredths. That's twenty-four bucks a contract. Two weeks ago, at one point, I had you up to two hundred contracts for a half-hour. I'm cutting way back. OK?"

"Good, Benny," Goren said. "I'm glad you see it that way. I might have cut back more, but I'll go along with you. Now come on. I'm going to get some hot food into you and send you home. You need to catch up on your sleep. Then, I'm going to see Bobo. I better go to him before he sends for us."

***

The next day, the beans dropped. Benny closed out the contracts at a loss. Then he went short. The beans went up. He covered at a loss. For the day, Goren and Bobo each lost about $1,000. Benny lost $440. I lost $180. My account was down from $10,791 on September 26 all the way to $4,222. I had lost over $6,500! Incredible. The figures were mind-boggling. I was playing with thousands.

Goren reported that he had a few uncomfortable moments with Bobo. Bobo gave him that look from under the eyebrows, then waved the tension away. He said, "What the hell! I got out my original five grand and five grand more. It's the house's money."

The next day was worse. Benny was wrong again. Our accounts were shrinking. My account dropped below $4,000. Secretly, I wished we would close out the accounts. But that decision had to come from Goren or Benny. It was their game. I was only along for the ride.

I tried to imagine having $10,791 in cash in my hands. That's what my account was worth only three weeks ago. Suppose I had to shell out the losses every day, day after day, almost $7,000 of losses. I couldn't imagine it. I would have to stop and keep what I had. I wondered if Benny and Goren thought of it that way: real money being lost, vanishing. It wasn't the same, looking at numbers on

Goren's chart. If it was money in hand, we wouldn't be so reckless. On the other hand, I probably would have stopped and cashed in after the first three weeks, when my account was all of $316.

Meanwhile, my life as a fifteen-year-old schoolboy was about to push to the fore. It was the Mackeys again.

60

Encounter With the Mackeys

O N OCTOBER 8, the second Sunday in October, I took Alice for a
ride on the boardwalk. We were headed to Garden Pier, where
Glen Gray was performing with his Casa Loma Orchestra. Alice
was perched on my bike in her sidesaddle position, and I pedaled
furiously to get enough momentum to carry us up the ramp to the
boardwalk. Once on the boardwalk, we headed up-island at a
relaxed pace. It was the middle of the afternoon. It felt good to be
with Alice. It was a nice day, one of those bright October beauties
that no place does as well as Atlantic City. The sun sailed through
a cloudless sky, high above a sparkling sea. A sailboat slipped
through silver water, three hundred yards from shore, abreast of
our bicycle. As always, Alice was full of enthusiasm. "This is wonderful, Jack," she said, turning her head to me. "What a glorious
day! On, on to Garden Pier!" Her smile lit up her face, bright as the
day itself.

About three blocks south of Albany Avenue, I saw the Mackey
brothers. They were carrying fishing poles and tackle boxes, obviously headed to the surf-casting beach at Albany Avenue. The part
of the boardwalk we were on was only eighteen feet wide. The
Mackey brothers filled more than half the boardwalk with their
bulk and fishing gear. Briefly, I thought to go off the boardwalk,
ride one block along Atlantic Avenue, and come back onto the
boardwalk safely beyond them.

I guess that would have been the smart thing to do, and I guess I would have if I were alone. The trouble was that Alice would ask me why. I didn't want to tell her about my beating in May and my apprehension about the next encounter. So I decided to treat the Mackeys like any other pair of men walking on the boardwalk. I rang my bell to signal that I was passing. That was a mistake. I should have pedaled around them without the bell. Tom, who was on the left, turned to see the source of the bell. He saw it was me. He stopped and turned to face me. His face was expressionless as I neared him. I moved pretty far to the left, giving him plenty of room.

As I passed, he half-turned, stepped toward me, and shot out that powerful left arm. He caught me on my right shoulder, like a battering ram. Down we went on our left side, skidding a dozen feet along the boards in a tangle of legs, arms, wheels, pedals. Alice screamed as we fell. Tom Mackey grunted a malevolent chuckle and resumed walking.

We lay still for a few moments. Alice was crying. She was sprawled on her stomach, her skirt and slip twisted around her hips. Slowly I extricated myself from the tangle and lifted the bike off Alice. I leaned it against the railing. I knelt beside her.

"Alice, are you all right?" I asked. "Can you sit up?" I was afraid to move her. I remembered from First Aid Class that it is dangerous to move an accident victim until you know the extent of the person's injuries.

She continued to cry for a few more moments. Then slowly she began to sit up.

"I don't think anything is broken," she said. "How about you?" I held her in my arms and helped her to her feet. We made for a nearby bench and assessed the damage.

My left palm was full of splinters. I must have broken our fall by throwing out my left arm. My left wrist, arm, elbow, and shoulder throbbed with pain from having absorbed most of the impact of the fall. My left forehead was scraped. My left leg was badly bruised by the bicycle frame. My left ankle was cut where the pedal mechanism scraped across it. My entire left side—ribs, hip, leg—felt like I had suffered a beating. Nothing seemed broken. I stood and walked. My right side seemed uninjured. I tried to move my left arm. It hurt, real bad, but I could move it. I was a mass of pain. The side of my forehead was bleeding. So was my ankle.

Alice was pretty beat up as well, but nothing was broken. I had absorbed most of the force of our fall and hit the ground before her. Her dress was torn. Her right leg had a big scratch and was bleeding. Her left thigh was badly bruised and full of splinters. She also had splinters, a lot of them, in both palms.

"Wait here," I said. I climbed back on the bike. The Mackeys were about a block and a half away, walking unconcerned toward Albany Avenue.

No bell this time. I pedaled up to a furious speed. I must have been doing thirty miles an hour. As I reached them, I aimed at John on the right, but at the last moment, I turned a sharp left. The bike skidded, sideways, into them, sending them sprawling in a jumble of fishing poles, and hooks. Their tackle boxes flew open, their contents flew in all directions.

The impact knocked my bike over on its left side, but I was prepared. I stopped my fall with my left leg, sort of stepping off and throwing my right leg over the bar. I didn't even fall. Where did I learn such a stunt? I never had. I acted in rage. My body did it. There was no plan. Just rage.

I picked up the bike. The Mackeys were still sprawled on the boardwalk. I noticed that the hook from Tom's line was caught in his right ear lobe. *That must be fun. It's not gonna come out so easy,* I thought, as I mounted up and rode back to Alice.

Alice and I spent the rest of the afternoon in her kitchen picking splinters out of each other. We told her parents we had an accidental fall. We scrubbed our hands with Ivory soap. Then we burned a sewing needle and picked at each splinter until it surrendered and until we got them all out, maybe fifty of them.

"Shall we count them, Jack?" Alice asked. She was back in good humor, as she ministered to my bruises and cuts, first with warm soapy water, then with hydrogen peroxide and mercurochrome. She applied hot compresses to my aching left arm and shoulder and my left side. She half pulled down my underwear to get at my left hip. "Ooh," she said, "I almost can see *itself*. Let me hold it."

The thought of it made me squirm. "Better not, Alice. Not with your folks in the house."

I told her about the May beating. She became anxious. She was frightened for me. "He'll lay for you, Jack. What will you do? You have to tell somebody. Your father, the police. He's such a brute. He could hurt you real bad. Especially after today."

I explained that Eddie and I had thought it through. There was no help to be had. If I told my father, he would go to the Mackeys and do something rash, and get hurt or get into trouble. If I went to the police, they might go to see the Mackeys, but that would only heat them up more. It was a dilemma. I didn't know what to do except to stay away from them.

***

That evening, I told Eddie what happened. He wanted to know how I figured out that stunt with the bike. I told him I wasn't sure how I did it. I probably couldn't do it again. He said he was proud of me, but he was worried. He said he thought maybe the Mackeys forgot about us over the summer and that there didn't have to be a showdown. "Now," he said, "it's worse than I thought. You're lucky you and Alice didn't get hurt worse than you did. Let's stay out of their way until we figure out what to do."

"Sure, Eddie," I said, "but it ain't goin' away."

My entire arm hurt. Everything turned black and blue, from my palm all the way up to my shoulder. My shoulder hurt, my wrist hurt. My elbow hurt when I bent my arm. But fifteen-year-old boys are made of rubber. I healed quickly. In a couple of weeks, I was just about 100 percent recovered.

What next? I wondered. Those fuckin' Mackeys were ruining my life.

61

Calling It Quits

TUESDAY AFTERNOON, OCTOBER 10, after school, I rode to Krieger's on my bike, as usual. I arrived at 2:45. I brought the early edition of the *Philadelphia Evening Ledger* and the *Evening Bulletin* and ham and cheese sandwiches for Goren and Benny. We'd been losing money every day since our meeting at Zena's last Wednesday. Our accounts were being eaten away.

I found Goren seated, reading the *New York Times*, seemingly relaxed in one of the red-leather easy chairs. He had a small table at his side with a half-smoked cigarette resting in an ashtray, a whiskey tumbler, a pitcher of water, and a bottle of Jack Daniels Black Label whiskey.

"Ah, Jack, good, you brought lunch," he said. "See if you can find Benny. I think he's in with Junior."

"How're we doing today, Mr. Goren?" I asked. I thought from the way Goren was relaxing that maybe we were having a good day.

"It's no good, Jack," Goren replied. "Between you and me, I think Benny's lost it. And I don't think it's coming back."

"Why do you look so comfortable, Mr. Goren?" I asked. "You look like you don't have a worry in the world."

"Let me tell you something, Jack. Ever since Chateau-Thierry, things like this don't bother me. I am a solitary person. I don't intrude on anyone. I don't want anyone to intrude on me. It's nineteen years since I quit Bache and Company. Since then, I don't have to account to anybody and nobody accounts to me. I always got by."

He stopped to refill his glass and take a bite of the sandwich. Then he continued. "I have a small Army pension. I make a little money every so often on a real estate deal. And until I met up with Zena and Benny, I always managed to make a little money trading commodities. I based my buys and sells on all the hard facts I could gather. And I usually did OK. Nothing big, and when I took a loss, it was usually small. That was my life. I hardly knew any people. My landlady still doesn't know my first name."

He drew at the cigarette. A long slow drag. He pursed his lips into an oval and puffed out three well-formed smoke rings.

"Nice trick, Mr. Goren," I said.

"That's my only talent," he replied. "That and maybe, *maybe* being able to call the direction of a commodity once in a while."

He went on. "Here's what I decided. When I met Zena, my account was worth less than three thousand dollars. When I met Benny, it was worth more than five thousand. Whatever Zena says otherwise, she steered me to my first big score. I never made that kind of money. A good week for me was a couple hundred dollars. I felt rich. Five thousand dollars is a lot of money. That's about double what I've been making a year. Now, even with the bad last couple of weeks, my account is still over $48,000, and that's after I pulled out $10,000. I'm rich. Richer than I ever hoped to be. So my account is down about $27,000 from its high. So what? When my account crossed over $20,000, I was actually embarrassed at being so rich."

He stopped for another bite at the sandwich and a sip of the whiskey. "I don't feel bad, Jack," he said. "I'm grateful for what I've made, and I'm grateful to have new friends. I shouldn't even say *new* friends, 'cause I haven't had *any* for years and years. You and Benny and Zena are more important than the money."

"Thanks for saying that, Mr. Goren," I said, "but the way Benny is going, we could get wiped out. Aren't you nervous?"

"A little," he said, puffing on the cigarette, another couple of perfect smoke rings. "I look at it like this: Benny might get hot again, but if we keep on dropping, I'll have to convince him to quit. We'll all be way ahead. If he doesn't quit, I can pull out alone. And I'll pull out Bobo. I don't like the feeling I have that Bobo won't want to understand what's happened. I think we're going to have an uncomfortable time with him. Even though we've made a lot of money for him. I'll be satisfied for myself. More than satisfied. I'm not a sore winner. I feel bad for Benny. You see what he's like these days. He is nervous and unstable, and he is not eating or sleeping. Like that time back in August when he blew up on the pavilion. He's like that again. Worse. Because then he was playing with hundreds and he was making money. I think his account was only worth about $800 that day. Now, he's playing with thousands. His account today is about $11,000! He is a rich man. What's eating him is that his account is down from a high of over $28,000. He can't stand it that he gave back $17,000. I try to calm him down but I'm not succeeding."

He took another bite. As he set down the remainder of the sandwich, he pointed and said, "There's Benny, coming out of Junior's office. Benny," he called out, "over here! Come, have a sandwich. Relax."

Benny approached. He looked terrible. His face was gray. His lips were gray. His clothes were wrinkled. He must have skipped shaving that morning, because there was stubble on his cheeks. He collapsed into a chair. "Thanks for the sandwich, Jack," he said.

Then to Goren: "There's about an hour of trading left. We're up for the day. I been short the last hour and a half. There's a turn coming in about fifteen minutes. I'm gonna cover and go long. This is the turn. I feel it."

Goren nodded. "Whatever you think, Benny."

Goren gave me an envelope for Bobo. "Take this to Bobo, Jack. It's last night's figures. He's probably at his office at this hour. If not, shoot over to Trucci's."

I delivered Bobo's envelope. He was at his bookie joint office in the alley behind the shooting gallery. He opened the envelope while I was there and studied the numbers on the slip of paper. He looked up at me and said, "What's happening over here, Jack? The money is evaporating. I had over fifty-eight grand here a little while ago. Since then, it's down, down, down. This paper over here says I'm down to $37,590. And there's a note over here from Alan. It says don't forget I took back ten thousand. Tell him that's old news. I had over fifty in the account over here. Now, it's thirty-seven. That don't sound kosher over here. Better tell Alan and Benny to pay me a visit."

I hurried back to Krieger's and reported.

Benny said we should meet at 7:30 at Zena's. Then he told me to go back to Bobo and tell him we will pay him a visit tonight at Trucci's.

***

We met that evening, at Zena's. The day turned against us in the last half hour. The day was another loser, the ninth out of the last ten trading days.

When Benny arrived, it was hard to believe he was the same person I left at Krieger's three hours earlier. He looked like the old Benny James. He was relaxed and neatly dressed. He lounged comfortably on Zena's sofa, smoking a cigarette. He was a picture of casual relaxation.

"Hi, Benny," said Goren. He almost did a double-take. "Benny, you look like a different man. You look so cool. What's happened? You were all stressed out three hours ago."

Zena agreed. She said so. "Benny, you're looking better than I've seen you since you went into the cocoa business. What's up?"

I added my agreement. "You look great, Benny," I said.

"My friends," Benny said, expansively, "I'll tell you why I feel so terrific. When I left Krieger's this afternoon, I decided we should call it quits. Whether I lost the touch or whatever, I say we quit while we're ahead. I went home. I took a nap and a shower and shave and put on fresh clothes and here I am. The wealthy and well-groomed Benny James."

He jumped up. He threw his arms around Goren, then me, then Zena. "We're getting out, guys. We're cashing in. We're rich. I don't know what's gonna happen with the war. I don't care. We made ours. We'll get out of the game for a while. Maybe weeks, maybe longer. Maybe Alan will teach me bonds. Whatever. Tomorrow morning, before I change my mind, Alan, I want you to close us out of everything. What do you figure our accounts are worth?"

Goren produced his journal:

Alan	*$48,317*
Benny	*$11,071*
Jack	*$3,664*
Bobo	*$36,990*

"Jack," Benny said, soberly, "I cost you a lot of money. When Alan cut back from 160 contracts to 120, I cut back Bobo, too, from 130 to 100. I stayed with 110 and kept you at 45. I cut back later, but I overstayed. I was so sure I was on the right track. Sorry. I should have eased up more for you and me, too."

"That's OK, Benny," I said. "I always said I'll go along with you. I'm not gonna second-guess you. And I'm like Mr. Goren. I'm not a sore winner." Benny laughed.

"What do we do with the money?" I asked. "Do we leave it at Krieger's or what?"

"I say *or what*," was Benny's response. "I wanna close out our positions and take out all the money except for a little bit to keep the accounts open. I wanna put the money in the Boardwalk National Bank. I wanna let it earn some interest for a while. Let it rest. It's been workin' too hard. Like us. We all need a rest. Agreed?"

"Sure thing, Benny." We all agreed.

"OK. Now c'mon," said Benny, "we're gonna celebrate. You, too, Zena. Dinner is on me. We'll go to Trucci's. I'm in the mood for a big steak, well done, with the works. We'll tell Bobo the good news. We're gettin' out. He invested five grand. He took out ten and he'll have thirty-seven more. He can't be too sore about that."

***

The four of us made for Trucci's. Zena had never been there. She washed her face clean of the dark coloring she wore as the Occult Reader and put on regular street clothes. We were in a festive mood except for just a little bit of apprehension about Bobo's reaction to the final value of his (or Loretta Mauriello's) account, which was $36,990.

Date	Price	Alan	Benny	Jack	Bobo	Contracts				Trades

— CONTINUED

Date	Price	Alan	Benny	Jack	Bobo	Contracts				Trades
10/2	.0558	58 655	17 099	6164	45 516	160	110	45	130	3
10/3	.0540	52 653	12 983	4448	40 600	160	110	45	130	4
10/4	.0542	52 493	12 873	4403	40 470	160	110	45	130	3
10/5	.0538	51 437	12 431	4222	39 590	120	50	20	100	1
10/6	.0532	49 997	11 802	3974	38 390	120	50	20	100	0
10/9	.0528	49 037	11 388	3 801	37 590	120	50	20	100	0
10/10	.0525	48 317	11 071	3664	36 990	120	50	20	100	0

When we arrived, Goren asked the *maitre d'* if Bobo was in the dining room. He was not. He was upstairs in his office. He might be coming down later. Benny said he wouldn't enjoy dinner until we broke the news to Bobo. He asked me to go with him to Bobo's office. "Alan," he said, "how about you and Zena take a table? Have a glass of wine. Wait for us. We won't be long."

Benny and I walked up the backstairs and knocked on Bobo's office door. Georgie opened it. He announced over his shoulder to Bobo that it was us. Frankie stood off to one side.

"C'mon in, guys," Bobo called out. "What's up?"

Benny told Bobo that we would be closing the accounts tomorrow. He apologized that he lost money almost every day since he switched from being short to going long on September 28. He apologized that Loretta's account was down to under $37,000, down from a high of almost $59,000.

"I don't like that," Bobo said. "Last I saw, Loretta's account was still in the middle forties."

"I'm real sorry, Bobo," Benny said. "I lost the touch. Around the end of September. I was sure the war was going to heat up and turn real. So I went long. I read the signals wrong. My charts stopped talking to me. I started to analyze the news, and I started looking at the crop reports. Like Goren always did. Today, I decided to call it quits. Hey, we all made a killing. Loretta put in five grand. She pulled out ten grand already. And she's got almost thirty-seven grand coming. That's a big win, Bobo. Her five thousand into forty-seven. My six hundred bucks turned into fourteen thousand. Jack here put in a hundred and seventy-seven bucks. It grew into almost five grand! We did great! Aren't you pleased?"

Bobo rubbed his chin, thoughtfully. You never knew what he was going to do or say. He half-closed his eyes, as if in deep thought. Then he straightened up and in a cheery voice, he said, "Georgie, Frankie, set up some drinks over here. For *all* of us; you, too, Jack, you're one of us over here."

Bobo stood and grabbed Benny into a big hug. "You did good, Benny. I appreciate that. And I appreciate even more that you know when it's time to get out. You're no sucker. The suckers never quit until they're broke. Good work."

"Thanks, Bobo," Benny said, smiling. "I'm glad you're happy with how it turned out. I felt real bad, losin' that money the last coupla weeks. But like Alan says, I'm not a sore winner."

Bobo laughed. "Hey, that's a good line. I'm gonna use it." He slapped Benny on the back. "Where's Alan?" he asked. "Why ain't he here?"

Benny explained that Goren was in the dining room with Zena. Bobo said, "The hell with that. C'mon everybody. We're goin' down to celebrate. Frankie, get ahold of Loretta over here. This is a big day!"

It would have been great if it ended that way.

62

Closing the Accounts

WE MET AT Zena's at 3:30 the next day. Goren was there. He looked like he'd been there for hours, relaxed in a half-sleep on the sofa, his shoes off, half the newspapers covering him and the other half in an untidy heap on the floor. Zena was sitting at her table reading a book that compared the Egyptian pyramids with the Mayan and Aztec pyramids.

Goren stirred and sat up. "Well, Jack," he said, "this is a great day. Sit down, relax, have a cup of tea. You're a rich young man. Your account is $3,621. If you leave $1,000 in your account, you'll have a check next week for $2,621, five business days for the trades to settle."

"I still can't hardly believe it, Mr. Goren," I said. "I don't know what to do with the money. Now that it's for real, I guess it's time to tell my folks."

Goren stood and poured a cup of tea. "That's right, Jack. Tell them about it. No. Wait. You know what, wait until next week. When we pick up the checks, I'll take you into the Boardwalk National Bank and get a savings account opened for you. Wait until the money is in your hands—in the bank. Then tell your folks, and you'll be able to show them the passbook."

"What happened at Krieger's today?" I asked.

Goren told me about the morning.

"The market opens at ten. I got there about 9:30, before the market opened. Benny was already there. Usually we arrived before 9:00 and studied the prices from the previous night in London. So Junior asked how come we're late today. We told Junior we're closing out our positions. We asked him to put in our sell orders at the opening. He asked if we were reversing positions. Were we going short? No, we told him we're closing out the accounts. We said we're going to get out of the market for a while. Maybe buy some Treasury Bonds. Or maybe do some bond trading. Benny said he wants to learn bonds. Meanwhile, we'll take a rest. Call us when the trades come through. A little after ten, Junior asked us to join him in his office. The trades went through. We were out. We had no contracts in position. Only money."

Goren described what happened next.

Junior said, "Well, congratulations, fellows." He leaned back in his chair. "I had your accounts brought up-to-date. I asked the margin clerk to post this morning's trades as if they settled already. Here are your statements." He handed them to Goren. They showed Goren with $48,077; Benny with $10,968; Loretta Mauriello with $36,790; and me with $3,621. Goren folded the accounts into envelopes.

Junior continued, "Until a couple of weeks ago, you fellas traded as though you knew the next move, to the hour, and the tops and bottoms. I never saw anything to equal it. And all those tickets; ten, twenty tickets a day. I have to thank you for the commissions. I would give you a rebate to show you my appreciation, but you know it is illegal," he smiled. "I never saw a run of good luck like you fellows had. Too bad you gave some back the last two weeks."

"Good luck!" Benny exclaimed, good humoredly. "Good luck, you say. What do you think I been doin', flipping a coin every day? I been workin' harder on this than anything I ever did in my life. I doped out every move on my charts. Luck has nothing to do with it."

"That's right," Goren added. "Benny is a genius. He studied and charted every move. He worked hard at this. Meeting Benny was my lucky day. Look at all the years I have been your customer. I made a few bucks. I thought I knew what I was doing. I studied everything. I read everything. I thought I knew everything. Hah! I didn't know *anything!*"

"So what now, fellas?" Junior asked. "Where are you going to put your money? Another commodity? Have you looked at any of the metals? Copper looks interesting. Maybe you ought to put some of your money in some quality corporate bonds and diversify into some blue chip stocks. I think there is real opportunity in the high-quality industrials. They've been beaten down so low."

Goren answered, "No, Junior, we are going to get out of all the markets for a while until we decide what is our next move. Our trades settle on the eighteenth. We'll stop in then. We'll leave two thousand dollars in my account and Benny's and a thousand in Jack's. The Loretta Mauriello account we'll close. If you'll have the checks ready, we'll be by to pick them up on the eighteenth."

Junior was not happy. Goren couldn't blame him. He was losing four active trading accounts. No telling when we would be back.

"So," Goren said, rising, "thanks again, Junior, for all your excellent service and your quick executions. We'll probably be hanging around every day out of habit, but no more trades for a while."

Goren and Benny stood and shook hands with Junior.

"See ya, Junior," Benny said as we left. "Give my best to your dad."

"Sure, fellas," Junior said. His smile didn't look genuine.

Then Benny took a deep breath. He flashed the big smile. "Alan, know what I'm gonna do? I'm gonna climb in the sack with some girl, if any are still around, and I ain't coming out for two days. Maybe Gwen, if she'll have me."

Goren concluded, "So I took a walk and then I came here. It feels good, not having anything at risk."

"Where *is* Benny?" I asked Goren. I wanted to see him. I wanted to share the moment with him.

"I don't know if we'll see him for a while," Goren answered. "You know I think he was close to a breakdown. He said he's going to climb into bed for a few days. I'm glad we're out. He'll be OK now. And he's a rich young man. He can do anything now. With that personality and money behind him, he can do anything he wants. I am going to teach him bonds and stocks. He has a good head. He'll do well in the traditional markets. Maybe he'll stay in a few commodity contracts, just for some excitement.

"When we left Krieger's, he was already talking about going long on some crude oil futures. He thinks the war is for real. He thinks it is hardly even started.

"As for you, Jack, you have to be serious about school. It will seem tame to you now, after all this, but let me tell you, *learn, learn, learn*. Learn everything. Read everything. Open up your horizons."

At that moment, Benny showed up. Gwen was on his arm. She looked as pretty as ever. "Alan, Zena," he said, "this is Gwen. Jack, you already met Gwen." We all exchanged greetings. Then Benny sent Gwen on her way.

"Let me at that special tea of yours, Zena," Benny said. "And look, I brought the sandwiches. I took over your job, Jack."

So we relaxed for an hour, exchanging recollections and anecdotes of the cocoa days, feeling good, friends who survived a contest, scored a big victory, emerged unscathed.

We broke up at five, after arranging to meet a week later at noon. Goren said he would pick up our checks on that morning. I said I'll cut school so I can be here by noon.

"Oh, no, you don't," said all three in unison. Goren said I can show up at 2:45. He said he'll take me to the Boardwalk National Bank. It's open until 3:30.

As I left, I realized that I was going to miss them terribly. I had been with them almost every day since Benny and I met Goren back in the middle of the summer. What a summer! I pedaled home feeling a big emptiness. Nothing could match the adventure of being in the cocoa business with those two. I missed them already.

I thought the cocoa excitement was over, but I was wrong. A different, more dangerous part of the game was going to hit us the next day.

Date	Price	Alan	Benny	Jack	Bobo	Contracts				Trades
— CONTINUED										
10/2	.0558	58 655	17 099	6164	45 516	160	110	45	130	3
10/3	.0540	52 653	12 983	4448	40 600	160	110	45	130	4
10/4	.0542	52 493	12 873	4403	40 470	160	110	45	130	3
10/5	.0538	51 437	12 431	4222	39 590	120	50	20	100	1
10/6	.0532	49 997	11 802	3974	38 390	120	50	20	100	0
10/9	.0528	49 037	11 388	3 801	37 590	120	50	20	100	0
10/10	.0525	48 317	11 071	3664	36 990	120	50	20	100	0
		CLOSE ACCOUNTS								
10/11		48 077	10 968	3621	36 790	0	0	0	0	1

63

The Second Worst Day
in Goren's Life

THIS IS THE way Goren described the second worst day of his life; the worst being that day at Chateau-Thierry.

Goren headed for Krieger's the morning after we closed the accounts. He went there almost from force of habit, to look at the prices, read the papers, and plan his next move. He was in good spirits when he climbed the stairs and headed for the double doors to the Krieger and Son office. The doors were locked, with a handwritten note taped on them, *Closed October 12 for Inventory.* He looked at his watch. Eleven o'clock, the middle of morning trading. Inventory shouldn't take more than a couple of hours, and usually it's done at the end of the day, or very early in the morning, not during trading hours. They must have started early. They ought to be done by now. He knocked. He tried to turn the doorknob. He peered into the office through a frosted glass side panel. The lights were on, but he saw no one inside. He thought they must all be in one of the back offices.

He went downstairs to the coffee shop where he spent an hour nursing a cup of coffee and reading the paper. Then he climbed the steps again, expecting to find the office open. The doors were still locked. With growing apprehension, he went to a pay phone and called Krieger and Son. No one answered. He knew the Kriegers' home telephone numbers. He tried Carl Senior, then Carl Junior. Both calls went unanswered. Apprehension graduated to dread. He wanted Benny, but he didn't know where to find him. He was probably holed up somewhere with Gwen.

Goren left Central Pier. He walked a few blocks, trying to think. Something bad was happening. Where was Benny? He needed Benny.

Not knowing what else to do, Goren drifted toward Zena's parlor. He told Zena he was afraid the Kriegers made off with our money. Did she have any ideas? What should he do? She said he should go to the police. No, he knew that was not the answer. He had to find Junior Krieger. Or Senior. They had his money! And Benny's, and mine, and Bobo's. *Ohmigod! Bobo's money!* Worse than losing our own. He decided to tell Bobo and get his help. Better that he should bring the news to Bobo than Bobo should hear it from another source. Sure, and Bobo will find the Kriegers.

Goren walked to Bobo's bookie joint behind Royce's Shooting Gallery, rehearsing how to break the news. Bobo wasn't there. Goren headed for Trucci's. When he arrived at Bobo's second-floor office, he forgot what he had rehearsed. "They're gone," he exclaimed, "with our money! You have to find them! Quick, before they get too far."

What? Bobo wanted to know. *What did Goren mean, "They're gone!" The Kriegers? How could that be?* Bobo dispatched Georgie and Frankie. "Find the bastards. Bring them over here. And find Benny James. Bring him over here, too. And the kid, Jack, bring him here, too. The kid won't give me any bullshit. He don't know how to lie."

He turned to Goren. "And you, Goren. You stay right here. You're not goin' anywhere for a while."

***

At 2:15 that afternoon when school let out, I came through the front doors of Atlantic City High School and started down the steps. I was not going to Krieger's. Usually I ran down the steps, unlocked my bike out of the bike racks and headed straight for Krieger's. Not that day. I intended to head for the athletic field to watch the football team practice for an hour, and then make for Frederick's Pharmacy. Our cocoa adventure was over. I was rich! My head was swimming with the amount of money I had—almost five thousand dollars! I still hadn't told anybody. I didn't have any plans for the money. I was still overwhelmed at being rich and still not quite believing it.

I was surprised to see Frankie on the pavement at the foot of the steps. *Bobo must want me*, I thought. *That's bad.* I always got nervous when Bobo summoned. "Frankie," I said, as I approached him, "what's up?"

"You're coming with me, kid. Leave your bike." His Buick was at the curb. "Get in."

I climbed in. "What's up, Frankie?" I repeated.

"I'm takin' you to Bobo's office," he said.

"How come?" I asked. "What's up?" I didn't like it.

"Serious trouble, kid. You'll hear about it when we get there."

I was mystified and scared. It was 2:45 when Frankie brought me into Bobo's office. Bobo looked up but gave no greeting. He motioned me to sit. Frankie took off. Goren was there. I sat next to him on the red leather sofa. When he told me what happened, I really got scared.

Bobo sat at his desk in the big judge's chair. He was absorbed in paperwork, making notes on a yellow ruled pad.

"Where's Benny?" I asked.

Bobo looked up. "Frankie will bring him. Do you know where he is? Could save us some time."

"Don't know," I answered. "He may not be home. Maybe he's with that girl, Gwen."

"Frankie will find him," Bobo said. "Frankie can find anybody in this town."

Goren told me to relax. Read a magazine. He was reading a paper. I picked up an issue of *Life* magazine, but I couldn't concentrate on it. We sat like that, in silence, for an hour. Bobo continued to pore over the papers on his desk and make notes on the yellow pad.

At 4:00, Frankie returned with Benny and left again.

"What's up, guys?" Benny asked. He looked chipper. "What's the mystery? Frankie interrupted a tender moment."

Goren filled him in. Benny sagged into one of the red leather chairs, like the air was let out of him. "Oh, shit!" he said. "How can that be? I don't get it. You think those bastards ran away with our money?"

Goren shrugged. He lifted his eyebrows and raised his hands; the classic *I don't know* gesture that is the same in every language.

"Bobo," Benny said, standing, "you got to find them."

"If they're anywhere on this here island, I'll find them." Bobo said in a soft monotone. "Meanwhile, maybe I oughta be askin' you guys some serious questions over here. Got anything to tell me? If you do, now's the time to tell it."

Goren said, "You know what I know, Bobo. I hope you can find them before they disappear with the money."

At 4:30, Georgie arrived. He had Krieger Senior with him. Senior was wearing a pair of worn khaki pants and a worn green corduroy shirt hanging outside of his pants. His silver hair was disheveled.

Wisps of it stuck out all over his head. He was unshaven. I'd never seen him other than well-groomed and well-dressed. He stumbled into the room. It looked like he'd been shoved. His eyes betrayed panic. When he saw Goren and Benny and me, some of the panic faded, but only momentarily. Bobo looked up. Georgie positioned a wooden straight-back chair in front of Bobo's desk. Bobo motioned Senior to sit.

Bobo rose from his judge's chair and walked to the front of his desk. He half-sat on the front of the desk, one leg on the floor. He leaned forward, bringing his face to within a foot of Senior's. He held that position for a few seconds. There was no expression in his face. It was that look of his, the one that looked like he might spring at any moment, like a giant cat.

Senior's right hand lay quietly in his lap. His left hand wouldn't be still. It shook as though he had palsy. He spoke, in a tremulous voice, "Who are you? What is this place?" He tried to straighten up, to recover some dignity. He turned to Goren, "Alan, what's going on here?" Goren did not respond.

At last, Bobo drew back and spoke, quietly, courteously. "Do you know who I am over here, Mr. Krieger?"

Senior shook his head negatively.

"My name is Bobo Truck. Does my name mean anything to you, Mr. Krieger?" Bobo asked politely.

Senior's whole body began to shake, like a man with the chills. He knew who Bobo Truck was. He said so.

"So you know not to fool with me over here, right?"

"Why am I here, Mr. Truck?" Senior asked, his voice cracking.

Bobo said, "Call me *Bobo*." Then his voice sharpened. "I'm uncomfortable with people who call me *Mr. Truck*." He paused, "You have a customer, name of Loretta Mauriello, right?"

"Yes, she is a customer," Senior acknowledged. A great illuminating fear seized him. He seemed short of breath. "Can I use your bathroom, Mr. Truck?" he asked. He was squeezing his legs together and squirming in his seat.

"Whattsamatter, Pop? Got to pee? Sure. Georgie, take Mr. Krieger to the toilet before he pisses all over my carpets." Georgie lifted Senior by the one arm. Senior almost made it to the bathroom. Not quite. A wet stain ran down the left leg of his khaki pants.

None of us spoke. Goren and Benny sat quietly, impassively. Bobo returned to his big judge's chair and resumed studying papers.

Georgie brought Senior back and sat him down in the chair. Bobo came around the desk again and resumed that half-sitting position on the front of the desk. Again, he allowed a few seconds to pass in silence. Then he thrust his head forward and spoke, quietly, but with great menace. "Miss Mauriello has, excuse me ..." he rooted around his desk for a few moments and produced the Krieger and Son monthly customer's statement for September 30 for Loretta Mauriello. "Here it is, she *had*, at the end of September, an account with you that was worth $44,346. And now, as of yesterday," he produced Goren's final memo of October 11, "you have $36,790 of her money. *She wants the money, Mr. Krieger.* I'm going to collect it for her. When can I have it? By the way, Mr. Krieger, one of my men is looking for your son. I'm surprised he's not here yet. Where is he, Mr. Krieger? Did he leave town with Miss Mauriello's money?"

"No. No. He's around," Senior whispered. "I think he went to the office."

"Mr. Goren over here tells me your office is closed."

"Yes, we told everybody we are closing for the day. I'm sure that Junior is there with the doors locked."

Bobo motioned Georgie to leave, to fetch Junior from the Krieger and Son office, if Frankie hadn't already found him.

"Back to my question, Mr. Krieger. When can I have Miss Mauriello's money?"

At that, Senior shook so violently I thought he was going to fall off the chair or faint. He tried to speak, but nothing came out. Finally, he croaked, "*There isn't any money!*"

We all stiffened in surprise. Bobo, too. It took a few moments for Bobo to respond.

"*Whatya mean?*" Bobo's words snapped at Senior like a whip. "Whatya mean there isn't any money?! Listen, Krieger, you better start comin' clean. I don't like jokes, or tricks, or *thieves*."

Senior looked like he might faint. Bobo slapped his face, gently, almost like a caress. "Pull yourself together, Pop," he said, "and start talking."

"Jack," Bobo addressed me, "get Mr. Krieger a glass of water." I was glad to be able to do something. I brought it. It was a long time before Senior was composed enough to tell his story.

64

Senior's Story

Carl Krieger Senior's father was a customer's man who earned a comfortable living with Merrill Lynch, Pierce, Fenner and Beane in its Philadelphia office, but never managed to accumulate more than a few thousand dollars. He put Carl through the Wharton School at the University of Pennsylvania. Upon graduation, Carl joined his father at Merrill Lynch in Philadelphia as a customer's man. After a few years, he married. A year later, Carl Junior was born. Senior was the model of a customer's man, as they were called: educated, well-mannered, handsome, married into a good family, and now with a baby boy. All was perfection except he was barely making a living. He was drawn to the commodities market. It was the high leverage that intrigued him. He began to trade commodities for his own account, with modest success. Merrill Lynch's Philadelphia office had no commodities section, and none of the customer's men at the Philadelphia office dealt in commodities. When a customer wanted to do a commodity trade, his customer's man had to spend a half-hour arranging it through the New York office. Senior decided to make commodities trading his specialty, and within a short time, customers of the Philadelphia office who wanted to do commodity trades were being referred to him. His income rose. He managed to accumulate five thousand dollars, a substantial sum in 1897—enough to buy a seat on the Chicago Mercantile Exchange and later on the New York Board of Trade. He left Merrill Lynch and moved his family to

Atlantic City, where he formed Carl Krieger and Company as a commodities specialist firm. It was a good decision, and he was the only commodities broker in Atlantic City. He had little trouble attracting his former commodities customers at Merrill Lynch.

He left Merrill Lynch's Philadelphia office on good terms. The Merrill Lynch people were happy to recommend Carl Krieger and Company to anyone who wanted to trade commodities. Commissions are small in commodity trading. There was not enough in it to interest Merrill Lynch, but for Carl Krieger and Company, who made it a specialty, there was enough activity to make for a moderately successful business. About two-thirds of his customers were Philadelphians, referrals from Merrill Lynch. The Merrill Lynch people in the Philadelphia office felt justified in recommending Krieger because he didn't compete for stocks and bonds business but rather reciprocated by referring such business back to Merrill Lynch. Krieger was a safe referral, while the big brokerage companies that traded commodities were competitors for Merrill Lynch's stocks and bonds business.

Carl had a good marriage. After forty-seven years, he was still married and still in love with his wife.

At that, Bobo interrupted. "I know all about your wife, Mr. Krieger. Katherine, isn't it? Good-looking woman for a woman of sixty-five. I hope she stays well over here. You could help in that department. But go on … continue."

I saw that Bobo's remark hit its target. Senior's composure broke down and the shaking started again.

"I'm sorry, Krieger," Bobo soothed. "I didn't mean to upset you. Go on. I'm interested in your story."

Carl Krieger and Company developed a good reputation. Brokerage firms other than Merrill Lynch liked to send commodities customers to him. He always reciprocated when he had an opportunity to steer a new bond and stock trade. He stuck to commodities and became very good at it.

His life was just about perfect. Carl Junior grew up to be a carbon copy of Senior. Senior put young Carl through Wharton School, just as his own father had done for him. There was never any discussion about Junior's career. Senior got a job for him as a customer's man trainee at Merrill Lynch in Philadelphia, so he could get good training in all the financial markets and understand the culture of the brokerage business. Senior steered Carl Junior to commodities. Like Senior, Carl Junior was attracted to the high leverage characteristics of commodity trading. After two years at Merrill Lynch, Carl Junior left to join Carl Krieger and Company. Carl Senior changed the name to Krieger and Son. It was a proud day for Carl Senior. His life was 100 percent on course.

Father and son were a good team, and the business flourished. Carl Senior and Katherine led a comfortable life. They lived modestly, but Senior gave off an air of prosperity through the way he dressed and his courtly manner. It was good imagery for business. In reality, however, his earnings, while substantial for the times, never reached the level of real wealth. No matter, Carl Senior and Katherine thought themselves rich enough. They had everything they wanted.

Junior moved to his own apartment. He was one of Atlantic City's most eligible bachelors. Senior became a little troubled when he saw that Junior was developing an appetite for expensive things. The 50–50 profit split provided everything Senior needed, but Junior wanted more.

In 1934, at the age of forty, Junior decided to abandon bachelorhood. He married Emily Featherton, a pretty and vivacious young woman from a good family. Emily loved society and socializing. Junior bought a big house in Margate, suitable for gracious entertaining, far downbeach of Atlantic City, in an upscale area known as *The Parkway*. The new Mrs. Krieger turned out to be a spender too, and the financial pressures on Junior started to become serious.

Carl Senior, trying to satisfy his son's needs, changed the profit split to 40–60, the sixty being for Junior. That didn't do it for Junior's lifestyle. Soon the split became 35–65. That didn't do it either, and worse, the thirty-five percent split wasn't enough for Senior and Katherine. The relationship between father and son became strained.

Senior's world was losing its serenity. Junior's needs were too much. Junior began to draw more than his profit split. Arguments became frequent. Senior was distraught. He worried. He pleaded with Junior to cut back. Junior was hooked. He couldn't cut back.

Once, at Senior's prodding, Junior and Emily spent an evening making a list of their expenses. Senior wanted his son to write down every expense and question the need for every one, and in the process decide which to curtail or discontinue. The next morning, in response to Senior's question, Junior said, ruefully, with a twisted smile, "Yes, Dad, we did it. I went over everything with Emily. She agreed to cancel our subscription to *Look Magazine*. I can't control her. I know I opened the door for her spending. But I never dreamed it would get like this. And now I can't shut it."

Junior's remarks led to a heated argument. "What kind of joke is this?" Senior asked, aghast at the flippancy of Junior's remark, his speech slurred with frustration.

Later that day, during another argument over money, Senior grasped at his chest and collapsed. It was a double whammy, a

heart attack and a mild stroke—a doubleheader, as Senior liked to
call it later on. He barely survived the first 24 hours. Then he was
in intensive care for seven weeks. Then it was home for Senior and
a course of physical and speech therapy for several months. The
doctors ordered him not to think about business, only about his
health. Katherine tended to him. She never left his side. Gradually
he responded to the therapy. His recovery from the stroke was
almost complete. It took a long time.

Junior visited him every day. Senior never asked about business.
Even so, Junior volunteered that things were good. The money
problems were under control. Senior didn't ask questions. He
thought his life as a businessman was over. He wanted only to
exercise, sleep, and read. He read books, not the financial pages.
Business no longer interested him. He thought his remaining time
was short. Why fill it with anxiety and stress? Junior seemed to
have things under control. Katherine received the same amount of
money every week. However, Junior was doing it, it worked. Junior
was more relaxed. He spoke casually of the things he was doing at
home, the parties, the new car. All the tension between the two
men was gone. One day, Junior capped the good news with an
announcement that Emily was expecting. She was in her third
month. Senior and Katherine wept at the news. Without understanding it, Senior decided that Krieger and Son was more prosperous without him. He wondered why, briefly, but he put the
thought away. The reality was that he didn't want to know.

Ten months after the heart attack and stroke, Senior felt up to
returning to Krieger and Son. He told Junior that he would come
back to his office for a few hours, maybe read a commodities journal, maybe look over the firm's accounts. Junior welcomed the
idea. Senior looked no different than before the doubleheader, but

he was slower in every way. He noticed new faces in the back office. He had difficulty remembering their names. He spoke slowly. Sometimes he groped for a word. Most serious was that his mathematics sense was impaired. A simple problem, like adding a couple of two-digit numbers, required pencil and paper. When he studied a financial statement or a customer's account, comprehension came slowly, and sometimes, he couldn't remember it minutes later.

The customers were glad to see him. He greeted everyone with a ready smile and a firm handshake and inquired of their wives and families. All of his social skills were intact. His slowness added a new dimension of grace to an already attractive package. He did nothing at the office, really, just acted as host, read the paper, sat at his desk, and dozed off periodically.

One day, a call came in for Junior, but Junior was in a meeting and had asked not to be disturbed. Senior overheard the receptionist. The caller was Elliott Graham, a longtime customer. Senior motioned to the receptionist to give him the call. Graham asked about Katherine and how Senior was getting along. They chatted a bit, then Graham asked whether Senior could answer a question about his statement. Senior said certainly. He set down the phone and went to the customer files. Graham's account wasn't there. Then he went to the customer ledger, which, in those days, was a thick post binder book with green ledger pages for every customer.

There was no page for Elliott Graham. Senior was puzzled. He returned to the phone and told Graham that Junior must have the file. He told Graham he would call back when Junior's meeting broke up. Senior was afraid he might forget, so he wrote a note to himself and set it in the center of his desk.

Later that day, while Senior was at his desk, Junior came in to see him and saw the note. It said *Call Elliott Graham.*

"What's this?" Junior asked.

"Oh, yes." Senior had indeed forgotten. "Elliott wants me to call him. He has a question about his statement. Let me have his account. I couldn't find it in the customer file or in the customer ledger."

"I have the file," Junior said.

"But Graham's account isn't in the customer ledger. How can that be?" Senior asked.

That was when Junior decided it was time to tell his father where Krieger and Son's new prosperity was coming from.

After pausing briefly to collect himself, Senior continued with Junior's story.

While Senior was in the hospital, Junior was struggling, worse than ever. Senior's medical insurance was not covering all the medical costs and Junior's expenses kept on rising. The firm's capital was dwindling. Krieger and Son's capital, which at one time was as high as $85,000—quite substantial for a small brokerage firm in the 1930s—was all the way down to $6,000 and sinking fast. The firm would soon be in default of the Securities and Exchange Commission's minimum capital requirements. The firm was already in default of two key ratio requirements: the ratio of customers' balances to capital, and the ratio of the firm's own trading account to capital. The next quarterly SEC questionnaire would reveal the violations. That would be the end of Krieger and Son. Junior was trapped. He saw no way out. He had no place to turn. He could not deal with the idea of failing. A bankruptcy would devastate his wife. And their little girl? What about his little girl? They would all be social outcasts. He couldn't face it. After days of anguish, without coming up with a better plan, he decided to kill himself.

It was at this point in the story that Georgie and Frankie pushed Junior into the room.

65

Junior's Story

GEORGIE HAD FOUND Junior at the Krieger and Son office. The locked double doors couldn't keep Georgie out. Minutes after Georgie broke in, Frankie showed up.

Junior looked like he might have been manhandled a bit by Georgie and Frankie, though he was as well-dressed and well-groomed as always. He was even wearing his indoor shoes, the ones with the pristine soles. I guessed that Georgie and Frankie had hustled him out of the office pretty fast.

As Georgie and Frankie shoved Junior into the room, he stumbled and almost fell. Fear showed in his eyes. He straightened up, fussed briefly with his suit jacket, and jutted out his chin as he straightened his shirt collar and necktie. He looked around the room.

"Dad, Alan, Benny," he passed me over, "what are you doing here? What office is this?" He addressed Bobo. "Who are you, sir? And who are the gentlemen who broke into my office?"

"Sit down over here, Junior," Bobo said, motioning him into a wooden straight-back chair that Georgie had placed next to Senior's chair. "You'll be here a while."

"If this is about Krieger and Son, I'd better call my lawyer," Junior said.

Bobo snorted. "Your lawyer. That's very funny. Very funny." Bobo got into Junior's face. "Listen to me, Junior." Bobo's words were clipped, menacing. "Maybe better you should call your *undertaker.* Do you know who I am? My name is Bobo Truck. I'm a friend of Loretta Mauriello. I'm looking for Loretta Mauriello's money over here. You know Loretta Mauriello, don't you? She has $36,790 with you. She used to have a lot more, more than $58,000, but my friends, Benny and Alan over here, they pissed away *twenty-two grand.* Or did they? Did you have somethin' to do with that?"

"Well, Mr. Truck," Junior shifted in the chair. He drew himself up, tried for a display of authority. "Is that what this is about? I closed up because I think Krieger and Son might be in default of capital. *Might be,* I said. Perhaps not. But even if we are, I expect our customers will receive *one hundred percent* of their account balances. Please tell Miss Mauriello that her money is safe. It will take some time, however. The first thing I intend to do is to review the situation with our auditors. Why don't I keep you informed as things unfold? This meeting is premature."

With that, Junior rose and moved toward Bobo with his hand outstretched for a handshake, the image of dignity and authority. "But at any rate, Mr. Truck," he said, "it was a pleasure meeting you. Dad, I think we can leave now."

Bobo pushed Junior back down into the chair with a powerful two-handed thrust on his shoulders.

"You sit right there, Mr. Carl Krieger, Junior," Bobo snapped. "You'll leave here when I'm done with ya. If you wanna leave in one piece, don't fuck with me. You better start talking to me over here. *Where's the money?*"

Junior looked like a trapped animal. Senior spoke first, addressing his son. "Junior," he said, "I told them there is no money. I was telling them the whole story. This is the time to tell the truth. The game is over."

"Yeah, Junior," Bobo said, "time to come clean. No lawyers, no auditors, no SEC. Just you and me over here. I wanna hear the truth from *you*."

"What did you tell them, Dad?" Junior asked, nervously.

Senior filled his son in briefly and then reached out to touch his arm, reassuringly. "You finish it, son," he said. "Get it off your chest. Finally."

"Did my father tell you I considered suicide? Did he tell you that?"

"You tell me," Bobo said.

Junior continued the story.

He couldn't face the disgrace of failure. He couldn't see a way out. It was not an emotional decision. He thought it through and reached his decision by reasoning it out. The house was in joint names. It would become Emily's upon his death. He had a $50,000 life insurance policy that was seven years old, well beyond the contestable period. Emily was the beneficiary, and creditors couldn't get any of it. His wife and their little girl would be all right.

But what about Senior and Katherine? They would be penniless. Their home was paid for, and they owned their 1937 Buick. That was it. What would become of them? No, suicide was not an option. Not because he couldn't or wouldn't do it, but because it wouldn't solve their problems.

How about running away? Disappearing? That would work for Junior, but he couldn't abandon his family and his parents, leaving them disgraced and penniless. No good. Maybe steal all the customers' money and *then* run away. A little better. He could send back money, secretly, from time to time. Sooner or later, though, he knew he would be caught.

The inspiration came to him one night, sitting at his desk, alone in the office, poring over the books, hunting for a way out.

What he focused on that night was the phenomenon of how so many of his customers lost money in commodities yet continued to trade them. He and Senior had discussed it many times over the years. Why did these people persist? Senior said it was the gambler's conviction that a big win is coming.

The typical Krieger and Son customer was reasonably well-to-do, maintained a serious portfolio of stocks and bonds at Merrill Lynch or some other big brokerage firm, and dabbled in commodities at Krieger and Son with relatively small money. Krieger and Son had almost two hundred customers. The typical account was worth somewhere between $3,000 and $5,000. Junior knew that the typical customer *lost* $800 a year. The customers paid their margin calls. They groused a little about bad luck and unexpected turns, but they paid up. They were like casino gamblers. They covered their losses and continued playing.

If casino gambling had been around in those days, these respectable businessmen would have been casino regulars. Of the $800 or so of a customer's annual losses, only about $300 represented commissions. Krieger and Son operated on about $60,000 of commissions per year. The office rent was $150 per month; the receptionist earned $20 a week; the margin clerk's salary was $30 a week; the trader's salary was $40 a week; and the bookkeeper's salary was $35 a week. Other than the payroll, the biggest expense was the telephone bill and teletype, at about $250 per month. The firm earned about $2,500 per month for the Kriegers. That's $30,000 a year, which should have been enough for both families to live very well. But Junior needed more than that for his family alone.

That night, alone in the office, Junior calculated that his two hundred customers were losing $160,000 a year. Of that, only the commissions, about $60,000, went to Krieger and Son. So the idea was born: *Krieger and Son would back their customers' play!*

The trades would be fictitious. The customers would get confirmation slips, monthly statements, margin calls, everything as before *except* there would be no actual trades. Krieger and Son would become a casino, with customers playing against the house. The customers always lost. Krieger would rake in their losses.

It looked like Junior had found a solution. Immediately, he shifted his attention to the mechanics of his plan. He would have to take over all the bookkeeping. He would have to operate as before, with some of the customers, legitimately. There would be an official Krieger and Son and an official customer list.

The other customers—he thought of them as the X-accounts— would be a completely separate second set of customers. The X-customers' trades would be fictitious. Junior himself would have to maintain the X-accounts. He would have to prepare the monthly statements personally. He would have to send out the X-account margin calls himself. He would have to open all the mail himself and pull out everything that pertained to the X-accounts.

It would work. Krieger and Son's liability for the X-account credit balances would disappear from the Krieger and Son books and reappear on a new set of books, the official books, as *capital.* Presto! Plenty of capital. Thereafter, all of the additional investments by the X-accounts to cover their losses would go straight to Junior. He would share it with Senior. It was only a matter of time for each X-customer to lose his money. This way, the X-customers would lose it to Junior instead of to some unknown trader somewhere in the world. The details and mechanics of the changeover were monumental. Junior would have to lay off his trader and his margin clerk and his bookkeeper and do their jobs himself for several weeks while he restructured the books and made sure the plan would work.

Once he had everything restructured, he would hire new back-office people for the official customers. Junior would have to be the trader and entire back-office for the X-accounts. He would arrange an elaborate system so the office would seem exactly the same as before. Customers had to be able to mingle with one another, to visit, to call. All calls would have to come to Junior. The new back-office people would have to be isolated from *all* customers. The back offices had to be kept closed. Signs would say *Krieger Personnel Only*. Customers had to be kept away from the new back-office people. If an X-account customer got to speak with a back-office person, the game would be up.

The added work burden for Junior would be immense. Where would he find the time? His days would have to begin at 6:00 instead of 9:00. His normal days would end at 7:00 instead of 4:30. He would have to work at least two nights a week until 9:00, and he would have to work Saturdays—the morning at least, all day if necessary.

That was the plan. The workload was brutal, but it worked.

Junior worked harder than he ever imagined he had the capacity to work. The hardest part was at the beginning. Later, everything functioned smoothly although Junior had to put in seventy-five to eighty hours a week to keep it working. And the money started to roll in, just as Junior had planned it. The X-account customers continued to lose money, but now it was

Junior who profited from their losses rather than anonymous traders.

By the time Senior returned to work, the new system was operating smoothly. Junior even rationalized that no one was being cheated. Sometimes an X-customer made money, which meant that Junior lost it, but for the most part his selection of who to make into an official customer and who to make into an X-customer was on the money. He knew his customers. He made few mistakes in deciding which pool got which customer. When an official customer lost money, Junior was really sorry—sorry that the customer was official. When an X-customer *made* money, Junior managed to act congratulatory even though the profit would have to come out of his own pocket. He was very good at being sympathetic about X-customers' losses and developed a great style for urging them to stay in the game. He had a repertoire of big success stories. He hummed to himself, cheerfully, as he did the monthly X-accounts, alone, in the evening. *These people. They are such chronic losers.*

Junior knew he would have to tell his father what he was doing. He kept putting it off. Senior was not as sharp as he had been. Junior started to think Senior might never have to know.

When Elliott Graham called that day and reached Senior, Junior knew it was time to tell his father what he was doing. If he didn't, sooner or later Senior would tip off an X-customer, unwittingly.

Senior was outraged. "We're a *bucket shop*," he whispered. "I can't believe it. Forty years of integrity down the drain. We're common crooks." He slumped in his chair. He was afraid he was having another attack. A small voice told him that he had known something was wrong. He just didn't want to know about it.

Junior worried about his father. He tried to soothe him, calm him. When Senior regained his composure, Junior told him everything. He was persuasive. He told his father how low he had sunk, that he came close to suicide, that the only thing that stopped him was the thought of Senior and Katherine becoming paupers. Furthermore, look at the facts. No one is being hurt. These X-customers are losing money. They *always* lose money. Why shouldn't Krieger and Son take it from them instead of some nameless trader? Senior protested, but it was only a protest out of good form. He soon became a willing and helpful accomplice. No one could imagine that behind Senior's charm and grace was a bucket shop crook.

Goren was an X-customer. That was Junior's big mistake. He should have put Goren in the official pool. Goren's history showed years of small profits. That meant he belonged in the official pool; however, in the six months before Junior established the X-accounts, Goren's account was a small loser. This resulted in a small miscalculation by Junior, from which all of Krieger and Son's present troubles stemmed. When Benny and Jack opened accounts, naturally Junior assigned them to the X-pool. Same thing when Goren brought in Loretta Mauriello's five thousand dollars ten days later.

Junior became nervous when the four accounts began to make money. He made another mistake. He should have moved the four accounts to the official list then. He didn't because he didn't want to make good the profits. Greed got in his way. Junior was betting that, like just about all the commodity speculators he ever knew, Goren's lucky streak would end, and Goren would give back the gains. Even so, the gains meant nothing until and unless Goren and his friends wanted to withdraw money. Even if Goren wanted to switch to bonds or stocks, Junior would pretend to accommodate him. It didn't matter how big the accounts grew so long as they did not want to withdraw cash.

When Goren and Benny hit the big score in late August, their phony accounts were close to $30,000. Junior was scared, but he was in too deep. Then the war started. The damn accounts shot up to $55,000 in one day. He had a bad sinking feeling on the day after Labor Day when Goren and his friends accounts' shot up again and they pulled out $11,300. Suppose Goren had pulled out more? Suppose Goren had decided to cash in? Even after the withdrawal, the accounts were still over $53,000, and Junior couldn't produce that kind of money. His scheme would collapse if Goren decided to close the accounts.

A few days later, Goren pulled out another $13,000, and Junior began to worry big time. Day after day, the damn accounts kept on soaring. Goren and this Benny James were geniuses. It was as if they could see tomorrow's *Wall Street Journal*. By mid-September, the accounts were over $140,000! And the number of contracts Goren controlled? Over four hundred! The typical customer played with ten to twenty contracts, the way Goren did for all those years before Benny came on the scene. A tenth of a penny meant $20 a contract. On four hundred contracts, that was $8,000. Goren was killing him.

Even when the price of cocoa peaked and then started to fall, the accounts kept growing. Goren and Benny really were god-damn geniuses. They went short when the price started to fall. Their accounts got bigger still. Over $170,000! Junior was in a panic, worse than before the scheme. This time, his situation was much worse. This time, he would not only face bankruptcy, he would be a criminal. So would Senior. What a mess!

Then, starting around September 27, Goren and Benny seemed to lose their touch. They took some losses. Then more losses. Their losses started to mount. Just as once they couldn't seem to do anything wrong, now it looked like they couldn't do anything right. Junior started to relax. He told his father to relax. Goren and Benny were like everybody else. *You'll see, they'll go broke after all, like all the others.* Their accounts were dropping like a stone. Down they went; by the end of September, they were down to $123,000. Yesterday morning, they were down to $100,000. Junior started to think the crisis was passing.

Then came yesterday. Junior was not prepared for the shock. Goren was closing the accounts. They wanted to withdraw the money! That never happened. Customers stayed and lost money, and stayed and lost some more. There were customers who had been covering losses every year for twenty years. Nobody ever quit. Junior's game was up. There was no way Junior could find close to $100,000 to pay off the four accounts. It was a miracle that he managed to put on a good front for Goren and Benny. His heart was racing and his temples were pounding. Could they hear the pounding? His blood was coursing. Could they hear the swishing sound? He managed to smile and congratulate them. He held on until they left. He thought he was going to collapse. He had to think. He had to be alone.

Junior told his employees that he was closing early and that he was shutting down for a day. As an excuse, he said he discovered that there might be a small ratio problem with the firm's own trading account. Not a capital problem. If indeed there was a ratio problem, he would figure it out tomorrow and sell off enough to get back in ratio. No problem. Just a technical ratio glitch. He had allowed the firm's trading account to get a little too big. Everybody take tomorrow off.

Junior knew the game was up. He told Senior to go home and stay there. *Do not answer the phone.* Junior needed to think. He had five business days to find a solution. Goren would be in for his money on the eighteenth. Junior stayed late into the night, hoping to find a solution. He could mortgage Senior's house. It was worth $20,000. He could get a mortgage loan for $15,000. His own house was worth $35,000, but it had a mortgage of $12,000. He could refinance. That would get him another $12,000. Some personal loans would produce another $8,000 to $10,000. That's about $35,000 to $37,000; not even close to the almost $100,000 he needed to pay off Goren's four accounts. He didn't mind stealing from customers, but there was nothing left to steal.

My God, he thought, *just one mistake, but what a mistake!* If Goren's accounts were official accounts, none of this mess would have happened. The contracts would have been real. The profits would have been real. Even the commissions were wasted. At one time, the four accounts had been carrying over four hundred contracts. Every time Goren made a trade, it was worth $2.50 a contract, a thousand dollars a trade. Some days, they made four trades. Some days, as many as five or six. Back in the middle of August, when they were carrying ninety-six contracts, they made *eight* trades a day, three days in a row. The commissions would have been $1,920 a day. If the Goren accounts were in the official pool, the commissions alone would have been enough to lift Krieger and Son out of trouble. The Goren accounts were generating as much commission as all the official accounts combined. As it was, because the trades were fictitious, so were the commissions. The phantom commissions got absorbed into the four phantom Goren accounts. The phantom commissions reduced Goren's gains, but Goren's trading profits were overcoming the commissions easily.

Junior left the office at 3:00 AM. He didn't wake Emily. He tried to sleep but couldn't. At 5:30 he got up, showered, dressed and returned to the office, alone. He was going over all the accounts, looking for an idea. He ignored knocking on the door, several times. Then Georgie burst in.

"That's the story," Junior concluded. "The four accounts show credit balances of $99,456. And there is no money. I can't pay."

66

Bobo's Solution

"THAT WAS A very interesting story over here, Junior," Bobo said, his demeanor almost pleasant. "But you know what? This ain't a complicated story. All that shit about X-accounts and margin clerks. It's simple as ABC. You backed my bet. And you lost. And you don't wanna pay. You want to welch on Bobo, for thirty-seven grand. Is that it?"

Junior squirmed. "It's not like that, Mr. Truck. Krieger and Son is a business enterprise that is in trouble. I have it all in focus after last night and this morning. If the firm goes bankrupt, I calculate that the recovery for all the customers—the official ones and the X-customers alike—will be about ten cents on the dollar. Dad and I will get wiped out and most likely I will serve a 2–5 year sentence. I don't think they will put Dad away. He'll get a suspended sentence. So, I believe, sincerely, that it is in your best interest and in the best interest of all our customers to accept informal settlements and let Krieger and Son get out of business quickly, without lawyers for the creditors and lawyers for the firm and auditors, and SEC examiners. Of course, I have a very selfish reason also. I don't want to be in criminal trouble. It's bad enough that I'll be broke. If my customers agree to informal settlements, I can pay fifteen cents on the dollar to everybody. It will take me about a month to marshal the assets. What do you think? Does that seem reasonable?"

Bobo pushed off from the desk. He stood in front of Junior, who was looking up at Bobo hopefully. With no hint of what was coming,

Bobo's arm shot out like a piston. He drove his fist into Junior's mouth. His fist was big and meaty. The blow smashed into Junior's mouth and the lower half of his nose. The force of the blow knocked Junior's head back into the high back of the chair with such force that the chair fell over backward with Junior in it. Junior's face squirted blood.

"Georgie," Bobo said, "quick, get a coupla towels. Don't let him mess up the carpet. Jesus, between Pop pissin' and Junior bleedin', this carpet over here is going to get all messed up." He turned to Frankie. "Frankie, pick up this piece of shit."

Frankie lifted the chair into an upright position with Junior in it.

Bobo resumed his seat on the edge of the desk. He put on the pleasant face again. "Now, then, Junior, do you get the idea that I don't like your plan?"

Junior's face was a bloody mess. His nose was broken, his lips were split. It looked like several teeth had been knocked loose.

Georgie returned with two wet towels. Junior held them over his face. Frankie stood behind Junior, casually, like a sentinel, his hands clasped behind him. Senior's trembling and shaking started up again, bad. His whole body was shaking as if attached to a vibrator.

Goren stood up. "Bobo," he said, "that was uncalled for. That was a brutish thing to do."

"Brutish? Is that what you said, Alan? Are you tryin' to insult me over here, or what?"

"The way I see it," Goren said, "it's only money. And it's money that we won. We got our original money out. And we pulled out a profit besides. What's left is all profit. If we have to settle for fifteen percent of it, we're still way ahead."

"Now, you look here, Alan," Bobo answered, giving Goren that dangerous squinty-eye look from under his eyebrows. "I like you. You're a friend and you're a sportin' guy. I ain't forgot that you was at Chateau-Thierry, because that fuckin' hellhole I was in was only twenty miles away, so I'm gonna forget you called me a brute. OK? But this is what you gotta unnerstan'. I back bets. Horses, numbers, ballgames, you name it. That's my business. When I lose, I pay. When I win, I get paid. That's how it works. Now this piece of shit over here, he backed my play. I won. He lost. He's gotta pay."

Bobo turned to Junior. "Who knows about this, Junior?"

"Nobody," Junior's voice was muffled behind the towels, "just us in this room."

"That's good, Junior," Bobo said, "because if it got around that I was stiffed … that would be no good … you unnerstan'? I'd have to do something terrible to you. You, too, Pop. And your families. Nobody stiffs me. Get it? That's my stock in trade. You ain't nothin' special. You're just another fuckin' welcher. Terrible things happen to welchers. So here's what you're gonna do. You're gonna bring me twenty-five grand, in cash. I'm a reasonable man. I'll give you two days. You'll bring it here. In a briefcase. In twenty dollar bills."

"Mr. Truck," Junior mumbled from behind the towels, "I can't assemble that kind of money. Be reasonable."

Without warning, Bobo pushed off from the desk and delivered another piston blow, this time to the upper nose and between the eyes. You had to admire his accuracy. It was obvious that he struck where he aimed. Junior and the chair started to go over again, but Frankie, who was standing sentinel behind the chair, must have expected it. He caught the chair as it went over and stood it up again. More blood.

Bobo spoke calmly, "Be reasonable you say? Don't you get it, Junior?" Bobo rubbed his fist. "You're gonna do what I tell you.

Unnerstan'? Or is it comin' to you maybe that you oughta go to the police? Now, *that* is a funny, funny idea."

Bobo's brows knit. His expression turned malevolent. He thrust his face to within inches of Junior. "Now look here, you piece of shit," he snarled, "you'll be here two days from now, on Saturday, at 4:00 sharp with twenty-five grand, like I said. And that ain't all. You'll come here every Saturday, the same time, with a grand. *Every week* until I tell you to stop. You're gonna owe me *vigorish*. I'll figure it out. I'll tell you when to stop. Is all that clear, *Mr.* Krieger?"

Junior nodded, pressing the towels to his face.

"OK, you two can go. Go 'head, Pop. Take your boy home. Tell him to open the business tomorrow, like nothin' happened. He's gonna have to fuck all the other customers so he can pay me. Look at my carpet over here, Junior. I'm gonna have to get it cleaned. I'll add that to your account."

As the Kriegers rose to leave, Benny called out, "Hey, Junior, what about Alan and me and Jack? How you goin' to pay us?"

"Let them go," Bobo said. "*I'll* deal with you guys." The Kriegers left.

Bobo turned his attention to us. "I don't know what to do with you guys. It's a goddamn puzzle. On one hand over here, you made me some money. Five grand at least. If I collect from Junior, maybe more. Maybe more than forty grand. That ain't peanuts. But you are an unusual problem. You see, when I back a bet with some-body I don't know, the guy what introduced me is responsible. If I win and don't get paid, I look to the guy what introduced me. Unnerstan'? Unnerstan' my problem? You brought me Krieger. I didn't know him. You're responsible for him."

"Krieger is a forty-some-year-old company," Goren said, "with a good reputation. I've been doing business there for seventeen years. How could I know it's a bucket shop?"

"Too bad, Alan," Bobo answered, "Krieger is your man. I look to you. The trouble over here is that I like you guys. And you, kid," he said, pointing his finger at me. "I owe you one. I don't forget favors. But like I told Junior, business is business. I'm gonna think about this. I'll let you guys know about it next week. Be here next Monday, 4:30 sharp. Stay away from Krieger's. Don't talk about this to nobody. I'll see you then. By the way, Alan, what's a bucket shop?"

Goren explained, "It's a phony brokerage company that pretends to buy and sell for you, but really doesn't. All make-believe. They take in the customers' money, and one day, they disappear and nobody can find them. Then they open up under a different name in another city. Krieger turned into a hybrid. Half their business was legitimate. We got stuck in the bucket shop half."

"How about that," Bobo said. "Ya gotta be so careful. There's such crooks out there."

67

Pinochle Game

W<small>E LEFT</small> B<small>OBO</small>'<small>S</small> a little after 6:00. It was Thursday. I sped home to dinner. From Bobo's to home, from one world to another. Could the two be any more different?

Our weekly pinochle game began at 7:30 on Thursday evenings in our kitchen. I had trouble focusing on the game. What was Bobo's plan for us? I kept turning over the problem in my mind as the game went on. I must have played very badly. I don't know how I managed to play at all. Evie was the fourth, still taking Bernie's place. Blinky had been teaching her the game, and we were keeping up the Thursday night tradition, doggedly. Evie was dreadful, but she was improving. If we could have found a better fourth, we'd have dumped her. We were patient with her. We had to be. She was our only available fourth.

Evie loved the game. She loved being part of the foursome. I knew she had a crush on Eddie, but he was oblivious. To Eddie, she was a thirteen-year-old kid. She was just my little sister, and she could just as well have been my brother.

Blinky, on the other hand, was quite aware that Evie was a girl, and developing, but I knew he wouldn't try anything. I'd given him my warning, and I knew he would heed it. We paired Blinky with Evie because he was so much better than Eddie or me. Evie was his handicap. That pairing made the two teams pretty even.

Mom put out homemade cookies and milk for us. At 8:00, we stopped for a half-hour to listen to our favorite radio program, *Big*

Town, with Edward G. Robinson as Big Town's crusading newspaper editor. Then back to the game, until 9:30, which was bedtime for Evie.

"How did I play tonight?" she asked. She and Blinky had scored the only *schnitz* of the evening (winning all twelve tricks), thanks to Evie interpreting, correctly, Blinky's *peetie* (a no-value discard on your partner's winning trick).

"You're improving," Eddie said. "You're almost up to real bad."

She made a face. "You're mean," she said.

Blinky was generous. "Oh, yeah," he said to Eddie, blinking twice, "how about that *peetie* she picked up on? You're improving," he said to Evie. "Don't listen to Eddie. He don't play so good himself."

Eddie and Blinky and I talked some about school and how the Yankees were doing and made some uninformed comments about the war in Europe. These were my best friends, and this was my favorite kind of evening—at home with friends, conversation, a card game, a favorite radio program. It was crazy that a few hours earlier I was watching Bobo mess up Junior's face and wondering if Goren and Benny and I were going to be next. I shuddered. My life was too complicated. I was only fifteen. I was in over my head. What was Bobo going to do with us, or *to* us? I still hadn't told anyone that I was part of the cocoa game.

My father came in a little after 9:30. He was tired but feeling good. "Big day," he said, "business is getting good. Since Labor Day, I'm up every day over last year. The district manager told me he's going to recommend me for a $3.00 a week raise." He slipped off his suit jacket and necktie, washed his hands and face, and sat down to the hot supper that mom had waiting for him. *He is so solid,* I thought. *His life is so straight, so tough, ... so dull.* I didn't want his life. Not after being exposed to Goren and Benny and cocoa.

Until I went to work at Krilow's, my father's life looked good to me. It was safe and predictable. He paid his bills and took care of us and made us feel secure. He epitomized the American Way of Life. He was a Norman Rockwell painting. I was proud of him. I admired him. I loved him. But his life was not for me. No thanks.

68

Sunday Night at Zena's

I ARRIVED AT Zena's parlor at 7:30 on Sunday evening for a meeting we'd agreed to after leaving Bobo's on Thursday. Benny had just arrived. It was a cool evening. He was wearing a topcoat. He was on the boardwalk outside Zena's entrance with Gwen, who looked adorable in a woolly jacket and knit cap with a pom-pom on it. She was holding his arm with both hands and smiling. Benny was his old self, neatly dressed, lively and alert, with that big smile and the dancing eyes.

"Hey, here comes Jack," Benny said. "Say hello to Gwen. Gwen is leaving. Bye, dear." He planted a quick kiss and patted her backside. "I'll see you later, about 9:30."

She gave me a big smile, reached up to kiss Benny's cheek, and took off. *She sure is a good-looking girl*, I thought, watching her walk away, with that bouncing step she had.

Goren was inside. It looked like he'd been there for awhile. The parlor was invitingly warm. Goren and Zena looked the way I was getting used to finding them: Goren, half-asleep, sprawled on the sofa, shoes off, newspapers on him and on the floor, the radio playing classical music. Zena was reading at the round table. The samovar was working. It made its *bloop, bloop* sound every few seconds. The aroma of tea filled the room.

"Well, everybody," Benny said, energetically, his arms spread as if embracing the entire scene, "here we are again. Alan, you look like you belong here. Zena, you're getting better lookin' all the time. Is Alan doing something? Or is it seeing me so often? C'mon, give us a hug."

He lifted her out of her chair with a big bear hug and kissed her cheek. "I love you, Zena. Let me steal you away from him." They laughed. It was one hundred percent Benny James. Goren sat up.

"You seem pretty chipper," he said to Benny with a smile, "considering you just lost eleven thousand dollars and Bobo is liable to break your legs tomorrow."

"No way, Alan." Energy poured out of him. He was in constant motion. "Bobo is our friend. He *likes* us. We made money for him. If he doesn't collect a dime from Junior, he still doubled his money. In a coupla months. What's so bad about that? And he'll probably squeeze something out of Junior. He's putting on a show for us. Not to worry, Alan. How about some tea, Zena? Any cookies? And hey, Alan, I only started with six hundred bucks. If I have to give Bobo the whole three grand I pulled out, I'll be out six hundred bucks. No big deal. I never had any money to speak of. I'm used to not having money. I'll go out on the circuits. I'll be OK."

Goren was very sober. "You're right about the money, Benny," he said, thoughtfully. "If I end up with what I had before all this began, I'll be fine. I got along all these years. I'll get along again. I don't need Bobo for a friend. I just don't want him as an enemy."

"Forget it, Alan," Benny said. "I tell you, Bobo is not goin' to do anything to us. We're his friends. He'll probably ask us to open an account for him at Bache and trade it for him. He saw what we can do. I figure I'll take off a little time and then dive back in. This time, I'm gonna go long crude oil futures. I *know* this war is gonna be bad and long. Oil is gonna go through the roof. I'll make a killing. Bigger than the cocoa." He paused. Then, he said, softly, almost to himself, "Of course, it depends on whether or not Bobo leaves me with any money."

"Anyway, fellows," Goren said, "why are we meeting? Can you think of anything we can do to influence Bobo's decision for what he's going to do with us, or *to* us?"

Zena answered, "Alan, I don't think you can do or say anything. A lot depends on whether Junior brought the twenty-five thousand dollars yesterday. If he did, or even any part of it, Bobo may be satisfied to go after Junior and let you fellows alone."

"Well, I made a decision," Goren said. "I'll give up the profit I collected. My account was worth $5,600 when we took Bobo's money. I pulled out ten thousand. I'm willing to give back the $4,400 profit. But no more. That $5,600 is mine. I didn't ask Bobo to give us his money. I tried to discourage him. He just about forced the money on us. I told him the risk."

"Yeah, Alan," Benny replied, "you told him the *trading* risk. That's different. I think Bobo would have accepted losing the whole five grand without a peep. Like betting on a baseball game. What's crazy is that he may not be satisfied with a five grand profit. Because he placed his bet and won, and he wants to get paid. That's his life. That's what his whole organization is based on. To him, every day that we didn't pull out, we were making a new bet. His mindset is as if he collected his winnings every day and then gave it back to us to bet some more. That was *his* money. Not profits, like *we* think about it. To him, that was hard cash, every day. I think I understand him. He's not like us. We think the profit was the House's money. I remember how many times I told Jack it's not ours until we pull it out."

"Anyway, Benny," Goren said, very calmly, very seriously, "I won't suffer abuse from Bobo. Or anyone else. I'll give up $4,400.

That's it. No more. And he's not going to lay a hand on me. Nobody can do that to me."

"Alan, you're scaring me," Zena said, full of concern. "You will have to give him the whole ten thousand if that's what he wants. You could get hurt, physically. I'm frightened for you. He's a dangerous man."

I studied Goren. He was not a big man. And he certainly was not tough looking. Yet, there was an essence about him that warned, like the flag of Vermont in Colonial times, *Don't Tread On Me*!

"Well, we'll know soon enough," Benny said. "I'm goin'. Alan, you're depressing me. See you tomorrow at Bobo's."

"Me, too," I said. "I have to get home."

Eddie was coming over. We had homework to do. *Homework— isn't that droll?* I thought.

69

Settling Up With Bobo

"C'MON IN, GUYS," Bobo waved us into the office the following day. He consulted his watch. "You're right on time. I like that about you, Alan. You're precise."

Goren spoke. "Did Junior show up yesterday?"

"That's right, Alan, come right to the point. Yes, he did. He brought fourteen grand. He was so scared over here, he could hardly talk or stand straight. He said he needed more time."

"What did you do, Bobo?" Goren asked.

"I took it and I let him go. I didn't lay a hand on him. I gave him until next Saturday for the other eleven grand *plus* the first thousand of the thousand a week. He'll bring it. I could tell. I didn't have to get tough with him. Anyway, sit down, guys. Make yourselves comfortable. Want some sodas? Sandwiches? Anything to drink?"

"Like you said, Bobo, let's come to the point," Goren said. "What are your plans for me and Benny and Jack? I am not going to try to sell you on anything. You know how I feel about things. You wanted in. You made some money. As far as you and us are concerned, that ought to be the end of it. Whatever else you get from Junior, so much the better for you."

"What about you guys?" Bobo asked. "Junior owes you, too."

"I will go and see him," Goren said. "I will settle with him if he wants to. If I can't get anything out of him, I'll forget it. We three talked it over. We are ahead of the game just from what we pulled out. We are satisfied even if we get nothing else. We're not going to

the police or the SEC. That will not get us anything except satis-
faction, maybe. And we do not want to be the cause of putting
Junior in jail and breaking Senior's heart. He's been hurt bad
enough. Like I told you, Bobo, I'm not a sore winner."

Bobo stood, came out of his chair, and took up that half-seated
position on the front of his desk. When he was like that, you didn't
know if he was going to embrace you or break your nose. When he
spoke, it was with a serious but friendly manner. "Well, Alan. Well,
Benny, Jack, tell you what. I took a likin' to you three. I'm gonna do
something for you. *I'm* gonna settle your accounts. I'm gonna *buy*
your accounts for fifteen percent. You'd never get a dime outta
Junior. You *know* that. So I'm gonna do you a favor. I'll *buy* your
accounts for fifteen percent. And you don't have to thank me,
cause I'll collect them in full. Every fuckin' dime. A thousand a
week. He'll be bringing me money for the next year and a half.
That's without the *vigorish*. I'll figure that at the end. I got it all figured out what you guys get.

"Alan, your account is $48,077. I'm buying it for $7,211.

"Benny, your account is $10,968. I'm buying it for $1,645.

"Jack, your account is $3,621. I'm buying it for $543.

"I got the money right here."

He went into his drawer and brought out three envelopes. They
were marked "A, 7,211," "B, 1,645," and "J, 543."

"Here, take 'em."

We were stunned. Nobody spoke. For the first time since I knew
him, Benny had nothing to say. Finally, I spoke up. "Thanks, Mr.
Truck. I don't know what to say, except *thanks*. The money is great.
What's better is that we're still friends."

"You said it, Jack," Bobo gave me one of those backslaps that
almost knocked me down.

"Well, Benny, Alan, whatcha say?"

Benny came to life. "Bobo, you're the greatest. Like Jack said, the money's good, but your friendship is more important."

"Alan?" Bobo asked.

Goren hesitated. When he spoke, it was with regret in his voice, "I appreciate this, Bobo, but I can't take it. Not on those terms. I think Junior is bad. Real bad. He's a crook and all that, but I can't take this money and have you go after him for the rest. I would rather lose everything he owes me. It doesn't feel right. He is not an evil person. He got caught in a trap. He married the wrong woman. I'm angry at him. But I don't hate him. I feel sorry for him.

"Look. I'm OK. I am like I was before. Better, because through the cocoa business, I met Benny and Jack and Zena. And you, too, Bobo. I'm glad you're going to collect what Junior owes you. I would like to make that fifteen percent settlement with him. It is a lot of money for me. But I can't let you buy the account. I can't even explain it. He's not worth my concern. He's a bucket shop operator. So why should I care if you buy my account and make him make it good? I shouldn't. I should be glad to see him punished. But I can't. Forgive me, please, Bobo. Don't think I'm ungrateful." He placed his envelope on the desk.

"How about you, Benny, and you, Jack?" Bobo asked.

Benny gave the big smile. "I guess I feel like Alan. I don't know why." He leaned toward Goren. "Alan, you're fuckin' nuts. I knew it the day I met you. You have these goddamn principles. You're full of 'em. You're a pain in the ass ... I don't know why I even like you, you're such a *schmuck*." Benny returned the envelope.

There was nothing left for me to do. I returned mine as well.

"You guys," Bobo shook his head, "you guys. I don't know whether to admire you or send you to the funny farm. Here," he pushed the envelopes back. "Take these. I'll settle with that prick for you, for fifteen percent. Don't worry that I won't get it. I will. I won't make a dime on it. No *vigorish* or anything. I'll just get made whole for what's in those envelopes. And Alan, don't forget, I already got fourteen grand out of him. I ain't gonna be a loser, no how. And to quote a good friend of mine, *Me, a sore winner? Never!*"

70

Last Meeting of the Four

B ENNY ARRANGED FOR us to meet at Zena's the following Sunday, October 22, at 4:30. It was the last time the four of us were together.

Benny was wearing a trench coat and a hat and was carrying two suitcases. He said he was catching a 6:00 bus to Baltimore. From there he was taking the train to Florida. He was headed for Miami Beach. There was a kitchen gadget booth on Lincoln Drive. They offered him a good deal.

"I'm gonna spend the winter down there," he said. "I'm gonna get my head cleared. I can't hang around here. I'll get in trouble. I have all this money, forty-six hundred dollars. I never figured to have that much money at one time. I thought about going back into commodities. And maybe I will. But not yet. I don't know if I understood anything about it. Maybe it was just a run of good luck, and a *real* lucky guess on picking when the war would start."

Benny sat at the round table and lit a cigarette. He tried to imitate the Goren smoke rings, but he wasn't good at it. "I'm practicin'," he said. Then he continued, "I remember what Junior said. All those customers of his, all those years, none of 'em made any money. Well, maybe a few guys, like you, Alan. But what did you or anybody ever make? A couple thousand dollars a year? Hell, you can't make a living on that. And it is hard work. Since we quit, I'm a new man. I feel good and relaxed and healthy. I feel great. And I'm rich! Thanks to you, Alan. And you, Zena. And you, too, Jack.

You started the whole thing with that arithmetic contest. Hey, wasn't that *somethin'*?" He laughed.

The arithmetic contest seemed like ages ago. I could see Benny standing behind the counter, hands resting on the countertop, calm, with a half smile, waiting for Bobo to say *Start!*

"Benny, don't go," I said. "Stay here. Your friends are here. You have money. You can go into business."

"You're a good kid, Jack," Benny said. "I'm gonna miss you, and you, Alan, and you, Zena. But it's time to move on. Hey, don't look so sad. I'll be back next summer. How about you, Alan?"

"More of the same for me, Benny. I'll open an account at Bache. I think you're right about crude oil futures. I'll try them. Not big. I don't have to go big time. Just ten or fifteen contracts. I'll do some real estate deals. It will be like before except now I'm rich, and I have friends. I'm worth over $17,000. Before I met Zena, I was worth all of thirty-five hundred. I was up to a little over five thousand when you took over. What an adventure! I'm not going to try to talk you into staying in Atlantic City. You go, get yourself together. Don't speculate. Hang on to your money. Next summer, you and I will do things together."

Zena said, "Sit down, Benny, I'll pour you a cup of tea. One for the road."

"Look in the ball, Zena," Benny said, "and tell us what's gonna be."

"Oh no, Benny, none of that stuff. I can't see past the next minute and you know it. I can hope for things, though. I hope you'll be OK. I hope Jack forgets all of this grown-up stuff and becomes a fifteen-year-old boy again. And Alan, I hope you'll keep your barrier down, and I hope I'm gonna see you a lot, maybe all the time. Look, I'm blushing. How about that, an old bag like me, blushing."

Zena poured tea for all of us. We reminisced for a while. Then it was time for Benny to catch his bus. "Well, guys, and lovely lady, time for me to say *so long, 'til we meet again.*"

Goren extended his hand for a handshake, but Benny ignored it and gave him a huge hug and several energetic back slaps. Then Benny embraced Zena and kissed her, loud, on her cheek. He saved his farewell to me for last. "Remember everything I taught you, Jack. Pay attention to your schoolwork. And stay close to Alan over here. Did I say *over here*? I'm pickin' up bad habits from Bobo. Good thing I'm leavin' before I pick up something worse." He embraced me. I managed to say, "I'll miss you, Benny," before I choked up and couldn't say more.

He backed away toward the door, tossed us a salute, turned, and was gone.

"What a guy," Goren said. "I am going to miss him terribly. But listen, Jack, I don't want you and me to lose touch. Stop in here at Zena's any Sunday afternoon. Maybe I won't be here, because she might get tired of me hanging around. If so, you know where I live. Find me there. Oh, yes, and look, I brought you something. I'm taking over from Morris." He handed me a beautiful leather-bound book, *The History of the World in One Hundred Pages*, by Hendrick Van Loon.

"Thanks, Mr. Goren," I said. "I really appreciate this, and I'm glad I'll still be seeing you and Zena."

"Jack," Goren said, "I am also getting like Bobo. Please drop the *Mr. Goren.* Call me *Alan.*"

71

What Happened to Evie

NOVEMBER 5, 1939.

It was Sunday, a sunny day, warm for November. Evie spent the morning doing homework. Mom left to visit her cousin, but first she fixed a peanut butter and jelly sandwich for Evie's lunch, with a glass of milk and two homemade oatmeal cookies. Evie finished her homework, had an early lunch, then headed out to a girlfriend's house about five blocks away, downbeach. It was 10:30 AM. She wore a plaid skirt, knee-high knit stockings, saddle shoes, and a woolen cable-knit sweater with a round neckline. The collars of her white blouse lay over the round neckline of the sweater, a Little-Bo-Peep look. She was carrying her loose-leaf schoolbook. She was going to review homework with her friend.

She crossed Annapolis Avenue. There were the Mackey brothers. It was their hangout corner. Tom was leaning against the wall. John was leaning against the light pole on the curb. She passed between them, trying to look straight ahead as if preoccupied with her thoughts. She was afraid of the Mackeys. She wished she had walked around the block in the other direction to Atlantic Avenue, and crossed Annapolis Avenue at Atlantic Avenue instead of at Ventnor Avenue.

"Hi, Evie," Tom Mackey called. "Howya doin'?" He gave her a big smile, more like a leer. She started to say *hello* without stopping. Before she could finish the word, Tom shot out his left arm, and in one sweeping motion, grabbed her left arm with his left hand, turning her back to him, clapped his right arm around her shoulders and across her mouth, and pulled her backward into the narrow windowless alleyway between the first two houses. There was no one else on or near the corner to witness what was happening. It happened swiftly, in seconds. John moved into the alley. His bulk concealed from Ventnor Avenue what was happening. The Mackeys had Evie inside the narrow alley. Tom held her off the ground in front of him, her feet kicking in the air, her back pulled against his chest, his right arm across her chin and mouth, her mouth squeezed into the crook of his elbow.

Evie tried to scream but her mouth was sealed off, smothered by the massiveness of Tom Mackey's huge right arm. The whole maneuver took only a few seconds. John still stood in the narrow alleyway, blocking Tom and Evie from view. Tom pulled her deeper into the alleyway. All the way in. John followed in, effectively sealing off the alleyway.

"Don't kick, Evie," Tom grunted. "Don't squirm. I don't want to hurt you." He began to pant from the exertion of trying to hold her still. She felt his hot breath on the back of her neck, smelled the foulness of his breath, felt the stubble of his chin.

She tried to scream. Only a tiny muffled sound escaped from behind Tom's massive arm. She kicked, her legs pushing and kicking and pumping. She tried to flail her arms. With his left arm, Tom locked her arms in place, pinned to her sides. She raised her knees and pressed her feet against one brick wall of the narrow alleyway. She pushed backward with all her might. The thrust was unexpected. Tom's back was slammed against the opposite brick wall. *Whoosh!* He lost his breath. His grip loosened momentarily.

She struggled to break free and run away. She started to scream, but Tom was already recovered. He grabbed her by the back of her neck. He turned her around and punched her, hard, in the stomach. "Little bitch," he snarled. The blow was massive. Evie fell to the ground, almost unconscious. She gasped for breath. She could hardly breathe. Her lungs and stomach were on fire with pain. With what strength she could muster, she tried to struggle to her feet, a wounded bird. She was crying. Silent cries. Tears filled her eyes. Her lungs could not find the air to scream. Tom propped her up against the wall with his left hand under her chin. He slapped her. She slumped but could not fall. She was pinned against the wall. Now she was still, limp, gasping for air.

Leisurely, Tom reached forward with his free right hand. He palmed her little breasts, pinched her tiny nipples through her sweater. "Ya got nice little titties, Evie," he panted. Then he reached under her skirt and pushed his hand between her legs. She tried again to kick and squirm, but his left hand pressed her against the wall like a vise. Her cries were choked off. Silent screams.

"Ya got a nice little cunt here, Evie," he grunted, his foul breath a hot blast in her face. He hooked his thumb into the top of her panties. With a quick yank, he pulled her panties down to her knees. She kicked and flailed her arms again. Tom's vise grip held firm. She kicked her feet in the air. She tried to cross her legs. Tom was not to be denied. "Let's see what your little cunt looks like," he panted. He started to push a finger into her. A thick sausage of a finger. His fingernail scratched her. He pushed. A spear of pain shot through her. She fainted. He let go. She slipped to the concrete. She lay still, her slip and skirt up above her waist. Her panties around her knees.

John was frightened. "You hurt her, Tom. This could be bad. You went too far."

"Fuck you, John. I didn't do this by myself. Stop yer fuckin' whining."

Tom lifted her up, gently, carefully, a monster lifting the broken bird, a passerby would have thought his gentleness was the gentleness of love.

"Evie," he whispered in her ear. "Evie, wake up. You're OK. Wake up."

She came to. She started to scream, but he clapped his hand over her mouth.

"Don't scream. Don't fight. I'm lettin' you go. Go home. You're all right. Nothin' happened. You're fine. Go home. But listen, Evie, you better keep quiet about this, or next time ... *and there will be a next time* ... if you tell anybody about this. Get me? Keep quiet and we'll all forget all about this. I won't bother you no more. But you go blabbin', you'll be sorry. I didn't hurt you none. But *next time*. You know, I might do somethin' *real bad*. Now get goin'."

She pulled up her panties. She gathered up her loose-leaf book and ran home, sobbing. Salty tears of humiliation and rage ran down her face. No one was home. I was at Frederick's Drug Store, hanging out with Alice and a bunch of guys and girls. Alice was perfecting my jitterbug technique to the rhythms of the big bands on Frederick's jukebox. My father was not home from work yet. Mom was visiting her cousin.

Two hours later, I came home and found Evie sobbing in her bed. She was curled up on her right side, facing away from me. Her long, fair hair, usually so neat and groomed, covered her face in tangled disarray, moist with tears and perspiration. Her knee-high stockings drooped around her ankles, revealing dirty scratches and bruises on her legs. Her sweater was soiled. So were the collar points of her white blouse that hung over the sweater's neckline.

"What's wrong, Evie?" Her sobs frightened me.

More sobbing. Deep full-throated sobbing. She didn't answer.

"Evie, what's the matter?" I sat on the bed. I touched her shoulder. She turned to me. Her eyes were red and swollen. Tears stained her cheeks. A dirty, reddish welt covered the left side of her neck.

"Oh, Jack, it was horrible," she shook with sobbing. "He … he …" she turned away and buried her head in the pillow. She was trying to be quiet. I sensed that she wanted to scream, but she was afraid to be heard in the apartment below. She was choking back the screams and trying to stifle the sobbing.

I held her in my arms. I tasted the saltiness of her tears. "What, Evie? What happened? Who?"

"Oh, Jack," she sat up, suddenly, and threw her arms around my neck. She buried her head in my shoulder. "He … he … he …"

"What, Evie, what? Tell me."

Between sobs and tears, she told me. I boiled with stifled fury. I tried to comfort her. I held her tight and rocked back and forth with her in my arms.

"It's OK, Evie," I said it over and over while I rocked her. I was choking with rage, but I tried to soothe her. "It's OK. It's OK. It's OK." I held her like that until she fell asleep. Gently, I took off her shoes; I opened the top sheet and blanket and lay her down, carefully, quietly. She slept. The rage consumed me. I trembled with rage as I pulled up the blanket and lay it over the sheet. I brought the sheet and blanket up under her chin. I wet a washcloth with warm water. I washed away her tears as gently as I could. She slept. An angel. I loved her. I kissed her. I rose to leave. I pulled on my windbreaker. I looked back at her, sleeping. "Don't worry, Evie," I whispered. "I'm gonna kill 'em."

72

Vengeance

I WASN'T THINKING. Only feeling. Rage. Hot, like something heating my blood almost to a boil. They say that an adrenaline rush gives you strength. Power surged through me. I felt myself swell with power. I had no plan. Just rage. But as I headed down the stairs, an image came to me. I could see it in my mind's eye. A length of iron pipe, lumpy with several coats of white paint, lying near the trashcan at the rear of our alley. A plumber discarded it after replacing a hot water riser a few days ago. I went into the alley and searched for it. Yes, there it was, lying on the concrete, up against the wall, an eighteen-inch length of inch-and-a-half iron pipe with the knuckle of an elbow soldered to one end. I slipped it up my left sleeve, cupping the iron elbow in my left hand. I knew Tom Mackey would grab at my right arm with his left hand. I had to hit him and stop him before he hit me. The first blow would decide the outcome.

They saw me approaching. Tom advanced a couple of steps nearer to the Annapolis Avenue curb. John stood a pace behind to Tom's right. "Well, well," Tom grinned. "Look who's here. It's Jackie-ass. Tell you what, Jackie-prick, don't cross the street, and I won't beat the shit out of you."

I continued to walk forward, fast. I noticed a flicker in his eye as I started across Annapolis Avenue. Was it fear? He stepped back a half step and half crouched and bowed his arms in readiness like a wrestler. He curled his lips in a snarl, like a dog getting ready to attack. But there was a question in his eyes. He hadn't expected me to cross over toward him.

I never slowed down. I was ready for his cat-like lunge. As I approached him, I let the pipe slip out of my sleeve and caught it with my left hand near the end. I was ready for his lunge at me. Sure enough, as soon as I got in range, his left hand shot out to grab my right arm, just like the last time, last May. I was prepared. I was still walking toward him as I swung the pipe up at him with my left hand, a sharp, short swing, too quick to give him time to deal with it. His left hand just reached my right arm as the elbow end of the pipe caught him under the right side of his jaw. *Crack!*

An instant realization came to me as the pipe hit him that I was bigger since the May beating. He staggered from the blow. An animal sound came from him. A howl of pain. I shifted the pipe to my right hand. The second blow followed an instant later. *Crack!* I grunted as the pipe caught him behind his left ear. Blood spurted. A third blow struck down at his left shoulder as he fell. *Crack!* I broke his collarbone. He was down.

John moved toward me. He was a little late. He'd wasted a few precious seconds watching the quickness and ferocity of my attack. Now he approached, crouching, looking to grab the pipe. He reached for it, but my swing came from below, like an uppercut. It caught his left hip, then skipped up to catch him under his chin. He fell back and went down.

I returned to stand over Tom. He was on the ground writhing and groaning. I took careful aim and shattered his left knee. I aimed again. *Crack!* I shattered his right wrist. I was about to crack his skull when a strong pair of arms grabbed me from behind. It was Eddie. Where did he come from? "Stop it, Jack!" He pulled me back. "You're killing him."

"Let me go, Eddie." I struggled to break free. He held me fast. I grunted, "I'm not finished."

"Yes, you are," Eddie said. He took the pipe from me. "Now go home. I'll get them to the hospital. Go!" He pushed me. I saw that several people were watching from across Ventnor Avenue. I headed home. I felt weak. I was shaking. All the rage and strength and power were gone. What had I done?

Eddie had been coming to take me out to toss a football. He'd just walked out of his house as I landed the first blow. He saw all of it. He stopped me. I think I would have killed Tom Mackey. Maybe John, too.

73

In Jail

THEY CAME FOR me that night: two detectives from Central Police Headquarters, in double-breasted suits. The big one was the younger of the two. The older one was slight. He seemed bored. His expression said he'd seen it all. "Come with us, son," he said, quietly. "Gimme your wrists. I have to 'cuff you." He sounded apologetic.

My mother, standing behind me, began to crumble. My father caught her, led her to the sofa.

"Please, guys," my father said, "don't take him. I'll bring him in the morning."

"Sorry, mister, no can do. He's charged with attempted homicide. Maybe murder, if the guy dies."

Mom tried to rise off of the sofa, but her legs gave way. She fell back. In the dimness of the dining room, I saw the paleness of Evie's anxious face before she stepped back into the darkness.

They led me out of the building and into the night. A red police car was at the curb, motor running. A dozen neighbors were gathered on the sidewalk. They all knew the story. The arrival of the police car had drawn them outside. The car's red dome light rotated lazily in the darkness. Each slow sweep of the beam bathed the onlookers' faces in its red light, briefly, then returned the impassive faces to the darkness. My father followed us outside. "Let me come with you," he said, trying to block the car.

"Better stand aside, mister. No point you coming. We're gonna book him. Come tomorrow for the arraignment."

Mr. Dunauskas drew my father to the side. He offered to drive my father to the police station.

The younger detective held the door open for me and held my head down as I climbed into the back of the car. As the door closed, I saw Alice racing along Ventnor Avenue toward the police car. She leaned into the car door, hands pressed against the window, her face almost touching the glass. "Jack, Jack," she sobbed. "Jack." Tears ran down her face. "Jack, Jack."

"It's OK, Alice," I said, pressing my hand to hers against the window. She moved with the car as it started away from the curb until my father took her by her shoulders and drew her back to the sidewalk.

Dad reached the police station a few minutes after the detectives walked me in and had the desk sergeant book me. He tried to get me released into his custody. The desk sergeant shook his head as he told him to come to the arraignment the next morning in Courtroom Six at 10:00.

"But he is only a boy," my father said. "He's only fifteen."

"Come to the arraignment," one of the detectives repeated. "We can't do anything for you here. Do you know he almost killed that one fellow, and he fractured the other one's jaw? That first one will never be the same. The other one will talk funny for the rest of his life. He bit off his own tongue when the pipe hit him under his chin. Your boy is a killer. If his friend didn't pull him off, your boy was goin' to kill both of them. Your boy is goin' away. For a long time."

"But do you know why he did it? Did you hear what they did to my daughter? She's only thirteen."

"Yeah, we know all about it. But there's a way to deal with that. And it ain't the way your boy did. Do you understand that he premeditated? He went with a weapon. He's in big trouble."

I spent the night in a cell with two drunk and disorderlies, a car thief, a man who stabbed his girlfriend, and a mugger. At 9:00 the next morning, the six of us were taken out in handcuffs and led to Courtroom Six, guarded by six policemen. I saw that my father and mother and Eddie and Evie were in the courtroom. They tried to approach me, but the police stopped them. They had to remain behind the railing.

The judge didn't show up until 11:00. "All rise," the court clerk cried out as the judge climbed up to his bench, arranging his robe and smoothing his hair.

My case was last. When my name was called, my handcuffs were removed, and I was led by two policemen to stand before the bench. An assistant prosecutor came up. He said he intended to charge me with assault with a deadly weapon, aggravated assault, and attempted murder. My father was asked to come up. One of the detectives came forward and told the story. He displayed the pipe. There was a bloodstain on the elbow.

"Does your boy have a lawyer?" the judge asked my father. "No? Well, you'll have to get him one."

"Meanwhile," he addressed me, "what do you have to say, son?"

I explained what happened to Evie. I said I didn't know what I was going to do until I did it. My father asked to speak. He told the judge that I was a good boy, a hard worker, had never been in trouble, had never hurt anybody, that if Evie had told my father what happened, he would have done what I did, except that he would have killed both Mackeys.

The judge waved away my father's remarks. "I'll forget you said that," he said, in an icy tone, with narrowed eyes. Then the judge said the assistant prosecutor would have to recommend whether to keep my case at the juvenile level or waive it up to the Grand Jury for indictment on an adult charge. "This is a serious case," he told my father. "Your boy needs counsel."

Meanwhile, he said he had to hold me over to be indicted, but he would let me out on $2,500 bail.

"That's not enough," the assistant prosecutor objected. "This is an attempted murder case."

"He's a juvenile," the judge said, "and he doesn't look like a flight risk to me."

My father said he will have to borrow some money. He only had about $1,800 in the Boardwalk National Bank. The judge pointed to a man seated in the courtroom. "See him," the judge told my father. "He is a bail bondsman." My father did not know what a bail bondsman was. The bail bondsman rose and came forward. He explained that he would post a $2,500 bail bond for a $150 fee. "And your boy can go home with you, right now." There were papers, and things for my father to sign, including a $150 draft on my father's bank account.

I was released.

"Get yourself a lawyer, son," the judge said. "I won't set you down for the Grand Jury yet. Your lawyer may convince the assistant prosecutor to keep your case in the Juvenile Court. I want to hear from your lawyer."

"Yes, sir."

We left. I was a criminal. Out on bail.

74

Out on Bail

AFTER I WAS released, we headed straight for home: Dad and Mom and Eddie and Evie and me. My father said he had to get a good criminal lawyer. He didn't know one. He went next door with Eddie to ask Mr. Dunauskas for a suggestion. Mr. Dunauskas said he didn't know any criminal lawyers, but he once used a lawyer when he bought his property. He could ask that lawyer for a name. My father said that was too remote. Then Mr. Dunauskas offered to lend my father two hundred dollars. "No interest," he said, "pay back whenever you can." My father was very grateful, but he declined. He said he could manage on his own. Then Dad went to see Mr. Michaelson and got a similar response. Mr. Michaelson used a lawyer many years ago to buy his property. He didn't even remember his name. "But I can let you have a few hundred dollars if you need it."

I knew where to go. To Bobo. I told my father that during the summer, I ran some errands for Bobo Truck. Bobo would know the right lawyer.

"What were you doing with Bobo Truck?" my father wanted to know. "Do you know who he is?"

"Yes, Dad, I know who he is. He is Alan Goren's friend," I said, which was a half truth. Then I poured out the whole cocoa story. My father was stunned. He said he knew I was into something over my head, but he didn't know what. Then I told him I had almost $1,600 hidden in a handkerchief box in the bunk bed mattress.

He stared at me in disbelief. "You have more money than me," he said. There was a sadness about the way he said it, as if I thought he was a failure. He said he would go with me to see Bobo. I felt terrible to have to tell him that wasn't a good idea. I told him Bobo was a strange man, and unpredictable. I thought I would do better alone. Bobo liked me.

My father said he'd sleep on it. He said we'd talk about it at dinner tomorrow.

I said OK, but I knew I wasn't going to wait. I knew that I had to go to Bobo, alone. I decided to go after school the next day.

75

Popularity

IF YOU WANT to be the most popular boy in high school, try to beat someone to death with an iron pipe.

The morning after my arraignment, I found Alice standing outside of Michaelson's when I came out of our apartment to go to school. "Jack," she said, anxiously, looking up at me, "I had to see if you're all right. Are you? I'm so worried. What's going to happen?"

I embraced her. "Thanks, Alice. Don't worry. Everything's gonna be fine. Anyway, whattya doin' here? You'll be late for school. Better get goin'. I'll see you soon." She gave me a quick kiss on my cheek and ran off. Eddie arrived on his bike, and we headed off to school together.

When we showed up at school, I was surprised to see that I was a big celebrity. Eddie was a minor celebrity.

"Hey, look, it's Jack," I heard a half-dozen kids announce my arrival when Eddie and I parked our bikes and climbed the stairs. A crowd pressed around us. Everybody knew the story. I was the killer. Eddie was the one who stopped me from killing Tom Mackey. I was out on bail. I was a criminal.

Girls who never knew me or knew I was alive approached me to say hello and ask me how did I feel. Rhoda sought me out at recess. She bore down on me, together with three other cheerleaders. She took my arm. "Hi, Jack," she said. "How's it going?" She reached up to kiss my cheek.

I knew what she was doing. She was showing me off. She was advertising that she had a relationship with the school's newest and most famous celebrity. In spite of the effect her physical presence had on me, which was unchanged, I felt irritated that she would be so shallow. I just said, "Hello, Rhoda," and turned away, leaving her to explain to her friends that I must be very preoccupied with my legal problem.

Blinky, the pacifist, the appeaser, told me he admired what I did, but it was wrong. He said I should have told my father, gone to the police. He said that his original plan was the right one back in April when the trouble began. I should have humbled myself and apologized to the Mackeys for calling Mrs. Mackey a fat pig, regardless of what the Mackeys said. They were only words. No one was hurt. I should not have escalated the damn thing. That was Blinky's view of the world. I told him his ideas stunk. There's such things as pride and honor. "Yeah, see what it's got you," he said, his eyes squeezed closed. "Anyway, my father said he can let you have three hundred dollars. He said you'll need a good lawyer." I was touched by the offer. Poor Blinky. Somehow he felt responsible for my problems with the Mackeys. I guess he thought he should have done a better job getting me to turn the other cheek.

At Evie's school, the junior high, her celebrity was different. She was not a heroine. She was a victim. She was not admired. Victims are never admired. Victims are lessened by their ordeal. Through an upside-down psychology, the victim is brushed with blame. People feel safer holding the victim responsible, believing the victim must have done something wrong; maybe she provoked it or maybe she shouldn't have been at that place at that time, or maybe she should not have tried to resist or maybe she *should* have resisted. She should have screamed. She should *not* have screamed. She should have run, or she should *not* have tried to run.

Poor Evie. The other kids looked at her with that *you poor thing* expression, you poor *tainted* thing. Alice sought her out. She offered none of the insincerities that most people use to make themselves feel good. She embraced her, silently, and then walked away. Her embrace spoke volumes. Evie's two girlfriends who were with us at the Miss America Pageant became very protective. They were the ones who let all the boys know that Evie's friend, Alice, is Jack's girlfriend and that bad behavior to Evie will be reported promptly to Evie's brother, to Jack, the iron pipe killer. So Evie didn't have to endure any wisecracks from the boys.

At Atlantic City High School, I was greeted by every one of the varsity football players, the first string team, the school's Princes, who used to look through me as though I were transparent.

Eddie stayed near me as much as he could. Eddie was sure somebody would pick a fight with me, like in the Westerns. Now that I had the reputation of being the toughest dude in the school, Eddie figured some tough kid might want to beat me up so he could claim my title.

I had no such confrontation. I must say, however, that giving Tom Mackey that beating changed me. I thought I could do it again, even without the pipe. I think that ninety percent of winning a fight is being willing to beat the other guy to death with whatever you have—a club, a pipe, or your fists, if that's all you have. Most of us are burdened with the constraint of being civilized. The consequence is that most of us contain our fury and try to measure it out, stopping short of maiming or hurting the other guy too bad. That isn't the way. You can't think about not hurting the other guy too bad. On the contrary, you have to try to beat him, real bad. Hurt him real bad. You have to be vicious and quick, the way Eddie was with that kid at the Memorial Day Parade, the way Bobo was with Junior. Even Tom Mackey, for all his brute strength, didn't have it. He was a bully, not a killer. I guess something like that showed in me after I beat Tom Mackey with the pipe. No kid in Atlantic City High School was going to mess with me.

76

Lawyer Durells

A FTER SCHOOL, TWO days after my arraignment, I went to see Bobo, in search of a lawyer. I looked for Bobo and found him in his office behind Royce's Shooting Gallery. He knew the whole story. He knew about Evie. He said I did right, except I should have thought it through. I should have lain in wait for Tom someplace where I could jump him by surprise, alone, with no witnesses, and beat him to death. "You should never act in a rage," he said. "It's sloppy. You leave a trail. Look at the trouble you're in over here. Because you acted in heat. You gotta think these things through."

I told Bobo that if I hadn't gone after Tom Mackey that moment, if I stopped to plan and figure, probably I wouldn't have done it. I told Bobo about the beating Tom Mackey gave me in May and how I put off the confrontation all summer. I told him also about how Tom Mackey knocked me and Alice off my bike and how I ran them down afterward, without thinking. I never would have tried that stunt if I had thought about it.

I said if I had taken Evie to the police, that would have been a joke. Bobo agreed. "Anyway, it's done," I said. I wasn't sorry. They deserved what they got.

"Relax, Jack," Bobo said, trying to put me at ease. "Don't get all fired up again. I'll see what I can do over here. Come to my office at Trucci's at 5:30. I'll see what I can do." When Bobo was in that mood, you wanted to think he was the kindest, most thoughtful, most considerate man in the world. He knew how to be a charmer.

403

"By the way, Bobo," I asked, "is Junior paying?"

"Like a clock," Bobo answered. "He caught up the next week, and he's been comin' across every week."

When I arrived at Bobo's office later that day, at 5:30 like he said, I found he had a visitor, an impressive, well-dressed man, relaxing on the sofa with a cigar and a drink in hand. Bobo introduced me to Lawrence Durells, Managing Partner of Durells, Clarke, Wister and Levy. Durells wasted no time. He looked at his watch.

"You don't have to tell me the story, Jack," he said. "I heard the story. I think I can help you. I know the county prosecutor. When he hears the whole story, he may be inclined to go easy on you." He stuffed out the cigar and set down the drink. "Can you pay me, Jack?" he asked. "If I take your case, I'm stuck with it. If it goes to trial, that's a lot of time and expense. If I keep it in the juvenile system or kill it altogether before you get indicted, I'll want a thousand dollars. If you get indicted, you go on the clock. Could run to four or five thousand. Do you have it?"

"I can pay you the thousand," I said. "I have almost sixteen hundred dollars. My father has about the same. We have about thirty-two hundred dollars between us. I think we can borrow another thousand. That would get me up to about four thousand altogether. I don't think I can get to five thousand."

Durells looked at Bobo, questioningly. I saw Bobo give a half nod.

Durells looked at me again. "All right, son, I'm taking your case. Come to my office next Tuesday. Four o'clock. Bring your father. Bring the thousand dollars. Here's my card."

"I don't know if my father can get off work," I said.

"Bring him," Durells ordered, "and bring the money."

He rose, picked up his black leather briefcase, shook my hand, and left. He was a no-nonsense man.

"No wasted motion, hey, Jack?" Bobo said. "He's the best. He's taking the case as a favor to me. He don't lift a finger for a thousand dollars. After this over here, I'll owe him. But I owe you one, Jack. I'm gonna pay you off. I don't like owing."

"You don't owe me anything, Mr. Truck," I said. "You're being generous. I don't know how to thank you."

"Once and for all," he said, "will you drop that *Mr. Truck* business? It's *Bobo*."

"Sure … uh, Bobo. What can I do to repay you?"

"I'll call you when you can do something for me. Now scram. Go home. Do homework or something. Like other kids do."

77

Thursday Pinochle

ARTHUR KOESTLER, IN *The Act of Creation*, says that life goes into partial suspension while important decisions are being made. It's true. It's hard to concentrate on anything else. School and schoolwork seemed irrelevant in the face of my problem with the Atlantic County Prosecutor's Office. I tried to go through the motions of being a high school student. It was a waste of time. I couldn't concentrate on what I read. I couldn't absorb what I was being taught. The image of the prosecutor drove everything else out of my mind. I saw him in my imagination, a faceless man in a dark gray suit, a good-looking man, even though I couldn't make out his face. I knew he would *prosecute* me like one of those fearless DAs I saw in the movies at the Saturday matinee—tough and strong and good-looking, like George Brent or Herbert Marshall or Pat O'Brien. But then, I told myself, the movie DAs had heart. They found a way to make things right. What I did to the Mackeys was wrong. But did I have a choice? Surely, a compassionate DA would understand. What if it was *his* kid sister?

Sometimes, I would daydream of being let off with a stern warning by the prosecutor. Secretly, I imagined, he admired what I'd done, though he allowed no hint of his approval to show. When I wasn't daydreaming, which was most of the time, I was just plain scared.

The day after I met Lawyer Durells, it was time for the Thursday evening Pinochle game. Eddie and Blinky came over. Evie was ready. I said I really didn't want to play. They persuaded me to give it a try, which I did. The three of them tried to make light conversation while we played. Eddie and Blinky talked about the kids at school. Evie told us how she and her two best friends were starting up the Atlantic City Frank Sinatra Fan Club. She said even some of the ninth grade girls were going to join. Like Alice Keever. She said Alice finds her in the schoolyard at lunch recess every day and asks about me. I told Evie to tell Alice that I'm OK. Not to worry about me. I have the best lawyer in Atlantic City.

After a few hands, we gave up. It was obvious that I couldn't focus on the game.

"OK, Jack," Eddie said, "let's call it off for tonight. Blinky, how about you give Evie a lesson on how to remember who plays what cards, and Jack, I'm taking you out for a walk. You need some fresh air to get your head clear."

Blinky didn't need any coaxing to spend an hour alone with Evie. Eddie and I headed for the boardwalk.

The air was clear and fresh and cold. A light frost was on the boardwalk. There was no wind. A full moon lit up the darkness as it slipped through the few clouds, splashing silver on the dark water. Our shoes made a crunching sound in the light frost.

By now, Eddie knew just about everything about my adventures. He knew about my short flirtation with wealth. He knew that my account was worth $10,791 at its peak, after I pulled out $1,300. I told him that Benny lost his touch and gave back almost all of it. I didn't tell him that Krieger and Son was a bucket shop and about how Bobo settled accounts. That was *appena fra noi*, as Bobo said.

I told Eddie how hard it was to be serious about school, not because of the Mackeys' case. That was only part of it. There was something else. It was that I lived in the real world for a while. I learned big lessons. I knew there was a lot to learn in three years of high school. It's just that it's so slow. If only there was a way to cram it all in, real fast, and get out into the world.

"To do what?" Eddie wanted to know. "Do you have any plans?"

"No, that's just it," I said. "I need a plan but I can't put one together. I been thinkin' about that all summer and couldn't get a grip on it. I don't know what I want. I know what I *don't* want. I don't want to manage a paint store."

"Well, you must be slow," Eddie said. "I *know* what *I* want. I'm gonna take over the deli, or open up my own garage. Or buy a farm. Or be a lawyer. Or maybe a doctor or an engineer. See, I have it all figured out." He punched me on the arm. "C'mon, lighten up," he said. "You shouldn't be thinking about this stuff. Not now. We're only fifteen. That's the good thing about school. It's slow. We learn slow because we're too young to do anything else. So we learn and maybe by the time we get to the end of school, we'll know what to do. Don't push it. Getting laid a couple times and fooling around with Alice doesn't make you a grown-up. You're just a kid like me. We got to get you past this Mackey thing. Then you'll be OK."

"You're right, Eddie," I agreed. "If only I can get out of it, get past it. Boy, if only ..."

"Yeah," Eddie said, "and you could use an Alice Keever treatment. That wouldn't hurt you one bit."

"Yeah. If she is still interested in the Atlantic City pipe murderer."

78

Meeting With Lawyer Durells

ON TUESDAY, MY father and I arrived for our 4:00 appointment with Lawyer Durells. My father had permission from his district manager to take off at 3:30. The district manager knew my story. Just about everyone in Atlantic City, it seemed, knew the story. The district manager's sympathy for me was considerable. He told my father he could have off from 3:30 until 5:45 and he wouldn't be docked for the time. "Is that enough time, do you think?" he asked. He was really being very helpful. Time off for personal matters was frowned upon at Nu-Enamel.

We waited in the reception area of Durells, Clarke, Wister and Levy, but 4:30 came and passed. Then 4:45 came and went. My father was fidgeting. He consulted his watch every half-minute. He didn't want to abuse the district manager's generosity. He calculated that he had to leave the law offices by 5:35. If he ran, he could make it back to the store in under ten minutes. He was nervous. He didn't want to leave in the middle of our appointment. He didn't want to return to the store after 5:45. I was angry that Durells did this to us. My father told me to stay calm. "Don't let's antagonize our lawyer," he said. "He is a busy man. We're not an important case." I told the receptionist that my father had to leave by 5:35. Could she do something to help us? She said she could not disturb Mr. Durells.

At 5:05, Durells's secretary came for us and ushered us into his office. It was the biggest, most impressive office I ever saw, including in the movies.

He came forward to greet us, asking to be excused for keeping us waiting. His manner was abrupt, just as in Bobo's office.

"Did you bring the money?" he asked.

I handed it over. He counted it and placed it in his drawer.

"I've been working on your case," he said, motioning us to be seated. "I've been in touch with the district attorney and the county prosecutor and the assistant prosecutor who has the case. I've been successful thus far in keeping this as a juvenile matter. We will have a pretrial conference in about a month. I hope to persuade the Prosecutor's Office to keep this in the juvenile system."

Durells explained that the prosecutor might think the crime was serious enough to justify trying me as an adult, in which case the assistant prosecutor would recommend to the court that I be brought before the Grand Jury as an adult, for a criminal indictment, which would lead to a trial. "In that case," Durells said, "the State will ask for a jail sentence, maybe four to ten years, maybe more, depending on the extent of Tom Mackey's permanent injuries."

Durells explained that if that is the prosecutor's decision, Durells and the assistant prosecutor will have to argue the issue in a formal hearing before a judge; that is, whether to keep me in the juvenile division or have the court waive me up to the Grand Jury. It will be the judge's decision.

"My theory is this," Durells elaborated. "The best way to deal with this case is to kill it before you get indicted. The prosecutor's whole case rests on the Mackey brothers' testimony. Maybe they won't want to testify. They don't come to court with clean hands. They've been in trouble themselves—a couple of drunk and disorderlies, an assault, a petty larceny, two shopliftings. And I could make a molestation case out of what they did to Evie. If they won't testify, the county prosecutor won't waste his office's time. We don't have to worry about your friend Eddie, and I'm not concerned about other witnesses. They will never be identified or located. We don't want to win a trial. We don't want a trial to begin with. Does that make sense?"

My father and I agreed.

"Now then," Durells went on, "I'll see if I can get someone to interview the Mackeys in the next day or two. All of them, Mr. and Mrs. and the brothers. That's my next move. I'll let you know when I want you back here." He stood up. The meeting was over. It lasted less than ten minutes.

79

Trying for Normalcy

EDDIE AND BLINKY came to my home every evening so we could do our homework together. Without their help, I wouldn't have done any. They persisted in the Thursday evening Pinochle games. They pushed me into trying to do normal things, generally doing their best to restore some normalcy to my life even while my case hung over me and overshadowed everything else. They even arranged for a Saturday evening triple date at the movies with Alice and her friends, Marilyn and Sandra.

For Eddie to go on a date was a genuine act of friendship. He was uninterested in Sandra. He went through the motions for my sake, trying to pull me out of my gloom. Blinky, on the other hand, was an eager participant. He wouldn't have mustered the nerve to ask a girl out on a date on his own, and I doubt Marilyn would have accepted an invitation from him, if it were just the two of them.

Alice was wonderful. She could talk up a storm. She talked about everything. She laughed at her own stories. She didn't need me to participate. An occasional comment from me was enough. I was happy to be with her, with them, but the dark cloud never left me.

Alice asked if it was all right for her to come to my house once or twice a week, around 5:00 so she could see me for a half hour or so when I got home from work. I said, "Sure, that would be great." Don't you know that the next Tuesday when I got home she was sitting across from Mom, stuffing envelopes and chattering away while Mom concentrated on her work, wearing an amused smile.

The days passed. Routine took over. I went to school, called Durells every afternoon. Alice was at home waiting for me a couple of times a week. Then it was dinner, homework with Eddie and Blinky, Pinochle on Thursdays.

Thanksgiving came. Mom made the usual feast. It was dispirited. Days grew short. Alice reminded me that Winter Solstice was only three weeks away. "After that, the days start to lengthen. We'll be heading for spring. You'll feel better. Things will look brighter."

I appreciated her loyalty and how she tried to infect me with her own optimism. I was lucky to have such a girlfriend.

80

An Invitation

O
N A WEDNESDAY, early in December, I found Rhoda waiting for me in the hallway when my Algebra class let out. She was wearing her white, woolen turtleneck varsity sweater with the big blue chenille AC that made her look so wholesome.

"Hi, Jack," she said, smiling, pretty as ever. She took my arm and reached up to kiss my cheek, pressing her breasts against my arm, just for a moment. It stirred me. *What was that all about?*

As she stepped back, she said, "Come to the bakery this evening after work. I want to show you something."

"What is it?" I asked, feeling a small arousal from touching her.

"It's a surprise. You'll like it." Big smile and off she went.

Eddie saw what happened. "Careful, Jack," he warned. "She collects guys. You're a target."

81

Surprise

IN EARLY DECEMBER, the sun sets at 4:15. I arrived at the bakery at 7:00. It was nighttime. The store's bright lights were an inviting beacon in the darkness. The aroma of warm bread and pastries greeted me. Rhoda was alone. She was wearing her customary bakery shop uniform of white shirt and white apron. Again that look of purity. Her long black hair was gathered into the white baker's hat.

"Hi, Rhoda. Where's your dad?"

"He and Mom went to the movies. They left me to close up."

"Well, here I am. What's the surprise?"

"It's downstairs. C'mon."

She closed the lights and locked up the store. She led me to the basement apartment that the Michaelsons closed during fall and winter.

It was like entering a crypt. It was dark. The furniture was covered with sheets. The air was stale, but surprisingly, it was warm and there was none of the dampness I always noticed in the summer.

"That's because the heater is down here," Rhoda explained. "The heat is not on in the summer."

Mendelsohn, Rhoda's cat, approached us, mewing softly, a green-eyed shadowy form in the darkness. He rubbed against my leg, purring like a motor, the sound amplified by the concrete floor and cinder block walls. Rhoda swept him up, held him against her chest, briefly, nuzzled him with her nose, then set him down. He retreated to the warmth of a folded quilt near the heater. Rhoda turned on the lights.

"What have you got for me, Rhoda?" I was getting fidgety. I was uncomfortable being alone with her. I wished I hadn't come.

"You have to help me," she said. She produced a clothesline and pointed to two wall sconces facing each other across the living room.

"Here, Jack. Let's string up this line across the room."

We tied the line to the sconces. It divided the room in half. What was she doing?

"Now then, watch this," she said, taking a sheet off the sofa and draping it across the clothesline. "You sit there on the sofa and watch."

I sat. "What am I watching? Is it a movie?"

"You'll see in a moment."

She turned off all the other lights except for a table lamp behind me with a red lampshade. It bathed the room in deep red light, like a photographer's darkroom.

There was a gooseneck lamp on a table on the other side of the sheet. She turned it on and aimed it at the sheet. The sheet lit up like a movie screen. The lamp projected her black silhouette onto the white screen of the sheet.

There was a record player on a table on her side of the sheet. The silhouette turned it on, filling the room with Cole Porter's *Begin the Beguine* and the throaty voice of Jo Stafford.

When they begin ... the Beguine

The silhouette swayed dreamily to the music, as though unwinding before bedtime, alone, enjoying the supple grace of her own body.

It brings back the sound ... of music so tender

Her moves were smooth and sensuous. It was erotic. My apprehension of being alone with her faded into disbelief. This is Rhoda, the most beautiful girl in the entire school, poised and sophisticated beyond her years. She had no time for me, the tenth grade kid who lived upstairs. Her boyfriends were seniors, even some college boys. What's going on here?

The silhouette removed the baker's cap. Long hair spilled out onto the silhouette. The arms lowered, slowly. They untied the apron. It fell to the floor. The silhouette opened the top button of its shirt, slowly, to the rhythm of the music.

It brings back a memory ... ever green

Another button opened. Then another. She seemed unconscious of me. I was a voyeur, unseen, hidden in the reddish darkness, watching through a neighbor's window. I was mesmerized. I began to swell.

I'm with you once more ... under the stars

"Rhoda, what are you doing?" My voice intruded on her performance. The silhouette spoke, but its seductive movements never stopped.

"Wait for the surprise, Jack."

And down by the shore … an orchestra's playing

The silhouette disrobed, slowly; the fluid movements never stopped. The shirt slipped off and fell to the floor. An interval, then the skirt … then the rest, piece after piece dropped to the floor: slip, bra, panties, until the silhouette was nude, a black study in perfection.

And there we are … swearing to love forever

She faced forward, legs apart, elbows out, hands clasped behind her head, hips rolling from side to side in time to the music. It was the most erotic thing I ever saw. More than if I were watching Rhoda herself rather than her silhouette. The silhouette lowered one hand, hesitated, then touched itself. Hot blood filled me. I got bigger.

And promising never … never to part

The silhouette picked up a robe that was folded on the table beside the lamp. She slipped into it, slowly, languid movements, pulsing to the beat of the music. It was as exciting as the disrobing.

Let the love that was once a fire … remain an ember

She paused.

"Now the surprise," she said, throwing aside the sheet. She fell on me, the silken robe opening in the dim red light. Her lips parted. She smothered me with kisses, her tongue flicking in and out as she kissed my lips, my eyes, my cheeks. She took hold of me; I was huge. "Oh my," she spoke to it, in a whisper, "you *are* a big fella. I knew you would be."

"Ohmigod, Rhoda. Why are you doing this?"

"Surprise, Jack. I've been wanting to do this for a long time. I know all about you. You're the most man I know."

Oh yes, let them begin the Beguine ... make them play

I laid her down on the sofa. I ran my hands all over her. Her body was like nothing I had ever felt or imagined. Smooth, firm, a silken body inside a silken robe, supple, thrusting, thrusting. I felt the hidden cheerleader muscle under the smoothness of her long legs. I slid my hand along the inside of her thigh ... and higher. She was smooth, completely shaven. I was wild. I pushed her down and made to enter her.

"No, Jack, not that," she said, smiling.

"Why not?" I demanded, hungrily. "Who's it for?"

"Nobody's had it yet," she said with a smile, "but some things are even better." She slipped to the floor and bent her head over me.

Til you whisper to me once more ... darling, I love you

"Ohmigod!"

Afterward, she stood up and cut off the music abruptly. The needle scratched, ending the song with a screech. She dressed, quickly.

"Let's rearrange everything and get going," she said. I leaned toward her to kiss her, but she turned aside, offering her cheek. I think I understood her. There is a rush you get when you're near a notorious person, or someone dangerous. I used to feel it when I was near Bobo, an aura of power that excites you and makes you apprehensive at the same time. Rhoda was experiencing that rush. I was notorious, maybe even dangerous—a magnetic combination. I was a prize she had to win, the most popular boy in the school. I'd been had, collected. I was angry with myself. It occurred to me that her performance was too polished to be extemporaneous. Others had preceded me.

Mendelsohn never left the comfort of his bed near the heater. I guess he'd seen it all before.

As we passed through the bakery on the way out, I ran my finger across a tray of powdered sugar. I sucked on it as I left.

How about Alice?

For sure I would be Rhoda's secret. Rhoda would never tell what she did with me, a tenth grader. Did I even have to tell Alice? I knew the answer to that one. I could have no secrets from her. "It was an accident," I told myself. "I was a victim." It would never happen again. Was it really so terrible? I would tell Alice tomorrow.

But I didn't see Alice the next day, or the next. That was troubling. Usually I saw her every day. Did she know? By Saturday morning, it was obvious that she was avoiding me. I went to the beach to collect my thoughts and plan what to say.

82

Telling Alice

THERE IS AN Atlantic City other than the golden one of summer, other than the silvery-blue ones of spring and fall when the skies are clear and the air is sweet. There is a mid-winter Atlantic City with brief days and long nights. There are inviting wintry days when the sun glances off the ocean and a bundled-up walk on the boardwalk is invigorating. But there is also the bleak Atlantic City of those winter days when there is no sun and the air is damp and all is gray and the surf freezes on the beach.

This was such a day, a cold December day. Rain was coming. Nature's palette was hidden. The sky was gray, hard as steel above a steel-gray ocean. Sky and ocean merged, seamlessly, in the distance. There was no horizon. Only a pale spot in the southeastern sky hinted that a sun was still there, invisible above the cloud cover. The ocean was turbulent; a fifteen-knot northerly wind blew off the tops of the swells into long sheets of spray, leaving deformed waves that raced to the shore in crazy patterns and crashed on the beach in clouds of spray and foam. Sea birds stood at attention at the water's edge, silent, wings feathered, pointed into the wind, beaks buried in their breasts.

The boardwalk was desolate—the stores were closed, not a person in sight. The lamppost lights glimmered weakly inside misty coronas. I wore a heavy sweater under a hooded sweatshirt. It was not warm enough. I walked the beach for an hour, huddled into the hood of the sweatshirt, planning my words. They sounded plausible. Was it such a terrible thing I did? I didn't initiate it. Can't we put it aside?

The cold wind hurried me. It was time to go to her, but I had little confidence in a good outcome. A light rain began as I climbed on my bike. When I reached Alice's house, my clothes were heavy with dampness.

Her parents were out. She was alone.

She opened the door for me.

The radio was playing a Haydn symphony. The house was warm and inviting. Alice was cool and distant. She turned off the radio.

"Come in, Jack." Her voice was flat. She sat on a chair and motioned me to sit across the room. I was uncomfortable in my damp clothes, perspiring under the clamminess of the sweatshirt and heavy sweater. I wanted to be closer to her, but her look suggested that I keep my distance.

"Are you all right, Alice?" I asked from across the room. "I've missed you. What's wrong?"

She raised her eyebrows, "*Is* something wrong, Jack?"

"Alice, I have something to tell you. Please hear me out."

She silenced me with a raised palm. "Never mind, Jack. I know. She made sure I would know."

"Alice, it was nothing."

"It's OK, Jack." There was no emotion in her voice. She paused for a moment. "You can have her. Don't worry about me."

I felt like a little boy, being scolded. I pleaded with her. I said everything I had practiced saying on the beach. Here with Alice, the words sounded false and weak.

"I feel betrayed, Jack," she said. "I tried not to cry, but I did. I'm all cried out now. You and I are finished. It's best you should go."

Her words cut. Like a knife wound, there was an instant of disbelief before the pain set in. I expected what? Anger? Maybe tears? But I didn't expect this. She was sending me away. I was being dumped.

I sprang to my feet. "Alice, I'm not interested in Rhoda. I want *you*. We have something special. How can you turn me off just like that?"

"*You* did the turning off, Jack. *You* threw it all away. Just like that."

Before I could respond, she rose from her chair. "Don't make this any harder, Jack. I've thought it through carefully, and I've lost my trust in you. Our relationship is broken. It was good, but it's over. You're just not for me anymore."

She wasn't yet fifteen. How did she come to talk like a grown woman?

"This can't be," I said, moving closer. She stepped back. "I have to make this right," I said. "What can I do?"

"Listen, Jack, nobody ever died from this. In a little while, it'll be as if we never even knew each other."

"Alice—"

"Goodbye, Jack." She opened the door and nodded toward it, averting her eyes.

I tried to reach out to her, but she backed away.

"I hope she'll be good for you," she said as I walked out. As the door closed behind me, I heard her say, half aloud, as if to herself, "but I don't think so."

The rain had become heavier, and the wind whipped it into my face. Halfway home, my rear tire went flat.

83

Durells's Reports

Now I HAD twin obsessions. When I wasn't worrying about the Mackey case, I was thinking about how I'd lost Alice. Some days I felt hopeful that things would work out, but most of the time, I was wracked by misery and anxiety.

I waited for Lawyer Durells to tell me the outcome of the interview with the Mackeys. He said I should call his office every afternoon and ask if he wanted to talk to me. I did as instructed, and the receptionist would try to transfer me to his secretary, who, invariably, was away from her desk, on the phone, or otherwise unavailable. I should call back. It always took several attempts just to reach the secretary, and each time she said the same thing: nothing to report, call again tomorrow.

My life was in partial suspension, just as Arthur Koestler said. My father tried to pull me out of my funk by putting me to work at the Nu-Enamel store as stock boy, janitor, and general gopher. My work schedule was every afternoon from 3:00 to 5:00; Saturdays, 8:00 until 5:00, with an unpaid hour off for lunch. I had Sundays off. My salary was twenty cents an hour.

What a comedown from the heady cocoa days; days when my account jumped as much as $1,000, $1,300, $1,600 in a *single day*. At the end of my first week at Nu-Enamel, I opened my pay envelope and counted out the mournful result of eighteen hours' work: three dollar bills and sixty cents in change.

One day, after four weeks of calling for news, Durells's secretary said to please hold, that the attorney wanted to talk to me. What he had to say was disappointing. He had three reports for me: First, Tom was still in the hospital, in serious condition. He was going to have a lot of permanent damage. Second, John was home. He was wearing a cast to immobilize the lower part of his face and jaw. The cast followed the contour of his jaw and neck and then spread out to rest on his shoulders. His jawbone was fractured. He had lost two teeth and bitten off a half-inch from the tip of his tongue, which would need to be reshaped surgically. Third, Durells's investigator had met with Mr. and Mrs. Mackey. He was an experienced investigator who knew how to lend a sympathetic ear and was expert at getting people to open up and speak freely.

The investigator reported that the Mackeys were consumed with hate for me. They wanted me sent away for life. Their boys were good boys, hard-working boys. The few misdemeanors on their record were pranks, nothing serious. The incident with Evie was just a prank. They never intended to hurt her. That rotten kid, Jack, had goaded them into acting out of character. First, he insulted Mrs. Mackey, and then he escalated an exchange of words into a physical confrontation. Jack started it. Jack escalated it. Jack had a henchman, the Dunauskas boy, Eddie—a decent boy who Jack had led astray. Jack got Eddie to join him in an unprovoked attack on Tom last May. Jack ran them down in October with his bike, another unprovoked attack. The Mackeys were afraid of what Jack would do next. Jack should not be out on bail. He is dangerous, a killer. Were the Mackeys going to testify? You bet. Tom will be there, probably in a wheelchair or in a hospital bed, if necessary. John will be there. That Jack is a killer. The Mackey boys are good boys. They never hurt anybody.

"So," Durells said, "I'm going to meet with the county prosecutor. I know him very well. We belong to the same country club. I consider him a friend. I will try to convince him to keep your case in the juvenile system. I don't know how he will react. There is a lot of pressure these days to be tough on juveniles, and vigilante justice scares him. The whole county knows your case. If you get off, that will be perceived as an endorsement of vigilante justice. My guess is that the prosecutor will want to take your case to the Grand Jury and get an adult indictment against you. I intend to try to soften his attitude by giving him all of the background. I am going to have my investigator take statements from Eddie Dunauskas about the May incident, and from Alice Keever about the October incident on the boardwalk, and, of course, from Evie. I want the prosecutor to know what kind of boys the Mackeys are. Call me every afternoon to find out if I have more news. Goodbye."

Durells's news was discouraging, and my spirits went into a real tailspin. I tried to focus on the one positive thing he said, about letting the prosecutor know what kind of boys the Mackeys are and that they were the provocateurs, not me. Not much comfort there, but it was the only small ray of hope I had to hang on to.

Over the next several days, Durells's investigator met with Eddie, Alice, and Evie. He brought a stenographer who took their statements in shorthand, then typed the statements and had them signed, witnessed, and notarized. I read the carbon copies of the statements. They lifted my spirits a little because I thought they made it clear that the Mackeys were the real criminals. I felt a faint ray of optimism.

***

In Europe, the war took a strange twist. The Russians invaded Finland in mid-November, expecting to roll over it in days, the way the Germans rolled over Poland. To their chagrin, and to the surprise and admiration of most Americans, the Finns didn't collapse. They put up a dogged defense, beating back one Russian offensive after another. The Finns held firm all winter behind their fortified Mannerheim Line, which was fashioned after the two opposing fortified lines on the French-German border, the Maginot Line and the Siegfried Line. It wasn't until early 1940 that superior Russian numbers and resources finally prevailed, and the Finns sued for peace.

December 19 was the next time Durells spoke to me, to tell me the pretrial conference was set for February 6. He said nothing happens in the Prosecutor's Office from the middle of December until after New Year's. Usually, Durells did all the talking. On this occasion, however, I managed to tell him that I read the three statements and asked if he thought they were helpful. I could tell he was impatient with my question, as I was taking up his time by asking it, and he would have to waste his time by answering.

Nevertheless, he responded. "I gave the prosecutor the three statements. We talked about them at the club, but evidence related to the Mackeys' prior acts is not admissible. If he wants to help you, the statements will encourage him. If he wants to throw the book at you, they will not stop him. The attack on Evie was hours earlier, meaning you acted with premeditation. You sought out a weapon. You concealed it. Carrying a concealed weapon is one more charge he can bring if he wants to. Call me every afternoon to see if I have more news for you. Goodbye."

The man had the warmth of an iceberg.

84

Death of the *Graf Spee*

O NE FRIDAY IN December, when I got home from work at the Nu-Enamel store, Mom had a message for me from Goren. He'd phoned to ask me to visit him at his apartment on Sunday morning at 9:00 and said I shouldn't have breakfast before I came. I didn't have to respond unless I couldn't come.

That Sunday, I rode my bike to Goren's apartment. On the way I decided not to tell him about my break-up with Alice. I guess I was still hoping for a reconciliation. His apartment was in a four-story walk-up, a red brick building on Montgomery Avenue, only six blocks away. It looked like two buildings standing next to one another, except the entrance was an arched doorway in the center of the two buildings. It had a grand name, *The Versailles*—too grand for the building—carved into the concrete archway above the entrance.

Inside was a central stairway. Goren's apartment was a fourth-floor front in the left building. I thought, as I ran up the stairs, that this was good exercise for Goren, probably the only exercise he got.

I sort of knew what his apartment would be like. I was correct. It was furnished sparely, other than all the books. Everything seemed fine quality. Sunlight poured in the front windows, through sparkling white enamel Venetian blinds. The predominant colors were pale gray and white, except for colorful Oriental rugs and a number of handsomely framed paintings on the white walls. The books added color. They were everywhere, hundreds of them. One entire wall of the living room was a floor-to-ceiling bookcase, overflowing with books. More books were on tables, in bookcases in his bedroom, and in neatly stacked piles on the floor.

Goren was dressed in his khaki trousers, gray ragg socks, brown loafers, and a white shirt under a dark gray cardigan sweater with brown leather elbow patches and brown-leather pockets. He was smoking a pipe, something I hadn't seen before. A radio was playing a Mozart symphony. An unopened Sunday *New York Times* lay on the coffee table, next to a chessboard, where the pieces were in the middle of a game. Nearby were two books on chess by Emanuel Lasker, *Common Sense in Chess* and *Morphy's Greatest Games*.

"Hi, Jack," he said with a smile, "come in. It's so good to see you." He gave me a warm handshake. "Here, you see what a bachelor's apartment looks like. I've been here over fifteen years. It's very comfortable, but I'm either going to have to get rid of some books or move to a larger apartment. Here's a surprise for you. Zena is in the kitchen making breakfast. And you thought she could only make tea!"

Zena came out to greet me. She was without any make-up at all, wearing a white chef's apron. She gave me a big smile and then said, "Sit down, fellas, breakfast is coming."

Breakfast was tomato juice, fried eggs with bacon and potatoes, fresh rye bread with strawberry jam, and coffee. Zena joined us. We sat at the dining room table. Goren wanted to know about my case. He said he knew some details from Georgie at Bobo's bookie joint and the newspaper.

The story was in the *Atlantic City Press*, with photographs—Tom Mackey in the hospital bed, John Mackey with part of his head in the cast, me at the arraignment, even a picture of the corner of Annapolis and Ventnor avenues. Goren said he read the newspaper account, but he didn't trust newspaper reporting. I told him all the details, starting back in May when Tom Mackey gave me the beating, and the October incident on the boardwalk when Tom pushed over my bike with me and Alice on it. And, of course, I told him what happened to Evie. I told him that Lawyer Durells said the Mackeys' testimony was the central thing. Even if the prosecutor wants to treat me as a juvenile offender, he may not be able to because of the Mackeys. They want my head. It's a high-profile case. Durells says that the district attorney and the president judge want to get tough on juveniles who commit adult crimes.

Goren said he would have done something like I did. Maybe he would just have shot them. That way, they wouldn't be around to do any testifying. He pointed to his Army service revolver in its brown-leather holster, hanging by its brown leather strap from a hook on his living room wall. "Sometimes," he said, "there's no justice to be had except what you mete out yourself."

"That's what Bobo said," I answered, "except Bobo said I should have beat them to death in a place where there were no witnesses. The prosecutor is calling what I did *vigilante-ism.*"

"The Mackeys are the criminals," Zena said. "What could Jack do? Run to the police? Evie would have been in worse danger if he did that. I think Jack did the right thing. Doesn't the legal system understand that?" Then she asked Goren, "Alan, do you have the short story, *A Cask of Amontillado*, by Edgar Allen Poe? Jack, you should read it. It's about revenge. Poe says you need three things for revenge to be complete. The victim has to know it's you, he has to know why you are doing it, and he has to be helpless to stop you."

"As Bobo said," Goren added, "revenge has to be planned. And it's best served cold. I'll look for the story. I have it here somewhere. Anyway, Jack, I want to help. I don't know how. I know you have the best lawyer. He must be expensive. So here, take this." He handed me an envelope with my name on it. "There's two thousand dollars in there. Maybe you'll need it. I know how you are about accepting money, so call it a loan."

I was touched. "Alan," I said, calling him Alan for the first time, "I can't thank you enough for this. But I don't need it. At least not now. So thanks, but please take it back. Can I come to you if I do need help? If I do, it could be that much, maybe even more. Or maybe my lawyer will get my case settled without a trial. If that happens, it's only the $1,000 I already paid him."

"Sure, Jack," Goren said. "I'll keep this for now. But it's yours whenever you ask for it. You won't forget?"

He wanted to know how I was spending my time besides worrying about my case. I told him I was working for my father at the Nu-Enamel store. I told him I was having trouble concentrating on schoolwork and that my friends were terrific support, especially Eddie.

"And how about you, Alan?" I asked.

"Little to report," he answered. "I opened an account at Bache. I'm trading a few crude oil futures. Benny was right. The war is turning real. You see that the Russians started a war with Finland. The German Navy is doing a great job in the Atlantic. Between the U-boats and the surface raiders, they've sunk over a hundred merchant ships. The British economy is suffering, and their war effort is hurting. We're going to get dragged into this war. Roosevelt is going to help the British every way he can. Do you follow the news, Jack? The fighting along the Maginot Line is like two boxers sparring and testing each other and looking for an opening. In the spring, there will be an offensive. I don't know by which side.

"My guess is the Germans will launch it. The French don't have the belly for this war, especially after the way the Germans ate up the Poles so fast and so easy. And my guess is the British wish they weren't in it either. They're telling themselves if only Hitler would be satisfied with Eastern Europe, they wouldn't be in this rotten war. In the spring, it will become a big war. That's my guess, with lots of casualties, lots of poor young fellows getting killed or maimed, lots of kids lying face down in the mud. Like the last time. You see what's going on in China and Korea. We might even get into a war with Japan. Most people think the Japanese are too primitive militarily to pose a threat to us, and the Japanese know we carry around that misconception. But, you know what? Everybody thought the same thing when the Japanese beat the Russians in 1904. Big surprise. Well, maybe *we* are in for a big surprise." He drew on the pipe again, and blew out a narrow stream of fragrant smoke through pursed lips. "One way or another, we will be in a war. I hope it's over before you have to go.

"But, like Benny said, at least we should make a few bucks out of it. Oil prices will skyrocket. They're up already. Just like the cocoa shot up. But cocoa slipped back. Oil prices are strong."

"How many contracts do you have?" I asked.

"I'm long twenty Junes. I made about three hundred dollars so far. Hey, I'll tell you what. I'm going to open an account for you. What do you say? A small one, $200. Are you game for it?"

I hesitated. I might need that money for Durells. But the idea of being back in the game was irresistible. "Sure," I said, "I'll drop off the money tomorrow evening."

Goren unfolded the *New York Times*. It was Sunday, December 17. On the front page was a picture of a battleship. "Did you follow the story about the *Graf Spee*?" he asked.

As a matter of fact, I had. It was the first serious military engagement of the war. Until then, the war consisted of German U-boats and warships sinking unarmed merchant ships and passenger liners. The *Graf Spee* found herself in her first real fight, with warships, not merchantmen.

The 1919 Treaty of Versailles, which ended World War I, imposed limits on German rearmament, including the size and firepower of German warships. When Hitler came to power in 1932, he ordered construction of the most powerful battleships that could be built within the size limitations of the Treaty. A few years later, he ignored the Treaty and started construction of bigger warships and the world's most powerful army and air force. Before he renounced the Treaty, German naval architects designed the *Graf Spee*. It complied with the size and tonnage limitations of the Treaty, but it had the guns and firepower to equal a full-size battleship. Naval experts called the *Graf Spee* "a pocket battleship." She was a magnificent warship—fast and heavily armored. Her armor-plated hull was electrically welded, a new and radical departure from the riveted hulls of those days. She had eleven-inch guns, capable of hitting a target over ten miles away. Her full capabilities were secrets carefully guarded by the Germans. Clouded in mystery, *Graf Spee* was admired and feared by the world's navies. It was an era when battleships ruled the world's oceans. It wasn't until December 7, 1941, that battleships lost their preeminence in naval warfare, when the Japanese demonstrated that the aircraft carrier was the new ruler of the seas.

In early December 1939, the *Graf Spee* was sighted in the mid-Atlantic by a light British cruiser, which then tracked it, carefully staying out of range of the *Graf Spee*'s guns, while two other British warships sped to the scene. The three British ships caught up to and attacked the *Graf Spee* on December 13. They were *Ajax* and *Achilles*, light cruisers with six-inch guns, and *Exeter*, a medium cruiser with eight-inch guns.

So, the battle was joined.

Graf Spee's eleven-inch guns could reach the three British ships before the British could come close enough for their guns to reach *Graf Spee*. Despite that, the British ships fought through *Graf Spee*'s barrages until they got into range to fire their own guns. *Exeter*, with its eight-inch guns, was crippled and knocked out of the fight. Then, *Achilles*, with only six-inch guns, was hit and severely damaged, but managed to hit *Graf Spee* in the stern at the waterline, damaging its steering. *Graf Spee*, its maneuverability limited, turned and ran, heading south, looking for sanctuary. She limped into the Plate River in Uruguay and up the Plate to Montevideo Harbor. The British ships waited outside the Plate, outside of Uruguay's territorial waters. The *Graf Spee* sought asylum long enough to arrange for repairs.

Uruguay was a neutral country. Fearful of antagonizing Britain and afraid to risk the displeasure of the United States, which, while neutral, clearly supported Britain, Uruguay ordered *Graf Spee* to leave within forty-eight hours.

Overnight, hundreds of journalists raced to the scene. On Sunday morning, December 17, *Graf Spee* steamed down the Plate River, a crippled giant. Broadcast journalists, photographers, and reporters lined the shores of the Plate and raced along with *Graf Spee* in a flotilla of small ships and fast boats. The whole world listened and watched. Dozens of small aircraft circled overhead, filming the drama below and broadcasting from the sky.

Graf Spee headed out to sea. *Cumberland*, an eight-inch gunned cruiser had raced to the scene to replace the damaged

Exeter and joined *Achilles* and *Ajax*. The three British warships were waiting. *Graf Spee* was a doomed ship, unable to maneuver, and inside the range of the British ships. The outcome was not in doubt. A sudden series of explosions tore open the great ship, as *Graf Spee* killed herself. She sank in a cloud of black smoke. Almost all of the crew had been sent ashore in Montevideo. The remainder left the ship moments before the scuttling. The *Graf Spee*'s captain, Hans Langsdorff, depressed and humiliated over the loss of his beloved ship, shot himself two days later, after first sending a congratulatory message to the captain of *Exeter*, expressing admiration for the bravery and skill of the British crews and their captains.

Goren explained how uneven the fight should have been.

"Captain Langsdorff made a bad mistake. When he realized he was being chased by the three British ships, he should have run away, keeping at least 10 miles ahead of them. He could have fired at them at will with his eleven-inch guns, and the British couldn't have reached him with their six- and eight-inchers. Instead, he sailed at them, brave Captain, meeting them head-on." Goren thought Captain Langsdorff must have received an order from Hitler himself to engage the British cruisers. They were steaming at each other at 22 to 25 knots, so the gap between *Graf Spee* and the three British ships closed at the rate of about 47 miles per hour. There was only a fifteen-minute period when *Graf Spee* could hit the British without risk of their hitting back. *Exeter*, with eight-inch guns, got knocked out of action in those fifteen minutes. After that, *Ajax* and *Achilles* were able to reach *Graf Spee* with their six-inchers. The fight became more even. Still, the *Graf Spee* had the advantage. Her guns were bigger. The British ships were clad in lighter armor, but Brits were the better naval warriors, centuries of tradition, and all that. The Germans will make Langsdorff out to be a hero. No such thing. He was a blunderer. He was good for sinking unarmed merchant ships, not for fighting warships.

"There is something revealing about this *Graf Spee* business," Goren continued. "The Germans have a superior military machine. Their General Staff and field commanders are the best. They have a long tradition of brilliant generals and imaginative new tactics, using up-to-date equipment in new ways. The French and British will try to fight World War I all over again, but the Germans will be fighting a new war, like they did in Poland. The French and British are in for a terrible surprise. But here's the rub. My guess is that Hitler will run the war. He has contempt for his generals because they come from the German aristocracy. Hitler will override their strategies. He trusts his instincts because they have got him everything he wanted until now, but war is something else. He will be facing soldiers instead of politicians.

"The *Graf Spee*'s mistake was too basic to have been made by an experienced naval officer like Langsdorff. I think it was Hitler's mistake—bravado; he thinks the Germans can do anything he orders. He doesn't respect the French and British as soldiers. He doesn't realize the Brits are the world's best naval warriors. If the *Graf Spee* is a symbol of the way Hitler will micromanage the war, then Germany will lose, even though the Germans have the best war machine.

"Let's see, what else?" Goren looked at Zena. "Do we have anything else to tell Jack, Zena?"

Zena blushed. "Not that I can think of, Alan," she said, as she stood up and began to clear the table.

I asked about Junior. Goren said he asked Georgie at the bookie joint about Junior, and Georgie says he comes every Saturday, like clockwork, and the joke is he is trying to get Bobo to become a customer. Is that rich? Bobo had a good laugh. He wanted to know if Junior wanted Bobo as an official customer or an X-customer and which customers were getting fucked the worst.

Goren led me to the parlor. We sat on his sofa. He drew on his pipe, tilted his head, and let out another narrow stream of smoke. "Do you play chess?" he asked. "No? I'll teach you. It's the greatest of all games, you know, the Royal Game, the King of Games. If you want, come around next Sunday, and I'll give you the first lesson."

Then he turned very serious. "Jack, for the last twenty years, I have been avoiding friendships. You know how I feel about that. Friendships bring obligations. You can't be a friend unless you're willing to stand by and help when your friend needs you. A friend has a claim on you. That's why I always avoided friendships and personal entanglements. And I was right. Now I have friends— you, Zena, Benny. I worry about you. I want to be here for you. I want to help you. You got in trouble, and it became my trouble. And I think about Benny. I haven't heard from him. I don't know where he is or what he is doing. I worry about him. And Zena. I would do anything for her.

"So you see, I was right all along. Who needs friends? They are nothing but trouble and responsibility. You know who needs friends? I'll tell you—everybody! Me most of all. I realize that I short-changed myself all those years. And I aim to make up for it."

85

Alone

FOR TWO WEEKS, I held onto the hope of a message from Alice, but none came. A terrible loneliness surrounded me. Nothing could give me peace or pleasure. Alice was gone, really. I tried to imagine going to her to ask for forgiveness, but her dismissal of me was so cold and so final. If I went to her, it would only be humiliation for me and unpleasantness for her. No, she was the one who broke us up. I knew this about her; if she relented, she would come to me without feeling diminished or having "lost." There was no false pride in Alice.

The combination of depressed loneliness and the anxiety of the Mackey case was coloring everything. I had to get some relief.

So, no more Alice. I might as well get with Rhoda. She could certainly get a fellow's mind off his troubles. I approached her for a date.

"OK, Jack, maybe next week. I'm kinda busy this week. Wait, not next week. Try me the week after."

She flashed her big smile, touched my arm, and was gone. It wasn't exactly the brush-off, I told Eddie. He said she just wanted to keep me in the collection, available at her choosing.

My spirits sank even lower. Then the humor of it came to me. Sure, she collected me, but guess what … I also collected her! It was the most erotic experience I'd ever had. Even now, I remember every moment and every detail and Cole Porter's music. And it didn't even cost the usual seventy cents for a movie date followed by hot dogs and soda. I laughed, my first laugh in weeks. It made me feel better. She didn't know it yet, but I had just left the reservation.

A week later, our football captain, Roger Balkin, stopped me in a corridor. There was no platoon system those days. Players played offense and defense. Roger was big and strong. He was a sixty-minute player. He was just named All New Jersey High School Left Tackle. That boosted him into first place in Rhoda's collection, edging out me and the fraternity president and several lesser competitors. He was, without doubt, the top campus celebrity. My own celebrity was waning. I hadn't done anything lately to refresh my reputation.

"Listen, Jack," Roger said, getting a little too close. "I want you to stay away from Rhoda. She's *my* girl, understand?" He smiled, confidently. He must have rehearsed the scene. But as I had learned, such scenes don't always play out as rehearsed. I was supposed to be intimidated. *His girl.* I smiled. Might as well say his *sun*.

"Roger," I said, smiling, "you're supposed to say *or else*."

He moved back, a reflex, only a few inches. He didn't know how to respond. The confrontation was not going right.

"Yeah," he said. "You know what I mean." He was puzzled by my casualness.

"No, Roger," I said, moving into the two-inch space that he just vacated, "what *do* you mean?"

Poor Roger. This was all wrong. Did he really think he could scare me? I decided to spare him.

"Not to worry, Roger," I said, "she's as much yours as she ever was. See ya around."

I turned and walked away. Oh, that Rhoda, you had to admire how she played her game.

Roger hadn't rehearsed a scene where *he* would feel threatened. I let him save face. He was grateful. He always made it clear, thereafter, that he considered me a friend.

86

A Letter from Benny

GOREN LEFT ME a message to please visit him next Sunday. I did. It was the day before Christmas. He was in his customary relaxed-at-home attitude. He looked like he hadn't shaved that day. He had a letter to show me.

Miami Beach
Saturday, December 16, 1939

Dear Zena, Alan, and Jack:

You guys are not going to believe this. I hardly believe it myself.

I am working a kitchen gadget booth on Lincoln Drive, which is a classy boulevard near the south end of Miami Beach. I am doing great. Making better than $150 a week. Not so great compared to the good old cocoa days, but good enough for a carnival bum like me. The girls are gorgeous. They are all blondes with great golden tans. The weather is gorgeous. The scenery is gorgeous. I am feeling gorgeous myself. I got an apartment nearby so I can walk to work. And everything is great.

I put my money in the Flagler National Bank. Everything is under control. I am settling in for a good winter.

Then, a week ago, a guy comes up to me after my 4:00 pitch and asks me am I Benny James who used to work at Krilow's in Atlantic City? His name is Brewster J. Barrington, an Englishman (why do the English always have two last names?). He talks so English I have trouble understanding him. Now get this. Some guy who saw the arithmetic contest at Bobo's joint told this Barrington guy about me, and he tracked me down to Miami Beach.

What for? I wanted to know. *Who is looking for me?* For a minute, I thought I was in trouble with Bobo.

Try to believe this. The English are trying to build an electric calculator that can do thousands of arithmetic calculations *per second*! Do you believe that? Well, I did not believe television until I saw it. The machine is going to be used for code breaking. Beats me how. Well, anyway, will I come to England and let some neurologists from Oxford University Medical College examine me to find out how I do the addition thing?

I tell Mr. Brewster J. Barrington he must be nuts. I am not leaving the good old USA to go to a country that is at war. And anyhow, do I want somebody poking around in my brain?

Next day, here comes Barrington, together with a US Army Colonel. They take me to a hotel and feed me dinner. The Colonel has six three-by-five-inch cards. Each one has a column of numbers. He wants me to give him a demo. I ask how many numbers are in the column. The smaller ones I tell him to show me upside down, the larger ones right side up. He flashes the cards, one at a time. I know the answer as fast as it takes me to scan the numbers, right side up or upside down, it doesn't matter. He says it is unbelievable. They need me.

The Colonel asks me how I feel about the war. I tell him I just want us to stay out of it. He asks me would I rather see England win or Germany. I tell him England, but I am not about to go to war to help.

The Colonel tells me that the USA will be in it before it is over. I can help to end it quicker, maybe, if the neurologists can figure out how my brain adds numbers and use it in the machine they are building. Anyway, he tells me it will only be three months. They will fly me to England from Canada in a British bomber. They will put me up in a good hotel. And they will pay me fifty pounds a week. That is about $250! *Oh, yeah*, I say, *how many pounds does it cost for a dinner?* thinking they are going to tell me that a dinner costs five pounds. *About a shilling*, they say. That is 25 cents. Cheaper than here. But then they say I will have no expenses. They will take care of everything. And I will be helping a good cause. So I figure to come back with more than three grand! Well, guys, I been thinking about this pretty hard and I am going to do it. I don't know anything about what they are trying to build except I heard Barrington use the word *enigma*, and later on, the Colonel asked Barrington if I would be staying at *Bletchley Park*. That is all I know.

I closed my account at Flagler National Bank. So, Alan, I am enclosing my check for $4,000. I will take the rest with me. Please invest it for me. Anyway you want.

If I was you, I would be going long crude oil futures, as far out as they go. This is a real war. It will get bad. It will be a long one. We will be in it before it is over. But you do for me whatever you do for yourself. I am sorry to put this responsibility on you. But who else? You are my best friend.

I am taking off for Boston tomorrow. From there, my route will be Newfoundland, Greenland, Iceland, Ireland, London. I am getting a geography lesson. What an adventure!

I may not be able to write to you. But I expect I will be back in the USA around the end of March or April. I guess I will come straight to Atlantic City as the season will be over down here by then.

Say *hello* to Bobo for me if you see him. Give Zena a big kiss for me and a big hug for Jack.

Your friend,
Benny

"I guess he doesn't get the *Atlantic City Press* down there," Goren observed, puffing away on his pipe. "He doesn't seem to know about your trouble. Is anything new?"

"Nothing he could do about it anyway," I answered. "No, nothing is new. I guess nothing will happen until the pre-trial conference. That's going to be February 6."

Zena said, "It's going to be all right, Jack." I asked her if that was an occult reading or her personal hope for me. She laughed. "I thought you believed in me, Jack. Don't you?" I sure wanted to. Then Zena said, "What a great adventure for Benny. Maybe they can learn something from him. They do all kinds of miraculous things these days."

"Let's hope he'll be safe," Goren said.

Then Goren said, "Come on, Jack, have some breakfast while I give you a chess lesson. Lesson Number One: how to set up the board. And I guess you can stop worrying about your case. You heard Zena. I think it was official, even without the glass ball."

87

Marking Time

ICALLED LAWYER Durells every afternoon. The receptionist got used to telling me to call back, and Durells's secretary got used to telling me that Durells had nothing to tell me, except once, when he got on the phone to say he used up $800 of my $1,000; he said he'll send me an itemized bill. He said our deal was $1,000 up to and including the Grand Jury. He is sticking to the deal, but he reminded me that if indicted, I go on the clock.

Our family's Christmas was quiet and somber. Like Thanksgiving was. Mom made a wonderful turkey dinner. It was just the four of us. After dinner, Eddie and Blinky showed up and dragged me out to the boardwalk to look at the moon and the ocean. I couldn't enjoy anything. I missed Alice.

88

A Visit to the Mackeys

GEORGIE AND FRANKIE visited the Mackeys on the day after Christmas. I never knew about it for six years. It wasn't until 1945, when I came home from World War II, that Bobo let Georgie tell me what happened back in 1939, on the day after Christmas.

At dinnertime that evening, Georgie and Frankie climbed the six steps to the Mackeys' porch. The Mackey house, like all the houses on Annapolis Avenue, was decorated with Christmas lights. They rang the doorbell. As Mr. Mackey opened the door, Georgie pushed it, hard, throwing Mr. Mackey off balance. Georgie entered the Mackeys' parlor. Frankie was close behind.

"What is this?" Mr. Mackey demanded, rubbing his nose where the door caught him when Georgie pushed it. "Who are you guys?"

Without a word, Georgie shot out his right arm, the same kind of piston blow that Bobo delivered to Junior, except Georgie used an open hand, his arm angling upward as it struck Mackey, so that the meaty part of his palm smashed up into Mackey's upper lip and the bottom of Mackey's nose. The upward angle of the blow broke the bottom of Mackey's nose bone instantly and jolted his head backward. Mackey fell. Blood erupted from his lip and nose. He clutched at his face and moaned in pain.

Mrs. Mackey emerged from the kitchen, carrying a big bread knife. "Put down the knife, Missus," said Frankie in a voice that she didn't want to disobey. She took in the scene and screamed, dropping the knife and kneeling beside Mackey. She was followed into the room by John, his lower face and neck still covered by the cast. Mrs. Mackey ran back to the kitchen and returned with several towels, which she applied to Mackey's face. Mackey moaned, "Oh, my nose. It's broken."

Georgie extended his hand to Mackey to help him to his feet. It almost looked like a friendly gesture. Mackey was a huge man. Georgie pulled him up off the floor. Frankie helped.

"Now, sit down, everybody," Georgie said quietly. "We don't wanna hurt nobody. Look, you got blood on your rug. That's too bad. Now then, this must be John. Sit down, John."

Georgie approached John. He slapped the cast. John howled. "That hurt, did it?" Georgie asked, innocently. "I'm sorry. I don't wanna hurt anybody … any more than I have to."

"Who are you? What do you want?" Mrs. Mackey whimpered.

"A small thing is all I want," said Georgie. "I want you to leave that boy alone, you know who I mean. I want that none a you should appear or testify against him. I don't wanna hurt any of you, but if you don't do this small thing for me, I will hurt you bad. Worse than you could ever imagine. All of you, including Tom. If there's anything left of him to hurt, I will find it and hurt him. Real bad."

Georgie paused to let the words sink in. "This is just a warning. Don't disappoint me. If you do, we'll be back." He paused again, studying the Mackeys without emotion. "And if you're thinkin' you'll go to the police, forget it. Nobody can protect you. If you do, I'll know, and I'll be seein' you. Maybe here in your house, or maybe somewhere else. Like where you park your rig, Mackey, or the warehouse where you work, John, or you, Missus, I might find you on the way to the grocer or to the cleaner or here in your own kitchen." Georgie paused again. He looked at each one with hooded eyes. "Now then," he said, "you got anythin' to say?"

Mackey lifted a towel, "I don't know why you had to come here," Mackey said. "The other guy already delivered me the message. Tell whoever sent you that we ain't gonna appear. Give me a break. The other guy was just here yesterday. He said I gotta call the prosecutor and tell him we're not gonna testify. I will call him, don't worry. I will call tomorrow."

Georgie and Frankie looked at each other. "Tell me about the guy from yesterday," Frankie said.

"Jesus Christ, wasn't he one of your guys?" Mackey asked, in between pressing the towel to his battered face. "He scared me more than you. Look at these two bullet holes. He shot me out of my wedding picture, and he shot the crucifix off the wall. Can you imagine? A crucifix. He shot a crucifix. He's crazy!"

"Describe him," said Frankie.

Mrs. Mackey gave a good description. Georgie and Frankie exchanged glances. They gave no indication of surprise.

"We're leavin' now," Georgie said. "The prosecutor will want to know why you and your boys ain't gonna testify. You're gonna tell him *nothin'*. He will ask you why, fifty times. You will tell him *nothin'*. If you tell him about our visit, you will regret it. Now, we're leavin'. Don't make us come back."

When Georgie and Frankie reported to Bobo, they said they believed the Mackeys were silenced, but who was yesterday's guy? Georgie described the mystery man as Mackey described him to Georgie. And he shot a crucifix! On Christmas! He must be crazy. Who is he?"

"Well, I'll be damned," said Bobo. "That Jack is somethin' else over here. He beats these guys with an iron pipe, and lookit the friends he has. He'll go places, that kid. I knew it. He's a good boy. I got no idea who that mystery guy could be. Do you? And I can't even ask Jack. Your visit is *appena fra noi*, unnerstan? It's called *intimidating a witness* and *obstruction of justice*. If the Mackeys shoot off their mouths, the assistant prosecutor might try to guess you came from me, but he's got nothin' to tie me to Jack, and anyway, the DA is mine. But, you never know, so keep it quiet.

"However," he mused, stroking his chin, "I want to know who was that other guy. Let's see, dark skin, dark glasses, heavy black sideburns, thick black mustache, a sailor, or a stevedore, spoke like a Greek, looked like a Gypsy, or an Armenian, wore a navy watch cap and a pea coat. Write it down. I don't want to forget any details. Who the fuck is he?"

89

Good News

ON JANUARY 30, 1940, a week before the pretrial conference, Durells took my call.

"I have good news for you, Jack. The county prosecutor is dropping the charges. You're off the hook. No indictment, no juvenile hearing, no probation, nothing."

I was stunned. I could barely croak out, "What happened?"

Durells never wanted to waste time, but this time, he must have been feeling good about the news he was giving me, or else he figured he could afford to give me a little more time, seeing as how my $1,000 didn't get all used up, but it was all his anyway. "I told you," he said, "that the county prosecutor is a friend. I see him all the time at the club. Last night, I was having dinner with my wife and he came to my table; he wanted to talk to me in the library after dinner. In the library, he told me that his assistant prosecutor lost his two key witnesses, the Mackey brothers. He said they wouldn't explain why they won't testify, just that they won't do it, that it will serve no purpose. They want bygones to be bygones. The prosecutor tells me his assistant thinks he detects the fine hand of Bobo Truck because he knows I represent Bobo. Then he said *Where does this boy, Jack, come to Bobo?* He can't see a connection, and anyway, the Mackeys are not saying they were intimidated. They say they just want to drop it and get on with their lives.

"Then he says, needless to say, his assistant tried to wheedle more out of the Mackeys. He even went to visit them. They seemed relaxed enough, not frightened, not intimidated. Mr. Mackey's nose was bandaged. He said he broke it changing a tire. The jack snapped loose and hit him. John was still in a cast. Then the assistant went to visit Tom Mackey in the hospital. Tom is able to communicate now. Tom said the same thing, *Leave it alone, let bygones be bygones*, like it is a family slogan. *Larry*, the prosecutor tells me, *I'm not going to make a career out of this case. It stinks, he says, vigilante justice and all that, and juveniles who commit adult crimes should get adult punishment. You know how we feel about that in the Prosecutor's Office. Maybe there's been some witness intimidation here, but at the moment, we have no case, and I'm not going to waste time and money trying to coax witnesses who don't want to be witnesses.*

"Anyway, Jack, you're free. It's over. Congratulations!"

"I … I don't know what to say, Mr. Durells," I stammered, "except thanks. You're great. Bobo was right when he said you're the best."

"I *am* the best, Jack," Durells agreed, "but not this time. Something changed the Mackeys. Maybe it was a touch of honesty, knowing that they deserved what they got. Or maybe it was something else. We'll never know. Goodbye, son, stay out of trouble."

And that was it. It was over. Just like that. I'd been telephoning Mr. Durells from the Nu-Enamel store. I hung up and told my dad. He hugged me and started to cry. He said I should go home and tell mom.

I was a free man.

Before heading home, I wanted to see Bobo. I found him in his little office behind Royce's Shooting Gallery. Georgie was out front. Frankie was with Bobo. I told them the case against me was over. I told him what Durells said.

"Mr. Truck," I asked, "tell me the truth. Did you do something with the Mackeys?"

"Jack, what do I have to do to get you to call me *Bobo*?" Bobo replied. "Listen here, I always tell the truth. The truth is that intimating a witness is very serious business over here, and I wouldn't be caught dead doin' it. Is there somebody else you know what might do such a thing?"

"You must be kidding, Mr. ... Bobo," I answered. "My friends are kids, except for you and Benny. And Morris Rubens, too, I guess, but Morris got married and moved away, and Benny. Hey, I have to tell you about Benny."

I told Bobo about Benny's letter. Bobo said he knew Benny would do something good with that machine in his head and if he helps to beat the fuckin' Nazis, that's great.

"And the only other adults are my father and Mr. Goren," I said, "and neither one of them would even try to talk to Mr. Mackey. So either the Mackeys decided to drop the case on their own, which I don't believe, or else you helped them make that decision. C'mon, tell me."

"You're annoyin' me, Jack," Bobo said. "I already told you I don't know nothin' about it. The only help I gave you was to get you Durells. Durells is the guy. He and the county prosecutor are real tight. The prosecutor did a favor for Durells. That's the answer. You're a lucky kid, you had the right lawyer."

"Well, anyway, Mr. ... Bobo, I'm around if you need me. And thanks for everything."

"Be seein' ya, kid," Bobo said, with the only gentleness I had ever detected in him. "You're a good boy. If I had a son, I'd want him to be like you. Stay in touch, y'hear?"

I was sure Bobo fixed it for me. If he did, he wasn't about to tell me.

90

Hero

A T SCHOOL, THE news was electrifying. The Mackey case was dropped.

He beat the rap. He almost killed the Mackeys, and he got away with it.

My celebrity got a soaring recharge. Everyone pressed forward to congratulate me, even kids I didn't know—and Rhoda. She bore down on me in the lunchroom, smiling. She was getting better looking all the time. She threw her arms around me. She kissed me and pressed close.

"Congratulations, hero," she said. "I've missed you. Where have you been? How about we get together."

"Sure, Rhoda," I said, "I'll call you." I squeezed her arm and turned away.

91

Starting Over

IWENT BACK to being a normal fifteen-year-old. I went to school. My grades improved. I worked. Eddie and I remained best friends.

The weeks passed, uneventfully. I continued to work part-time at the Nu-Enamel store. Winter ended. March arrived. The days lengthened. April came, with its promise of summer, and color returned to the city. I longed for Alice. I missed her touch. I missed her presence, the way she filled my life. You know the expression, *we're so close, she's a part of me*. It's true. There are relationships like that, where one feels incomplete without the other. That's how I felt, as if part of me was gone with her. She had become so much a part of my life.

I did all the usual tenth grade things. I spent time with Eddie and Blinky. I studied the chess book that Goren gave me, Emanuel Lasker's *Common Sense in Chess*. I learned about Paul Morphy, the incomparable mid-nineteenth-century champion, probably the greatest of them all. He swept aside all the European champions before he was twenty. I played out some of his games. Little as I understood, I could appreciate their elegance and precision of movement. Chess became a good and absorbing pasttime for me because of Paul Morphy.

Alice had been part of my family. She was much-loved and missed, especially by my mother, whose instincts told her I was to blame for the breakup. She never questioned me, but it was obvious that I was a disappointment in respect to Alice.

Evie was not so circumspect. She asked Alice for an explanation, but Alice would not discuss it. So Evie formed her own opinion, that I did something bad. She said that to me, hoping to learn something if I tried to defend myself. I disappointed her with my silence. Poor Evie. Adoring me was conflicting with her loyalty to Alice. Only my father avoided the subject. It couldn't be that he was unaware. It was part of his make-up not to touch on such matters. He drew me closer, spent more time with me. We discussed business at the Nu-Emanel store, and the war in Europe, and the effect the war was having here at home. There was a melancholy in him since the war started. In later years, he confessed that he had an overwhelming fear that war was coming to America, and the return to prosperity was going to be paid for by me and my generation going off to war in far-away places.

Eddie's sixteenth birthday arrived. Mr. Dunauskas gave him two dollars to treat him, me, and Blinky. We went to the Warner to see *The Road to Singapore*, starring Bob Hope, Bing Crosby, and Dorothy Lamour, followed by hot dogs with everything—mustard, relish, onions, and cole slaw—and ice cream sodas. I managed to keep Alice out of my thoughts for a few hours. We had a good time on Mr. Dunauskas's two dollars. Eddie even had twenty cents left over.

My sixteenth birthday came a month later. Mom made a banana ice cream cake and arranged a small celebration, just our family and Eddie and Blinky. I worked hard to generate enthusiasm and good spirits, but I couldn't feel it. I didn't fool anyone. Alice was missed. I realized that she had turned fifteen only two weeks earlier. We should have been together, then and now.

***

The second Sunday in April was clear and sunny. I went to visit Goren and Zena. A visit to them was always uplifting.

Goren was alone.

"Zena's not here?" I asked. I was disappointed. I wanted to talk to her about Alice. Or, more accurately, I suppose, I hoped she would tell *me* about Alice. I wanted to talk about Alice. With Zena, I would be able to bare my feelings in a way I couldn't with anyone else.

"She is at the parlor," Goren said. "On a nice day like today, there will be tourists on the boardwalk."

I told him I lost Alice. His only comment was *Too bad.* He asked no questions. That was so Goren. I'm sure he would have liked to say that's the problem with such relationships. They make you vulnerable. They can hurt.

Instead, he talked about the war. "Spring is here," he said. "The war in Europe is about to get real." He started to explain how the Germans were going to fight the war, but suddenly he interrupted himself. "I almost forgot to tell you, Jack," he said. "Remember I went into crude oil futures and I put you in as well? We're making money, and when the war gets real, we're going to make real money. And Benny, too. He gave me four thousand dollars to invest in crude oil futures when he left for England. He had it right. He'll be a rich man when he comes back."

If he comes back, I thought. It had been months since we heard from him.

Goren proposed a game of chess. He won easily, of course, but he complimented me. "For a beginner, you're quite adventurous. That's good. Practice. Learn from Morphy. Never be timid."

"In fact," he added, "never be timid about anything."

Good advice from Goren. He was a tonic. The visit lifted my spirits.

But the loneliness returned by the time I reached home.

***

I encountered Alice once, walking along Ventnor Avenue with her friends, Marilyn and Sandra. They were returning from school, chattering and laughing, hugging their schoolbooks against their bosoms with arms folded across them, the way schoolgirls carried their books those days. It was a scene worthy of Norman Rockwell—a 1940 picture of three pretty teenage girls in the full bloom of youth, in pleated skirts, knee-high socks, and saddle shoes. When they saw me, they became quiet. I hesitated for a moment; maybe ... but Alice continued on. She half-nodded as they passed, barely a sign of recognition.

The Thursday night Pinochle games continued. Evie's game was improving. I think she felt she was betraying Alice by playing in the game with me, but the attraction of being near Eddie was irresistible.

I spent a lot of time alone on the beach. I dated several girls. None refused me, the famous one, on the loose. Aside from some teenage kissing and groping, pleasant enough, I was not attracted to any of them. But I knew I would continue the search. The hurting started to heal, slowly. Alice was fading. She was right. She was always right. Nobody ever died from this.

92

The Real War

THE WAR WAS good for business. It looked like Roosevelt would run for an unprecedented third term. Although it was clear that his sympathies were with the British and the French, he promised to keep us out of the war. *Let the Europeans make war. America will supply them.* The belligerents needed everything—textiles, steel, grain, trucks, engines, chemicals, tires, everything. All over America, closed factories were coming back to life, and men were returning to work. Unemployment vanished. Work was there for anyone who wanted it.

The Atlantic City Chamber of Commerce predicted a good season. The nation's growing prosperity, it said, will make 1940 the best season ever. The anticipation of good times made everything and everybody look and feel vigorous. Business improved everywhere. At the Nu-Enamel store, my father planned to ask for a raise right after Memorial Day.

***

Looking back at that time, knowing what was to come, it seems the world was sleepwalking through the Phony War. The war at sea was real, but the war at the French-German front was a charade. In Paris, the new spring women's fashions were introduced, as usual. Most Frenchmen hardly noticed they were at war. They believed the war was a sham, that the politicians would posture for a while longer, then settle it. Roosevelt tried to broker a European peace. He sent his Under Secretary of State, Sumner Welles, to meet with Hitler in Berlin. Nothing came of it. Hitler had a different plan.

On May 10, the war exploded. The Germans launched an offensive that wiped out the Belgian Army in three days and sliced through the French Army and the British Expeditionary Force with the same swiftness as in Poland. The American radio networks patched together improvised long-range hookups and relays to bring the war into our living rooms. We gathered around our radios to hear the scratchy voices of on-the-scene commentators: Edward R. Murrow, *this … is London. German bombers were over the city again last night*; and Eric Sevareid, *reporting from Paris;* and William L. Shirer, *here in Berlin.* Their voices faded in and out, amid crackling of static and whistling sounds and frequent loss of signal.

***

The Germans occupied Paris on June 14. The main French Army Group surrendered on June 22. The French government capitulated June 26. The French Army, considered the best in the world, was crushed in 47 days. It was stunning. The radio spoke of nothing else. The newspapers screamed the news in thick black two-inch type, FRANCE FALLS! It seemed impossible. No more talk of Phony War or quick peace. It was to be a long war. It could go on for years. We'll be in it. *I'll* be in it. Suddenly, I felt very alone. The wound of Alice's leaving wasn't fully healed. The scab was torn off. The wound felt raw again. The pain returned. A flood of feelings and remembrances of Alice overcame me—her generous smile, her quick laugh, her inquisitiveness about everything, the way she felt, yielding to me. I needed her. I had to get her back. I was going to risk the humiliation of another rejection. This time there would be no rehearsed speech. I wanted to open my heart to her. We shouldn't be on the outs while the world was going to hell. I had to be with her again.

So I went to her.

93

Saturday, June 29, 1940

I~N THE MORNING,~ I rode my bike to Alice's house, but she was not there. Her mother said she left at 8:00, on her bike. She didn't know where she went. "Maybe she is with Marilyn or Sandra," she said. "Try them."

Alice hadn't been to see either of them. Sandra suggested the boardwalk, the pavilion near Albany Avenue. "Sometimes she goes there to read."

That's where I found her, seated on a bench looking out to sea. A pair of binoculars were hanging from the bench. I recognized the curve of her back. Any notion that I was beginning to get over her dissolved the moment I saw her. I ached for her.

An open book was in her lap, but she wasn't looking at it. Her eyes were on the ocean and the horizon.

The sun had been up for a few hours, climbing high, picking its way through feathery clouds. The summer solstice was near. Sky and water were painted in spring pastels, cheerful colors after the gray of winter. The sun touched the freshly painted ivory-and-gold domes of the Shelbourne and the Traymore and set them ablaze. Atlantic City was dressing up for the season.

The air was cool and fresh, the ocean calm. Waves rolled in quietly and rose up as they neared the shore, displaying their glistening undersides, leaning forward, getting ahead of themselves, then falling over and sliding onto the beach. Gulls circled and wheeled and filled the air with their cries. A flock of sandpipers scurried along the water's edge. Across the horizon lay a low bank of white clouds, looking like a distant range of snow-covered mountains.

"Alice," I said, "it's me. Can I sit with you?"

She turned. A shadow of a smile played on her lips, only for a moment.

"Nice to see you, Jack," she said. Was there any welcome in her voice?

"Alice, I had to see you. Everything is so crazy. The war. Everybody says it's going to be a long war. We'll be in it."

"Look out there," Alice waved at the horizon. "Everything is so beautiful and peaceful. It's hard to imagine what's happening on the other side."

She pointed to the binoculars. "This morning I saw a Navy blimp headed out to sea, and last week I saw a Coast Guard ship on the horizon."

"And how about right near here, in the ocean," I said. "The subs sink a few freighters every day and forty English Navy ships since September. That's thousands of sailors killed. If they don't get killed when the torpedo hits, they end up drowning. The subs don't come too close to us, though. They stay outside our territorial limit, but they're close enough. The wreckage drifts in.

"Did you see the wreckage that washed up on the beach last week, at Missouri Avenue? I went to see it. It gave me the creeps. It was all covered with thick black oil, pieces of wood, mattresses, furniture, ropes. Somebody said there were bodies, too, but the Coast Guard pulled them out a few miles before it all floated onto the beach."

"It *is* frightening," she said. "We are so far from it; it seems we are in a different world. But I think it's coming here."

"That's what I think, Alice. I am sure I'll end up in it."

I was interrupted by the roar of five husky-looking Brewster Buffalo fighter planes coming out of the newly built Naval Air Station on the mainland, at Pomona. They roared across the city, passing almost directly overhead and headed out toward the horizon. Tough and powerful as they looked, they were a flawed design. Later on, they were called *Flying Coffins* by the pilots who flew them.

"Alice," I leaned closer after the roar of the planes receded, "I came looking for you. Because this is not right. The world is going crazy. We belong together. You have to forgive me. You have to take me back. We were like one person. Half of me is missing. You must feel the same. I couldn't feel this way if you didn't feel the same thing. I need another chance."

"Sure, Jack," she said with a smile, startling me with the easiness of her surrender. "I've been expecting you. I believe you. I saw Zena. She said you'll come to me, and I have to take you back."

Zena!

"You'll never hurt me again, will you, Jack?" she asked, looking deep into my eyes, a bit anxiously, her eyebrows raised. She smiled questioningly, so wistful and vulnerable. Is that a tear she's trying to hold back? My heart burst for her.

I took her in my arms and lifted her from the bench. "Alice, you'll never regret this. I'll never do anything to make you unhappy again. I promise."

"But you're early," she said, resting her head in my shoulder. It felt so good. "Zena didn't expect you for another month."

"Well," I said, hugging her tighter, "how could Zena know that France would fall in seven weeks?"

94

Endgame and Revelation

A S FRANCE LAY prostrate, hours away from complete capitulation, Mussolini jumped in on Hitler's side, in one of history's most craven acts, like a jackal, to feed on the corpse of southeast France. Roosevelt described Mussolini: *The hand that held the dagger plunged it into his neighbor's back.* Hitler was master of Europe. The war spread to North Africa.

In September 1940, the Selective Service Act became law. The draft age was 21 to 35. Alice and I became closer than ever. Goren became my mentor. The books he gave me were better than going to college. He even gave me books for Alice on astronomy, paleontology, anthropology, and ancient structures. That man knew *everything.* The book about ancient structures caught my interest. I learned about Stonehenge, the Egyptian Pyramids, the Mayan and Aztec Pyramids, the Easter Island figures, the Great Wall of China, the Palace at Knossos. Alice already knew all about them.

In June 1941, the Germans invaded Russia, the worst of Hitler's many military blunders. On December 7, 1941, the Japanese attacked Pearl Harbor, and as my father, and Benny, and Goren predicted, we were in the war. I knew it was coming. The draft age was lowered to eighteen. The calendar moved closer to the day when I would be drafted.

Some historians say that history is not influenced by individuals. Their theory suggests that events are shaped by great social and political forces, that leaders are thrust into their roles by events, that events produce the leaders that the times demand. You have only to look at the World War II leadership to see the weakness of that theory.

Hitler was a force that shaped Germany, not the other way around. Churchill's bulldog stance against Hitler was another example of a leader bringing his people along. Imagine a Britain with Edward VIII as King, and Neville Chamberlain as Prime Minister. There would have been no British resistance after Germany's stunning victory in France. A Chamberlain–Edward VIII government would have made a quick peace with Hitler, leaving him to plunge all of Europe into the blackness of Nazi rule. Hitler boasted that his Third Reich would last a thousand years, and for a while, it certainly appeared to be indestructible. The credit for Hitler's destruction goes to two great leaders, Churchill and Roosevelt. They led their people in the right direction.

I graduated from Atlantic City High School in June 1942. I didn't wait to be drafted. I enlisted on the day I graduated. So did Eddie and Blinky. All three of us made it through the war. So did Benny. He came out as a Major in the OSS, the Office of Strategic Services, the forerunner of the CIA. Blinky almost got his wish to fly a fighter plane. He didn't make it as a pilot. He became a navigator. He flew twenty-five B-17 missions over Europe, the last fifteen as his squadron's lead navigator, before he was rotated back to the U.S. to become an instructor. He was mustered out as a Major, a different person from little Blinky who enlisted three years earlier. I made it into the Marines' OCS (Officer Candidate School) Program, where they cranked out Second Lieutenants in three months—ninety-day wonders we were called. I served in the Pacific, where the average combat life of an infantry Second Lieutenant was two and a half days. Those of us who survived the first engagement usually were promoted to First Lieutenant going into the next engagement, and up to Captain going into the next. OCS produced a steady stream of freshly minted ninety-day wonders to fill the gaps. I came out a Captain.

Roger Balkin, ACHS's football captain, turned out to be a decent guy after all. I think our confrontation over Rhoda peeled away some of his arrogance and left him better for it. He graduated from Atlantic City High School in June 1940. Football earned him a West Point appointment. He played on the powerful Army football teams of 1942 and 1943. He graduated from West Point a Second Lieutenant, in June 1944, only to die in January 1945, at a now forgotten battle to clear the Germans out of their last stronghold west of the Rhine, at a place called the Colmar Pocket in the Alsace province. It sounded so antiseptic, *to clear out the pocket*, as a dentist clears out an abscess. The newspapers said that casualties were light that day but Lieutenant Roger Balkin was just as dead as on a day of heavy casualties. He died on the same day, at the same place, that Audie Murphy's heroism earned the Congressional Medal of Honor. Audie Murphy made it home, the most decorated soldier of the war. Roger Balkin was buried at Colmar.

Eddie Dunauskas was a radio operator on a heavy cruiser. In later years, he attributed his big success in communications electronics to his wartime days in the Navy.

Bernie Resnos never did get back to high school. He stayed in Asbury Park to run the diner. He tried to get a draft deferment because he didn't want to leave his aunt alone with the diner. In 1943, he was drafted. He was killed in Belgium at the Battle of the Bulge in December 1944.

In July 1942, Rhoda Michaelson moved to Washington. It was the center of wartime power and wealth, a place where she could use her good looks and special talents to good advantage. Roger Balkin and I and the others had just been practice. She joined the WAVES, the Navy's auxiliary for women. Probably she chose the WAVES because she would look so handsome in the trim navy blue uniform, worn over a white shirt and navy tie, and the good-looking navy-and-white cap. She focused on a rich, 30-year-old Navy pilot. He never stood a chance. They were married within three months. He shipped out only a month after their marriage, never to return. Brief as was their time together, I'm sure she gave him his money's worth. He flew an Avenger, a carrier-based torpedo bomber. He was killed in the Pacific during the Battle of Leyte Gulf in October 1944, leaving Rhoda, at age 20, a wealthy, young, beautiful widow. She knew how to make the most of that, and she did.

We know how World War II ended. Knowing that, we cannot feel the fears of those days. On the day France fell, the odds-makers were betting on Germany triumphant. And, indeed, it seemed that way for a long time as German arms scored quick-and-easy victory after victory.

Today, because we know, the outcome seems inevitable. Not so then, as we witnessed in disbelief the destruction of the combined French and British armies. Weren't they the most powerful in the world? The Germans seemed invincible.

It was a near thing. Hitler made all the big German decisions. But for his mistakes, he might have won that war.

You probably can guess that right after the war, I married Alice. I was twenty-one, old for my years. War does that to you. Not long after, Eddie married Evie and became my brother-in-law, and later on, my partner in our electronics company.

***

In October 1945, six weeks after I returned home from the war, I paid a visit to Bobo. His office was still on the second floor, over Trucci's. Georgie was with him. Bobo told Georgie to tell me about his and Frankie's visit to the Mackeys on the day after Christmas back in 1939. When Georgie finished, I asked, "Well, who *was* the Christmas Day guy?"

Bobo did the Italian thing, pulling down the lower lid of his right eye with his right forefinger. "You mean you don't know?" Bobo asked, suspiciously. "C'mon, Jack, don't bullshit me. You gotta know. Who else woulda sent him?"

"I don't have a clue, Bobo," I said. "Who could it be?"

"Yeah, Jack," Bobo said, "who could it be? I been wonderin' for six years."

That was a surprise twist. I always thought Bobo had silenced the Mackeys for me. Now, six years later, I knew it for sure. But the Christmas Day mystery man? Who could he be? Together, Bobo and I went through the possibilities. Neither one of us knew anyone who answered to the description of the mystery man. Somebody must have hired him, but who? We thought of Benny James first, but he didn't even know about my problem, and besides, he was on his way to England a week before Christmas. Who did that leave? My father? Goren? Morris? Could it be one of them? Could one of them have kept such a secret from me for all these years?

Georgie said, "Wait a minute. Maybe it was somebody we don't even know. Somebody with a hard-on for the Mackeys. Somebody who thought those boys were long overdue for a beating. Somebody who hardly knew you, Jack, or maybe didn't even know you at all. Ever think a that?"

"Listen, Jack," Bobo said. "Don't go pokin' around in this over here. It's six years. Leave it alone. Whoever it was, it was a criminal act. Somebody done ya a favor. Leave it be. You could hurt the guy whoever he is if you start pokin' around in it."

"I guess you're right, Bobo," I said, "but how about you? How come you're telling me what Georgie and Frankie did for me?"

"That's different, Jack. Me and Georgie and Frankie done so much shit over here, that was nothin'. And maybe I like that you should think you owe me."

I did owe him. Far more than he realized.

So who was that guy?

***

It was in the spring of 1950, five years after the war, five years after Georgie told me about his and Frankie's visit to the Mackeys. It was on one of my Sunday visits to Goren that Zena finally convinced him to come clean.

It was Goren! He was the mystery man who appeared at the Mackeys' house on Christmas Day 1939. He did it alone. He didn't even tell Zena about it for eleven years. She made him tell me the story on the very day she heard it. It was hard to believe that Alan Goren was capable of what he did that day.

He disguised himself. First, for three days before, he let his beard grow some stubble. Then, he used a chestnut-colored dye on his face and blackened his eyebrows with a makeup stick. He pasted on a thick black mustache and pulled on a heavy black wig with long hair and heavy sideburns. He put on old navy dungarees, a black woolen turtleneck sweater, an old Navy peacoat that he bought for the purpose at a used clothing store, and scuffed six-inch work boots. He wore a pair of dark prescription sun-glasses and a dark navy watch cap, pulled low over his forehead and halfway over his ears. He had bought a second-hand .38 cal-iber automatic. He didn't want to use his Army service revolver.

He looked like a seaman, like a Gypsy or an Armenian. The col-oring made him look ten years younger. When he studied himself in the mirror, he thought he was quite good-looking in his dis-guise. He stuck the pistol in his pants.

That's how Goren went to the Mackeys. He was surprised at how calm he was. He'd thought it through for weeks. He wasn't sure he could do it. He expected, at the last moment, to be too nervous to go through with it. Remarkably, he was not nervous at all. He thought back to Chateau-Thierry, blowing the whistle and climbing out of the trench. This couldn't be as bad. He tried to deepen his voice and affect a thick Slavic accent. He'd been prac-ticing. He practiced as he headed to the Mackeys. *Sit don. Dunt muv. Dees vot I vant.* He thumped on the Mackeys' door. As it opened, he pushed himself in, pointing the gun. He told them what he wanted. He was calm and cool as ice water. He warned them that he would kill them if they didn't obey him or if they went to the police.

Nubuddy ees protec' yu frum me. Nubuddy. He tapped John on the side of his cast with the gun, hard enough to make him scream. In parting, he shot out Mr. Mackey's head in the framed wedding picture and shot the crucifix on the wall, striking it exactly in the center. He backed out, ran down the steps, and disappeared into the darkness. He threw the gun into the bay and later burned the peacoat. He had been calm at the Mackeys, but his heart raced and his head pounded violently for several hours afterward.

I couldn't believe it. There was always that fearless something about Goren. But this? It was Jimmy Cagney stuff. Only in the movies. I could hardly believe it.

"Alan," I said, "I'm speechless. I've been wondering about the mystery guy ever since Georgie told me about him."

"Georgie? How does Georgie know?" Goren asked, puzzled.

I laughed. "That's the biggest joke of all. Georgie and Frankie went to the Mackeys the next day!"

I told Georgie's story, including what Mackey said, that Goren's Gypsy-Armenian-Greek was scarier than Georgie and Frankie.

"Alan, you missed your career," Zena said. We were all quiet for a moment, and then she said, "Come, boys, let me pour you some tea."

"Yes, dear," Goren said, "you may find a message in the leaves."

"Wait, Zena," I blurted. "No more predictions. *Please*. I don't think I can take it!"

There was a long, awkward silence. As Zena exchanged glances with Goren, I hoped I hadn't offended her. Suddenly, without warning, Goren burst out laughing. Zena joined in. I hugged them, the three of us in a circle. Together, we laughed until we cried.

A week later, the Korean War started. If Zena saw it coming, she never said.

About the Author

J. Louis Yampolsky is a graduate of the Wharton School of the University of Pennsylvania. He practiced public accounting for 40 years before retiring from public practice to become a financial manager of trusts and investment partnerships.

Mr. Yampolsky lives in Wynnewood, Pennsylvania, and in Margate, New Jersey, with his wife, Judith. They have five children, nine grandchildren, and one great-granddaughter.

A Boardwalk Story is Mr. Yampolsky's first novel.

MORE GREAT FICTION AND HISTORY
FROM PLEXUS PUBLISHING, INC.

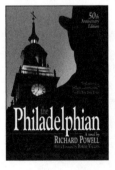

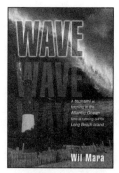

WAVE
By Wil Mara

As this exciting thriller opens, it's a beautiful spring morning on New Jersey's Long Beach Island. High overhead, aboard a 747 bound for the U.S. capital, a terrorist's plot has gone awry. The plane nosedives into the Atlantic and a nuclear device detonates, creating a massive undersea landslide. Within minutes, a tsunami is born and a series of formidable waves begins moving toward the Jersey shore. The people of LBI are sitting ducks, with only one bridge to the mainland and less than three hours to evacuate.

Hardbound/ISBN 978-0-937548-56-1/$22.95

WRONG BEACH ISLAND
By Jane Kelly

When the body of millionaire Dallas Spenser washes up on Long Beach Island with a bullet in its back, it derails Meg Daniels's plans for a romantic sailing trip. As Meg gets involved in the unraveling mystery, she soon learns that Spenser had more skeletons than his Loveladies mansion had closets. The ensuing adventure twists and turns like a boardwalk roller coaster and involves Meg with an unforgettable cast of characters.

From the beaches of Holgate and Beach Haven at the southern end of LBI to the grand homes of Loveladies and the famed Barnegat Light at the north, author Jane Kelly delivers an irresistible blend of mystery and humor in *Wrong Beach Island*—her third and most deftly written novel. Meg Daniels, Kelly's reluctant heroine, may be the funniest and most original sleuth ever to kill time at the Jersey shore.

Hardbound/ISBN 978-0-937548-47-9/$22.95
Softbound/ISBN 978-0-937548-59-2/$14.95

To order or for a catalog: 609-654-6500, Fax Order Service: 609-654-4309

Plexus Publishing, Inc.
143 Old Marlton Pike • Medford • NJ 08055
E-mail: info@plexuspublishing.com
www.plexuspublishing.com